MATCHED BY MISTAKE

KATHERINE GARBERA

THE RANCHER MEETS HIS MATCH

J. MARGOT CRITCH

MILLS & BOON

First Published in Great Britain 2023
by Mills & Boon, an imprint of HarperCollins*Publishers* Ltd
1 London Bridge Street, London, SE1 9GF

www.harpercollins.co.uk

HarperCollins*Publishers*
Macken House, 39/40 Mayor Street Upper,
Dublin 1, D01 C9W8, Ireland

Matched by Mistake © 2023 Harlequin Enterprises ULC.
The Rancher Meets His Match © 2023 Harlequin Enterprises ULC.

Special thanks and acknowledgement are given to Katherine Garbera and J. Margot Critch for their contributions to the *Texas Cattleman's Club: Diamonds & Dating Apps* series.

ISBN: 978-0-263-31763-3

0723

This book is produced from independently certified FSC™ paper
to ensure responsible forest management.

For more information visit: www.harpercollins.co.uk/green

Printed and Bound in the UK using 100% Renewable Electricity at
CPI Group (UK) Ltd, Croydon, CR0 4YY

MATCHED
BY MISTAKE

KATHERINE GARBERA

This one is for my good friend Joss Wood.
Thanks for always being there when I need to talk
and for all the writing sprints!

One

Jericho Winters took his VIP credentials and walked through the atrium of the Winters Expo Center with more than a little pride. His architecture company, RoyalGreen, had won the bid to build the new center in Royal, Texas, his hometown. Jericho had personally designed the center using cutting-edge eco-design elements to create a convention space that blended seamlessly into the landscape and incorporated energy-saving measures.

His brother Trey had urged him to come to ByteCon and check out the presentation of the wildly popular k!smet app that Trey was a financial backer in. There was a bit of in-family controversy as the creator of the app, Misha Law, had hired her best friend, Maggie Del Rio, to design the graphics and promotional elements for the app.

The Del Rio and Winters families had been feuding for more than a century since Eliza Boudreaux had dumped her beau Fernando Del Rio and married Teddy Winters.

For Jericho's part, he didn't get too involved in family

politics, preferring to bury himself in his work and watch his beloved Dallas Mavericks play.

He rubbed the back of his neck. Somehow being in this space was stirring up mixed emotions that he'd long ignored about Royal and his place in it. He could have gone anywhere in the world to open his company but instead he'd stayed here. He liked his hometown, liked the people and their friendly faces. He even tolerated the local gossip because it was part of the charm of living in a midsized town. But he felt the pressure of the feud more and more lately.

The scent of jasmines and then the staccato sound of heels on the tiled floor of the atrium brought his head around and he saw the very reason for his feelings toward the feud walking blithely through the crowd.

Maggie Del Rio.

She was tall and curvy with long black hair that she habitually wore in a long fall down her back. He'd noticed her for the first time in the bar at the Texas Cattleman's Club. He'd recently joined the TCC, a local country club that had been thriving in Royal for over one hundred years, having originally been founded by local cattle ranchers. He'd been on his way over to introduce himself when Trey had pointed out who she was. So he'd turned his attention to another woman but… He wanted Maggie.

Rationally, he knew it was just lust. It had to be because he had never met the woman, but his obsession with her had led to him reading up on her online. She was impressive. Thirty years old and she'd made a huge splash as an art director and graphic artist. Her high-profile client list had made it easy for him to check her work out, and he realized that her reputation was well earned.

There'd been scant personal information available except

for a two-year-old article on *Royal Tonight*'s website that mentioned a broken engagement. So he wasn't even sure she was single. That had been his only thought. Not the fact that someone had broken the engagement and maybe there was a valid reason.

His body just didn't care, which was typical of him. He wasn't afraid to admit that part of the reason he wanted her as much as he did was that she was forbidden fruit. At best they could have a one-night stand. Neither of them was going to risk all-out war with their families to start anything.

Which suited his life.

He rubbed the back of his neck again and shook his head. He wasn't going to sleep with Maggie, no matter that he'd had torrid dreams of hooking up with her since that one moment in the bar more than six weeks earlier. It was time to force his attention away from her.

He walked through the exhibition hall seeing old friends like Brian Cooper, whom he'd gone to school with.

"Hey, man, love this place. I heard you got the bid and was really looking forward to seeing what you did," Brian said after shaking his hand and giving him a one-armed bro hug.

"Thanks. I wanted to get a lot of eco-friendly things into it but didn't want the design to suffer," Jericho said.

"Piper said she loved it. She said that you had an artist's eye," Brian said.

Brian's partner, Piper, was an artist herself and a successful gallery owner in Dallas, which was a little over two hours from Royal. The couple split their time between Dallas and Royal. Brian worked in a law firm in Dallas as well. The couple had gotten together a few years ago when someone had been sabotaging Piper's family.

"Tell her I said thanks," Jericho said. "What are you here to see?"

"K!smet. Piper downloaded it and recommended it to me for business. But I'm not sure yet. Have you used it?"

"Nah. Not for work. I mean I downloaded it, but I've been busy," he said. Plus he wasn't sure he wanted to be matched romantically with someone based on an algorithm. The app had been gaining attention and traction for the matches it had made.

Today at the event they were going to debut a new function—Surprise Me!—something that suited the mood Jericho was in.

Despite his attraction to Maggie, he normally dated other people in his industry, either architects or other building developers. He'd been seeing a woman who lived in Dallas off and on for the last three years. But that was just for sex, which was what they both wanted. This app… Well, he had no idea what would happen.

"You might as well. Piper used the business app and it matched her with a graffiti artist who she's mentoring. The connections that she's experienced have been solid."

"Maybe," he said.

They made their way to the main exhibition stage, where the k!smet banner hung. There was a large computer screen with the company's logo. Brian excused himself to go and talk with some family members. And Jericho found a quiet spot and pulled out his phone, opened the k!smet app and toggled the looking-for-a-match button. When in Rome, right?

"God, it's hot today. I mean August in Texas is worse than purgatory," Maggie Del Rio said as she entered the backstage area and the greenroom that had been allocated to the k!smet app. Her best friend, Misha Law, was looking in the mirror, touching up her lipstick.

Misha wore her auburn hair cut in a wavy bob. She'd accented her hazel eyes by wearing thick mascara that made her lashes seem even longer than they naturally were. She was really good with tech-com stuff and Maggie was very excited to see the app she'd designed doing so well.

"Good. I'm glad. That means more people will be inside and come to our presentation. There is some talk that the investors might take the app public, which is the dream," Misha said. "I just hope the Surprise Me! function is well-received. When my brother first mentioned it I was really excited for it but now that I'm about to go onstage and debut it…"

Maggie reached over to squeeze her friend's shoulder. "It'll be great. You are really tuned into what people want and Nico is a genius."

"He is. I wish he was here today."

"I know. But I'm here. I know I'm not Nico but I've got your back."

Nico was recently out of prison after serving a sentence for assault even though he'd been framed. Most people still didn't want him around Royal, which ticked Maggie off. Even if Nico had committed the crime, he'd definitely done the time and been rehabilitated as far as the state was concerned so that should be enough.

"I know you do. Thanks, Mags. I'm glad you're here."

"Me, too."

"So…"

"So?"

Misha rolled her eyes at Maggie. "Did you sign up in the app?"

Maggie dug through her purse for her phone, deliberately not looking at her friend. Misha knew better than anyone how reluctant Maggie had been to date—even online dating, where some of the interactions were just over text—since Randall had dumped her two years ago.

There was something about being so wrong that she'd never been able to let go of. It wasn't just that Randall hadn't wanted to marry her. He was free to make his own choices to be happy. It was that Maggie had loved him and how could she have fallen in love with a man who'd only seen the Del Rio name and fortune? It was only after her father had insisted on a prenup that Randall had started to get cold feet.

"I'm not going to go away," Misha said, coming over, looping her arm through Maggie's.

Maggie sighed. "I don't want you to. I just… I'm scared."

"That's why you should use the app. No pressure on you to pick the right person—the app does that for you," Misha said.

She hugged her friend. "I don't know. I think I've made this first date after Randall into something bigger than it should be. It's just a date but I've made it into something huge in my head."

"I can tell. That's why you are going to give me your phone," Misha said, holding out her hand.

Maggie reluctantly put it in her friend's hand. Misha held the phone up to Maggie's face to unlock it and then scrolled to the app. She looked at Maggie's profile. "Are you kidding me with that profile photo?"

She shook her head. "It's a good photo."

"Of your back in silhouette. Was this at the beach last summer?" Misha asked.

"Yes. You said to pick a photo where I was happy."

"I did but somehow I assumed you'd know people want to see your face, too," Misha said, laughing.

"Hmm."

Misha shook her head. "Well, stand over there. We are going to get you set up."

"Shouldn't you be doing something important?" Maggie asked.

"Helping out my best friend is important," Misha said. "Listen, if you don't want to get matched, I'm not going to push you into it. But you have been alone for a long time and if you were happy, then I'd be happy, too, but you're not. I'm not sure if you're punishing yourself or just scared… You said *scared*, but you're the least timid person I know."

Maggie chewed her lower lip and then nodded. "I think I am punishing myself for being so stupid."

"Well, stop. You're not stupid and we all make mistakes when it comes to emotions, especially love. Do you want to do this?"

She nodded. "Yes. Go ahead and take my picture."

Misha smiled at her before giving her some directions on where to stand. She snapped the photo and Maggie went back to her side to watch as Misha uploaded and cropped the photo and then toggled the button to look for a match in the dating category before handing her phone back. "There you go. Now you can wait for the matches to come in. And you don't have to accept any of them."

"Thanks," she said.

"You're welcome. Now help me get ready. I'm going to

be livestreaming the presentation. Would you mind keeping an eye on the comments?"

"Not at all. That's why I'm here. What am I looking for?"

"Just any of those creepy, spammy things that pop up," Misha said.

Maggie nodded. She'd been to a few of Misha's livestreams and for the most part her followers were great and supportive, but she had a few haters and some spam from men who made wildly inappropriate comments. "I'll block them."

"Thanks. I'm so excited for this. It's nice to be doing this in Royal and to have so many people turning out," Misha said.

"It is. When I walked through the hall, I heard a lot of positive buzz. You're going to kill it," Maggie said. "The public is going to love the Surprise Me! function."

"Thanks. I guess I better go," she said, as her theme music started to play. Maggie hugged her friend and then stepped to a place just off the stage out of view where Misha had set up her laptop so that Maggie could monitor the comments.

"Hello, ByteCon! I'm Misha Law, the creator of k!smet. I'm so excited to be here today to share the app with you and we are going to match a couple live. So if you haven't downloaded the app, then do it now. You don't want to miss out on being the first to try the new Surprise Me! function and finding your perfect soul mate today!"

Misha went into her spiel about the app, describing the different streams that were available. She finished her overview presentation after about fifteen minutes and then switched to live mode and broadcast it on the jumbo screen behind her.

"Now the moment we've been waiting for. We are going

to use the Surprise Me! button. K!smet, let's make a match," she said, hitting the button.

The screen was populated by a crowd that Maggie had provided the graphics for and slowly the group was whittled down to just two figures. The faces were revealed at the same time and a gasp went through the crowd. Maggie looked up to see her own face on the screen and then gasped herself when she realized she'd been "matched" with Jericho Winters.

She glanced at her phone and saw the alert and then the button asking her to accept it.

Misha looked over at her, her social smile frozen on her face. Maggie knew her friend needed this launch to go well, and she wasn't going to be the one to let a centuries-old feud mess it up for her. Without another thought, she hit Accept on the match.

The ball was in Jericho Winters's court now.

Jericho Winters cursed succinctly under his breath. Several people near him had turned and were waiting to see if he was going to accept the match. Some who knew him and were aware of the bad blood between his family and the Del Rios stared. But this…the woman he'd been trying to get out of his head for six weeks being matched with him. His hormones were trying damned hard to convince his brain that there was more to this than he was sure there was.

He hit Accept.

"Jericho Winters, if you could make your way backstage," Misha said, as the Jumbotron confirmed it. "I want to have a word with our matched couple. But I think this perfectly demonstrates the unpredictability of possibility."

He heard Misha continuing to talk as he made his way around to the roped-off section that led to the backstage area.

The scent of jasmine was in the air as he walked around the curtained corner. He saw Maggie standing off to one side chewing on her nails. She dropped her hand as she seemed to become aware of him and looked up.

"Jericho Winters."

Just his name, but it sounded like the worst sort of curse.

He walked closer to her until only a few inches separated the two of them. "Maggie Del Rio."

He tried to put the same edge in his voice but the truth was, this close he could see the amber flecks in her eyes and he noticed how thick her black lashes were. She had high cheekbones and as he let his gaze drop lower, he couldn't help himself—he almost groaned when he saw her full lips.

Oh, he'd noticed her mouth before this. Had spent hours at night fantasizing about how it felt under his. God damn. He needed to get laid. And this app business was a mistake. A big one.

She sighed. "I'm sorry. I shouldn't have said your name like that. I mean, we've never even met."

"No we haven't," he said. "Should we at least introduce ourselves before we jump straight into family animosity?"

"Probably. I mean, you could be totally decent," she said, wryly.

He couldn't help the slight grin. "I could be. But you might have me confused with my brother."

She gave him a shy smile back. "I'm Maggie Del Rio, owner and lead art director for MaggieInk."

She held her hand out to him and he couldn't help noticing her brightly colored manicure. He took her hand. "Jericho Winters. RoyalGreen Architects."

A shiver of awareness went through him, not surprisingly. The intensity of his obsession with her had pretty much guaranteed that there'd be a spark. But he hadn't expected to like her. She flushed and then pulled her hand back and rubbed it with her other hand.

"You designed this space, didn't you?" she asked.

He nodded, not sure if she wanted him to launch into a description of the building like he'd almost done with Brian earlier. Instead he looked around, hearing Misha still talking on the stage.

"What are we going to do about this?" he asked. "My brother is an investor in the app so I don't want to do anything to generate any negative publicity."

"Same. Misha's my best friend. We could do it, just go out on a date and then say we don't have any chemistry or something like that," she said. "My family is probably going to have a conniption."

"The entire family?"

"Like yours isn't going to," she said, raising both eyebrows at him.

"They are. I get it. I kind of think it'll be fun. People won't be expecting us to go on a date."

"No they won't. I hate being predictable," she said. But he wasn't sure that was the truth. Something in her eyes made him realize she was hiding something.

Before he could ask her about it, Misha came rushing up to them.

"Oh my gosh. Y'all, I had no idea that you were going to get matched. So what do we want to do?" Misha asked. "I had to practically twist your arm to get you to do this, Maggie. Do you want to back out? I can say it was a glitch."

"I'm pretty sure you don't want to say the Surprise Me! button made a mistake on your live match," Maggie said.

"You didn't twist my arm," she said, giving Misha a look that Jericho couldn't read.

"We both decided to just give the people what they aren't expecting," Jericho said. "What does this match entail?"

"It's up to you. The app will suggest dates that fit y'alls profile and then you go on them," Misha said. "I had been planning to set up the first one live but if you'd rather do it privately..."

Maggie chewed her bottom lip again and he realized she was nervous. He looked at Misha and asked her to give them a moment. She looked over at Maggie first before stepping away to give them some privacy.

"What do you think? If we hamper her demonstration, it could hurt the appearance of our match," he said, realizing he wanted her to say yes to this. Wanted to do whatever the app thought would be a good date for them. So why was he acting like he just wanted it for Trey's investment? His brother would do fine if the app didn't go public. And he'd never been someone to hedge before.

"Let's do it," she said.

Two

Seated on the stage next to Jericho was doing nothing to stop her racing heart. Misha had asked Jericho his thoughts on the dating app, and though she knew she should listen to his words, it was the deep timbre of his voice and the cadence of his words that distracted her.

From the side profile, his strong jaw and sharp blade of a nose were visible. There was strength in his face and, as she let her gaze dip down, in his broad shoulders as well. There was something substantial about Jericho. In a way, he was the opposite of Randall, who'd been more gym muscles than body strength.

"Maggie?"

"Hmm...?"

Jericho's neck was corded with muscles, and as he turned to face her, humor was in his expression and in his dark brown eyes. She smiled back and she heard murmurs from the crowd and snapped out of it. "Sorry about that. I guess I like the unpredictability of Surprise Me! matching me with

Jericho. Let's face it—the two of us weren't going to ever hook up on our own."

That drew laughter from the crowd and a nod of agreement from Jericho.

"That's one of the very things that I had in mind when I designed the app," Misha said. "I think we are limited by our perceptions of what we want."

"I agree with that," Maggie added, remembering her own "perfect" match who'd left her high and dry. She wanted to get this back on track. They were up here to help show the benefits of using the k!smet app. She remembered that the program that Misha had written had search parameters different from other dating apps. "So what did the app see in us?"

"Great question. We can look at the back end and see where you two overlap and where you might each bring a quality the other is lacking," she said.

Misha started tapping on her smartphone and the screen behind them lit up with their profiles side by side. Jericho's photo was clearly taken on the lake on a boat. He smiled easily at the camera, he had his shirt off and she could clearly the strength of him that she'd only guessed at earlier. He was tanned and had thick muscles on his pectorals and then a flat abdomen. The photo cut off at his waist.

"Jericho's profile shows an outdoorsy guy who is active. Maggie, you have checked the same box," Misha said.

"I sure did. You know how much I love to walk on the weekends," she said.

"I do," Misha agreed. "So this is a clear like-to-like category. But if you look further down, here is where the magic of k!smet comes into play. Maggie has checked that she is spontaneous and isn't much of a planner. Jericho, on the other hand, is prepared for every eventuality. So k!smet sees that this might be an area where opposites attract."

Maggie looked over at Jericho. "What do you think?"

"That I didn't plan for this and I'm rolling with it," he said.

"And?" Maggie asked.

"Well, hell, Maggie darlin', I am already working out a plan for asking you to dinner and trying to figure out what kind of place would suit you."

She raised her eyebrows at *Maggie darlin'* but she wasn't upset by the endearment, though the way it rolled off his tongue, she had a feeling that he'd had a lot of "darlin's" in his dating life. "Dinner would be great. Sheen?"

"Of course," he said.

"Wow. I think you can see that k!smet has stumbled onto a match that might end in love," Misha said. "I think we'll leave the interview here. Thank you, everyone, for coming to this demonstration today. Help me wish Maggie and Jericho the best."

There was a round of applause and cheers from the crowd as Jericho offered her his hand as they hopped off the high stools they'd been seated on. That heat from him sent a tingle of sensual awareness up her arm and straight to her center. She was hyperaware of the warmth of his touch and how close he was. He smelled good, too. Spicy and exotic, and she almost closed her eyes and leaned closer to him before she caught herself.

She admitted to herself that she was having fun with this but she knew that once her family caught wind of it—especially her father, who never seemed to approve of anything she did—there were going to be issues. They stepped backstage and she turned to Jericho.

"Were you serious about dinner?" she asked.

"Weren't you?"

"Are you one of those guys?" she asked.

"No. I'm one of a kind," he returned.

She couldn't help the smile that danced around her lips. He was flirty and fun but she suspected that, like her, he was playing a part. Being what he thought she wanted him to be.

"I can see that," she said, reaching up and running her forefinger along the edge of his jaw. His pupils dilated and his body stiffened under her touch.

Interesting that he was just as affected by her as she was by him. They had chemistry, which wasn't a bad thing. If nothing else, they could hook up and maybe he'd be what she needed to break her long dating dry spell.

"I like you, Maggie," he said. His voice was rough and the words low, brushing over her senses like a warm breeze on a cold day.

"That's good because we're going to have to at least try to make this look real for Misha's and your brother's sake."

"Oh, I think I can deliver on real," he said, putting his arm around her waist and pulling her closer. She put her hand on his chest and felt the heat of him through the fabric of his shirt. Other than his arm at her waist and her hand on his chest, they weren't touching but she felt as if he was pressed to her body. In her mind, she was already wrapping herself around him, kissing him deeply and proving to herself and to him that she could be real, too.

But only in her mind. "Jericho."

He nodded, dropping his arm. "Sorry. I'm also a see-what-I-want-and-take-it kind of guy."

"Noted. I'm not saying no. It was more a 'not right now,'" she said to clarify to him. Her body was at war with her common sense—her brain saying to keep her distance and protect herself from her own bad judgment, and her body saying fuck that. He was hot, he wanted her and it had been too long since she'd slept with anyone.

"Good to know," he said.

Misha waved them over to do an interview with the press and local television show *Royal Tonight*. Maggie nodded but turned away to fix her lipstick, needing a minute to herself. It was one thing to think of hooking up with him but something else entirely to do it. And though she'd checked *spontaneous* on the profile, she knew she wasn't. She was cautious and overthought everything—including agreeing to do this.

Touching Maggie might not have been his smartest idea but he had no regrets. He was happy with the match and, given the fact that his sister and brother had both texted him, he was pretty sure that this time with Maggie might be all he had. He ignored the family group chat for now.

Misha looked shell-shocked but impressed Jericho with her professionalism. Her smile had only faltered once and she just kept on talking, like matching up rivals was the best thing her app could have done.

To be honest, Jericho still wasn't sure if it was a good or bad thing. His body was like *hell, yes* but his mind was throwing up all kinds of objections. Not the least was the fact that the Del Rio clan hadn't been trustworthy in all the time they'd been feuding. True, he himself had very few interactions with them, but genuinely was he knew this was going to be a hard sell to his family and he suspected hers as well.

Maggie joined them.

"Given your families' histories together, do you think that this match is simply hijinks, or something that is written in the stars?" Mandee Meriweather from *Royal Tonight* asked.

Misha and Maggie looked at each other and Jericho stepped forward. "I think that we are going to have to wait and see. As we said earlier, this isn't a match that would have happened outside the app and the chance to explore the possibilities entices both of us. The k!smet app and Surprise Me! function are meant to create opportunities you wouldn't make yourself in all avenues of life and I think myself and Maggie are a perfect example of that."

"I agree with Jericho. Our families are important to both of us but my parents also want what's best for me and I'm sure the Winters family is the same."

"Indeed," Jericho said.

"Thanks, everyone, for the questions and I'm happy to answer more about the app but we should probably let these two go for now," Misha said.

"Can we get a quick photo?"

Maggie looped her arm through his and through Misha's. "Sure."

"Great. Now one of just the two of you," the photographer said.

He was glad he'd put his arm around her earlier because he was almost prepared for the jolt of awareness that went through him when he did it this time. He pulled her into the side of his body and she put her arm around his waist, and he felt himself stir and adjusted his legs as he hugged her to his side. They both smiled for the cameras, and then when they were done, he let his arm drop and they walked away from the press and Misha.

Maggie's stride was quick, as if she wanted to get as far away as possible. From him or the press? He didn't know but followed her out of the backstage area.

"We need to talk," she said.

"I agree. There's an office space just over here that I think we can use. We'll have some privacy there," he said, pointing to a door marked Private.

She nodded toward him and they went through the door. She immediately stopped as soon as it closed behind them and leaned back against the painted wall. She put her head against the wall and closed her eyes.

"Are you okay?"

"Yes. Just needed a minute. My smartwatch hasn't stopped vibrating in the last five minutes and I'm pretty sure my entire family knows about this. I'm not sure what to say," she admitted.

"The Winters family WhatsApp chat is blowing up, too. Do you want to call it off?" he asked.

"I don't see how we can. Misha needs this live match to be a success. What about you?" she asked.

"I agree. I don't want to back out," he said. "I'm going to tell my family that we are going to go to dinner. Just a test date to see how this works out."

"I like that. I'm sure that my father is going to balk at the thought but my mom will get it," she said.

"On the plus side, we're both grown-ass adults," he said.

"Has that ever stopped your parents from butting into your life?" she asked. "If so, I need some tips."

"Well, not really but I do remind them often," he said. And he had. His family was close but they didn't really try to control his life. But Maggie was a Del Rio and that meant that his family was going to have some concerns. He got that. But he also wasn't going to miss the chance to have dinner with her and maybe more.

Time would tell if this was a match written in the stars or just one more online snafu. But for now he wasn't going to back down.

Maggie looked at Jericho. Hotness aside, she needed to start figuring this out. Dating shouldn't be this hard, but for her it always had been. Even before Randall, she'd never just been chill about meeting someone of the opposite sex. She knew a lot of the pressure was self-inflicted. Her mom had always been someone to point out her strengths and give her the tools she needed to build her own confidence.

Jericho was watching her and she knew she was showing him all the wrong sides right now. She straightened from the wall, putting her shoulders back. Time to remember she was Maggie Del Rio.

"I like that thought. So for this first dinner, there is going to be a lot press and public speculation…"

"You're right. And since I announced it publicly, we can't blame them," he said. "Instead of Sheen, want to come to my place or I can go to yours? Might be better for our first date to be out of the public eye."

"Sounds good to me. Why don't you come to mine tonight at eight," she said, using the private chat in the k!smet app to send him her address. "Is that too late?"

"That works. I'll see you then. You can get out of the expo hall down that way or go back through the crowd."

"I think I'll choose the private route. I need to get to a client meeting in forty minutes," she said.

"I'll walk you out," he said.

"Why?"

"It's the gentlemanly thing to do," he said.

"Are you a gentleman?"

"I try. I know I came on too strong earlier, but I do try," he said.

"Why did you do that?"

"Seemed like you were looking at me like you wanted to kiss me," he said.

She blushed and chewed her lower lip. "I was thinking about it."

"Were you? Then why'd you stop me?"

"I don't always have the best instincts when it comes to men," she said. She wasn't going to pretend this was easy for her. She wanted him, but that made her doubt that she should have him. Her own gut was so unreliable when it came to the dating choices she'd made she couldn't trust it. Could she trust Misha's app? God, she had no idea.

"Why is that?"

"I'm not sure. I was left almost at the altar, which doesn't help," she said.

"I read about that. What happened?"

"That's not a barely know-you conversation," she said.

"Isn't it? I find that people are most honest when they don't know you," he said. "I mean there's nothing really to lose by being honest at this point. We might not even go on more than one date."

She tipped her head to the side studying him. She'd never thought of it that way. But it made her realize that he must have a lot of experience with first dates. "Been out with a lot of strangers?"

"I have. I keep things casual. So if your gut is saying he's not looking for forever, it's right," he said.

"I'm not looking for forever, either." She didn't know if

she'd ever be able to be engaged again. All the pressure that came with it wasn't something she was sure she wanted to sign up for. But more than the pressure was the broken hopes and dreams. The life she'd thought she'd have with Randall that was suddenly gone. And as much as she knew she'd gotten lucky that he'd bailed before they were married and had kids, she wasn't sure she'd ever trust a man enough to get that close to marriage again.

"Maybe the app knew that," he said. "Damn. I can't even believe this."

"I know, right?" She couldn't help the giggle that came out of her. She'd spent the last two years avoiding any man. No dates, no fix-ups when her mom had subtly mentioned trying to set her up. Nothing. And then this very public match to a Winters.

He laughed, too, and then shook his head and rubbed the back of his neck. "Crazy. Trey is a big believer in this app, which is why I downloaded it."

"Yeah? Misha's a genius and I trust her, which is why I did," Maggie admitted. "And if I'm being totally honest, and since by your reckoning, I can be with you—I'm intrigued to see if there's more to you than meets the eye and where this leads."

"Into my arms?" he asked.

"Let's figure out if our families and us dating is going to happen first," she said. "I know I checked *spontaneous* but I'm not. I'm cautious. I'm not a planner, but I don't ever just leap."

He nodded. "I do when it comes to dating. Seems like when you try to plan a relationship…"

"It never works out," she finished.

"Exactly."

They'd gotten to the end of the hall and he opened the door for her. The heat of the Texas August afternoon wafted in, wrapping around her and stirring her hair, making the strands wrap around her neck. She reached up to push it back.

"It's been interesting meeting you. See you tonight," she said, then turned and walked away.

He was too intriguing. It wasn't just the sex thing. It was the way he looked at life and the contradictions between what she'd expected of a Winters and who Jericho was. To be fair, she hadn't really thought of him as a Winters. Not really. Jericho was too big a presence to lump in with that rival clan.

But she knew she was going to have to face that. She put her sunglasses on as she walked toward her car and finally looked at the messages in the family chat.

Preston: Sis, you good?

Mom: Call me. Since when do you online date?

Dad: Family meeting tomorrow 9 a.m.

She shook her head. Then took a minute to write her response.

Maggie: Yeah, I'm good, Pres. It was about time I tried dating again. I will look at my schedule and let you know if I can make the 9 a.m.

Her phone rang and she glanced at the caller ID before answering.

"Preston."

"I like your ballsy response but Dad is going to lose it."

"I know, I was being bratty. I'll text that I can make it in a few minutes. I just can't deal with him being autocratic sometimes."

"I get it. So Jericho Winters…"

"Yeah. It's Misha's app, so I couldn't bail," she said, realizing she didn't feel like letting her brother know how she really felt about Jericho and admitting to herself for the first time that she was excited to see him again.

"I doubt Dad will see it that way."

"You're right," she said. "But I'll make him see it."

"Good luck with that. See you tomorrow morning," he said.

"You, too. Bye."

She texted back that she could make the meeting and her mom sent a thumbs-up and then a smiling face and then the kissing face.

She didn't delude herself that the family meeting was going to be easy and neither was this "date" tonight with Jericho.

Three

Jericho showed up at Maggie's place just a little before eight. He had a bottle of wine in one hand and a bouquet of gerbera daisies that he'd been unable to resist picking up. He'd said he was a gentleman, and gentlemen brought flowers.

He wanted the gesture to be sincere but he wasn't sure. What was he playing at? Her honesty, combined with her physical hesitancy, had thrown him. Part of him said to make this an act. To play that they were dating to help his brother and her friend, but another part… That gut-deep, lust-driven part of him wasn't having it.

She opened the door to the sound of Santana's guitar blaring in the background. She had pulled her long hair up into a high ponytail, changed into a pair of wide-legged shorts that ended at the top of her thigh and made her legs seem endless and wore a slim-fitting halter top that enhanced the curves of her breasts and her nipped-in waist. He swallowed and then smiled as if she hadn't blown every thought from his head. As if he wasn't standing on her doorstep with wine when what he wanted was to open his arms and take her into them. Kissing her so long, so hard and so deeply that he wouldn't lift his head until they were both naked.

"Evening," he said.

"Hey. You're on time, something I can appreciate. Fair warning, I tend to always run late," she said, with a wink. "Are those for me?"

"They are." He handed her the bouquet and the bottle of wine.

"Thanks. Come in and grab a seat in the kitchen at the bar," she said, then called out to her in-home assistant to lower the volume. "Sorry about that. But I love 'Supernatural' and it can only be played at full volume."

"Don't be sorry, I agree with that. So what's for dinner?"

"Taco salad. In this heat I can't be bothered to cook," she said.

"Agree. I'd be grilling if I was home."

"Do you do that often?"

"Well, since I like to eat and keep late hours, yes. Sometimes I stop at the TCC but then I'm distracted," he said as he took a seat at one of the wrought-iron-backed tall stools at her breakfast bar.

She put the daisies in water and then went back to a large wooden bowl where he could see she had the salad already prepared. She put in a few finishing touches. "Corona with lime is my go-to drink with this, but I have lemonade, wine or tequila if you'd prefer those."

"Corona works for me. Can I help?"

"If you want to grab two beers from the fridge, we should be good to go," she said. She put the salad bowl on the table that she'd already set with two places. She also got some wedges of lime, which she placed in the center, and he twisted the caps off the bottles and went to join her.

She was so casual that he should be at ease. But he wasn't. He was conflicted, and he knew that nothing was going to change until he figured out if he was going to try to sleep with her. Also, there was the slight issue of his family.

They sat down and she dished up a portion of the taco salad for him. She did the same for herself, then tapped the top of her beer bottle against his. "Cheers."

"Cheers," he said.

"So… I've been summoned to a family meeting tomorrow morning," she said.

"I suspect I'm going to be as well. So far I have the family chat on mute," he said. But he knew he was going to have to respond some time tonight.

"Good idea. But if I do that my mom freaks out and comes to my place," Maggie said. "She worries."

He smiled. "Yeah, parents do that. Why'd you bring up the meeting?"

"I want to get ahead of this. I know my dad and your dad really hate each other and I've only heard my father's side, but I get where he's coming from."

"Same. And then adding in all of the bad blood that each new generation adds to the feud, it's a big ask for us to date," he said.

"It could be," Maggie admitted. "But maybe it's time to get over the feud and move on."

"Do you think your dad will go for that?"

"No." She shook her head and laughed. "He's the most stubborn man on the planet."

"I bet my old man could give yours a run for that title. What are you suggesting, then?"

"That we figure out what we want and then call a meeting with both of our families. Maybe get an unbiased third party to mediate," she said.

"To what end?"

"Well if we are going to support the match made by k!smet, then I think we are going to have to go on some public dates, and it might be better for us if we set the terms," she said.

She was making a lot of sense. He didn't want to have his father or the rest of his family interfering in dates with Maggie. Or would that interference be the excuse he could use to keep his hands to himself?

"What are you thinking for the dates?" he asked.

"Just a set number of public outings where we can look like we are out together. I think the app will continue to suggest things."

He leaned back in his chair and nodded. "Why a set number?"

"Well, I think we both know this isn't going to work and a set number gives us an out," she said. "And it will make our families happy."

"What if we both don't know it's not going to work?"

"You think this could be a real match?" she asked.

"I don't know. Maybe we table all this talk about our families and try to really get to know each other."

Inviting Jericho into her home had been a calculated risk. But after she'd almost kissed him, she knew she needed to test herself with him before they were in public. See if what she'd felt had just been nerves and the excitement of having a date again after all this time.

Which she knew was her own fault. She could have dated

after Randall left her. Some of her friends had encouraged her to find a super-hot guy and hook up just to make Randall jealous, but she hadn't. She'd been too in her feelings and those feelings had been all the worst, ugliest things she could say about herself.

Now he was suggesting they get to know each other.

Let down her guard and let him in.

No way.

She wasn't going to do that. And she had a feeling he wouldn't, either. Or maybe he would now at the beginning of their relationship. As he'd said, strangers could be honest in a way that intimate partners weren't.

"Like how?" she asked.

"Something simple," he said.

She arched both eyebrows at him. Her brother could arch one, which looked totally cool, but she'd had to settle for both. She remembered seeing a photo of him at the opening of an art gallery in Houston recently. "What kind of art do you like?"

"Photos or realistic things that show the Texas landscape or portraits. You?"

"Impressionist mainly. I do like some of the surrealists, and I truly love what some modern artists are doing, but I'm not a fan of when they do something just to shock," she said.

"I forgot you're not just a graphic artist," he said.

"Graphic artist and art director," she said. "I'm not really that great at the fine arts, like hand drawing and painting."

"There's more to art than perfect lines," he said.

"Says the architect."

He gave her a wry grin. "Indeed. But a straight line isn't necessarily perfect if you haven't taken into account the entirety of what you are working on. Take the expo center.

I went through ten drafts before I had a design that I was happy with. Each of those straight lines had to add up to something that would be more than a standard convention center. I wanted to create something more."

"Art. So I think we can add a check in the we-both-like-art column," she said.

"Agreed. Do you like sports?" he asked in a very casual manner.

She knew in an instant that he did and that he was probably very passionate about at least one. And she wanted to know what kind of man he was when he met some opposition, and she could never resist teasing her brother about his passion for baseball, which she couldn't get into. "Not really, but I do like hot guys so sometimes I tune in to a football match."

He flattened his lips and shook his head. "Dang. I thought we were going to be a match for the ages but that's a deal breaker for me."

"Is it? Can't live without your sports?"

"I *can* live, but really, what is life without basketball?" he said.

"Pretty much what it is with basketball. I don't know that I've ever watched a game. My brother is into baseball and my dad loves football and golf," she said. "So that's a non-match. What about food?"

"What about food?"

"Are you a foodie? Do you cook?"

He shrugged. "As I mentioned I grill, and I can make a mean omelet. You?"

"Same. Salads and soups are my go-tos year-round. So it's either chop veggies and toss them in dressing or grill veggies and blend them up into a soup. Not exactly a gourmand."

"Something else in common. We're not doing too bad here," he said.

"No we're not," she admitted. But did she *want* to like him? He had been funny about basketball, not angry, which was important to her. She didn't want to date a man whose default emotion was anger.

They talked about books and movies and they were sort of fifty-fifty on them as well. They had some similarities but he didn't share her love of 1940s rom-coms and she definitely wasn't into gangster films. Though it was fun to watch him do some impressions.

When they were done with their meal, she still was torn about going through with dating him. She liked him. But as she'd mentioned when he'd arrived, her father's anger toward his family was justified and as much as she didn't let him dictate her life, she had never been one to deliberately anger him.

And there was the attraction. She'd been sitting across from him all night trying her best to ignore the fact that his mouth was strong and looked firm. She remembered the feel of his arm around her and the warmth of his body pressed to her side. She wanted him.

She'd been denying that she was a sexual being for the last two years. Masturbating when she could no longer deny her needs. But with Jericho sitting across the table from her, watching her with his big brown eyes and that intensity that she couldn't help feel was more than a little bit sexual…

She wanted him.

She wasn't sure that was wise. For all the reasons she'd listed in her mind too many times. But this dinner was making her somehow believe she could have him, placate her father and help her friend.

She shook her head and thought wryly that there was

only one reason why she was contemplating this and it had nothing to do with her family or Misha, though she loved them both. It simply came down to Jericho Winters, son of her family's rivals and the only man who'd made her feel feminine and alive in the last two years.

She had no idea if the feeling was genuine or just some by-product of the fact that she'd finally decided to try dating again and the app had picked him. And somehow relying on anyone who wasn't herself seemed smarter than trusting her gut.

She had gone quiet, and he appreciated that the two of them dating was going to cause a lot of tension in their families. He wouldn't have put either of them through that just for a financial boon for his brother. But he liked Maggie. The more time they spent together, the easier it was for him to see the woman she was.

She was funny and smart. She laughed easily and wasn't afraid to talk about the things that mattered to her. He glanced around her house, which on the outside was a cookie-cutter suburban subdivision home but inside had been curated to reflect Maggie. There was richly colored Mexican tile on the kitchen floor and the walls had been painted a vibrant yellow. She'd incorporated a few paintings on the walls as well as plates and wooden serving pieces to create a space that was uniquely Maggie.

It was earthy, cultured and passionate. And as much as she was a passionate woman, he realized how much of it she kept hidden. She limited herself to showing him only the tip of her interest in any subject. She'd mentioned her broken engagement earlier and he wondered if that was at play here or if it was simply his last name.

"Does me being a Winters make you not trust me?" he asked bluntly.

Well, hell, he usually tried to be much more subtle than that. But it was getting late and he was going to have to leave soon and he needed to know as much about Maggie Del Rio as he could before he responded to his family.

"Yes. I'm sure me being a Del Rio doesn't help matters for you."

"It doesn't. But it's simply a wrinkle and I want to find a way around it. Do you?" he asked. To be honest, this evening had been a chance for them to decide what they wanted to do away from their families and the public. For himself he still wanted her and as much as he wanted her in his bed, he was a grown-ass man and didn't let his dick make decisions for him. Sure, it could influence him but this wasn't something that could be decided simply because he wanted her under him.

It had to be something they both wanted because as much as they were pretending they could coax an agreement out of their families, he knew this was going to be a hard sell to his parents and an uphill battle in public.

"I do. I'm not going to lie and pretend that I think this is actually going to lead to anything permanent between us. But I know I'd regret it if I didn't at least give it a try."

He smiled and leaned forward, putting his forearms on the table and reaching for her hand. He took hers in his, felt that electric jolt of awareness go through him. "Same. But I'm not going to rule out permanent just yet."

"Are you looking for that? I think you should know I will not ever agree to marry again," she said. "I can't walk around for months with a ring on my finger and then... I just can't."

She pulled her hand from his and twisted her fingers together. It was almost as if she'd pulled on a heavy coat and wrapped it around not only her body but her senses. She'd shut down completely.

"Forever doesn't have to mean a long engagement. If I did decide to marry you, Maggie Del Rio, we'd get it done in private and quickly."

"Promise?" she asked.

"Yes."

She chewed her lower lip and nodded. "Okay. So I'm meeting with my family in the morning. Do you know anyone who'd be unbiased we could ask to mediate? Then we can set up something with our families."

Mentally he went through his acquaintances. "Jack Chowdhry. He's well respected and a member of the board of the Texas Cattleman's Club. I think both of our families know of him but he's not connected to either."

"That's a great suggestion. Do you know him well enough to reach out to him? My brother might know him."

"I do but it might be good if your brother does as well so that it seems both families have agreed to it."

"Okay. I'm going to text Preston now. I want him onboard before I talk to my parents," she said.

"Then I guess that's my cue to leave. I'll be in touch tomorrow after I talk to my family," he said as he stood up. He carried his plate to the sink and turned to see that Maggie was standing behind him.

"Yes?"

"Uh…" She walked closer to him and put her hand in the center of his chest the way she had earlier in the day and then went up on her tiptoes and brushed her lips against his.

Immediately his blood felt like it was running hotter and heavier in his veins and he wanted to go slow, but as he opened his mouth against hers and deepened the kiss, he realized how impossible that would be.

She was a fire in his veins and someone he'd wanted for too long. He put one arm around her waist and pulled her into his body, felt the brush of her breasts against his chest and her fingers spread out against his chest as she tipped her head to the side and allowed him to deepen the kiss.

After a long moment had passed, she stepped back, licking her slightly swollen lips. "Just wanted to make sure the chemistry was real."

"I knew it was," he said. "But you can keep checking all you want."

She shook her head. "Not until we get everything sorted."

"Tomorrow, then?"

"Or the next day," she said.

He left a few minutes later and sat in his sports car thinking about Maggie and wanting her. No matter what happened between the two of them, that kiss had reinforced what he'd felt when he first saw her. And he wasn't going to let anything keep him from finding out if they were as hot in bed.

Four

Somehow when he'd been alone with Maggie he'd had a feeling that they might be able to actually date, but as he arrived at his parents' house the next morning in time for the breakfast buffet his mom put out, he knew that wasn't the case. He glanced at the familiar room with the painting of Eliza Boudreaux wearing the diamond, ruby and emerald necklace. She was the one who'd started the feud. She'd jilted Fernando Del Rio the first and married Jericho's great-grandfather Teddy.

But that was past. He had today to get through. He went into the dining room and kissed his mom, who gave him one of those looks down her nose.

"You're going to date a Del Rio girl?" his mom asked. Camille had dark brown eyes and long, naturally curly black hair and kept in shape. She worked at Winters Industries and was an integral part of their success.

"Maybe. Mom, it's more complicated than that. Trey is heavily invested—"

"Save the arguments until after breakfast. I'm more interested in why my always-playing-the-field son is suddenly keen to date someone an app picked," she said, taking a sip of her coffee.

Camille was actually his stepmom. His dad had married her when Jericho was eight after his mom had died in complications after giving birth to his youngest sister, Tiffany. But from the moment Camille had married his dad, she'd been mom to him and his siblings. Camille had a way of cutting past all the other bullshit that most people just accepted from him. He leaned against the counter trying to find something between the truth and a lie as he often did when he spoke to her. Finally he just shrugged. "I don't really know."

She smiled at him. "Don't say that to your father."

"Oh, I'm not planning to," he said. "I met with her last night just to see who she is, away from the business rivalries between our families."

"And?"

He realized he sort of wanted his mom's advice, which if he was honest, he hadn't actively sought since he was fourteen. "I like her."

His mom put her coffee cup on the counter and moved slightly closer to him. "Like her how? I've seen her around town. Is it just a fling thing?"

"Mom."

"Hey, I love you and want you to be happy but this affects the entire family. If it's just you wanting to hook up with a pretty girl, then you're on your own. If it's something more…"

She trailed off, but the look in her dark brown eyes just made him more aware of the stakes. His mom as usual had boiled it all down to the important stuff. Was he willing to put his family through a close encounter with the Del Rios, who had always been a thorn in their side? "I still don't know. That's why I waited so long to respond in the family group."

"The fact that you don't know might be the answer. I'd keep that to yourself until you know something more. But for now you are going to date the Del Rio girl?"

"I am. Her name is Maggie," Jericho said.

"The Del Rio girl?" Alisha asked as she walked into the kitchen.

He hugged his sister, who was only a year younger than he was. She was technically his stepsister since she was Camille's daughter from a previous marriage. But from the moment they met, they'd been close growing up and still were today. She hugged him back, then reached around him to get a mug and poured herself some coffee.

"Yes."

"Are you really going through with this?" she asked.

"Yes. Trey's invested heavily in k!smet," he said, realizing he needed to stop sounding like he was letting circumstances dictate what he wanted. Maybe that was what his mom had meant.

"So you're doing this for Trey?" Alisha asked skeptically.

"No. I like her. I saw her at the club a few weeks back."

"Have you been dating her on the down-low?" Alisha asked.

"No." But then Alisha gave him one of her knowing looks and he realized that fooling his family wasn't going to be any easier than fooling himself. He was pretty sure he should leave now before he ended up revealing more than he wanted to.

He headed toward the back door.

"Oh, no," Mom said. "You're not getting out of this that easily."

"Oh, f—"

"Watch your mouth."

"I was going to say *fudge*, Mom."

Alisha snickered.

"Breakfast is ready," the housekeeper said.

They entered the breakfast room together and Jericho was glad to see his father, younger sister Tiffany and his brother Trey along with Trey's eight-year-old son, Dez. Maybe it was just him but it seemed like everyone was watching him with heavy stares. He went to Dez at the buffet table and stooped down to hug his nephew.

"Sorry I missed you on *Nintendo Sports* last night," he said.

"That's cool. I played with Dad and beat him."

"That's not really hard to do," Jericho said.

"Uh, it's hard. I was distracted by the app mess," Trey said as he joined them at the far end of the room.

Dez chuckled as he started making his breakfast plate from the buffet.

"Yeah, about your app…"

"I didn't write the programming. Sorry. I saw your interview and you handled it like a champ but that had to be awkward."

"It's cool. Misha made sure we were all comfortable and even offered to say it was a glitch and try to do another match. But Maggie and I both thought that wouldn't look good for the app."

"You're not wrong. In fact, there's been a lot of online chatter about it. I wanted to talk to you before I make a push to the family, but I think you should do some dates with her. People aren't sure if it's an actual match or just a publicity stunt."

Since he planned on seeing Maggie again, he just nodded at his brother. When they were all seated at the long breakfast table and after they'd eaten and Dez had gone off to check TikTok or whatever he did, his father folded his hands together and looked over at him.

They'd talked about the Mavs and their chances earlier, but Jericho knew it was time for the discussion about Maggie Del Rio and what was next. He'd better start before his dad got rolling.

"Maggie and I talked last night and are going to do the dating thing. I know that given the tension between our families, neither of us is going to feel comfortable unless we lay down some ground rules," Jericho said. Having decided to see Maggie again, he needed to take control of this runaway car and start steering.

"And?" his father said.

"I've reached out to Jack Chowdhry to ask him to mediate something between us. I think given our family history, having something on paper would be good," Jericho said. Though, as Maggie was reluctant to get married, he wasn't worried about being left at the altar, but at the same time, her family had a history of coming out on top in personal skirmishes with his.

"Good idea. I'll phone our lawyer and get him to come along," his father said, pulling out his phone.

"That's going to be awkward. I don't want her to feel like I'm pushing her into something. I'll call Brian instead. He's a great lawyer, but he's also my friend," Jericho said.

He saw his mom give his sisters a look and Alisha shook her head at first and then sighed. "I'll go with Jericho so the girl doesn't feel weird."

* * *

Maggie arrived at her parents' house just after ten. She saw Preston's car in the driveway and was glad to see he was already there. She wore a pair of wide-leg trousers and a simple fitted blouse. Her mom opened the door as she walked up the drive and Maggie hurried to hug her. They'd always had a close bond and today she had a feeling she was going to need someone by her side.

"You're late. Did you do that thing I told you about setting every clock thirty minutes ahead?"

"No. That's silly. I'm trying to just…"

"Not be you?" her mom asked with a laugh. "You're not late, by the way, we asked everyone else to come at ten thirty."

"Thanks, I think. Who else is coming to a family meeting?"

"Cecily," her mom said. "Dad wants to make sure you're good."

Cecily Meachum was one of the Del Rio Group's lawyers and acted as their family attorney when needed. She was about eight years older than Maggie. Curvy and feminine, she used her looks to her advantage, as many people underestimated her because of them. Cecily was a ruthless attorney.

"I will be. You know I'm not going to let anyone walk all over me."

"I do, but you know your father."

"Is that Maggie?"

Her father entered the foyer and opened his arms. Maggie went to give him a hug. There was a bit of stiffness and formality to the hug. She knew her father loved her but he had always been more interested in running Del Rio Group than anything else.

"Morning, Dad."

"So you're online dating now?"

She kissed his cheek and then stepped back. "Yes. I thought you didn't want to discuss me dating."

"I don't but online dating… That seems sort of iffy."

"Iffy?"

Her mom came over rolling her eyes as she looped her arm though Maggie's. "He thinks you should meet a boy at the Cattleman's Club or at work."

"It worked for us," he said. "Let's go into the den so we can discuss this."

"Is he serious?" she asked her mom as they followed her father.

"Always."

When they got into the den, she saw Preston, who smiled at her, and then Cecily, who was looking at her phone and only put it down after they entered and waved at Maggie.

"Now that we are all here, we can get started," Dad said.

Maggie took a deep breath. She realized unless she spoke up now her father was going to dictate the terms of whatever he'd decided about her future. She'd never really been one to toe the line and she wasn't going to start now.

"Thanks, everyone, for coming," she said. "I know you are concerned that I'm going to be dating a Winters but that's what's going to happen."

"We haven't decided that yet," her dad said.

"I have. Listen, I know it's going to cause tension for both families. I talked to Jericho last night and we thought it might be nice to have a Del Rio and Winters meeting to make sure we're all on the same page. I reached out to Preston and we've asked Jack Chowdhry to mediate it."

Her father was obviously surprised that she'd beat him to

the punch on this, but he nodded. "I like it. Good idea. Cecily, you can go with her to make sure our family interests—"

"Dad, do you really think I won't represent the family?"

"I know you will but you also have your mother's kind heart. I don't want that Winters boy taking advantage of it."

"Then why don't I bring Preston? Even though he's my *little* brother and I was the one who had to defend him on the playground," she said.

"Hey," Preston said. "You're mad at Dad, not me."

She swallowed and looked at her mom. "Maggie doesn't need anyone to protect her, Fernando."

"Thanks, Mom," Maggie said.

"But I agree with your dad that Cecily should go with you. We just don't know Jericho Winters. If he's like his father, then he can't be trusted. The past has shown us that the Winters family will use anything to their advantage."

She nodded, knowing her mom was right. Last night in her kitchen it had seemed like maybe Jericho was the gateway back to dating and feeling normal, but this morning reality was staring her in the face and there was no way around it. Jericho's family and hers had more than bad blood. They had a history of battles in business that had left one side bruised and battered and the other victorious. While the winners changed with each battle, the truth was, she wasn't sure *what* Jericho wanted from her.

She didn't know if she could trust him or not and she wasn't willing to let herself be hurt by another man's hidden agenda. "Fine. Cecily can come."

"I'm coming, too," Preston said.

She just rolled her eyes. "Fine. Mom and Dad, you want to come?"

"No, honey," her mom said.

"Definitely not," her dad said. "When is the meeting?"

"Let me text Jericho and see if he's spoken to his family," she said.

She pulled out her phone and opened the k!smet app and used the private chat function.

Maggie: Family agreed to the meeting with Jack. Did yours?

Jericho: After some debate. What time is good for you?

Maggie: The sooner the better. When can Jack do it?

Jericho: Let me check.

She looked up from her phone and noticed Cecily watching her with a sympathetic smile. "You okay?"

Preston and her dad were talking quietly and her mom was checking the coffee service she'd had the housekeeper set up on the sideboard.

"Yeah, of course. Why wouldn't I be?"

"Because the last guy you dated turned out to be…well, worse than a Winters," Cecily said.

"This isn't dating. This is helping out a friend," Maggie said. Though the lie felt dirty even as she said it. The truth was she wasn't going to let anyone know what she felt for Jericho until she was sure he wasn't using her.

Jericho: Tonight at six thirty. Boardroom at the TCC. Work for you?

"Hey, can everyone do six thirty tonight?" she asked Cecily and Preston.

"Yes," they both said.

Maggie: See you there.

The boardroom at the Texas Cattleman's Club was richly paneled and had a long center table made out of mahogany and big leather chairs around it. There was a painting on the back wall of Texas longhorns grazing on a field. Jack Chowdhry waited at the end of the room with some papers in front of him. Alisha was by his side as Jericho entered.

"Jack, thanks for doing this," Jericho said. His sister nodded her hello.

"No problem. I'm all for our members getting along and putting old feuds to rest."

"Good luck with that," Alisha said.

"A," he said sardonically.

"J." She just sassed him back as she always did.

He shook his head. The door opened before he could say anything else and Maggie entered the room. Her long hair was in a braid that she'd somehow wrapped around her head to make it look like a crown. She had on another halter top that clung to the curves of her breasts. Alisha elbowed him and he tore his gaze from her.

But his mind was still on her figure and the look in her eyes that was very different from the one the night before. He forced a smile. Brian Cooper, Jericho's friend and personal attorney, came in after the Del Rios.

"Everyone, if you want to have a seat, I think we can get this started. Do you all know each other?" Jack asked.

"I know Maggie and I've heard of Preston but never had the pleasure of meeting him," Jericho said.

Preston Del Rio nodded. "Nice to meet you."

"This is Alisha, my sister, and my attorney, Brian Cooper," Jericho said.

"This is our attorney, Cecily Meachum," Maggie said. "It's nice to see you again, Brian."

He looked at Brian, unaware he knew Maggie. "Piper hired Maggie to be the art director of an installation in Dallas last summer."

"Well, now that the introductions are out of the way, let's get started," Jack said. "Maggie and Jericho have agreed to go on the dates that the k!smet app sets up for them and want to make sure there is no 'family drama' and that nothing happens to reignite the feud, which could ruin business for everyone involved."

"Any drama won't be coming from us," Alisha said.

"Since when?" Cicely asked smartly.

"Who are you again?" Jericho asked. The family attorney shouldn't be bringing that kind of attitude.

Maggie frowned over at him. "Don't do that, Jericho. You know that your family has stirred up a lot of—"

"Our family?" Jericho asked.

"That's right," Preston said at the same time.

"This is rich," Alisha said. "Why did we even bother coming here if they are just going to insult us?"

"Everyone, please sit down," Jack said.

Jericho sat down and looked over at Maggie.

"Do you still want to do this?" he asked her.

"Yes. I won't bail on Misha."

"I won't bail, either. I suggest we go on a set number of dates," Jericho said. Seeing her in this situation was making him really look at the how difficult dating Maggie would be. Alisha looked ticked and Brian...well, he was cool but Preston didn't seem happy to be in the same room as them, either.

And while he wanted Maggie, this wasn't going to be easy. His mom had been right when she'd said trust was going to be very hard to build. He got that and he knew that there was a pretty good chance nothing was going to come of this. At this point he wondered if he should just tell himself he was doing it for Trey.

"That works for me. Also let's set an end date. Two weeks?"

"That sounds fine," Alisha said.

"Thanks, sis."

"No problem. I am here to keep things from getting awkward."

Maggie laughed. "Preston is, too, but he obviously didn't understand the assignment."

"I thought I was here to protect you," he said.

"From who?" Jericho asked.

"You, Winters."

"Someone's going to have to protect you if you don't shut up," Alisha said.

"Families," Jack said. "I think we have enough for the attorneys and me to come to an arrangement."

"I don't," Maggie said.

"What is troubling you?" Jack asked.

"The Surprise Me! function is known for its unpredictability and I think we have to be open to that if we are going to help really promote it," Maggie said.

"That's fine with me," Jericho said. "We'll do these public dates that the app sets up for us and then when our time is up, go our separate ways."

Maggie looked over at him, and maybe he was just seeing what he wanted to, but it seemed to him that there was a hint of sadness in her eyes. But she nodded in agreement. Today had shown him that there was no way to broker peace with the Del Rio family. Her brother was obviously spoiling for a fight.

"It might be nice if each of your families could seem to be making peace while you're dating," Brian said.

"Uh, what?" Alisha asked Brian.

"Well, you mentioned that you want the app to get good publicity and for it not to seem like a stunt, right?"

"Yes, we do," Maggie said. "I think we could be cordial to each other in public, right?"

"Yes," Jericho agreed.

Alisha and Preston both left a few minutes later and the lawyers and Jack were in a deep discussion of the agreement that Brian's firm would draw up and he and Maggie would sign later.

"Want to get a drink while they hash things out?" he asked her.

"I'm not sure that's wise," she said. "Last night seems like a different life and today... I think we should face facts. There can never be anything real between the two of us."

Jericho shook his head, remembering the feel of her in his arms, and pulled her out of the boardroom and into the corridor that was empty. In the distance he could hear the sounds of voices downstairs in the bar.

"This feels real," he said, pulling her into his arms and kissing her.

Five

Maggie hadn't intended to find herself back in Jericho's arms but honestly, she was secretly glad she was. The meeting had been tenser than she'd expected. She had the feeling a few public dates were going to be all they actually had and she craved this kiss more than she should.

His mouth was firm and strong. He wasn't wishy-washy about kissing her, pulling her close into his body and turning so that she had the wall against her back. She put her hand on his jaw, felt the stubble on it and rubbed her fingers against it as his tongue tangled with hers and he thrust it deeper into her mouth.

Something deep and needy awoke in her soul. She put her arms around his shoulders, using that to pull herself closer to him. Letting the fullness of her breasts brush against his chest. His hand slid down her back, cupping her butt and rubbing along her hip. His hips canted forward and she felt the brush of his erection against the tops of her thighs.

He wanted her.

This was ridiculous. They'd just agreed to put on a show for their families but this… This was private. This was just for the two of them.

She tore her mouth from his as she heard the sound of footsteps at the end of the hall. He adjusted himself and stepped back from her as she glanced down the hallway and noticed whoever they heard had gone in another direction.

"That was close," she said.

"Yes," he agreed. He shoved his hand into his hair. "I'm not going to apologize for that."

"Good," she said, sighing and rubbing her finger over her lips, which still tingled. "We're too old to sneak around and I'm not sure where this is going."

"I agree on both counts. Could we do something for show and something private for us? Not necessarily sneaking—"

"We could. But to what end. I mean, my brother and your sister were pretty heated in there. It would have been even worse with our fathers," she said. "I think it's smarter for that to be our last kiss."

"Smarter? Maybe. But I'm not sure that it will be the last time I take you in my arms," he said.

She wasn't entirely sure, either. There was something about Jericho that was just making her want to let go. To reconnect to that part of herself that she'd let stay dormant for too many years. Why him? Why now?

But she knew that the answer wasn't something she could define. Maybe it was hormones or maybe it was the forbidden nature of it. Part of her was really attracted, not just to Jericho but also to the thought of having a secret relationship. After having been publicly dumped, her mind found it way too easy to justify.

"Ugh."

He smiled and shook his head. "I know. Why do you have to be a Del Rio?"

"Why do you have to be a Winters?" she countered.

He moved to lean against the wall next to her, his head turned to face her, and she couldn't help but notice how thick his eyelashes were and that he had a scar just near his left temple. She reached out to touch it. "How'd you get this?"

"Doing a sick scooter trick off a homemade ramp in our backyard," he said.

"You don't really seem like the X Games type. I assume that's what you were going for," she said.

"I'm not, but Trey was. He thought Dad would say yes to building a half-pipe in the backyard if we were both into it. Anyway, after I was rushed to the ER and had stitches, we gave up our X Games dreams."

She smiled remembering that summer she and Preston had decided they were going to be water ski champs. Their mom had been on board and had taken them out on the lake every day to practice jumps and stunts. But at the end of the summer, their passion for skiing had waned. It was funny to think that they would have something in common with the Winters family.

"You make your family sound almost normal and not like the competitive, driven demons I've always imagined you to be," she said wryly.

"Yeah? I always pictured your clan more as the devil," he said.

"To be fair, there is a lot of back-and-forth business competition and one-upmanship on both sides. I'm not going to pretend I'm not competitive."

"Me, either. But dating isn't a place where I normally want to feud." He paused, gazing straight into her eyes. "I do like you, Maggie."

"Not Maggie darlin'?"

He shook his head. "Of course, darlin'."

"Ah, I know you call all the girls that."

"How do you know?"

"Because it rolls off the tongue so easily for you," she said. "I can't make a decision based on lust."

"One-night stand?" he suggested. "I mean, let's face it—every time we come within a few feet, it's hard for us to keep our hands off each other."

"For you maybe. I have the famed Del Rio willpower."

He put his hands up near his shoulders. "Fine. If you don't want me, then we stick to the agreement and that's it. I won't touch you again unless you specifically ask me to."

She took a deep breath. Why had she said that? Because she knew that a one-night stand wasn't what she wanted. But at the same time, he'd put the ball squarely in her court. If she wanted to just do what they were going to legally agree to, then he'd abide by it.

Easy, right?

She could do that.

But she couldn't.

She wanted him and by his saying he wouldn't touch her unless she asked him to… Well, it was a challenge, and though she knew it would be wiser to just ignore him, a part of her wanted to see how far she could take things before he broke. Because she wasn't going to be the one to ask—he was.

"You're on."

Brian stuck his head out of the conference room and beckoned the two of them back in. He gestured for Maggie to go first but her words were heavy on his mind.

You're on.

He knew that maybe he should regret challenging her but he didn't. He wouldn't say he was overly competitive, especially compared with other members of his family, but in this case he was determined to win. Probably because it was Maggie.

She was a Del Rio. And just based on what had happened when they'd met, he knew that there wasn't going to be an easy way to ever have a relationship with her. But sex... Well, no one said they couldn't hook up. Except Ms. Maggie Del Rio. She'd dropped a barrier between them and he'd issued his challenge.

The truth was, no matter how long it took he was going to have her in his bed. If that meant making her think it was her idea, even better. But he knew that inevitably they were going to end up together.

There was too much passion for anything else.

"You coming?" Brian asked.

Jericho hurried into the conference room, where Maggie and her attorney had their head's close together. Brian drew him to the other end of the table. "I got them to narrow the dates down to five in two weeks. You two already announced a dinner. Sheen is the logical choice for that. A second one would be boating on a lake. We decided to let the app suggest two to show off the app's functions. Then you and Maggie can decide on the last one."

"After the five dates what happens?" he asked. He wasn't going to have very long with Maggie so he was going to have to work hard to get her to break.

"Well, Cecily and I are going to draft a press release and right now we're going back and forth on the language, but for now you can sign this agreement and we'll have an addendum with the press release," he said. "What do you think?"

He read the agreement, which had been drafted and printed out. It was pretty straightforward and honestly the weirdest thing he'd ever done when it came to dating.

"Looks good to me."

"Good. Jack, Mr. Winters is in agreement," Brian said as he moved toward the end of the table where Jack was.

"Ms. Del Rio is as well," Cecily said. "Once you both sign it and Jack witnesses it, we can leave. Brian, I'll draft the press release and send it to you for approval?"

"That works for me," Brian said.

Jericho watched Maggie, who'd put up some kind of barrier when they'd reentered the boardroom. Jack was saying something about the agreement and handed the paper to Maggie. Jericho watched the slashing motions she made with the pen as she signed her name with a flourish and then turned the agreement toward him. He took the pen from her and their fingers brushed.

An electric tingle went up his arm and he glanced up. Their eyes met and held, and he felt like all of the air had gone out of the room. How was he going to keep his hands off her? He wanted her more each time they touched. Even this exchange of a pen and brush of fingers had him hardening.

But he had determined he wouldn't break first. He just smiled at her. "Thanks, darlin'."

She rolled her eyes at him. "You're welcome, babe."

He grinned as he signed his name and handed the agreement to Jack for him to sign as the witness. Jericho realized he was going to have to come up with another endearment for Maggie. He wasn't going to get her to break by treating her the way he'd treated every other woman he'd hooked up with.

Which meant he was going to have to lower his guard.

Which seemed like the worst sort of idea. He didn't like the thought of being vulnerable to a Del Rio. Even the supersexy Maggie.

He'd figure it out and find a way to get what he wanted without putting himself in a vulnerable position.

"Thank you, everyone. I'll have copies sent to the lawyers. Maggie and Jericho, good luck with your dates. I'll see you all around," Jack said.

They all filed out of the boardroom and Maggie and Cecily left the club. Brian mentioned he had to get home to Piper and Jericho went to the bar to get a drink. The bar was busy. He saw a few single women whom he'd flirted with in the past and he briefly toyed with the idea of taking one of them home. Maybe the lust thing with Maggie was just him needing to get laid.

But it wasn't. He couldn't get her out of his head. None of the women he spoke to had that feisty spark that Maggie did. And he left a few minutes later. He drove toward the expo center and parked in front of it.

The building was a big project that he and his brother hoped would draw more business to Royal. But it was also a new phase for Jericho in eco design. He sat there trying to take his mind off Maggie and the remembered feel of her in his arms. This was where his head should be. On design. On the next big building project he had.

But it wasn't.

He sat there trying to force his thoughts to work but all he could remember was that almost kiss they'd had in the back corridor and how the two kisses he'd shared with her since that moment had only served to inflame his need for her.

And no agreement or dare was going to stand in his way. He wanted her and he wouldn't stop until she cracked and admitted she wanted him, too.

* * *

Cecily and Maggie stopped for drinks and dinner at a place close to Maggie's house. Maggie was glad that they'd reached an arrangement and wanted to talk about anything other than Jericho Winters.

But Cecily was still focused on the Winters family.

"Thanks for all your work today," Maggie said.

"No problem. I texted your father to keep him up to date on everything," Cecily said.

"Great. So we're good now?"

"Ah, yeah. I think you're in a good position to keep your eyes open," Cecily said after their order had been taken.

Maggie took a sip of her chardonnay. "What do you mean?"

"Just that you might be able to help your family out. We know there is something dirty going on with Winters' latest business deal."

"How do we know that?" Maggie asked. "You know I just do the graphics for the De Rio Group's promotional material."

Cecily took a sip of her vodka tonic and nodded. "Of course. It's just when you're with Jericho, he might let things slip."

"I doubt that man will let anything slip," Maggie said.

"I saw the way he was watching you. I'm pretty sure you could coax some information out of him," Cecily said.

Maggie didn't really like the sound of that. She had pretty well decided to try to get Jericho to break and kiss her but trying to get information... She wasn't even sure what kind of info Cecily expected her to uncover. "I don't know."

"I get it. I'm asking you to do something you're uncomfortable with. But we think that some of their investments aren't aboveboard and are being funneled through Winters

Industries. All I'm saying is keep your ears open. If you hear something that doesn't sound right, then just let me know."

"Sure, I can do that," she said, not wanting to let her family down. And she was also fairly confident that Jericho wasn't going to let anything slip. He'd been pretty clear where his allegiance was and it wasn't with her. He might want her in his bed but he wasn't ever going to trust her.

She was confident of that because she knew she'd never trust him. How could she? This dinner was a perfect example of why she couldn't. Their families. As much as she was glad they had an agreement for those dates to help out Misha, she knew it was going to be difficult.

This was part balancing family with her personal desire for Jericho. She wondered if she could do it. But honestly, after this, dating should be a whole hell of a lot easier. She hadn't thought of Randall and his douchey dumping of her. And she wasn't really dreading being seen with a man in public again the way she had been before she'd been matched by the k!smet app.

She finished her dinner with Cecily and went home. She found herself at the art studio she had in the back of her house. She blasted music and sat in her favorite chair with her tablet open to the drawing app. She started sketching, just trying to unwind, and wasn't surprised when she saw the lines taking on the shape of Jericho's strong jaw and piercing eyes. It was just a pencil sketch and she worked on getting his nose right.

His mouth wasn't an issue.

She remembered the intimate feel of it against hers and as she sketched it became clearer. She stopped as she realized what she was doing. Closed the app and left her studio.

Her phone pinged and she glanced down, surprised to see it was the k!smet app alert.

She opened it to a private message from Jericho.

Jericho: Thoughts on the fifth date?

She felt disappointed that his comment was about their family-approved dates. She thought about a fifth date. They were going to go to dinner at Sheen in two days. So something sooner?

Maggie: I'm hosting a wine and paint night tomorrow evening. Want to join me?

Jericho: Sure. Where is it?

She texted him the address. And he thumbs-upped it.

Maggie: Disappointed to see you've dropped into Winters clone mode.

She hit Send before she could second-guess herself. Their planned dates would only last for two weeks. So if she was going to make him break and win the challenge he'd set for her, she needed to move on it.

Also that sketch… It didn't take a genius to figure out she had him on her mind. She wanted more than five agreed-to dates. She wanted to actually be that woman whom she was going to pretend to be. Someone who had somehow become whole again and was ready to take on the world. Ready to stop hiding in her work and pretending that she wasn't affected by being dumped. She wanted to be strong again and stop hiding.

Jericho: Thought that's what you wanted.

Maggie: Really? You look smarter than that.

Jericho: A smart man knows when to back down.

Maggie: A smart woman knows when to push.

Jericho: What do you want from me?

Maggie: I don't know but not someone who's simply going through the motions.

She admitted to herself that she wanted the next two weeks to be more than she agreed to. She'd been dancing around it—and not doing a salsa where their passion and attraction reigned, but more of a formal dance. Something where they acted the parts that the app and their families had assigned them.

But it was time to end that. She wasn't going to play any more games. She wanted him but she also realized she *wanted* to trust him. And the only way that would happen was if she got to know him. Got to know Jericho Winters not because her family wanted inside information or because an app had matched them.

But because she liked him and wanted him and she was tired of pretending she didn't have desires.

Six

"Thanks, man, for doing your part. Alisha told Mom, who told everyone that the meeting with the Del Rios was a bit contentious."

He and Trey were sitting by his pool while his nephew played in it with some friends. Both men were drinking beer. "No prob. We agreed to two weeks of dates. Will the IPO happen in that time frame?"

"Yeah, we think so. If it doesn't, I might need you to extend things with Del Rio."

Del Rio. It was funny, but most of the time Jericho didn't see Maggie as the face of his family's bitter rivals. He had looked at the website of her company, MaggieInk, and he had to be honest—if he didn't know she was a Del Rio, he might have hired her. She was so accomplished and professional. Brian had sent him some photos of her work and a link to the exhibit she'd directed. Jericho had been impressed.

Which brought him back to his current dilemma. Normally he'd be honest with his brother and get some good advice. But he couldn't be. Not really. Maggie was the one woman that Trey wasn't going to be objective about. He rubbed the back of his neck and took another sip of his beer. He felt fucked. To be honest, he should stick to the public dates as they'd agreed.

No more late-night messages. Except he knew she wouldn't let his challenge go unmet. If he hadn't realized it earlier, it had become perfectly clear to him that Maggie Del Rio wasn't by any means meek. She might have given up on dating for a few years, but that was her choice.

"You look…intense. What's up?" Trey asked.

He shook his head. Having already decided not to burden Trey with everything that Maggie stirred in him, he changed the subject. "What's up with you and Misha? Is it just a business deal, or is there something more?"

"Just business. You know I don't mix business and pleasure."

"I know that we both say a lot of things," Jericho said.

Trey arched an eyebrow at him. "Like what?"

"Nothing specific. I mean we've both made statements in the past that we later retracted."

"Yeah, like that time you were going to go vegan and lasted about forty minutes into the barbecue," Trey said, snickering.

"Yeah. Like that." Jericho paused, taking another sip of his beer. "So, Misha…?"

"Where's this coming from?"

He downed the rest of his beer to stall for time but he could tell by the limited subjects his mind was coming up with that he wanted to talk about Maggie. "I like Maggie."

"What? How? I assume she's not a monster, since she and Misha are besties," Trey said.

"Yeah, she's cool, but I like her like her," he said.

"Fuck."

"Yeah."

"So, does she feel the same?" Trey asked. "Also, how is that even going to work?"

"It's not. I know it can't," Jericho said. "Forget it. I shouldn't have brought it up. I'm not going to let it go anywhere."

Trey turned his head and looked over at Jericho. "Truth?"

He shrugged. "I'm trying."

"Well, I guess if things go well on these public dates maybe things can change," Trey said.

Maybe. That was encouraging, but if things went badly, then he could add fire to the feud, which was the last thing he wanted. He changed the subject to the Mavs and he and his brother talked sports until Dez tried doing "tricks" off the diving board. Jericho and Trey looked at each other. They'd show the kid how it was done.

He forgot about Maggie as he horsed around with his brother and nephew in the pool, doing double flips off the diving board and helping Dez beat Trey in a race by grabbing his brother's ankle and giving Dez an edge.

Surrounded by part of his family, it reaffirmed to him that he wouldn't do anything to hurt them. He had a chance to protect not only Trey's investment but his family as a whole from any scheming by the Del Rios. He wasn't going to tell himself he'd stop lusting after Maggie, as he knew that was impossible, but he could try to resist the deeper pull she had on him.

That woman had gotten into his blood and into his brain. He couldn't sleep at night without her drifting into his dreams and turning them torrid and hot. He wanted her but not at the expense of Trey or Dez or the rest of his family.

He had dinner with them and then headed back to his gated house in one of the neighborhoods in Royal. Alone, in the big house that he'd had built when he'd landed his first big client at RoyalGreen Architects and had felt like he was solidly an adult. That it was time for him to start building his own legacy. He'd never been the successor to his father or Winters Industries. Which suited him because he'd always been drawn to figuring out how things were made and then creating buildings and designs.

Maybe that was his attraction to Maggie. Maybe he just needed to figure out how she was made. What made Maggie Del Rio the woman she was? She'd been hurt by love and had retreated and then come out of her shell in a big way by going on k!smet.

He'd never been hurt by love. In fact, he was pretty damned sure he'd never been in love, but then he hadn't been looking for it. He was thirty-three. Maybe it was time he started. Was this some kind of biological thing now that RoyalGreen was solidly established?

He walked through the well-designed rooms of his house and realized as he did so that he'd built it with his family in mind. The sports room with the large TV and the pool table where he hoped to teach his kids to play.

The large eco-designed bedrooms that used natural design elements instead of costly fossil fuels to cool and heat. He'd been thinking of something permanent and solid even though he was still living temporary.

And facing his family's past and their rivalry with the Del Rios was making him question everything. Especially as he entered the open plan living room space and could easily imagine Maggie standing in it.

"Was your family pissed about you dating Jericho?" Misha asked while they were getting pedicures at the Saint Tropez Salon.

"Sort of. Not really pissed but more concerned. I think that's what they were going for. More like 'we don't want you to get hurt,' but I could tell some of them still disapproved," Maggie said.

"Sorry."

"Don't be, I'm not. But I am nervous about the dates. The families both agreed to everything but…"

"But?"

She took a deep breath. Misha knew everything about Maggie; she never kept her in the dark. "I like him. But there's no future in it. My mind knows that but I can't get my body to accept it."

Misha reached over and squeezed her hand. "You've got this. I don't think the app would have put you two together if there wasn't something there."

"Are you sure? It seemed sort of random," Maggie said.

"I am sure. I had Nico look at the code and make sure it hadn't been tampered with," Misha said.

"I hadn't even thought of that," Maggie said. "Why did you?"

"We are hoping to release the IPO and there are those who'd like to see us fail. It was just something that I thought about and then couldn't let go of. What better way to make the app look like it didn't work than to match members of two rival families who would never normally date each other?"

"You're right but that wasn't the case?"

"No. It wasn't. The algorithm saw something in you two. I mean he's hot so there's that, right?" Misha said.

"Yeah. I mean he's really hot and a dynamite kisser," Maggie said.

"How do you know that?"

"We had a private meeting at my place before we talked to our families," Maggie said. "For my part, I needed to know if he was going to be serious about dating. I don't really want to get hurt again and especially not for revenge because of a business deal that we beat them out on."

"Makes sense…and the kiss?"

"He's wicked hot like you said. We have this really strong chemistry. Honestly, I've never been like this with any other guy."

"That's good," Misha said. "Maybe this match will work out."

"Maybe," Maggie said, but she wasn't sure. She was going to have to trust Jericho more than she was prepared to do.

"What's your fear?"

"That I read him wrong," she said. Misha was the one person she'd always been brutally honest with.

"I know, hon. But Jericho isn't Randall and you know he's not going to balk at signing any prenup. In fact he'll probably ask you for one."

"Mish—we aren't going to get married. We are going on five dates over two weeks. What are the chances we'll even fall into strong like?"

"Well, my app predicts heavy chances of that very thing," Misha said.

Maggie just rolled her eyes and shook her head. She hadn't mentioned the side bet. The one that she'd made with Jericho to see who could hold out the longest sexually.

After saying out loud how much she wanted him, she realized it was going to be harder than she expected.

But she wasn't one to back down. She never had been. That wasn't the Del Rio way. And though she didn't work for the Del Rio Group, she knew she was very much a Del Rio in temperament.

"When is the first date?"

"Oh, he's going to join me tonight at the wine and painting event I'm hosting. Want to come along?"

"I might. I'll have to check my schedule. I saw a bunch of matches from my app were going. Isn't that a date thing?"

"It is. Maybe use k!smet to find someone to join you."

Misha laughed and then sort of shrugged. "Maybe. I'm just slammed with work right now."

They started talking about their favorite TV show from the UK that had singles go to an island and hook up and try to find true love. As they were dishing about their favorites and the people they wanted to see go, Maggie realized in a way the public dates she and Jericho had agreed to might up being viewed by Royal as something similar.

And suddenly the behaviors of the participants weren't as funny as they had been before. She knew a television show was different, but the fact of the matter was, being viewed while you were dating was awkward.

"Ugh."

'What?"

"Do you think that *Royal Tonight* is going to cover our dates? What if people start rooting for Jericho to break up with me?" Maggie asked.

"Hon, I don't think that's going to happen. I mean you don't have a love chateau that you're going to retreat to and then discuss later. Or do you?" Misha teased.

"No," she said, blushing at the thought of being in a love chateau with Jericho. Honestly, maybe the fact that the participants in that show didn't hear in real time what was being said about them made it not matter. She would just ignore the gossip sites as she always did even as she knew they'd try to court them so that everyone could see the success of the k!smet app.

"What are you wearing tonight?"

"Something sexy. Jericho told me he wouldn't kiss me again unless I asked him to," she admitted. "I'm going to tempt him until he gives in."

Misha started laughing. "Yes. I love it. So you both decided it wasn't wise to sleep together?"

"Yeah."

" So you two have a side wager?"

"Yes. As soon as he said he wouldn't touch me again, I was like, 'Oh yes you will,'" Maggie said. "You know how competitive I can be."

"I do. Well, I'd say may the best person win but I know you will. You just don't quit," Misha said.

"No I don't," she said. And she wouldn't when it came to this bet with Jericho. In the midst of the stuff she was nervous about, she had no anxiety toward him. She knew that men wanted her and she knew how to turn on the charm and the attraction. And she also knew she needed a check in the "win" column when it came to intimacy and men.

Jericho parked his sports car in the parking lot at The Courtyard Shops where MaggieInk had a storefront and where her wine and paint session was being held that evening. He'd seen on the k!smet app that a number of meetups were using this event so he had a feeling that this would be a very public date.

He'd never really been a fan of painting but he could sketch and draw. He had always carried around a sketchbook when he'd been in college, mainly to jot down inspiration when he saw an element in the landscape that he thought would be challenging to turn into a functional building. But he had also at times sketched in it mainly architecture and building designs but sometimes he'd add in landscapes that he wanted to try and incorporate into designs.

He wore a pair of faded jeans and a designer button-down shirt and had toyed with shaving, but he liked the beard scruff so left it. He didn't want Maggie to think he was trying too hard, but he knew he was. He'd offered to pick her up but she had insisted they meet here. He was impressed with The Courtyard Shops, which were repurposed from a renovated old ranch. The design honored the ranches in the area and the complex was located about four miles west of downtown.

He was a bit early and when he walked into MaggieInk, he saw Maggie was running behind. Something he was beginning to realize she did frequently. "Want a hand?"

"Yes! I need each of those five-by-seven canvases put on the tables at the spots I've set up. Then I need the water pots filled. Do you mind?"

"Not at all," he said, getting straight to work. The music she had streaming in the shop was a funky mix of top forty songs from the last decade. Something he desperately tried to focus on instead of the image of Maggie, which he couldn't get out of his head.

She had her long black hair worn down this evening and it curled over her shoulders and down her back. Which he had noticed when she'd turned and he realized the dress she had on was backless. He had fought to tear his eyes from her bare tanned back. The skirt of her dress started right at the small of her back and was a pencil-type skirt so it hugged her butt and hips in a way that made him want to groan.

"Finished yet?" she asked, turning to find him standing there staring at her.

"No. I was just wondering if you had a pitcher to fill up the water pots?" he asked. Lame. He was coming up with dumb reasons for standing there when what he really wanted to do was lock the front door, take her hand and pull her into the back room and into his arms.

Something he'd told her he wouldn't do. Which he suspected was why she was standing there with her lips slightly parted as if she was begging for a kiss.

"I do. Let me get it for you," she said, turning and walking away from him, her hips swaying with each step.

She reached the sink at the back of the room and then bent over from the waist and opened the cabinet underneath it. His cock stirred and he realized that he might not mind losing if it meant that he got to put his hands on her waist and draw her back into his own body. He took two steps toward her with his hands extended.

"Aha," she said, standing and turning to him again. "You can use this one."

He dropped his hands and tried to appear chill, but since his blood felt like lava in his veins and all he could see now was her ass and all he could think about was taking her from behind, it was difficult, to say the least.

She held the pitcher out to him, and her face wore an expression that was a little too innocent.

"You know what you're doing to me, don't you?"

She shrugged, pursing her lips a little at first. "What? We agreed to do these public dates."

"And I said I wouldn't touch you, but damn, Mags, you are making it very hard for me to keep my vow."

"Am I?" she teased. "Glad to hear it."

"Minx. Fine, if that's the way you want to play it, I'm game. We'll see who breaks first," he said.

"I think it's going to be you. I don't lose," she said, handing him the pitcher as she stepped closer.

Barely an inch separated their bodies and he felt the heat of hers wrapping around him and the scent of her jasmine perfume. This close he could see the flush of desire on her cheeks and see the quickness of her breath.

She wanted him. Was it really worth winning not to take what he wanted?

But he knew it was. Nothing worth having was easy. He could play this game with her. And as much as he felt the knife's edge of desire, he knew that anticipation would make it even hotter when they came together.

He leaned in closer to her and her head tilted to the side the way it did when he'd last kissed her and he moved even closer but didn't allow his mouth to touch hers.

"Thanks."

She swallowed as he took the pitcher without touching her. He pivoted on his heel and walked back to the table where she had the supplies lined up, very aware of her eyes on him as he walked away.

He was still hot and horny but he felt as if she knew he'd come to play and that he wasn't one who lost, either.

He finished putting out the supplies she'd asked him to as couples started arriving for the lesson. She gestured for him to join her at the front and he saw they'd be seated very close together at a table for two. Perfect.

Seven

Her dress-sexy-make-Jericho-hot plan was working, she could tell, but she hadn't considered the fact that Jericho was definitely the kind of man who had more than a few tricks in his playbook. Luckily it wasn't her first rodeo, and as she flirted with him and came close but never touched him, she was reminded of how much she loved this part of dating.

The slow tease that came with being with a man she wanted but hadn't decided she was going to sleep with. She'd known that the last two years she was ignoring a critical part of herself but for so long it had felt safer to do so. Not any more, she thought. Never again would she let a man steal this from her.

The class was going well, too. She'd only introduced the wine nights this summer after doing some market research and also because she'd wanted to take advantage of the social part of the k!smet app. She saw notorious social media influencer Zach Benning and his wife, Lila, in the back and noticed Zach was streaming the class, which she thought would be a big boon for her business.

For the class she'd been demonstrating a very simple landscape design that was perfect for beginners. She looked over at Jericho's canvas. Dang. He was definitely not a beginner. She'd asked them to use a reference drawing that she had projected on the walls around the room so that no matter where someone was seated, they'd be able to view it.

Jericho had taken the basic Texas landscape and given it life. "You're really talented."

He glanced up at her, the graphite pencil he was using to sketch held loosely in his right hand. "Thanks. I'm okay with pencil but really am not great when it comes to adding color."

Which she guessed made a certain kind of sense given that he was an architect. She leaned a bit closer so that her breasts were almost brushing his shoulder and looked more closely at the landscape he'd sketched. She reached over him, again careful not to touch him, and spoke over his shoulder, hoping her words would be directly in his ear.

"I think if you keep it simple with a light watered-down wash on the bottom and maybe a few touches of sage green, you'll be good."

She noticed his hand shake as her breath brushed over the skin of his neck and ear. She smiled to herself and then took a deep breath and wished she hadn't as the scent of his spicy aftershave filled her senses. She took a step back as he turned to look at her. His pupils were dilated and she could tell he wanted her.

"Thanks for that. Let me see yours," he said.

She sat down on the stool she was using before realizing her mistake. He was on his feet, leaning toward her as she spun and used her knees to stop his advance. The very last thing she needed was him leaning over her, the warmth from his big body surrounding her and the yummy, manly aftershave enflaming her senses.

He arched one eyebrow at the move. She just gave him a quick smile. They were both playing a game after all. She pulled her canvas on to her lap and turned it toward him. Maggie's own art tended to lean more toward mixed media, so she'd put down a wash of color and then had used texture paste to create the cracks in the dried landscape and she had also made a few slashes with her palette knife in the paste to create fallen dead branches in other places.

"That's a very loose impression of the image," he said, leaning forward.

Even though she'd thought she'd created a barrier, she felt the heat of him. Or maybe that heat was coming from inside her. No *maybe* about it!

"That's sort of my style when it comes to my personal art," she said.

"But not for your graphic art business?" he asked as he went to sit back down.

She realized he was playing more in a thrust-parry-retreat manner. Something she wasn't used to. But she would let him set the tone for this round.

"No. I like something more retro-modern. One of my big influences for graphic design is Shag. I love the Disney-theme-park-inspired images and also just the cool, timeless feel that the prints give the viewer. I try to capture that in my business work."

"I do the same with buildings. I always want something timeless and classic but that is also modern."

"I can tell from the expo center. I'm also really impressed

at how many eco elements you were able to incorporate in something so beautiful," she said. The building's details had been in mind and she'd found herself sketching it after she and Jericho had met.

"Thanks. Most people don't see the beauty in modern buildings."

"Most modern buildings look like boxes or a cookie cutter of something else. Yours isn't."

"I try," he said blandly. "So do I have to color this in?"

"No, you don't have to do anything. This is really a chance to let your artist child out and let them play," she said.

"Ugh," he said.

"What do you mean by that?"

"I just hate the whole artist child idea, like there's another repressed person inside of me," he said drolly. "There isn't anything repressed about me."

She threw her head back and laughed. "Oh, I totally can see that."

He smiled at her and for a minute as their eyes met, she couldn't breathe in that wonderful caught-by-surprise way when emotions swelled without warning. They both sort of leaned in and she thought about kissing him when she heard someone clear their throat and she flushed as she turned toward one of her students.

"Yes."

"Sorry to interrupt. But I have a huge blob of paint on my canvas. Can you help me fix it?"

"Of course," she said, standing and following the student to their table.

A part of her knew she should be relieved she hadn't kissed him but the bigger part of her wasn't and wondered just how long she was going to be able to keep this game going.

* * *

Jericho watched Maggie walk away and turned his attention back to his canvas. She spent the rest of the class moving between tables and when everyone was finished, she wrapped up the evening with a thank-you speech and informed the participants there would be more classes to come in the fall.

He hung back as everyone filed out. The tables had been cleaned up by participants, but Jericho noticed some brushes and spilled water so took a moment to tidy things up. He knew that it probably seemed like he was looking for an excuse to stick around and he acknowledged to himself he was. After all, this was one of their official dates.

His phone started vibrating in his pocket and he took it out to see a flurry of messages from Trey and his sisters about him and Maggie.

There was a photo someone from the class had shared that showed the two of them when they'd almost kissed with the caption *k!smet magic??? Looks like one rivalry might fall prey to cupid's arrow.*

Trey: Nice work. I just got a high-level report that record traffic is being driven to the k!smet site.

Jericho thumbs-upped the message.

"Did you see this?" he asked as Maggie said goodbye to the last participant.

He wasn't sure how close he could safely get to her without breaking his vow not to touch her first. He was on the edge and each time he tried to turn the tables on her it backfired. There were no two ways about that. He wanted her and it seemed that he needed a twenty-foot or more distance to keep his body from forgetting what his mind had already dictated.

He held his phone out to her and she seemed to hesitate as she leaned in but kept her body a good distance from him. Seemed he wasn't the only one leery of getting too close. He wondered if they were both just torturing themselves by putting off the inevitable.

"No. I hadn't. That's great. Send that to me. I want to make sure Misha sees it," Maggie said.

He texted it to her, and as she walked by him a subtly scented cloud of jasmine followed her and he realized he need to get the fuck out of there. Now.

"Great. I guess I should go."

He turned on his heel, heading for the door, and his fingers brushed the door handle when she called his name.

He looked over his shoulder and saw her coming toward him with his canvas in her hands. "Don't forget this."

He nodded, taking it from her. "Thanks."

"No problem. For our date at Sheen tomorrow night, I guess I'll see you there?"

"I assume you still don't want me to pick you up," he said.

"It's not that I don't want you…to," she said.

Inwardly he groaned as he turned fully and leaned back against the door. "So I'll pick you up? I think after the kind of publicity we generated tonight, we should probably arrive together."

She chewed her lower lip, something she only did when they were alone and she wasn't feeling confident, he suspected. Because when she'd been trying to seduce him into touching her, she hadn't done it once.

Why was the thought of him bringing her out to dinner making her unsure?

"Mags?"

"Hmm…?"

He sighed. "Why is that the thing that bothers you?"

"Randall broke up with me at Sheen," she said at last. "I mean no one probably remembers it but me. I haven't been back since."

"Why didn't you say something? We don't have to go there," he said.

"We do, everyone eats there."

Everyone did. What an ass Randall was. Why break up with her in such a public place? "You won't be alone tomorrow night and I think if nothing else we are becoming friends."

She gave him the sweetest, most vulnerable smile and his gut clenched. He realized that despite her sexy moves and seduction techniques, Maggie Del Rio was very real. That realness appealed to him almost more than her teasing.

"Thank you, Jericho," she said. "I'm glad that I'm going back there with a friend."

"Me, too," he said. As much as he'd wanted to escape from her presence so he could get some relief from the sexual tension she had ratcheted up in his body, now he felt like a grade-A douchebag for leaving first. "I'll wait while you lock up and walk you to your car."

She tipped her head to the side. "You sure about that?"

"Very sure," he said. "I'm not a man to say things I don't mean."

"I'm the same kind of woman. Let me grab my bag and make sure everything's turned off and locked up in the back."

She left him alone and he stood there waiting, looking around her storefront and studio area. Unlike her home, which had shown the very intimate side of Maggie, this place was her business side. It was arty and edgy—more so than Maggie was—and it had the feeling of first-class professionalism.

She came back a few minutes later. "Ready. Also Misha texted back and said they are getting a flood of applications after that photo of us was posted. Apparently #k!smetmatch is trending everywhere. So kudos to us."

"Huzzah."

He held the door for her and then watched as she locked it and walked her to her car. A late-model Mustang. She leaned against the driver's door. "So are we going to both continue to pretend that we weren't about to kiss?"

"I was planning to. Unless you want to admit you can't resist touching me," he said. His seductress was back. The brief vulnerability she'd displayed when talking about Sheen was gone.

"I'm not. Sors."

Maggie knew she should keep her mouth shut but she couldn't. That one brief moment when she'd let the past in had rattled her, but the August night air was warm and the Texas sky was living up to its reputation for being big and bright tonight. And her confidence and competitive spirit were creeping back in.

"You don't sound it," he said, setting his canvas on the hood of her car and then leaning right next to her against the hood of the Mustang.

He'd left barely any space between them and her body reacted to his closeness as predicted. The breeze was strong, whipping her hair around her head, and she saw one of the strands brush against Jericho's cheek. She reached up to capture her hair and twist it a few times before pulling it over her left shoulder. "That doesn't count."

"Doesn't mean I enjoyed it any less," he said.

He wasn't pretending not to be affected by their closeness and his bluntness turned her on as nothing else could. Maybe it was that he was so very different from Randall. Maybe it was just his earthy sexuality that was calling at the sacred feminine inside her and making her want to claim him. To tempt him as she'd been doing all evening but up the stakes even more.

Except she wasn't confident he'd be the first one to break. There was no telling how much control he had but having seen that meticulously detailed pencil sketch he'd made this evening, she felt confident that it was going to take more than a brush of her hair against him to get him to crack.

And she admitted to herself she still wasn't sure she wanted him in her bed. Oh, she wanted... She just wasn't sure how wise it would be. So that meant she had to retreat. "Jericho, what am I going to do with you?"

The soft words were torn from her mouth without thought. As soon as she uttered them, she regretted it, but she couldn't call them back.

"I've got a few ideas," he said. "But you're going to have to touch me first."

Her palms tingled and she was so tempted to touch him that she wrapped her arms around her waist. "Not tonight."

He held his hands up near his shoulders. "I'm not in a rush."

"Me, either," she admitted. "But I do have to get home."

"Yeah. What's waiting for you?" he asked. "I thought you lived alone."

"I do," she said, wishing she'd made any other excuse

than needing to get home. She had nothing waiting for her. But… "I have to text my mom I'm home or she'll worry, and if I'm too late she'll want to know why. And I know I'm thirty but she still tracks us, so it's a thing."

He laughed, but sort of a commiserating one. "My mom does it, too, so I get it. I won't keep you, then. But maybe one day you won't mind explaining to her that you were with me."

"Jericho…" If he was any other man, she wouldn't be tempted, but with Jericho she wanted to say to hell with it and give in. But he wasn't any other man.

She'd told him about her fear of returning to Sheen. She'd never in her life enjoyed teasing a man and knowing that sexual ache was going to be with her for until their match was up. And she'd almost let herself forget that he was a Winters.

Honestly, when they were alone together she just thought of him as Jericho, but the fact that a photo of them was going viral had reminded her they were both very much bastions of their families. They were never going to be just Maggie and Jericho. Never.

The sooner she made her peace with that, the better.

"Good night, sweet Mags," he said, turning toward her and leaning slightly in as he scooped his canvas off the hood of the car.

He hesitated and she held herself back but her lips felt dry. *Don't lick them. Don't do it.*

But then she did. She saw his eyes track the movement and knew that he knew she wanted to kiss him.

Then he licked his own lips, winked at her and turned away.

Her pulse was racing and her center was moist, aching and needy. But she couldn't help admiring his willpower.

It made her realize that he was a man who wasn't afraid to wait. And that suited her more than she wanted it to.

She unlocked her car, put down the convertible top and got in it. The drive home was a blur, with music blaring in the speakers and the windows open. She tried to blow the tingling in her lips and body out with the wind, but the warm breeze wiped hair around her head and a strand brushed her lips.

In her mind it was the same strand that had touched Jericho's cheek, which made her breasts feel fuller and her nipples tighten. She swallowed as lust turned her traitorous body against her own willpower and determination. She was so tempted to just drive to his house but as she was at the stoplight and debating a turn toward Jericho, her phone rang and the in-car speaker notified her it was her mom.

She answered it.

"Hey, sweetie. Your class ended an hour ago. Everything okay?" she asked.

"Yes, Mom," she answered, turning on the signal toward her own home.

"Oh, good. I just wanted to make sure you didn't need any pineapple," she said.

Pineapple was their code word for I'm-in-trouble-call-the-cops. "I don't. I just had to clean up and it took longer than expected. I'm almost home now."

"Oh, that's good. Last time I checked you were still at the store. I'll let you go, then. Good night, sweetie. Love you."

"Night. Love you, too, Mom," she said.

She went back to her lonely house, wishing that she'd invited Jericho back. She could have done that without touching him…at first.

Eight

Sheen was made entirely of glass, a sleek modern restaurant that stood out in Royal. Maggie remembered how excited she'd been to come there with Randall just after it had opened. The new owner, Colin Reynolds, had just won Chef of the Year and the food was rumored to be spectacular. Not that Maggie knew.

She only had a pre-dinner cocktail before Randall had told her it was over, asked for the ring back and left. She remembered being shell-shocked for a few moments and then, to her horror, crying. She took a deep breath and felt her hands trembling. *Don't let Randall have anything else from you.*

He had long left Royal so this was just in her head. She had a favorite quote she kept taped to her laptop. "It's hard to defeat an enemy with outposts in your head."

That's all this was.

An old outpost that Maggie should have burnt down a

long time ago, but instead she'd ignored it, hoping it would crumble. But it hadn't.

"Hey, are you okay to do this?" Jericho asked, as he stood next to her.

"Yes. Well, honestly… No, but I'm doing it," she said, starting to reach for his hand but, remembering the who-will-touch-first dare, dropped it.

But Jericho noticed. "The touching thing is on hold tonight, agreed?"

She gave him a slight smile. "Yes."

He took her hand as soon as the words left her mouth, pushing their fingers through each other's in something that Maggie wished didn't make her start trembling in a very different way. His hand around hers was firm and she decided to stop censoring herself and her reactions to him. Just for tonight.

"Thank you."

"Only a really shitty man wouldn't offer you his support. So quick drink and nibbles at the bar and then we dash? Or keep our table res?" he asked.

He really was here tonight as a friend. She knew he wanted her. She could see the flush on his skin, and he kept rubbing the back of her hand with his thumb. But right now he made her feel as if she was the priority.

She took a deep breath. "I think we better do the reservation."

"Okay," he said and then held the door for her to enter.

She entered first and he dropped her hand, putting his on the small of her back as they approached the hostess stand, and she was vaguely aware of the low rumble of Jericho's voice as he spoke to the seating hostess. She was too consumed with looking around the restaurant and noting all the faces at the tables and bar.

Many people had turned when they came in, and given the publicity that photo from last night had generated, she wasn't surprised by their interest in them. But she also started to feel anxiety creeping in. It felt harder to catch her breath and she felt like she was sweating between her boobs and on her upper lip.

Fuck.

Get it together.

Surreptitiously she wiped her upper lip and forced herself to smile. She could do this. As the hostess turned to grab some menus, Jericho leaned over her shoulder and spoke directly into her ear.

At first all she was aware of was how intimately close he was as the words were whispered. "If you don't stop looking scared, I'm going to have to distract you in a way that will set us both on fire and probably give the good people of Royal more than they were expecting from a setup couple."

His words sent fire through her body. She turned, and he was so close her lips brushed the side of his face. "Deal."

He nodded, once again putting his hand on the small of her back, and subtly urged her to follow the hostess. She felt his hand drifting lower as he walked next to her. They moved past the kitchen, which was on full view from the dining area. The kitchen staff were busy and she allowed herself to be distracted by them.

The hostess stopped by a table in the center of the restaurant and before she could ask if it was okay, Jericho stepped closer. "Could we have that table in the corner?"

"Uh," the hostess stammered.

"Please," Maggie said. "I'm sure you don't follow gossip, but we were recently publicly matched up and a lot of people are staring, so it might be easier for us if we were over there."

"Of course," the hostess said. "I do know who y'all are. I think most people in Royal are just curious. Sorry I didn't think to move y'all."

She led them to the table that Jericho had indicated and Jericho held the chair for Maggie before seating himself. "Hope y'all enjoy your dinner."

The hostess walked away and Maggie looked down at the menu but couldn't read it at first. Why had she ever thought this was a good idea? She was sweating again and—

"Every time you get tense you breathe heavy and it makes your breasts move against that blousy fabric, which damn, Mags, I can't tear my eyes from."

She glanced up from under her eyelashes at Jericho. He was serious. He was distracting her but he was turned on by her body. "Only fair since I've had a hard time not staring at your shoulders in that jacket. It has to be bespoke."

"It is. My college roommate said only restaurant managers wear off-the-rack suits to important dates."

She started to roll her eyes until the he got to the important part. "Am I?"

"You know you are. Stop remembering the woman that man forced you to be and be the sweet, sassy Mags I'm coming to know. The one who gave me a hard-on without touching me."

He was right. His words were the little extra push she needed to remember who she was. Maggie Del Rio. She wasn't a woman who hid in the shadows or pretended she wasn't attractive and it was past time she remembered that.

Interesting that it had taken Jericho Winters to remind her.

* * *

Their meal was well prepared and Maggie seemed to lose her tension as it progressed. Now that he'd been to her studio and seen her artwork, he was getting a better idea of the woman she was.

"You mentioned a college roommate. Where did you go?"

"UT. You?" he asked as he took a sip of the shiraz he'd ordered with dinner. Though normally he preferred to drink beer in the summer, wine paired better with steak.

"A&M," she said, wriggling her eyebrows at him.

"So we're pretty much always rivals," he said, realizing that they were. On paper they made absolutely no sense at all. What had that app seen in the two of them or was it just a fluke?

"Seems that way. What did you study? I mean I'm sure architecture, but did you have to study any eco stuff? I don't know the proper term for that, as I'm sure you can tell," she said with a grin.

"Uh, I can. Yes, I studied eco-friendly manufacturing and business because I knew I wanted to have my own firm. I could always ask my brother or father for advice but that's not really how I operated when it comes to business. They tend to get a little too vested in what I'm doing.'

"I thought you and Trey partnered on the expo center," Maggie pointed out.

"We did," Jericho agreed. "But it was more Trey saying we should bid for the job and that they'd hire me to be the architect."

"I get it. That's sort of how things are with my business and the Del Rio Group. They hire me, and I do specific graphic design and promo work for them. Also my mom had me redo all the art in the corporate offices," Maggie said. "But it's contracted. Like you, I don't like too much outside input."

"I can see that. So what's been your biggest challenge so far?" he asked.

She tipped her head to the side, clearly giving his question some thought, and then shrugged. "I don't think I've had one. I mean every client has something that I have to overcome but it's not really a challenge."

"In what way?"

"I have to figure out what they want. For example, if a client says 'I want something classy and sophisticated,' that could literally mean several things, so I have to push them a little bit to get them to define *classy* to me. No lie, I had one client who said anything without neon lights is classy. That immediately told me what she didn't want."

He leaned back as he finished his meal. "That would do it."

"What about you—biggest challenge?"

That was easy. "All of them. I think that the challenge is making the design I have in my head work in a real-world scenario. It's one thing to want solar to power a building and another to find a way to hide the panels so that the building doesn't look like a big field of black panels. So those kinds of things. And each job seems to have a different challenge like that."

She smiled at him. "Have you ever not been able to make something work?"

"I did a job in the UK where I wanted to use the wastewater to heat a home, but I couldn't get the right pump system in place. I tried a number of different designs but eventually we had to go with something already on the market."

"And that was bad why?"

He shrugged, realizing he was telling her a little too much about himself. But maybe she wouldn't' notice. "It used more energy than I wanted it to consume. I was trying for a net-zero house. Meaning that it would produce the exact amount of energy it needed to consume."

"That's fascinating. The planet is really important to you isn't it?"

"It's the only one we have," he said. "I'm not like an eco-warrior or anything but if I can make a change and it helps, then I will do it. But full disclosure, I do love travel and probably take more flights than I should."

"That's fine. I don't take many so it probably evens out," she said with a wink.

He knew that wasn't the way it worked but he liked her logic. He liked thinking of them as a pair who balanced each other out. And he wasn't entirely sure when that had happened.

But he knew it had to be last night. When she'd been bent on seducing him without touching him. No other woman had ever made him so hot so fast. And tonight when he'd seen her struggle to enter the restaurant but not back down.

Damn.

Maggie was his kind of woman.

Fiercely feminine and not afraid of a challenge. He skimmed his eyes down from her face to the delicate curve of her neck and then lower to her breasts.

"You're staring at me and I'm not breathing heavy."

Immediately an image of her in his arms as he ravished her with kisses sprang to mind. "I'm thinking about another way to make you breath heavy."

"Oh, are we going that far with our touching moratorium?" she asked.

He wanted everything she had to give but she'd been the one to say they should take things slow. Maybe not even allow themselves to give in to the chemistry between them.

"We can go as far as you want," he said. "This is your night, Maggie."

"My night. I'd rather it be ours," she said.

He shifted his legs under the table. He wanted to say something clever but instead the truth was all he had. "I'd like that, too.

But the truth was he knew that "us" wasn't going to be easy for them. No matter how strong they both were in the face of their families.

Maggie forgot where they were and the fishbowl they were in for most of the meal. Jericho had that kind of power over her. She relaxed her guard and for a moment it felt like she didn't have any baggage. She knew it was still there. But right now it wasn't hanging off both of her shoulders.

Jericho suggested they split dessert, which made her give him a hard glare. "Uh, what?"

"Usually on dates dessert is a thing, but I have a sweet tooth… Why?"

"I do, too," she admitted. "If there is one thing I never split, it's dessert."

"Dang, Mags, you're making me wish…" He trailed off.

"What for?" she asked, even though she knew she probably shouldn't.

"That we were in a different situation. I think I could very well fall for you," he said.

But there was a light note to his voice. *Dessert, idiot. He was talking about your love of sweet treats. That was what*

would make him fall for you. It was just one more moment
of lightness in an evening that had been full of them.

He'd gone out of his way to make sure she didn't feel
uncomfortable and she knew her ease was due in no small
part to him. But her emotions were roiling through her again
like a tornado blowing fast and swift across the state and
she had no way to control them. She wanted him to like her.
Really like her. Which was a big freaking red flag because
the last time a man made her feel this way, he'd dumped
her in this restaurant.

"Hey, I was joking," he said, leaning in closer to her.

She did the same thing, putting her elbows on the table
and getting closer to him. She did like touching him and
when they went back to their challenge, she'd miss it.

"I know," she said. "I just wish you weren't."

"Damn, woman, don't be that honest," he said.

"You just told me to be my fiercest self and she doesn't
lie."

"Well, hell," he said.

"Y'all are so cute," a woman said as she walked by their
table. "I thought that the k!smet match was just a publicity
stunt. Glad it's not."

Great, Maggie thought. She'd known they were going to
be perceived by the public as a couple, but she hadn't anticipated how it would feel to know that all eyes were on
them. As much as she'd made that comment to the hostess
earlier, a part of her had just not wanted to sit in the middle of the restaurant where Randall had dumped her. Her
mind had been in the past instead of in the present, where
it definitely needed to be.

"Thank you, ma'am," Jericho said.

The lady just smiled and moved on.

"Well… That was interesting."

"Yeah, something like that," she said. "I'm going to need a big ole crumble with ice cream to take my mind off of it."

"I had my eye on the peach pie," he said. "My mom makes a really good one so I'm sure the one here will not live up to it. Right now I'm practically tasting hers on my palate."

"I know what you mean. My mom doesn't cook that often but she makes a party cheese dip that I could eat the entire serving dish of. So good."

She took another look at the menu. "I've heard the chocolate fudge cake is good."

"You did?" he asked.

"Yeah, my mom loves it. She sometimes Door Dashes just the cake when she's on a rest day."

They both placed their dessert order and after the waiter left, Jericho said, "What's a rest day?"

"She's a marathon runner so she has training days, weight days, running, all that, and then she has a rest day. And once a month she has a forbidden-fruits day."

She loved that about her mom. The discipline she'd given both her and Trey, but also that she always acknowledged that there were things that shouldn't be denied. Not over-indulged, either.

Maybe she could make this a forbidden-fruits thing with Jericho. She knew her family was expecting her to end the relationship after their fifth date and his was, too. But the more time they were together, the harder that was going to be. It was one thing to think about sleeping with him and trying to resist his magnetism. But tonight… He'd moved beyond sexy acquaintance she wanted to bang to someone real.

He could have taken advantage of her vulnerability in

coming here and the emotions she'd been dealing with. But he hadn't. And his revelations about trying to build a net-zero home showed he was a man who cared deeply about things. And she knew without having to say the words out loud that she wanted him to care deeply about her.

"I like the sound of that," he said.

"Well, you don't seem like someone who denies himself much," she said.

"Until you, you'd be right," he said.

Until her. She breathed in deeply and for a brief moment pretended she could believe him. But the line sounded… well, like a line. "Don't do that."

He cocked his head to the side. "Do what?"

"Say what you think I want to hear. You've been so real tonight… I can tell the difference," she said pointedly.

"Sorry. Was just trying to keep things light. The truth is this is harder than I thought it would be. I mean the no-touching challenge was always meant to be a bit of fun. But these dates keep showing me things about you that… well, that I like."

She licked her lips as she watched him. "And?"

She had to ask that because it seemed like he had more to say.

"And I feel a bit like I did trying to get that wastewater to heat the house. Like I'm close to figuring everything out and getting it to work but that I might be closer to failure."

Nine

"How'd the date go?" Misha asked as they sat down to coffee the next morning. They were seated outside across the street from the chamber of commerce.

It was a sunny August morning and luckily not too hot just yet. Maggie had opted for an asymmetrically cut dress that left one shoulder bare, then fell in a slim-fitting sheath. She had a meeting with the Del Rio Group board this morning to present her plans for the Christmas campaign's graphic art she'd designed and this outfit made her feel strong and powerful.

"Really good," Maggie said, smiling to herself as she remembered the evening with Jericho.

"How good?" Misha asked, pushing her large sunglasses up on top of her head.

"Well… I sort of freaked a little dealing with the whole last-time-I-was-in-there-I-got-dumped and he just… He was there for me," she said. She was still trying to reconcile all the things she'd learned about him with what she'd always thought of the Winters family. He wasn't cold or calculating and not one time had he tried to make her look bad. Though to be fair, he could have. In fact, she was hard-pressed to understand how a man like Jericho could have been raised in a family who was as horrible as she'd been led to believe.

"I'm sorry, hun, that you had to go through that. I'm not surprised about Jericho, though. Trey isn't what I was expecting, either."

"He isn't?"

"I mean he's sort of all about the business but he's not unkind. I think based on what I'd heard from your family at gatherings I'd been expecting something different from him."

"That's interesting. I was thinking that maybe Jericho was the exception because he's not really part of Winters Industries. You know?"

"Yeah, I do. I'm not a Del Rio so I can't say how Trey would be with you," Misha said as she took a delicate sip of her coffee.

Maggie's phone pinged and she glanced down to see a message from Cecily and groaned.

"What?"

"Nothing," she said. She wasn't going to tell anyone that Cecily wanted her to dig up dirt on the Winters clan. For one thing, Maggie didn't feel comfortable with it and for another she had decided that she'd only mention it if she saw something egregious, which she hadn't at dinner. "Just a family thing."

"That bad?"

"Nothing major, not like what you've got going on with Nico," she said. Misha's brother had been in prison for three years for a crime he didn't commit.

The story was basically Nico, trying to be the good guy that Maggie knew him to be, had been in a bar when a woman was accosted by a drunken man in a dark corner of the bar and Nico's friend jumped in to help. Just as Nico arrived to break up the fray, the accoster went down hard, hitting his head.

Bouncers stepped in to break it up as the police arrived. Everyone zeroed in on Nico because he was larger and more physically fit than his friend. Nico didn't resist, taking the blame for the blow knowing it meant spending the night in jail.

The accoster turned out to have a fractured skull and was too drunk to realize Nico wasn't the man who hit him. The accoster was also the nephew of a prominent politician. Still, Nico's lawyer was hopeful they could cut a deal with the DA since the most serious injury resulted from the fall, which was accidental.

But things went awry. The DA wouldn't make a deal. In too deep to back out and refusing to let his friend go to jail just months before his new baby was born, Nico stuck to his story and was convicted. Everyone was shocked and horrified by his three-year sentence. Only Nico's friend, Misha and Maggie knew the truth.

"That's good. I wouldn't wish that on anyone," Misha said. "But he's out now. New beginning."

Her friend looked sad and angry, and Maggie reached over to squeeze her hand. "Are you free for lunch?"

Misha was free and they made plans before her friend left to go to work. Maggie stayed at the café sketching on her iPad, finding herself drawn once again to the image of Jericho. Leaving him at her door after their date had been hard, but she had just felt too vulnerable to do anything else.

As much as walking into Sheen had restored her self-image and her confidence, she knew that she was going to have to take another big step and let herself trust her gut and her instincts when it came to Jericho. But this was much harder. There was no one's hand she could hold. This had to be her trusting herself. And it was easier in business, where she knew she had expertise and a good eye for art.

But men and love—that was something else entirely and there was a huge part of her that wasn't sure she'd ever be able to 100 percent trust herself again. Which was starting to feel unacceptable. She hated that she'd allowed herself into this state and she knew it was past time.

If there was a man she was going to trust… Could it be Jericho? A part of her was pretty sure it already was. Another part wasn't so sure. Which was just making her more determined to get over this.

That part that had sent him away last night instead of inviting him in. She got a flag that she had a message in the k!smet app. She clicked on it and saw that the message was from Jericho.

There was a tiny thrill that raced through her and her traitorous body practically went into seduction mode. Sitting up straighter, shoulders back, she tossed her hair and then shook her head. He couldn't see her, she reminded herself.

Jericho: Drinks tonight?

Maggie: We don't have a contracted date.

She had to point that out because she wanted to be clear that this was something else. Did Jericho feel that way?

Jericho: Does that matter?

Did it? Seemed he didn't care about the contract their families had carefully designed and had them both sign.

She knew that her family might want her to say yes but she wasn't sure it did matter to her. She felt the pull between her family obligation and what she personally wanted. This was a good test. She'd do it, trust her gut and see what happened.

Maggie: Was planning to check out a summer concert in the park. Want to join?

Jericho: Yes. I'll bring a picnic and drinks. See you at seven?

Maggie thumbs-upped his message and then smiled to herself. She felt both scared and strangely exhilarated. Not really strange since the no-touching dare was back in effect and she had enjoyed the teasing between herself and Jericho. And maybe tonight, as well as proving her instincts weren't wrong, she'd be able to shake Jericho's walls and make them crumble.

Her mom texted to remind her to leave if she was going to be on time to the board meeting and Maggie texted back the girl emoji with her hand on her face before she got up and headed to her car.

She had a busy day but in the back of her mind was the concert that evening and the plans she made for herself.

Jericho hit the gym after work and then went to pick up the basket of food he'd ordered from a local barbecue joint. It had taken all of his self-control to leave Maggie at the door the night before and he knew that the heat in both the long, hot summer days and that Maggie generated in him was starting to wear him down.

He'd found himself looking at that photo of them from the night at her studio more than he should. But he was obsessed with her. He wanted to believe that if they had sex, then maybe he could get her off his mind. But he wasn't too sure.

He was surprised at how likable and down-to-earth she was. Last night had shown him that despite what his family had always believed about the Del Rio family, they weren't cold-blooded and they didn't seem as calculating as he'd been led to believe. But the truth was even if her family was that way, it didn't change the fact that he was starting to really like Maggie.

Last night she'd let herself be vulnerable…or maybe she'd just felt safe enough with him to let her guard down. Something that Jericho had never really allowed himself to do. He admitted to himself that part of it was the fact that his parents had fallen hard for each other. Even though Jericho had always believed he'd do when he met the right woman— after he'd accomplished his plans for RoyalGreen.

But in the back of his mind, had he been looking? To be fair, most of the women he dated wanted the same things he did. Just someone fun to hang out and hook up with. Nothing serious.

Maggie might be the same but because of their families' rivalry and the pressure to make the k!smet app seem successful, they'd been placed in a weird pressure cooker. One that made the chemistry between them feel…more intense?

Well, that was what he was going for, he thought as he rubbed the back of his neck. He parked his car in the lot near the park and then got out. He slung an insulated cooler bag over his shoulder and tucked a picnic blanket that he'd borrowed from his mom under his arm.

They'd agreed to meet near the concert stage—a temporary structure that had been set up to accommodate the summer concert series. Mostly the artists were either up-and-coming bands trying to make their big break or artists from decades earlier who hadn't had any big hits lately but still liked touring and playing their old songs. Tonight it was a band from the '80s and he was surprised when he noticed his parents in the crowd.

"Hey! There are way more people here than I was expecting," Maggie said as she came up next to him. She had on a pair of high-waisted shorts that left her long legs bare, and honestly for a minute he couldn't tear his eyes off them.

Then he looked up, noting that she had tucked a sleeveless T-shirt into the waistband and had her long hair in a braided ponytail that hung over one shoulder.

"Yeah. Um. My folks are over there," he said.

"They are?"

"Yes. I had no idea they'd be here," he said. If he'd been with any other girl, he would have gone over to see them.

"That's fine. I guess it would probably be good for the app if I go and meet them," she said. "Right?"

She was probably right. But his dad had given him advice to stick to the contracted dates, warning him that Del Rios would take advantage of anything outside of what had been legally agreed to. When he'd talked to Trey earlier, his brother had mentioned he felt bad that Jericho was having to go on all these public dates but had admitted that the publicity was doing great for the app and the IPO.

"Yeah. Let's go and say hi to them so it doesn't get awkward," he said.

"Sure," she said. He started to reach for her hand, but she lifted both eyebrows at him and he knew they were back to the terms that he'd set for them that night in her house.

Which turned him on way more than he wanted to admit.

He walked over to his parents and her mom threw her head back to laugh at something his father had said just as they walked up. She glanced up at him and smiled before she noticed Maggie standing next to him. She cocked her head to the side and sort of gave him that What-are-you-doing-boy? look.

"Mom and Dad, this is Maggie. As you know, we've been seeing each other," he said. "Maggie, this is Camille and Joseph."

"Nice to meet you both," Maggie said, holding out her hand to shake his mom and then his dad's hands.

His parents nodded at Maggie and then they noticed that most of the people close to them were staring and his dad sort of smiled. "Why don't you two join us?"

"Are you sure?"

"Yes. We want to get to know Maggie better since you two are dating," his dad said.

That didn't sound like something that was going to make for a comfortable evening. He turned to look at Maggie but she just nodded and smiled at him. "Sounds good to me."

They spread their blanket close to his parents and sat down. His father was watching Maggie. Jericho wasn't sure what was going to break the tension between the four of them. He couldn't help but feel this was something that they both needed. He'd been ready to give in to the attraction he felt for her, but this was reality.

Their families had never been friendly and the truth was their life together would be full of meetings like this. Was there anything that could make this work?

Maggie wasn't sure how to act at first. The conversation was kind of slow and stilted and she could tell that Jericho wasn't comfortable, either.

"I was really impressed with the expo hall that Jericho designed. It's so nice to have something new like that here in Royal. I'm friends with Lila who works for the chamber of commerce and she mentioned that it's generating a lot of interest."

There was a moment of silence and then Jericho's mom smiled at her. "He's very talented so I'm not surprised to hear that. Seems like Royal is on a tech roll lately with the app and the expo center."

"The app seems to thrive on being unpredictable," Joseph said.

"I have to say, both of us were shocked when our names were matched," Maggie said.

"Definitely," Jericho added. "But Maggie's been a good sport about it."

"Why wouldn't I be? Anything that draws business to Royal is good for all of us," Maggie said.

"What is it you do? Graphic design, right?" Camille asked.

"Yes. And some art direction for projects. I redid the art in the Del Rio Group's corporate offices. It was a bit outdated."

"Sounds like the Winterses' offices. They haven't had anything new since the late nineties."

Maggie smiled over at Jericho's mom. She had the prettiest brown eyes, which were very similar to her stepson's. She also was making the effort to keep the conversation going, which Maggie appreciated. "That's how Dad kept his offices. My mom was after him to update things. He's so cutting-edge with business models but when it came to the space, he just liked things as they were."

"Some things don't need to be changed," Joseph said. "But we updated some of our building design in the last few years at Jericho's suggestion. I guess sometimes it takes a new generation to make those kinds of changes."

"I think so," Maggie agreed. "Have you two ever heard this band before?"

"We went to a few of their concerts when the kids were young," Joseph said.

Jericho's parents told a little more about the Texas blues alternative band who played covers of Stevie Ray Vaughn, a local legend in Texas, as well as their own hits. He and his band had played gritty, raw, sensual music that even Maggie's parents loved. "Texas Flood" was one of their favorites, and when she mentioned it, Joseph smiled and talked about some other Stevie Ray Vaughn songs.

The conversation had shifted into Southern blues, which was nice as they ate dinner. Maggie learned that Jericho had played the bass guitar in high school before some friends of Jericho's parents waved them over and they excused themselves and Maggie sighed.

"I'm sorry I just started talking but it was so—"

"Perfect," he said. "I was trying to think of something to say. Good idea to compliment me."

"You know I love that building. I've told you so," she reminded him as he poured her a glass of rose wine and handed it to her.

"I do. I wasn't sure how Dad was going to react when you mentioned your family, but he was cool," Jericho said.

"He was. It would be silly for us to ignore it. You know?" she asked.

"I do. I think you aren't what they expected."

"Fair enough, since not a single Winters I've met has been what I expected," she said. "So bass guitar?"

He groaned. "I was going to be a rock star when I was in the ninth grade and I'd seen this interview with Dave Grohl that said if you wanted a surefire way to get into a band, play bass. That most people pictured themselves as lead guitarists… So I learned."

"Sensible plan. What happened to derail your rock star dreams?"

"The Astros. We got to go to Houston for a summer camp that was adjacent to their practice field and my ambition changed. What did you want to be at that age?"

She remembered being fourteen and tried to remember if she wanted to be anything. "Lizzie McGuire or someone like that."

He laughed as she'd hoped he would. "Well, I see we both changed along the way."

"Yeah, my mom always said childhood is for dreaming so that when you are an adult, you'll be able to find something that makes you happy," she said. Maggie had realized that what she'd loved about Lizzie McGuire was the animated Lizzie who'd talked on the screen, and in high school she made her own comic strip. In college she'd found that she didn't really love comics, but drawing and art had stayed with her. So she saw the sides of Lizzie McGuire in her life.

"That's interesting," Jericho said. "I'm not sure I took anything from that time with me."

She thought about it for a minute. "There is something very methodical about you and architecture, and I can see that bass and baseball both could have helped hone that."

He tipped his head to the side. "I like that you see things in me that I've never noticed before."

She scooted closer to him, wanting to touch him but still very much in her feelings, and as much as she was ready to own her instincts, something about Jericho made her forget that she was conducting an experiment and more like she was in the middle of a tempest and out of control.

Nothing good ever came from that.

Ten

The music was heavy with electric guitars and that distinctive blues rhythm, and Jericho watched as Maggie moved to the music. His parents were on their feet, too, and an evening that he hadn't been sure would be anything but awkward was actual fun. Maggie sang along with a lot of the songs, which Jericho only half knew, but his dad actually knew all the lyrics as well.

His mom looped her arm through his while Maggie and Joseph clumsily duetted to a cover version of "Pride and Joy."

"She's not what I was expecting," his mom said to him as they swayed to the music.

"Me, either," he admitted.

"Does this mean we didn't need to get the lawyers involved?" she said dryly.

He smiled at her. "It's always easier when you don't have to have a contract to date someone. But Maggie and I are still figuring things out."

"Looks like you two are certainly on the same page," his mom said as Maggie turned and danced over to him.

She sort of shimmied at him and his mom dropped his arm as his father held out his hand to her and she went to his side to dance with his dad. Jericho reached for Maggie and then stopped himself.

She threw her head back and laughed. Strands had come free from her braid and curled around her face, one of the tendrils sticking to the back of her neck. "Still afraid to let me win."

"I don't know that *afraid* is the word I'd use," he said, coming so close to her that he could feel the heat of her body, smell that intoxicating perfume she wore without touching her. The band had switched to another Stevie Ray song, Texas Flood. This one was slow and sensual, and he moved his body to the music so close to Maggie's and she gave him one of those looks that made him hard immediately.

She wanted him and she knew he was hot for her. She timed her dance moves to his so that they were moving in sync. They never broke eye contact. It was one of the most sensual moments of his life. It felt to him like they both wanted the same thing. Each other. But they also both had their pride and wouldn't break first.

He was so tempted and more than once started to reach for her but kept his hands to himself. Dancing closer and closer, almost brushing but not allowing their bodies to touch. He leaned closer and she tilted her head to the side, her lips parting, and damned if that didn't make his cock twitch and his lips tingle.

She dropped low and then stood up slowly, her hands moving on her own body. And then he did the same thing, not one to let a woman out-move him. Her pupils dilated and her skin was flush as she watched him stand back up and move his hands down his chest. She licked her lips and he groaned.

"All you have to do is reach out," she said.

"Or you could."

She shook her head but just then they were jostled by the people around them who were also dancing and they fell into each other. He took full advantage of it, putting his hands on her waist, and she looped her arms around his shoulders. They both let out a long, low sigh as their torsos brushed against each other. He canted his hips toward hers and felt her hips brush against his erection. His hands started to drift lower to her butt but the crowd moved away from them.

Their eyes met and he wondered how much longer they were going to do this.

"Looks like it was a draw," he said.

"Looks that way to me," she said.

So he kept his hands on her hips until he heard his mom clear her throat and he dropped them. But Maggie just turned her back to him and he wrapped his arms around her and they sort of swayed to the music as the song changed to one of the band's own. His erection was nestled against her buttocks and she had her hands resting on his arms that held her close to him.

Her fingers were drawing a random pattern on his wrist and it felt like the most intimate touch. It felt like it was only the two of them here listening to the music. He felt a connection to her that he didn't dwell on. He wasn't going to do anything but take this end of the no-touching game they'd been playing as a win. There was no way either of them was going to be able to figure out how the other felt without sleeping together.

And while he'd enjoyed her teasing and flirting, he knew that he was also going to enjoy taking their relationship to a more physical level.

"I'm taking you home tonight," he said in her ear. "Unless you tell me differently."

She turned her head, her hair brushing against the side of his neck. "I was thinking the same thing."

"Glad to hear that," he said, moving them to the music. About an hour later, the concert ended and Jericho waved goodbye to his parents.

"Winters and Del Rio... Is that really you?" Mandee Meriweather from *Royal Tonight* called to them as they were almost to his car.

"It is," he said with a forced smile.

"Our viewers are split on whether the match is the real deal or if you two are faking it for ratings on the app."

"Well, I'd say half your viewers are correct," Maggie said.

"Which half?"

"You'll have to keep watching to find out," Jericho said, taking Maggie's hand and leading her toward his car. "We can pick your car up tomorrow. Let's get out of here."

"Agreed," she said.

He held open her door and his eyes lingered on her long legs as she swung them in. She noticed him watching and ran her fingers up her thighs and then winked at him when he groaned.

He hurried around the car, stowed their picnic gear and got behind the wheel, driving home at record speed as Texas blues music played in his head and his body still pulsed along to it, recalling the feel of Maggie in his arms.

* * *

Something had happened when she'd found herself sitting at the concert with Jericho's parents. It had been surreal at first, and then she noticed how much she'd been trying to control everything in her life and in her relationship with Jericho. As the covers of Stevie Ray Vaughn's songs had played, she'd let go of that need to try to manage something that she'd never been able to.

She was never going to know if she could trust her gut unless she just did it. She wasn't going to get a magic sign from the universe that Jericho was a good guy unless she started looking at him as one. And as the music had played and she'd sang alone with Joseph Winters, she'd realized that nothing was as it had seemed to her.

So she'd decided to stop playing a game that she'd started—out of fear, if she was honest. She'd been afraid to sleep with Jericho because she didn't trust herself. That was it. But she wasn't afraid anymore. She knew a big part of it was the man Jericho was. The way he just sort of rolled with the punches regardless of whether they were comfortable or not.

She turned her head against the headrest and looked over at him as he drove toward his house. She assumed that was where he was taking them, as he hadn't asked for her address. He stared at the road ahead, driving fast but safely. She watched as he shifted gears and saw how careful and thorough he was. Remembered the way he'd danced next to her and seduced her without ever touching her.

She might have thought she was teasing him, but the truth was she'd been responding to him. He had something indefinable that her body just responded to, and she was hot and wet and couldn't wait to get him in her arms again.

She put her hand on the top of his thigh and let her fingers caress him moving toward his cock. He put his hand over hers and shifted it closer, urging her to touch his erection, which she did. He was hard under her hand and she stroked him through his pants as he hit a button to open the gates to the guarded community on the outskirts of Royal. He slowed down as they drove through the neighborhood and he pulled into the driveway at a large house with landscape lighting. He turned the car off and got out in one smooth motion, coming around to open her door.

He reached for her hand, and when she got out of the car, she leaned into his body, having missed the feel of his mouth on hers for more days than she wanted to admit. His mouth under hers was firm and soft at the same time. His lips parted and she felt the brush of his tongue over hers as she sucked his tongue deeper into her mouth. He put one of his big hands on her ass as he lifted her off her feet into the cradle of his thighs, rubbing his erection against her center as the kiss deepened.

She felt him moving and she lifted her head as he set her on her feet. She saw him deftly key in a code on the pad near the front door and then he opened the door and led her into the entryway of his house.

The house smelled of sandalwood and leather, she noticed as he pulled her into his arms and leaned back against the closed front door. He lifted her up by her waist and she wrapped her thighs around his hips, trusting him in that moment more than she'd realized she did.

She put her hands into his hair, that thick, dark curly hair that she'd been wanting to touch since the moment they met. She brought her mouth down on his and realized how good he tasted. That there was something in his kiss that was highly addictive. She hadn't felt like that about any other man's kisses—not even Randall's. Which she tucked away to analyze later.

Right now she shifted her center along the ridge of his cock as she felt his hands sliding up under the legs of her shorts, his hands on her bare thighs. His hands held her firmly but not too forcefully. He spread his fingers out and she felt his touch along her center as he traced her pussy through the fabric of her underwear.

She trailed her mouth along the line of his jaw and over to his ear, sucking the lobe into her mouth and then nipping at it. "Why are we still wearing so many clothes?"

His mouth was next to her ear. "I like the way you feel through them."

She reached between their bodies and started to undo the buttons of his shirt and then pushed her hands into the opening she'd made. Felt his hot skin under her fingers, the light dusting of hair tickling the tips of them. She shifted around and he set her on her feet as she put her mouth on his chest, kissing him as she moved lower undoing more and more buttons.

His hands were at the tie at the back of her neck that held her halter top in place and he undid it. The fabric fell loose to her waist and she stopped undoing his buttons to push her top to the floor and then step out of it.

His hands were on her as soon as she did that. He palmed her breasts with one hand while pulling her closer with the other on her waist. She felt the tips of her hardened nipples brush against his chest.

His fingers were on the fastening for her shorts and undid his pants at the same time. After pushing her hand into the opening, she reached around to the back and pushed his pants and boxer briefs down his legs. He toed off his shoes before he stepped out of his pants and took off his shirt. He stood there in the middle of his entry, totally naked, and though she'd been shimmying out of her shorts and panties, she stopped to admire him.

He was fit, not overly muscled. His shoulders were broad and his chest firm, his stomach flat with a thin tapering of hair that led to his cock, which was hard and erect. She sighed as she wrapped her hand around him, stroking him and then reaching lower to cup his balls as she rubbed her breasts against his chest.

His hands were on her back, moving up and down in long sweeping caresses before his hands were back on her butt again.

"You like my ass…"

"I like everything about you, sweet Mags. Including your hand on my cock…"

She continued stroking him as he pulled her closer and his mouth was on her again. Starting at that spot where her neck met her shoulder, moving slowly down. She thrust her shoulders back and breasts forward. Felt his breath on her nipple a moment before his tongue touched her nipple.

She shivered delicately in his arms and then he suckled at her breasts. Her center clenched and she parted her legs, wrapping one thigh around his hips so she could rub the tip of his cock against her clit. His hand on her butt tightened, then she felt his finger running between the crack. She moved into his touch. Feeling everything in her building toward an orgasm.

She rocked her hips harder against his erection and he pulled back as she pushed him lower and positioned him at the tip of her body.

He cursed long and low. "Are you on the pill?"

"Would I be putting your naked cock against me if I wasn't?" she asked.

"Just checking," he said. "Don't want to take any chances."

Chances. Was that what she was doing with him? Who cared, she thought. Right now she needed him inside her.

He shifted her in his arms, lifting her off her feet and carrying her down the hallway. A light came on as he walked into the room. It was soft, not glaring. He carried her across the room and then he sat down on a large leather chair. She barely registered her surroundings as she straddled him and brought her mouth down on his. He pulled her forward and she positioned the tip of him at her entrance again.

She met his gaze as she slid slowly down on him until he was fully inside her. He was thicker than she'd realized and it had been a while, so it took her a moment to adjust to him. His hands caressed her ass and back, his mouth was on her breast and then she started to move. He held her hips, urged her to go faster and harder as she rode him, and she did, feeling like every inch of her body was ready to come but she couldn't get there.

She drove harder and harder, then took his face in her hands and lowered her mouth to his, kissing him long and deep as he fingered her clit, and everything clenched as she came. He continued rubbing her clit and then he moved his hands back to her hips and started driving up into her faster and faster, pulling his mouth from hers and letting out a long groan as he came and emptied himself inside her.

He shuddered underneath her and she collapsed against him, resting her head on his shoulder as he held her. They were both sweating and his hands held her loosely. She closed her eyes, trying not to think.

She'd made the choice to trust herself and live in this moment. But her mind was always going and now that she was in his arms a part of her realized that she didn't want to leave.

He held her close and she turned her head to face him and saw he was watching her. His dark brown eyes revealed nothing but there was a faint smile on his lips.

"Good?" he asked.

"Yes. You?"

"Very," he said. "Will you stay the night?"

"Yes," she said, realizing how spur-of-the-moment this was. She had no change of clothes, and her car was left at the lot in Royal. "I didn't plan for this."

"Neither did I. Regrets?" he asked.

Sex seemed to make him only able to talk in short bursts while her mind was waking up and she had a lot she wanted to say to him. But she didn't. "None."

"I'm glad to hear that," he said. He carried her upstairs to his bedroom, and she noticed that all of his lights were on motion sensors and shut off after they left. He offered to let her use the bathroom to wash up and gave her a RoyalGreen T-shirt to wear.

She got her phone and texted her mom that she was spending the night at a friend's so she wouldn't worry and then washed up. She looked at herself in the mirror, trying to see signs of changes in her face, but she saw none. There was no outer evidence that everything had changed inside her in the course of one night.

She'd let go of the insecurities that had been like chains wrapped around her after she'd been rejected by Randall. She'd let go of the expectations of the people in Royal who thought that a Winters and a Del Rio could never be together. She'd let go of not trusting her gut but she still wasn't sure she was ready for what it was trying to tell her.

That Jericho might be more than the key to moving on... He might be the key to her future.

Eleven

Jericho dropped Maggie off at her car the next morning, kissing her slowly because he didn't want to leave her, but they both had places to be. Something that lingered on his mind as he drove to work. He hadn't anticipated falling for her but there was no question he was. Seeing her in his home had twigged something in his mind, and as he'd made her breakfast while she'd been doing her makeup at the kitchen table, he couldn't help but think she belonged there. They told each other their plans for the day, as if it was the most natural conversation in the world.

She'd asked him a few questions about the family business and his dad, and he'd told her he wasn't really involved in the business, which was for the best since he tended to butt heads when it came to anything involving work. Joseph more than once had "offered" Jericho advice on how to run RoyalGreen.

He had a design meeting that took all morning, and when he got out he saw he'd missed a message from Maggie.

Maggie: Are you free for dinner tonight?

Jericho: I was planning to be with you.

Maggie: Great. Uh, do you mind going to dinner with my parents?

Yes, he thought. He didn't really want to spend the night with Mr. and Mrs. Del Rio. The impression he'd had when he met her brother was that he was persona non grata with the entire Del Rio clan… But maybe Maggie had felt the same when his sister and her brother were going at it. And she had met his folks already.

Maggie: I can tell by how long it's taking you to say yes that you don't want to go.

Jericho laughed at her text and then hit the video call button. She answered it immediately.

"Sorry, it's not that I don't want to meet your folks…"

"I totally get it. When you saw your parents last night, I wanted to bail but the truth is we had a lot of fun and I wondered…well, if maybe this entire feud thing hasn't been blown out of proportion. I just wanted to see you with my family."

He understood where she was coming from, and honestly, given that he was starting to think of Maggie as more than his summer fling, getting to know her family was seemed like a solid plan. "I think will work."

"I know," she said. "I'm smart that way. It's probably better that you know that at the beginning of this thing we have going on."

"Know what?"

"That I tend to be right."

"You do?"

"Yeah. So just go with what I suggest and we'll be good," she said and he saw the twinkle in her eyes and knew she was teasing him.

And it made him wish they were together so he could pull her into his arms and make love to her. "That might be awkward because I'm usually right."

She furrowed her brow. "How? All that means is you'll be agreeing with me."

He threw his head back and laughed. He didn't say it out loud, but damn this woman got him in a way that no one else ever had. Which was kind of hard to figure since they'd been raised by two families that were supposedly very different.

"I'll take that as agreement. I've got to go. I have a client meeting in ten minutes. I'll text you the details for dinner. Want to stay at my place tonight?" she asked.

"Yes," he said.

"Good. See ya later," she said, blowing a kiss at the phone and then disconnecting the call.

He sat back in his chair, remembering the feel of her in his arms last night and how she'd sucked his tongue deep into her mouth. Damn. He got hard just thinking about her and he still had a good six hours before he'd see her again.

Should he be worried that he was so into her? He hadn't felt this way in a long, long time. Since college when he'd thought he and Macy were going to get married. Of course, she'd texted him from Northwestern where she'd gone to school and broke up with him. He got it. They'd been young.

He'd sort of shut that part of himself down and focused on work. But work was coming in second to Maggie, which was fine now when he didn't have a big project in the final phase, but he knew he had to sort this out. Also, was he really falling for a woman that an app known for its chaotic suggestions had found for him?

But he didn't care how he and Maggie were matched up. She felt right in his arms and in his life and for now that was enough. If things went sideways with her parents tonight, he'd reevaluate. Hell, if things went well, he was going to have to think about it. But at this moment they were having an affair and they liked each other. That was enough for him.

Which he realized ten minutes into a videoconference about his latest project *wasn't* enough. One of the women had long black hair on the call and he couldn't help but notice it, which triggered a memory of Maggie's hair on his skin.

Getting laid usually meant he was satisfied for a few days but sleeping with Maggie had only made him want her again. So just waiting to see or pretending that he was totally cool with where they were now wasn't working. What more did he want?

Everything.

But he'd never been a man to need everything from a woman. And something told him that she wasn't going to just agree to that. He knew he still had a battle to ease her fears after she'd been engaged and dumped. He pulled the notepad closer to him where he was taking notes as one of his assistants was going over the sketch that he'd done for new solar panels and started brainstorming ideas on how to win Maggie's trust.

Dinner was a start, but she needed him to be there in trying times. She needed to know he wouldn't flake out on her.

He smiled to himself. As much as he hated it, everyone in his life knew he was reliable, and that boring label might just be the thing to help ease Maggie's fears.

Maggie didn't dwell too much on the fact that she'd picked a night when she knew that Preston wasn't available. But she wanted her parents to meet Jericho. She really wanted her mom's opinion, which was silly because everyone had liked Randall. But her mom had said later that she'd always had a feeling something wasn't right.

Maggie hadn't ever had that feeling. And she definitely was having all those loved-up feels that came from spending a really hot night in her lover's bed. She wanted to believe that it could last. She needed to stop letting herself be pulled into old fears and worries.

Last night she'd drawn a line in the sand and stepped over it. The past and her fears and insecurities were on the other side. She was moving on and not looking back.

But if only it were that easy to actually do. She felt the past back there. Felt the old fears like her most comfortable sweatshirt. That kids' XL that she'd bought when she was ten and still kept in her closet because she could squeeze into it for years after.

It didn't fit. She didn't love Napoleon Dynamite anymore but she couldn't throw it out because sometimes when she felt like that scared, unsure Maggie, she put it on and it comforted her.

She shook her head as if that would lose the thoughts and fears and texted her mom that she was bringing Jericho to dinner. Her mom texted back the thumbs-up emoji, and she smiled. The short response was due to her mom probably exercising. It was a leg day in the gym for her.

Misha dropped by with two iced coffees and lunch with a big smile on her face.

"What's up?"

"We are so close to going public. You and Jericho are driving interest in the app and last night after you two were photographed dancing at the concert we had another deluge of applicants. Girl, you're my secret weapon."

"Ha. Well, I'm glad. I actually had a lot of fun last night," she said.

"It looked like there was more than fun going on. I saw one photo that I could feel the steam coming off of."

"Well, it is August."

"Okay. Don't tell me if you and Jericho are just play-acting but being photographed with his parents was genius. Several social media accounts are touting it as the end of the rivalry."

"I don't think so," Maggie said. "But they were really nice. I thought they'd be cold or rude."

"Honey, they are Texan. You know they aren't going to be rude to your face," Misha said.

"It felt genuine," Maggie said. "And my mom saw that I met his parents, so Jericho and I are going to dinner with them tonight."

"Oh. Are you nervous?" Misha asked.

She shrugged. To be honest, she wasn't sure how she felt. She wanted to see how he fit in with her family. But she had no idea what she was looking for. Randall had been too good at fitting in. Too good at manipulating her by being what her father wanted in a future son-in-law. By doting on Maggie in a way that made her parents feel like she was a lucky woman. And Maggie had just eaten that up. She'd always been the princess in her family, but with Randall she'd felt like she had found someone whom she could start her own family with, which had never been a dream. Not really. Not until him.

She'd willingly let Randall manipulate her into changing her own dreams and vision of who she was. Which might explain why it had taken her two years to actually agree to a date.

"I don't know. It would be easier if Jericho wasn't a Winters, but the truth is I have a feeling he wouldn't be the man I like if he wasn't."

"So if things go badly, what then?"

"My family is dead to me and I spend the rest of my life having mind-blowing sex and avoiding everyone else in Royal," Maggie said.

Misha choked on her iced coffee and shook her head. "At least you have a plan B."

"That's what I was thinking," she said. They ate lunch and talked more about the app, then Misha hugged her before she left.

"Stay strong this time," Misha said as she walked out.

"I am."

And she was. New Maggie hadn't checked her common sense the moment that Jericho had kissed her. She was realistic. The chance that the first man she dated after a two-year-long dry streak being the one for her was slim. Sexual chemistry aside, there were other things that made her want to believe that it could be more.

And for now that was enough.

Just the belief that he could be. They were still getting to know each other. No pressure, she had another four dates before their contract was up. She was going to be chill and just let things happen.

Except when had she ever been chill about a relationship?

It wasn't like she hadn't already made a decision matrix about Jericho, and she knew that wasn't sexy or chill. But it was her. And the last time… She'd done things like a girl was supposed to. Just relax and be in love, trust her feelings. And that had gotten her dumped at Sheen in front of the entire town of Royal.

So this time she was going to be more Maggie about it. Do it her way, and if it all got screwed up, well, she'd be no worse off… But she knew that wasn't true. She'd be a lot worse because this "like" she felt for Jericho was more intense than the love she'd thought she had for Randall.

Trey texted him that the k!smet IPO might happen sooner than expected thanks to the success of his dates with Maggie. His brother had left things open by saying he'd heard that Mom and Dad had met her and liked her. Jericho wasn't one to talk about his emotions, but he almost wished he was. He just texted back that he liked Maggie and she was fun.

Trey sent a smiley-face emoji and the words, "Be careful. She's still a Del Rio."

Which he simply thumbs-upped before putting his phone away. What did he want Trey to say?

His mom had texted that she'd enjoyed meeting Maggie last night. Just that. He knew she'd been fishing, and he'd disappointed her by saying "she did too" and then "love you." She'd hearted back and let it be.

The plan he was working on for gaining Maggie's trust was also, at some point, going to involve brokering a peace between his parents and hers. Which was what tonight was about. Impressing the parents was kind of Basic Dating 101 as far as Jericho was concerned. So he brought a bottle of scotch whiskey he'd gotten from his friend in the UK and stopped by the local florist for a bouquet for Mrs. Del Rio before he picked up Maggie.

He'd also packed a change of clothes, and when he knocked on her door, she seemed more hesitant than she'd been when he'd left her this morning.

"What's up?"

He set his gym bag on the floor just next to her entry-way table. He'd left the scotch and the flowers in his car.

She chewed her lower lip and he recognized that as a sign of nerves. "Just had a long day with messages from a lot of people about us. And many of them were asking if it's real or if we're just going along with it to help Misha."

That was to be expected. "Yeah, my family all texted, too, but because Mom and Dad met you, they were nicer than they had been before."

"Really? I'm glad. I really liked your parents," she said.

"They liked you, too," he said, finally feeling like she'd relaxed and he could pull her into his arms and claim the kiss he'd been wanting.

She relaxed as she kissed him back, wrapping her arms around him. She laid her head on his chest. "I think my mom was…well, *jealous* isn't the right word, but disappointed and wondering why she didn't get to meet you when I met your parents."

He laughed. Moms were like that. At least his was. "So no pressure to not fuck things up tonight."

She playfully punched his shoulder as she stepped back. "That's right. Sorry I was having a moment when you got here."

"That's cool. I guess I'm the first guy you've brought home since the jerk who dumped you?"

"You are. So if things get odd, blame it on that and not the fact that you are the son of my father's mortal enemy."

She sort of smiled when she said the last part.

He shook his head and smiled back at her. "I'll definitely try not to give off too many of those vibes."

"I'm not even worried about you. It's more me. When I was a kid, I thought dating was going to be so much fun and I couldn't wait until I was old enough to go out, but the truth is it has always been nerve-wracking."

"Really? You're so pretty—"

"Jeez, glad I'm pretty."

"You know what I meant," he said but he knew he'd said the wrong thing. "I just meant I bet a lot of guys asked you out."

"You're not wrong, but some of them asked me out because I was a Del Rio or because I was pretty or popular, and the ones I liked didn't seem to notice me. I mean you're handsome, Jericho. Did you ever have any dating angst?"

"Well, uh, no. I dated the same girl all through high school and then when we went to college, she broke up with me and I sort of just had fun dating."

She gave him such a sour look he knew better than to smile.

"What?"

"How is it you can be so laid-back about it?" she asked.

"I'm not, but it seemed when I had planned for the rest of my life at eighteen, I didn't have a clue, so then I figured I'd just roll with it," he said.

She slid her feet into a pair of sandals near the front door as her phone alarm went off. "Somehow that makes me feel better. I guess that you don't really have it all figured out."

"No one does, Mags. And anyone who tells you they do

is lying," he said, then remembered that he was trying to show her she could trust him. "The truth is, until you, it didn't matter to me if the relationship ended."

"Until me?"

"You're different, and I'm not saying we should book a church, but I like you and I don't think moving on would be easy," he admitted.

She hugged him again. "Me, either."

He hugged her back and reached for that chill she thought he had, but it wasn't there. Because a part of him did want to book a church, and she'd already told him she was never getting engaged again. So he knew he still had a lot of work to do.

And he might screw things up with her parents or they might not get along after the heat wore off. Which he didn't anticipate happening anytime soon.

He tipped her head back with his finger under her chin and kissed her long and deep, but she pulled back. "We can't be late. Save that kiss for later."

Twelve

Fernando Del Rio III was a tall man with thick dark hair streaked with gray. His brown eyes were very serious when he held out his hand to Jericho. His handshake was firm but not overly so. It was easy to see why he was considered a shark with killer instincts in the business world. His petrochemical company was making strides by changing practices to be more environmentally friendly.

Maggie hugged her mom hello. Gayle Del Rio had a slim athletic build and an easy smile for her daughter but her expression was more guarded when she turned to face him.

"Welcome to our home, Jericho."

"Thank you, ma'am," he said, handing her the bouquet of flowers. "These are for you and, sir, I brought this for you."

"Whiskey? I'm more of a tequila drinker," he said, accepting the bottle.

Gayle cleared her throat and gave Fernando a hard look, which made him turn back to Jericho with a forced smile. "But I look forward to trying this."

"It's from a friend of mine. Like you, I prefer tequila, but it's not bad," Jericho said. "Thank you, both, for inviting us over tonight."

"You're very welcome, Jericho," Gayle said. "We're having cocktails on the back patio before dinner."

Gayle linked her arm through Maggie's, leading her down the large Spanish-tiled entryway toward the French doors that he could see from where he stood just inside the house. He looked at Fernando, who set the whiskey on the side table before looking back at him.

"So you're the son that's the architect, right?"

"I am."

"I've been impressed with the work you're doing," he said.

"Thank you, sir. Creating environmentally friendly buildings has long been a passion of mine," Jericho said, realizing he was nervous, almost like he had been when he'd first gone to the bank to a get a loan for his business. He hadn't wanted to use the Winterses money because he wanted to stand on his own.

"Glad to hear it. We have to look to the future, right? Preston has brought a lot of ideas to the table about making our business more environmentally friendly. At first, I wasn't too keen on changing things," he said.

"I get it. There are times when it would be easier to just draw the plans for a building and add on some solar panels or a field of wind turbines, but that isn't aesthetically pleasing," Jericho said.

"Damn, boy, you sound like my son," Fernando said. "Let's get a drink. I want to hear more about the energy-saving features you've been using in your designs."

Jericho followed Fernando out to the porch, where music was blaring and Maggie and her mom had already poured themselves a glass of summer sangria and were seated near the waterfall side of the large in-ground pool chatting away.

Fernando went to the built kitchen and bar, lifting the lid on the grill to check the heat. While he did so, Jericho glanced over at Maggie, who lifted her eyebrows at him and he just smiled and nodded. He assumed she was asking if he was okay.

He didn't really know if he was but talking about business was his comfort zone. And he could talk about his ideas for making the environment a priority in new and existing architecture for hours.

"Do you want sangria or tequila?" Fernando asked.

Noticing the other man had two rocks glasses on the bar, Jericho asked for tequila. The other man nodded, and something seemed to ease inside him. He'd been thinking of Fernando as the big, scary Del Rio monster that featured in a lot of his family tales, but instead Jericho realized he was just Maggie's father. And that was something else that he could deal with.

They talked about building and new environmental initiatives and measures that had been put in place and how it was impacting both of the family businesses for a while until it was time to start grilling and Maggie moved to help her father. He found himself sitting across from Gayle, who was watching him quietly.

"Ma'am?"

"Just trying to figure you out. So far, you've been everything that a Texas gentleman can be, and I'm wondering if it's real or not."

Given what Jericho knew of Maggie's former fiancé, he didn't blame Gayle for questioning him. "All of it. The environment is a huge part of every design I create so talking shop with Fernando was easy. And I like your daughter, so I want you both to like me."

She nodded, giving nothing away, and it suddenly occurred to him that she was going to be the harder one to gain approval from. "We'll see about that. Tell me about you. I heard you date around a lot."

"I did," he said. "I can be a bit of a workaholic, and my brother Trey and I were really focused on the expo center and getting that open. So I kept things casual." But he could tell that wasn't doing anything to appease her. He wasn't sure what she wanted and maybe he wouldn't be able to win her over tonight.

"I get it. Fernando is a workaholic, too."

"I can hear you, dear."

"I know, that's why I said it," she said in a teasing tone. "Why did you sign up for the dating app? Doesn't seem like you needed it to find a woman."

"I didn't. My brother is an investor and I joined to support him. Family is important to me," he said.

"It is to us, too. Maggie said she did it for Misha."

"But you think there was another reason?"

She hesitated, and he realized that whatever else she may be, Gayle was a protective mama bear at heart and didn't want to see Maggie hurt again.

"We both have been very honest with each other. I think we knew, given our families' history together, that our match was going to draw a lot of outside interest. And we both have committed to being a team."

"Good," she said. "That's all I wanted to know."

Maggie hadn't seen her dad so engaged in dinner conversation when Preston wasn't there in a long time. Normally her father kept his eyes on his phone until her mom made him put it down, but tonight he and Jericho had spent most of their time chatting. She'd noticed her mom had been grilling Jericho earlier or though she hadn't been able to hear all of the what her mom had said, she'd guessed that was what she'd been doing because of the way she'd been talking to him.

So when the evening eased down and it was time to go, she wasn't sure what to expect from Jericho on the car ride home. He was quiet until they were out of her parents' neighborhood.

"How'd I do?" he asked. "I feel like all I did was talk to your dad but your mom seemed cool with that."

"Yeah, I think she was. Honestly, I don't think Dad minded. What did you think about them?"

"I liked them. I mean your mom is going to take some time to warm up to me," he said.

Maggie felt a little thrill go through her at his words. "She's just overprotective."

"Oh, I got that," he said. "She definitely isn't sure about my motives but I'm pretty sure it has nothing to do with me being a Winters."

Maggie did, too. "Mom is just that way now. Hope it wasn't too uncomfortable."

He looked over at her as he coasted to a stop. "It's cool. She loves you and she's worried about you being hurt again. I get it."

She put her hand on his thigh and squeezed it. "Thanks. So now that you've met my folks… They aren't that dissimilar to yours."

He arched one eyebrow at her. "Do I need to be one hundred percent in this conversation?"

"Why?"

"If so, I need you to move your hand because all I can think about is how close it is to my cock."

That was all she could think about once he said it. She remembered the feel of him in her hand last night and she wanted him again. She was moist and her breasts swelled.

"Like this?" she asked, moving her hand up his thigh until she brushed his crotch with the back of her fingers.

He shifted his legs and took her hand in his, turning it so that her palm was toward his body, and pushed her hand lower until she could feel all of his growing erection under it. With a circle motion, she rubbed his shaft while cupping his balls with her fingers.

"That's good," he said.

She undid the zipper and slipped her hand into his pants under the elastic waistband of his underwear. His hips jerked forward as she wrapped her hand around him, moving it up and down, feeling him grow as she did it. God, she wanted him.

She didn't bother to think about anything but this moment. The late-summer romance she hadn't been expecting to find but didn't want to give up. She ran her finger over the tip each time she brought her hand up his shaft. His hips moved against her, urging her to continue touching him, and she looked down, seeing his big erection. She wanted him in her mouth.

She pulled her seat belt to loosen it and put her head in his lap. She felt his hand on the back of her head, his fingers in her hair caressing her as she took the tip of him in her mouth. He tasted good and earthy, filling her mouth. She sucked on his cock, letting her fingers stroke him at the same time. The angle was awkward but she was not uncomfortable. She felt his hand moving down her neck, his finger stroking the side of her neck as she sucked him deeper into her mouth.

His hips moved slightly, and after a moment she heard him curse, and then the car turned abruptly and he shut it off. He gently pulled her head away from him and reached down to put his seat back. She undid her seat belt and moved closer to him. Taking him back into her mouth. His hands were on her back, moving up and down it, his hand in her hair, holding her head down while she continued taking him deep in her mouth. Now that they had more space, she cupped and squeezed his sac gently, using her nails lightly as she started to take him deeper into her mouth and his hips were moving against her.

His fingers tangled in her hair and she heard the noises he was making, heard him calling her name, but she was only concentrating on the way it felt to have this powerful man at her mercy. To have control over herself and her part in this relationship with him.

He tasted salty as she swallowed until he was empty and he sighed. He ran his hands down her back and she rested her head on his lap, looking at up at him.

"Maggie...."

Just her name on a long sigh and she smiled as he said it. She felt the same when she thought about him. Jericho... this man whom she never would have gone out with if not for the dating app. This man who was making her feel like she owned her femininity again simply by letting her do the things that she wanted to do. Letting her indulge her own sexual needs and be the woman she'd been hiding away.

And she knew he probably had no idea he'd done that for her, but she knew it and that was enough.

"Thank you for that."

"You're very welcome. I enjoyed it, too."

"I'm glad," he said. "Let's get home so I can make love to you properly."

"Or improperly," she teased as she shifted back into her seat. He tucked his cock back into his pants.

"Whatever you want."

Him, she thought. She wanted him.

When they got to her place, he parked in her garage and then took her hand and led her upstairs to her bedroom. He wanted to take his time making love to Maggie and he wanted her spread out on the bed. He washed up in the bathroom first and when he came back, she waited for him on the bed totally naked.

Even though he knew it was going to take some time before he could come again, he got hard seeing her there. She was so confident in herself and her sexuality that he was turned on by her constantly. It was hard to marry the woman who had hesitated outside Sheen with this woman. He had a feeling they were both very much a part of who she was and both sides had been damaged by the same incident.

He stood there in the doorway and shucked off the rest of his clothes as his eyes moved over her. She was curvy, with full hips and breasts and a smaller waist. Her stomach was gently rounded and her nipples were a pinky-brown color that matched her lips. When he walked toward the bed, he realized he would never get enough of looking at her. Each time he did, he saw something else.

Tonight he saw the embodiment of some sort of fantasy woman that he'd never realized he wanted in his life. But now that he'd glimpsed her, he craved her.

Everything with Maggie from the beginning was borderline obsession. Since that first moment he'd seen her at the Texas Cattleman's Club to that moment he'd actually met her at the k!smet event. And now…well, enough thinking. He had this gorgeous woman lying in front of him and all he wanted was to touch and taste her.

Thank her in a very intimate way for what she'd given him in the car. He reached the side of the bed and she started to roll to her back. But he stopped her with his hand on her hip as he lay down next to her.

He looked into those deep brown eyes of hers, wishing they could tell him what she was feeling toward him. He knew she wanted him. Could tell by her hardened nipples and the slight flush to her skin, but he sort of wanted more than that.

He drew his hand down the side of her face. Her tanned skin was smooth to the touch and her lips parted as he rubbed his thumb over them. He leaned down and kissed her as his hands continued moving down her body, stopping at her breast to catch her nipple and rub it lightly with his thumb.

Her mouth parted under his and he felt the brush of her tongue over his and then he sucked hers deeper into his mouth as he skimmed his hand down her side, stopping at her waist. He traced his finger toward her belly button, teasing it with his touch before moving lower. She shifted her legs, parting her thighs, but he just skimmed his hand down the outside of her leg.

She shifted under him, her hands moving over his chest and tracing the hair on it. He felt her fingers teasing him and moving toward his erection. She took him in her hand and he reacted to her touch by getting harder. He pushed her onto her back and lifted his mouth from hers, kissing his way down her body.

He suckled at her nipple, making her back arch and her legs move restlessly on the bed, her thigh rubbing against his cock, which felt so damned good he had to stop for a second before he moved lower, dropping nibbling kisses against her skin until he reached her belly button. He licked it and then moved lower as he craved the taste of her on his tongue. He needed this.

He parted her lower lips and then licked her clit. She let out a soft moan and put her hands on his head and then moved them to his shoulders. He took his time, licking and sucking on her clit until her hips were moving frantically against him, and then he pushed one finger into her body. She arched deeply into his touch and her thighs tightened around his head as she drove her hips against his mouth until she called out his name.

"Come inside of me," she said.

He shifted back up her body and slid deep into her. He drove into her again and again, driving her higher and higher, feeling her body tightening on his as he drove himself into her again and again. She wrapped her legs high around his hips and leaned up to pull his head down to hers. She kissed him long and deep and everything in his body started to build. He shoved into her harder and faster, going deeper than before and taking everything she had to give.

She sucked his tongue deeper into his mouth and then he felt her body clenching down hard on his cock. She tore her mouth from his and cried out his name. He pushed his hand under their bodies, cupping her butt and driving into her faster and harder until he came again in one long release.

He kept thrusting into her until he was empty and then

collapsed on her body, careful not to let her take his full weight. He lay there, the smell of sex and Maggie in the air, her hands lightly caressing him, and he knew that nothing would ever be the same for him again.

She'd changed him and he wasn't sure he liked it. But he was pretty damned sure he couldn't live without it or her.

Which was more complicated than it should be. Or was it? Was he still living in the past where their families couldn't get along? Maybe it was time he moved them into the future where they got along and he could claim Maggie.

Thirteen

Maggie noticed Jericho's mom and sisters at the checkout counter when she arrived at the Royal Diner to meet Cecily for lunch. Normally she would have walked past without saying anything, but Camille Winters caught her eye and smiled.

"Hey, Camille, great to see you again," she said, walking over to them.

"Hello, these are my daughters, Tiffany and Alisha," she said.

"We've met," Alisha said.

"We have, and let me apologize for how heated Preston was at that meeting," Maggie said. "He can be a bit of a hothead at times."

Jericho's sister nodded. "We were thinking about having a girls' night at your art studio. We all saw it online and it looks like our kind of night out."

"I'd love to have you attend. If you have a big group, we could do a private event, or I have one coming up in late

September. I'll text Camille the details," she said. "I won't keep you since you were on the way out but it was nice to see y'all."

She gave them a little wave and then turned to walk to Cecily, who was seated near the back of the restaurant. Maggie felt a little thrill inside her as she walked to her friend. She and Jericho had been spending practically every night together still publicly doing the designated dates but having more fun alone together. Her feelings for him were growing deeper and she wanted his family to like her. She already liked them. His sisters seemed nice, and even Alisha had warmed up once Maggie had mentioned Preston's hotheadedness. Maggie was starting to think there was a very real chance that the feud was based on habit more than actual differences.

A germ of an idea took root in the back of her mind, and she didn't know if she was just riding the high of waking up in Jericho's arms and smelling the sweet flowers he'd sent her at work, but she thought maybe it was time for the parents to meet and just see what happened.

"Fraternizing with the enemy I see," Cecily said as Maggie slid into the booth across from her.

She furrowed her brow as she looked at the other woman. "What enemy?"

"The Winters. Or were you getting more information?"

She sighed. She'd asked Cecily to meet her today to tell her that she wasn't going to be able to get any corporate secrets or insider knowledge from Jericho. "No. There's nothing to find, Cecily. Also, Jericho doesn't really know much about the Winters' business. He's an architect."

Cecily nodded. "You're letting your feelings get the better of you. Remember what happened when Eliza Boudreaux left Fernando? Do you want to be hurt that way?"

"This is different," she said. Maggie didn't believe that Jericho would ever deceive her in any way. She hoped he knew that she wouldn't do that to him as well. The last few days had shown her just how different from Randall Jericho was. He might have started out trying to impress her parents at dinner, but she knew from a text via her mom that Jericho and her dad had been discussing environmentally friendly energy sources that he could use in his building designs. Something new her father and Preston had been brainstorming but hadn't been sure how to bring to the market.

Cecily tipped her head to the side and reached over to squeeze Maggie's hand where it rested on the table next to her phone. "I know. He's different and so are you, or at least it feels that way. I really just don't want to see you in a situation similar to the one you had with Randall…"

Maggie pulled her hand back, picking up her phone and setting it on the bench next to her. "Jericho is nothing like Randall. Shall we order? I think that Amanda put peach pie on the menu and I cannot resist it. So I'm leaning toward that. What about you?"

"I'm having the Greek salad with dressing on the side and the peach pie," Cecily said, reluctantly ending her line of questioning.

After they had both ordered, they talked about the upcoming Christmas campaign that Maggie was designing the graphic art for. Maggie was glad to have a chance to talk about something that wasn't Jericho or the feud. It made her more determined to actually end it. She and Jericho's relationship might have started out to help Misha and Trey, but it had turned into something else. She felt it, and she was pretty sure he did, too.

"I'm sorry if I overstepped earlier. I really do have you

and your family's best interests at heart," Cecily said as they were getting ready to leave.

"I know you do. It's just I think that it's time we moved on from the old rivalries and started doing more to build bridges," Maggie said. "Thank you for caring enough to say the tough things."

"That's what I do," Cecily said, giving her a hug and then getting into her car and driving away.

Maggie felt better and texted Jericho with her idea to make some permanent changes to the old tensions between the Del Rio and Winters families.

Maggie: Tell me if this sounds nuts but I think we should have our parents over for a cookout.

Jericho: It's totally bonkers, but I was thinking something similar.

Maggie: Okay, this Saturday?

Jericho: Two days?

Maggie: Yeah, that way they can't overthink it and back out.

Jericho: [[laughing emoji]] I'll text my folks.

Maggie: I'm going to say yours are already coming... I know it's deceptive but they won't say no if they think we'll be hosting your folks.

Jericho: You're diabolical but right. I'll do the same. Can't wait to see you tonight.

Maggie: Me, either.

She tucked her phone into her purse after texting her mom and sat in her car letting the air-conditioning cool her down. She cautioned herself not to get too excited but it was hard not to. She didn't want to say the *L* word. Or identify her feelings as that. But the truth was she was starting to think that was what she felt toward Jericho.

Jericho texted his parents and they immediately responded yes, they'd be there. His mom asked what she could bring and Jericho requested her potato salad, which was his favorite. She hearted the message and Jericho turned back to the design he was working on. He used an advanced CAD program and was trying to incorporate the idea that Fernando and Preston had talked to him about. They were trying to develop the basics of a revolutionary energy-saving way to heat and cool homes, but the design was... Well, *tricky* would be an understatement. That's where Jericho's expertise in building and architecture came in. Together they might figure it out.

He sensed someone watching him and glanced up to his brother standing in the doorway. "Hey, wasn't expecting to see you today."

"I was over this way for a meeting and decided to drop by," Trey said.

He arched one eyebrow at his brother. "For?"

"Mom said you and Maggie...that you seemed to really like each other."

"I told you it was complicated," Jericho said. "Please tell me you're not turning into some kind of Dr. Phil."

"No, but I want to make sure you've thought this through. She's a Del Rio."

"Thanks, Dad. I already cottoned onto that fact," he said, shoving his hand through his thick hair.

"Actually, Dad really likes her. Seems me and Alisha were the only holdouts but even she seems to have softened."

"Really?"

"Yes. So what am I missing? I mean the Del Rio family has been our business rival and more for decades."

Jericho saw the tension in his brother but also the worry. Trey was the heir apparent, the one who had been groomed by their father since birth to take over Winters Industries. But the truth was he'd also been indoctrinated as they all had in the legend of the feud with the Del Rio family.

Jericho got up and went to the sideboard in his office. "Want a beer?"

"Sure," Trey said.

Jericho took two out of the mini fridge, popped the tops and handed one to his brother before gesturing for him to sit down in one of the large leather guest chairs. Jericho sat next to his brother and took a long sip of his beer before he said anything else.

"I'm beginning to believe that our families have more in common than anyone wants to believe. I've had dinner with Fernando and Gayle and they were like Mom and Dad would be to anyone you or I were dating. And Fernando wants to make changes to the environment and we've been—"

"Oh, for Christ's sake. Are you working with them?"

Jericho sat up a bit straighter. "I am. I mean we don't have a project, we're just trying to find something that could be one."

"Tell me about the project," Trey said.

Jericho knew his brother was just as interested in the environment and had been hoping to bring his savvy investors on board once they had something to take to market. So he explained what they were working on. When he was done, Trey drained his beer in one swallow.

"I hate that I'm saying this, but I want in. That idea is good."

"We don't have a working model yet," Jericho reminded his brother. But he felt love for his brother and the fact that he was willing to put aside his own feelings toward the Del Rio family to move forward. This was why he'd thought Maggie's suggestion of getting their families together was a good one.

"It's you. You'll figure it out and have a working model in no time. How did this come about?"

"Honestly, Fernando. I was as surprised as you seem," Jericho said.

Trey nodded. "So you're serious about Maggie?"

"I am. I know you were grateful that I publicly dated her to help drive sales and applications of the k!smet app, but even if you'd asked me not to see her, I would have," Jericho said.

Trey didn't say anything to that; just got up and got them both another beer. He handed one to Jericho and smiled at him. "Glad to hear that you aren't just doing this for my profits."

"Yeah, me, too. Took me by surprise," Jericho admitted.

"Reminder I'm not Dr. Phil."

Jericho laughed and shook his head. "Yeah, you'd suck at it."

"But seriously, I'm happy for you. I hope that Maggie and the Del Rio family are exactly what you think they are," Trey said before changing the conversation to another Winters Expo Center he wanted Jericho to design for a new property in North Dallas.

They talked business and after his brother left, Jericho couldn't help but remember what Trey had said.

That Maggie and her family *were* what he thought they were.

It hadn't occurred to Jericho that they wouldn't be. He'd never been a man to see people as he wanted them to be. He prided himself on his ability to cut through the bullshit and see the real meaning behind anyone he met or did business with.

But he'd never experienced this kind of emotion with anyone else before.

His family he loved, he knew that. He'd been starting to think that what he felt for Maggie was well leaning that way. He liked her. He wanted her more than he'd ever wanted another sexual partner. They had another of their designated dates—boating on the lake which was a lot of fun. In fact, everything with Maggie was better because she was by his side.

And he'd been going with it. That was sort of his nature but Trey had raised something he had to consider. He had that big empty mansion in the gated community. His business was solid and successful. The only element that had been missing from his life was a genuine personal relationship. And Maggie fit that bill. She was giving him everything he wanted and had never realized he needed.

But was it real or was he just seeing what he wanted to see?

* * *

Jericho surprised Maggie with how involved he was with getting everything set up for their parents to come over to dinner at her place. Probably because her father would have sat in his home office working until her mom told him to come out to grill and play bartender.

But Jericho woke up early and started working on the meats. He was grilling a brisket, ribs and sausages. While he put rubs and marinades on things, he'd also made them breakfast. Maggie knew she was trying to be sensible, especially since their parents hadn't met yet and there was a good chance that they might not get along, but Jericho was making those dreams she'd thought were shattered forever by Randall seem possible again.

She didn't dwell on it as she started to make her grandmother's seven-layer dip recipe and made an emergency run to the liquor store. She was making sangria and beer margaritas to serve at dinner. When she got back to her house, the music was blaring from the patio and the fountain at the end of the pool was on.

Jericho had changed the bulb in one of the lights on the trellis that she'd mentioned was out and she stood in the kitchen watching her man dancing and singing as he worked in the backyard.

Her heart sort of slowed down as she watched him, and the realization that she'd been hiding from herself finally dawned.

She loved him.

She wasn't going to be able to act like she didn't. It didn't matter that she'd only known him for a few short weeks. She knew her heart. What she'd thought was love with Randall hadn't been because it was nothing like this.

Jericho glanced up and caught her watching him. He wasn't wearing a shirt and had on a pair of low-slung bathing suit trunks. He put his hands on his hips, shoulders back. "Like what you see?"

"You know it, baby," she said. He was sweaty from the work he was doing; his hair was mussed, and he wasn't perfect, but to her… She'd never seen a man she was more attracted to. This was what she'd been missing in her engagement to Randall. This was probably what she'd never understood about her parents' dynamic. But here it was the truth about love and emotion.

Love didn't look for perfection or the easy path. If their parents hated each other tonight, Maggie knew she wasn't going to not love Jericho. It would make their life together harder but she knew deep in her soul that they would be together.

Jericho rushed her and scooped her off her feet with his arms around her hips, lifting her and spinning her around as he rubbed his sweaty face against her neck. "Kiss me."

She did, putting her hands in his damp hair and kissing him long and deep. He carried her into the house and they made love in the shower. She kept her love unspoken as they got dressed and readied themselves for their parents' arrival, but it was hard.

He caught her smiling at him more than once and he sighed. "Woman, we can't keep our parents waiting while I make love to you again."

"We won't. But later…"

"Oh, definitely later," he said.

They went back downstairs dressed and ready to entertain. "I'm nervous."

"Me, too," Jericho said. "Silly, right? We both know our own parents."

"That's why I'm nervous. I mean Dad took a minute to warm up to you and you aren't Winters Industries."

"Yeah, that's what I'm thinking," he said. "Whatever happens tonight, I'm not walking away from you."

She turned from the hall mirror where she'd been putting on her lipstick, and looked at him. "Me, either."

He nodded and the doorbell rang before they could say anything else. She took a deep breath and finished putting her lipstick on, then set the stick in the basket on the hall table before going to open the door.

His parents arrived first. Joseph and Camille hugged them both. His mom had brought potato salad, which Jericho had warned her was his favorite and that he'd eat all of it if not closely guarded.

She led them out to the patio and poured them drinks before the doorbell rang again.

Jericho came with her to answer it. He squeezed her hand as she opened the door. She suspected he was thinking what she was. This was it. The moment they knew if the feud would die or if they'd have a new one. One, she thought, with her and Jericho on one side and their families on the other.

But their nerves turned out to be for nothing. Her dad was happy to see Jericho, and her mom had relaxed toward him as well. It was a bit tense when they got out on the patio, but Maggie just kept the drinks flowing.

"I'm going to get the side dishes."

"I'll help," both of their moms said at once.

"Great. I could use you both."

As they went into the kitchen, where there were windows that overlooked the patio and grill area, Maggie noticed her mom watching the men. "Lord, help me, I told Fernando to be on his best behavior…"

"Mom."

"I did the same, but you know how men are."

"I do," Gayle said. "I reminded him that we're here for the kids."

"Exactly," Jericho's mom agreed. They finished getting the side dishes together and went out to sit down to eat.

Maggie and Jericho weren't alone in keeping the conversation going. It seemed their moms were just as interested in smoothing things between the families and Maggie almost laughed when her dad turned to Jericho's and started talking about football. He was a huge Cowboys fan. Turned out Joseph was as well.

And though they hadn't talked about the past or the rivalry, Maggie felt steps had been taken to move them away from the past and toward the future. A future, she thought as she felt Jericho's hand on her thigh under the table, that would definitely involve the two of them.

Fourteen

After dinner had been cleared away, they moved to the seating area around the firepit. The weather this time of year wasn't really cool at night, but it had a nice ambiance. Maggie was surprised at how well the conversation had been going during dinner, and when Jericho served some after-dinner drinks and pulled her onto his lap in an arm-chair close to the love seat where his parents were sitting, she noticed his mom smiled at them.

She put her arm around his shoulders and looked down into his dark brown eyes. The knowledge that she loved him flooded her and she felt so hopeful that this time she had a man she could count on and trust.

"So Dad, Fernando and Preston have a revolutionary idea for an environmentally friendly way to heat and cool homes," Jericho said. "I've been working on refining their design for them."

Jericho hugged her close as he said it, and she noticed he held his body in a slightly tense way. She held her breath.

Jericho working with her dad had really been something she wasn't anticipating, but it had for the first time made her truly understand that no matter how standoffish her father was, he did love her. But bringing up that project tonight… Maggie had no idea how her father would react.

Fernando took a sip of his after-dinner drink and looked over at her and Jericho, and she saw a slight smile on his face as he sat back and put his arm around her mom.

"Your son has some good ideas, but we are both struggling with a way to make it at a price point that will actually be affordable," Fernando said.

She squeezed Jericho's shoulders. She knew her man was good at what he did. She'd seen the Winters Expo Center and countless other designs he'd shared with her since they'd been spending so much time together. Jericho wasn't just talented, he was constantly looking for ways to use his knowledge and skills to make things better. It seemed to her he was a man with his eye on the future.

"Winters Industries might be able to help with that," Joseph said with one of those nods that older men sometimes did to reinforce a point. "Maybe it's time we stopped working against each other and combined our resources."

Maggie couldn't believe what she was hearing. She knew the feud was something that both families had almost relished. She could remember the tension when her and Jericho's names were announced on the k!smet app. What would Royal do if their favorite feuding families weren't? But that thought was tongue-in-cheek. She had been sort of hoping for this since she realized how deep her feelings for Jericho were. And that she wanted him in her life.

"I like the sound of that. I've seen what the Winterses

have to offer by my discussions with Jericho. I'd really enjoy expanding them."

"Good, I already mentioned the idea to Trey," Jericho said to his father. "He's onboard with investing in the product."

"I'll need to see more before I can just sign off, but I really don't see why we can't figure out something that will work for both of our families," Joseph said.

"This calls for champagne," Maggie's mom said. "We're going to have a toast and seal the deal."

"Without lawyers?" Fernando asked.

"Definitely without lawyers," Gayle said. "You two should shake on it."

Jericho nodded. "Should we photograph it, Mom, just in case?"

Joseph laughed, shaking his head. "With you two as witnesses I don't think we'll need any other proof."

He held his hand out to Fernando and her father leaned in to shake it. "Might be nice to do business together. Really use our influence on the direction of the industry in this town."

Maggie got up off Jericho's lap. "I'll go get that champagne."

Camille and her mom helped by getting the champagne flutes. Over the last few years, Maggie had stopped keeping champagne in the house, though it had been her habit. She'd just felt like there was nothing that she'd be celebrating. But when she'd done her grocery shopping this week, she'd put two bottles in the cart just in case.

She smiled as she uncorked the champagne. That was another in a million little things that she'd abandoned when she'd been dumped. Looking back, it seemed like she should have known better than to let Randall steal that much of who she was. But at the time… Well, at the time she hadn't been able to see anything but the broken dreams and the hurt.

She couldn't help herself but think, as she watched her parents and Jericho laughing and talking on her patio, that this was something she wouldn't have anticipated. She thought she'd had a plan for her future all mapped out and one man had destroyed it. Or rather she'd let him destroy it.

Jericho glanced up and quirked one brow at her and she smiled. One man had changed everything. He hadn't asked her to marry him or tried to pressure her family into investing in anything. He'd just come into her life with his easy smile and hot, rocking body and changed everything.

She filled the glasses and they had a toast. As she let the bubbly wine sit on her tongue for a second before closing her eyes and making a wish before swallowing, she knew what she was wishing for. And the truth was at this moment she had her wish. Things that she'd never knew were important to her suddenly were. Tonight she was in love, and for the first time in a very long time, she believed that there was such a thing as happily-ever-after and Mr. Right.

And she'd found him through a dating app. A part of her was astounded by that. When she opened her eyes, Jericho was watching her, and he didn't say anything, just walked over to her and pulled her into his arms and kissed her.

Jericho had a late meeting and Maggie had been vague about her plans, but he thought she'd gone to Dallas with some friends, so Jericho was for the first time in a while on his own. Trey was busy doing something with his son, and his brother Marcus had texted to see if he wanted to meet up for a drink, which Jericho agreed to. Marcus was definitely the black sheep of the family, but that was only as far as the business was concerned. Like Jericho, Marcus had found his own path. He was an expert at networking and using social media to get results and more than once Jericho had turned to his brother for help in that area.

He walked into the Texas Cattleman's Club looking around for his brother, and he wasn't hard to spot. Marcus was six-three and stood out above the crowd. Marcus waved when he saw Jericho and he waved back.

He gave his brother a hug and they ordered drinks before taking them to a high table toward the back of the bar area where they could have some privacy.

"What's up? It's not like you to want to have drinks," Jericho said.

"I was wondering what's up with you. It's not like you to be all over social media. That's usually my gig," Marcus said.

"Yeah, I know. It's surreal."

"Add to that Mom and Dad talking about the Del Rio family and not cursing their name…figured it was time for us to catch up," Marcus said.

He smiled at his younger brother, who smiled back, flashing his dimple. "Not much to tell. I'm dating Maggie."

"I could get that from the viral posts I've seen of the two of you. Is it real? I think it must be given that Dad is actually talking to Fernando about possible mutual business deals," Marcus said.

"It is real. It started as sort of a favor for Trey."

"Trey asked you to fake-date a hot woman?" Marcus asked sardonically.

"Yeah, that's the kind of brother I am, so I said yes."

Marcus laughed. "You're the best about that. Seriously, though, you've only known her like what, two weeks? Now everyone is all nicey-nicey."

When it was put like that, Jericho sort of understood why Marcus had suggested they have drinks. "Yeah, I know it's been fast, but it feels real."

Once again Jericho had that moment where he wanted to talk about what he was feeling but honestly he had no words to express it. What was he going to say that wouldn't make him sound like some simpering idiot? *Somehow I really like her.* That might be true, but he wouldn't utter those words to anyone, let alone one of his brothers.

"Yeah? I'm on the k!smet app and have had a few matches, but they've all been casual."

Jericho had been exactly where his brother was. That was what he'd expected when he and Maggie had been matched. So why was it different? Was that what Marcus wanted to know? Was his brother trying to navigate things changing in his own relationships? Frankly Jericho wasn't the brother for that kind of advice.

"I don't know why it's different. I mean I guess I do. It's all down to Maggie. She's not like other women. On the surface she could be, but there is so much more to her than—"

"Bro, sounds like you're in—"

"Don't say it. Don't." He cut Marcus off. Was he in love? Hell, he thought he might be. No *might* about it. He knew he was. But he wasn't about to talk about it or admit that to anyone other than Maggie first. And he wasn't sure she felt that way. Sure, they had been spending all of their time together but at the same time, he knew he was the first man she'd dated since her broken engagement.

That in and of itself made him…wary. Which wasn't his MO at all so he was ignoring it.

"Okay, but you know if you feel that strongly about not saying it…you definitely feel it."

He just nodded. "Yeah, but I want to tell her first."

Marcus clapped his hand on Jericho's shoulder and squeezed it, looking like he was about to say more, when Jericho's phone rang.

"It's Dad," Jericho said to Marcus.

He answered the call. "Dad, what's up?"

"There's been a break-in at Winters Industries," Joseph said.

"Okay." He wasn't sure why his dad was telling him. "Did you call Sheriff Battle?"

"I did and he's on his way. But I think you should come down here, too."

"Why?"

"From the surveillance footage… Well, son, there's no easy way to say this. I think it was Maggie who broke in."

"Maggie? My Maggie?"

"Yes," his father said.

"I'm on my way," he said, standing up as he disconnected the call.

"What's going on?" Marcus asked.

Jericho looked at his brother and tried to ignore the feelings of hurt and betrayal that were swamping him. Instead he concentrated on anger. That was an easier emotion, one he had no problem showing.

"Maggie broke into Winters Industries."

"What the fuck?"

Marcus reached for him but Jericho stepped away from his brother, stalking toward the door. The other patrons in the bar at the Texas Cattleman's Club all cleared a path as he moved. There was no reason why Maggie would have broken into Winters Industries.

No reason for her to unless she'd had some sort of ulterior motive for dating him to begin with.

Had she only gone along with the dates so she could get… what? He had no idea what kind of information she would want to take from Winters Industries. In fact, the two of them had seemed removed from their families' interests, or maybe he'd simply been seeing what he wanted to in her.

Maggie texted Jericho when she was on her way back from Dallas. Piper Holloway had asked her opinion on a new art installation she'd been doing in the art district where she had her gallery. Maggie had helped Piper rearrange the artwork and then had dinner with Piper and her partner Brian, which had gone late. Brian was friends with Jericho and had acted as his attorney during the mediation they'd had. Brian and Piper had both said how happy they were for her and Jericho.

But Jericho wasn't answering her texts, and when she tried calling, he sent her to voice mail.

She started to get concerned that something was wrong and since she couldn't concentrate on driving and on worrying about Jericho, she pulled over. She texted her mom to see if she knew what was going on.

Her mom called back.

"Mom?"

"Maggie, where are you?"

"On the side of the interstate. I'm on my way back from Dallas. What's going on?"

"There was a break-in at Winters Industries," Gayle said. "I don't know the full details but Sheriff Battle wants to talk to you. Dad's on the phone with Cecily and you better get back here."

"Why do they want to talk to me?"

"Honestly, Maggie, they think you did it," her mom said.

"Who thinks that? Why would I break in?" she asked. But she remembered Cecily asking her to try to find dirt or information on Winters Industries. Was that part of this?

"Everyone."

"Everyone?" she asked. "Mom, does Jericho think I did this?"

"Based on how stone-faced he was when he showed up here with Sheriff Battle, I'd say yes."

Stone-faced.

How could the man who'd held her in his arms this morning after waking her up by making love to her believe she'd do something like this?

Maggie's hands started shaking. How could Jericho think she'd do something like that? But she took a deep breath. Until she spoke to him, she wasn't going to jump to any conclusions. "Okay. Should I go to the sheriff's office?"

"Yes, I'll meet you there."

"Thanks, Mom."

"Drive carefully, honey. Love you."

"Love you, too," she said, hanging up the phone.

She took a deep breath and almost got back on the road. But she couldn't stop thinking about the fact that Jericho might believe she'd broken into his family's business. She knew she should wait until they were in person to talk but she was both hurt and angry that he might believe the worst of her.

Maggie to Jericho: Just talked to my mom. I'm on my way back from Dallas, where I told you I'd be. I wasn't breaking into Winters HQ. You should know me better than that. I assume I'll see you at the sheriff's office.

Then she put her phone on airplane mode, tossing it on the seat beside her. She tried to stay calm, took a deep breath and then banged her fists on the steering wheel. How could she have been so wrong about another man? Did she have the shittiest gut instincts on the planet? How could she have once again trusted a man who literally felt nothing for her?

The rational part of her mind tried to caution her that maybe he didn't believe it, but she knew he did. He wouldn't have sent her calls to voice mail or ignored her texts if he thought she was innocent.

Instead he had assumed the worst. Was it because she was a Del Rio? Or was it something far worse? Was it because she was just the type of woman that no man wanted for who she was. She put her head on the steering wheel, crying and hating herself for crying. But unable to stop.

She loved Jericho. How could he not love her back?

And this wasn't like when Randall had broken their engagement. Because what she'd thought was love had just been a desire to have a husband. She knew that now. She could see through the lens of her relationship with Jericho how shallow everything had been with Randall.

She saw flashing lights and a car pulled up behind her. She wiped her tears as a highway patrol officer walked toward the car. She rolled down her window.

"Ma'am, are you okay?"

"Yes, sir. Just got some bad news and needed to stop driving for a minute," she said.

"Do you want me to call someone for you?"

"No, I'm fine. I think I'll be good to drive," she said.

"Okay, ma'am," he said, walking back to his car. She put the window up and signaled to pull back out onto the highway. She wanted to drive out her anger. To put the gas pedal all the way down and bury the needle on the speedometer and scream at the top of her lungs, but she didn't.

She drove as sedately as she could until the highway patrol made a U-turn and headed back toward Dallas. Still she kept driving slowly. In her mind she toyed with all the things she'd say when she saw Jericho, but she knew that was secondary. His family must have reason to believe she had broken in and she was going to have to do more than bring Cecily with her to the station.

She was going to have to live with the fact that everyone in Royal would believe she'd restarted the feud between their families.

For the life of her, she couldn't think why Jericho would believe she'd do that. She'd shown him how much he meant to her, shown him how much she wanted a future with him. Or maybe she hadn't and maybe that was a mixed blessing. Because even though she knew she loved him and how much his distrust in her hurt, at least he didn't know how much she'd cared. At least he wouldn't know what was in her broken heart.

Fifteen

Jericho read and reread Maggie's text. She was pissed at him. Had he been wrong? The woman on the video definitely shared more than a passing resemblance to Maggie. And she'd been cagey about where she'd been going.

"You okay, son?" Joseph asked.

He looked over at his father and for the first time realized he wasn't okay. He didn't have everything together and there was no way he was going to be blasé about Maggie. Or pretend he wasn't hurt by what looked like a massive betrayal by her.

"No. Dad, I can't believe Maggie would do this," he said.

His father put his hand on Jericho's shoulder and squeezed it. "To be honest, I can't either. It really doesn't fit with the woman I met or, to be honest, with her parents."

"Do you think they were just doing that? What was the reason?"

"I can't tell you, maybe they thought our business deals

weren't all legit. That's not how I operate so I'm not really sure what her motive would be," Joseph said.

Her motive.

Maggie had seemed to have no real connection to the Del Rio Group except as a graphic designer. What kind of information would she be looking for? Would she even recognize it when she saw it?

"Dad, I'm not sure—"

"Couldn't wait to stir up some more trouble with my family, is that it, Winters?" Fernando entered the sheriff's office with his wife. He'd never seen Fernando like this before and for the first time the reality of the feud was right in front of Jericho.

He could see not only the anger on his face but also something akin to…either hatred or hurt. Wasn't it funny how those two emotions could blend together? Jericho knew it firsthand because he was battling with betrayal and hurt.

"Calm down, Del Rio. We didn't just randomly decide to accuse your daughter. We have her on video surveillance. Also she's not in town and Jericho has no idea where she is," Joseph said.

All eyes turned to him and Jericho looked at the people he'd started to care for. He felt even more betrayed at this moment because he was sure that Gayle and Fernando would have had to put Maggie up to doing this. There was no reason for her to just do it on her own.

"She was in Dallas tonight," Gayle said.

"So she said," Jericho responded.

"Have you called your attorney? She had dinner with him," Gayle said again.

Jericho's brow furrowed. "Brian Cooper?"

Gayle just flicked her eyebrows up quickly and gave

him a disgusted look before she turned to the reception-ist at the desk.

"Where is Nathan?"

"He's not available right now," Officer Hatton said.

"Oh, he's available for me," Gayle said. "I'm not letting him take this ridiculousness any further."

"Gayle," Sheriff Nathan Battle said as he came out of the hallway that led to his office. "Calm down. We have questions for Maggie. We're not asking for a warrant for her arrest."

"Is that supposed to make me feel better?" she demanded.

Jericho had never seen Gayle like this. Normally she was calm and he'd seen her tough side when she'd questioned him about his intentions toward Maggie, but this was full-on protective mama bear.

"It is. As much as I want to believe that she had nothing to do with the break-in, the evidence is pretty damning."

"Can we see it?" Fernando asked.

Nathan looked at Joseph, who nodded.

"Fernando, honestly, after dinner the other night I was looking forward to putting the feud behind us. It's past time we moved on, but this… See for yourself."

Sheriff Battle had the video-surveillance footage on a large tablet and Maggie's parents, his dad and Jericho all leaned in as he hit Play.

There was no mistaking Maggie's long dark ponytail. She was wearing a trench coat, which was a bit odd consider-ing the weather and the fact that if Jericho knew one thing about Maggie, that wasn't her style. But he figured she was trying not to get caught.

The woman in the video also moved like Maggie. Her long stride and the way her hips moved from side to side with each step.

"Dammit. I know that's not Maggie," Gayle said.

"If it's not me, then who is it?" Maggie asked, walking into the sheriff's office.

Everyone turned to look at her and Jericho tried not to notice her. Tried very hard not to let his hormones react—it was just hormones, right?—to seeing her again. But it was impossible. He wanted to pull her away from everyone else and demand she tell him what was going on.

Why had she betrayed him?

But as he skimmed his gaze over her, he realized that she had her long hair down, curling around her shoulders, and she wore one of those body-contouring dresses she favored. She had a large bag over her shoulder and he could see that her eyes were red.

She'd been crying.

What was going on?

He'd seen her on the video. Her appearance wasn't that different that it couldn't be explained. But the tears? Maggie didn't cry. Not even when she'd shared her darkest fears.

"We'll need your alibi to start," Sheriff Battle said.

Maggie came forward, brushing past him without looking at him. She was ticked, too. That was fine. They were both in an impossible situation. Two people who'd been bound by a contract and a surprise match on a dating app. That's all they were.

"Sure. Are you going to question me here?"

"No, come into my office," Nathan said.

Maggie followed him down the hall. Her mom reached out to squeeze her arm and Maggie gave a short nod. He hadn't realized it earlier because Maggie was usually so genial and upbeat but there was a core of solid steel inside her.

And that made him realize something he maybe should

have sooner. Maggie wasn't the type to sneak around to try to get information. She'd always been brash and straightforward.

So as she'd said, who had broken into Winters Industries?

Maggie held herself tall as she walked past Jericho and his father. She was still so deeply hurt and mad that they thought she would commit a criminal act. Her mom had looked at her and Maggie shook her head, knowing if her mom showed her an ounce of sympathy her control would break and she'd start crying again.

Her mom just nodded and Maggie did what she'd done when she'd had to walk out of Sheen by herself after Randall had dumped her. She reminded herself whose daughter she was and that she'd been raised to be strong. And fuck Jericho Winters for not even hesitating before deciding she was a criminal.

Where was Cecily? She wondered if she needed to talk to her lawyer. Even though she knew she'd done nothing wrong.

"Do you want to wait for your attorney?" Sheriff Battle asked.

She shook her head. She knew she hadn't committed the crime and had been in Dallas all night.

"We can talk without her."

Sheriff Battle wasn't someone Maggie knew all that well. He'd come to the high school and talked about not doing drugs or drinking and then driving. And he'd come to her parents' Christmas parties over the years. But Maggie had never personally spoken to him.

"Okay, Maggie—do you mind if I call you by your first name?" he asked.

"No, sir, I don't. What do you need from me?" she asked as he gestured for her to take a seat.

She was nervous even though she knew she hadn't done anything wrong. Her hands started sweating and she almost wiped them on her thighs but then stopped in case he thought that meant she'd done it.

"I just need to know where you were from eight to nine tonight," he said.

"I was in Dallas with Piper Holloway and Brian Cooper. Mostly Piper. I had a quick dinner with both of them. I have GPS on my car and they can vouch for me... Also, I took this photo at the gallery of the art installation I helped Piper with."

She opened the photos app on her phone and handed it to Sheriff Battle after she'd swiped up so the metadata was visible.

He took it from her and then called in one of his deputies to verify her story. She was left alone in his office for a few minutes and her mind was whirring with too much. One thing that was so different about tonight versus the night Randall had broken their engagement was that back then her mind had gone quiet and calm. Of course, she'd been embarrassed and humiliated and mad. But not like this.

Her anger had been more because he'd taken her to a public place to end things. It hadn't felt like this. She'd been alone when she'd found out what Jericho thought of her and this hurt was so much deeper. She couldn't stop her emotions. She wanted to wrap her arms around her body to try to keep it all inside but she also didn't want anyone to see her that way.

She knew she just had to hold on a little bit longer. They'd confirm everything and she could go home and be alone and then she would let it all out. Just a little bit longer.

"It's confirmed. You're good to go," Sheriff Battle said as he came back into his office. "Though do you have any enemies?"

"What?"

"Someone went out of their way to look like you in this video," Sheriff Battle said.

"Can I see it?" she asked.

He turned the tablet to her and Maggie hit Play. As soon as she saw the long ponytail, she knew why everyone had thought it was her. It was her signature style. She wasn't wearing it tonight, but she almost always did. She leaned in closer. She didn't want to mention Cecily, but Maggie recognized those stilettos. And her friend had asked her to get dirt on the Winters family.

Would Cecily have done this and tried to frame her for it?

"I don't have any enemies, Sheriff. I mean, except for the Winters feud, and I'm pretty sure that isn't a Winters family member pretending to be me."

"Yeah, I thought so, too. It was a long shot," Sheriff Battle said.

"Maybe not. I… I'm not positive, but our lawyer Cecily did ask me to try to dig up some dirt on the Winterses since I was dating Jericho… I told her no, but maybe she tried to find some on her own?" Maggie said.

"Maybe. Thanks for the information. I'll have a talk with her," Sheriff Battle said. "I'm going to send you out with a deputy. I'm not ready to face your mama again."

Maggie smiled for the first time since she'd left Dallas. "Oh, I know she's tough but she's also fair. That video definitely looks like me."

"It does, but I don't think Gayle's going to be giving me a pass because of that."

Maggie nodded in agreement and said her goodbyes to the sheriff before following the deputy back into the waiting room, where her parents, Joseph and Jericho waited. Cecily was gone, which made Maggie worry that her family's attorney might have been the one to do the breaking and entering.

"My alibi checked out," she said.

"Officer Haddon informed us," her mom said. "Ready to go home?"

"Yes, ma'am."

"Maggie—" Jericho said her name.

She turned and gave him a long hard look and just shook her head no. Then she walked out of the sheriff's office with her head held high. Her mom followed her out but her father stayed behind.

As soon as they were away from the doorway, her mom pulled her into her arms and Maggie wrapped her own around her. She put her head on her mom's shoulder, knowing it was safe to cry, but there were no tears. She felt that icy coldness that had been so much a part of her for the last two years start to seep back in.

She knew that it was a protective thing and she realized that it was easier to feel nothing than to deal with the pain of heartbreak and disappointment.

Jericho knew from the moment that Maggie had walked into the sheriff's office that he'd made a mistake. Sheriff Battle wanted to speak to both his father and Fernando, so Jericho told his dad goodbye and nodded at Fernando as he went outside. Maggie and her mom stood off to the side of the entrance.

Jericho knew that it would be better if he just went home and tried to talk to her later but that wasn't his way where Maggie was concerned. He needed to talk to her. He wanted a chance to maybe explain, but more than anything he wanted to make sure that she knew...

What? he demanded of himself. Now that she had an alibi he believed her? Yeah, that wasn't going to go over very well.

He should wait to talk to her.

He should.

"Maggie, could I speak to you for a minute?" he called out.

Fucking asshole.

Her mom gave him a hard look but just turned to her daughter. Maggie said something softly that Jericho couldn't hear and then her mom walked past him without saying a word, going back inside.

She stood there, obviously not coming to him. So he walked over, his mind frantically going through words and rejecting them. He should have waited to do this.

"I know you're ticked."

"Oh, I'm more than that. How could you think I would do something like that?" she demanded.

"It looked like you," he said, and as the words left his mouth, he knew they were a mistake. He heard them and wanted to pull them back.

Camille would have had his head for saying something like that. One of the things he liked best about his mom was the fact that she had raised him and his brothers to understand how to treat a woman. He knew she would be disappointed in him tonight. "I'm sorry I said that."

Maggie nodded.

"Why would you believe that about me?"

That was the one question he hadn't been able to answer to himself. Sure, he could say maybe it was because his mom had died when he was a kid or that his high school girlfriend had ended things when they'd both gone off to college. But the truth was more nuanced than that. It wasn't that he didn't believe in love. He'd seen the evidence of it in his own home growing up between his dad and stepmom.

The truth was, he had never felt as deeply for anyone the way he did about Maggie. And that made him vulnerable, which he fucking hated. There was no two ways about that. So it had been easier to think he'd been wrong about her so he could just ignore those feelings. Easier was never the best path, his father had said more than once.

"I don't know," he said, even though that wasn't the answer he knew he should give her.

"Well, I have an opinion," she said.

He arched both eyebrows at her.

"You wanted to believe that somehow I was all the horrible things you were brought up to believe about the Del Rio family."

He shook his head. "I never thought of you as one of those manipulative Del Rios."

"Then why? And don't say you didn't know. I thought… I thought what we had was more than some contracted dates just to help out Misha and your brother."

Jericho shoved his hands through his hair. "Yeah, I had started to believe it, too. But I'm not sure if that was real."

Fucking hell. What was wrong with him? Why was he so afraid to just admit how he felt for her?

He had even been scared to admit that he loved her to Marcus earlier this evening. He wasn't ready to admit that those emotions were real. He wasn't even sure they were. He knew that he was a mess right now.

"Okay, then. We'll finish out the last few dates and then go our separate ways. I'll have the stuff you left at my place couriered back to yours. See you at our next contracted app date."

She walked past him and he was tempted to let her go. Hadn't he just hedged until this was the only option she had left? But he didn't want her to go like this.

Did he want her to go?

He started to reach for her and she stepped back so quickly she stumbled and then righted herself.

"Please don't touch me," she said.

It was then that he realized how much he'd truly screwed this up. He'd been looking for some sign that the feelings he had for Maggie were love. That they were real and that they'd last a lifetime. But he hadn't been able to find it until this moment.

When she was shoving him away and telling him in no uncertain terms she wanted nothing to do with him.

"Maggie."

"No, I can't. I know you want to hash this out and maybe become something like friends again, but I can't. I didn't think this was false and maybe that's on me. I decided to trust you and to believe the man I thought I saw," she said, then took a deep, gulping breath and he knew how hard she was struggling to keep her emotions in check.

"Maggie—"

"Stop. You're making this worse. You don't love me, fine. We gave our word and signed a contract. You'll get two more dates and then I never want to see you again. Goodbye, Jericho."

She walked away and all he could do was watch her go.

Was this what he wanted? He'd been so afraid to let himself be vulnerable, never realizing that he'd had no control over that. He wanted her. His life would be colorless without Maggie in it.

"Wait. Why were you so cagey about what you were doing tonight?" he asked her.

She opened the trunk of her car and pulled out a large, flat wrapped package. She walked over to him and handed it over. He could tell it was a canvas of some kind. She didn't wait for him to open it. She just got in her car and drove away.

He took it to his car and opened it and stood there for a minute. It was a landscape of the Winters Expo Center with him and Maggie walking out of it. He could tell that it had been freshly framed and the artist's initials in the corner were Piper Holloway's.

Sixteen

Maggie told her assistant she was going out of town but instead headed for her brother Preston's ranch. She needed time away to think, and nothing soothed her troubled soul like riding the horse she kept stabled there. Also Preston just let her be.

Her mom was understanding and suggested that Maggie "run her emotions out" but running had never really worked that way for Maggie. Running was a chore and didn't get her to that mindless state the way horseback riding did. Her father had texted her—something he never did—just to say that he loved her and he hoped she was okay.

Which meant more to her than she wanted to admit. But as she rode over the fields around Preston's property, she wasn't escaping her thoughts. Instead she was confronted with the landscape that very much mirrored the property where the Winters Expo Center had been built. And as she rode, she couldn't help but remember how effortlessly Jericho's well-designed convention space had melded into the landscape, seeming to be a part of it.

Which made her stop Dusty, her paint, and get off. She let the horse graze, knowing she wouldn't go far with her lead on the ground as Maggie herself walked toward a small copse of trees and sat down under it. She had brought her sketchpad with her and as she leaned against the trunk of the scrub oak, she started drawing. She always figured her life out in her sketchbook. It was easier to see things when she literally drew them.

So she did it this time. She drew Jericho as he'd looked at her when she entered the sheriff's office. She took her time recollecting his face and the lines around his eyes. The slight downturn of his lips that she had in the moment thought was anger but, as she went back over his face in her mind, might have been sadness.

Or was she once again trying to see in him something that wasn't there?

Her memories of them together at her studio on the painting night. When she'd been so on fire for him, wanting to touch him but determined not to let him win… She pulled out her phone, which had no reception on this part of Preston's ranch—another blessing—and thumbed back through the photos until she found that one someone had snapped of them and put online.

She looked at his face, trying to see some sign that he was faking his attraction to her. But she didn't think he had been. He'd made love to her like a man who wanted her. That hadn't felt fake. But sexual attraction didn't mean deeper emotions, did it?

Except as she thumbed forward, she got to a photo his mom had sent her of the two of them at the concert. Her back was to Camille so Jericho's face was the only one visible. She remembered they were negotiating in that moment if they were going to touch each other. The look on his face... She zoomed in, trying to make herself not see it, but he seemed to be really into her.

She tossed her phone aside. What was she doing? She was supposed to be falling out of love with Jericho, not trying to find proof he loved her.

But here she was surrounded by him in her thoughts, sketchpad and on her phone. The riding wasn't helping. It was just serving to make her face that getting over Jericho was going to take more than a few nights at her brother's ranch.

She knew she couldn't stay here forever. And getting over Jericho... Well, she was going to have to get back to her life to make that happen. She'd talked to Piper when she'd been in Dallas and her friend had mentioned there was an old gallery up for sale near her place.

Maybe... Maybe it was time she left Royal. She'd stayed because, if she were honest with herself, she loved her hometown. She liked seeing familiar faces when she got her coffee each morning and she liked being close to her family.

The feud with the Winterses hadn't been a big factor in Maggie's life other than overheard comments or discussions between Preston and her dad at the dinner table. But now she knew that she wanted to leave precisely because of Jericho Winters.

She no longer felt like this place was her home and maybe that was because she'd started to see the two of them everywhere. Which really ticked her off. Why couldn't she have been as in "love" with Jericho as she'd thought she'd been with Randall? Then she could have just licked her wounds and moved on.

But this hurt. The fact that he didn't trust her was something she didn't know how to get around. Her gut had never been reliable when it came to men, but she'd tried really hard this time to keep her eyes open and be realistic.

So how had she screwed up?

"Thought I'd find you here."

She glanced up to see Preston on his horse. He dismounted and came over, sitting down next to her. She looked into her brother's hazel eyes. He hadn't shaved for a few days and had some artful stubble. He picked up her sketchpad and looked at it.

"So...not sure if you want to hear this or not, but Jericho is here. He wants to talk to you."

"What?"

"You heard me," Preston said. "For what it's worth, he's apologized to Dad, Mom and me for thinking we had anything to do with the break-in. I think he might want to apologize to you."

"So?"

"Really, Mags? I get that you want to be just mad but—" he picked up the sketchbook "—it's more than that. You're hurt but it seems to me you're still hoping for something from him."

"I am, Pres. How stupid is that?"

Her brother put his arm around her. "Not stupid at all. I think it means something because when Randall broke up with you in front of most of the town, you ripped him a new one and walked out of Sheen like you were a queen."

"I did," she said, smiling as she remembered it. Somehow, she'd gotten used to hiding until the app had matched her with Jericho.

"But with Jericho, you crumbled. Even Dad mentioned it and you know he never notices those kinds of things."

She nodded, pulling her knees up and resting her head on them. "I just don't know what to do."

"Go talk to him. Maybe he'll say something that will help. Or don't. It's up to you," Preston said.

She hugged her brother one more time. "Okay, I'll do it."

"Great. He's on the patio," Preston said.

Maggie rode back to the stables with her brother but Preston lingered as she walked toward the house. She wasn't sure what she was going to find when she confronted Jericho but she knew that she needed to talk to him again for her own peace of mind and maybe, as Preston said, she'd be able to finally figure out how to move on.

It had taken Jericho two days to realize that Maggie wasn't in town. True, after they'd learned from Sheriff Battle that Del Rio family attorney Cecily Meachum had broken into Winters Industries on her own accord, unhappy that the two families were getting along, Jericho knew he should have called Maggie. But he'd had a meeting and he'd been unsure of his reception so he'd let it go for a day.

One day.

And then he'd gone to her place and she wasn't home. He'd gone to her studio and was informed she was on leave. He'd gotten desperate and gone to talk to Fernando, who accepted his apology but didn't offer his daughter's whereabouts. So he'd gone to Gayle, whom he had to track down at her tennis club. She'd refused to stop practicing with her automatic ball machine to talk to him.

Finally, he'd just sat down on the bench behind her. And told her he'd screwed up and he couldn't make things right if no one helped him find Maggie. Gayle still kept hitting balls but she had called over her shoulder asking him what his objective was.

In that moment Jericho knew he was going to have to admit his feelings for Maggie, but he still felt that she should hear them first so he'd simply said that he wanted a future with Maggie and he'd do whatever he had in order to make it happen.

Gayle had stopped her automatic ball machine and turned to him and gave him that level stare of hers. "I'll tell you where she is, but if you don't make things right with her, you leave and we never see you again."

"Yes, ma'am," he said.

So here he was on Preston Del Rio's ranch sitting in the sun without a beverage since he hadn't been offered one. He knew that he wasn't the Del Rio family's favorite person. He got it. He had heard via Trey that his dad and Fernando hadn't spoken since the night of the break-in. It seemed to Jericho they were back where they started before the k!smet app had matched him and Maggie.

The feud had new fuel to drive it for another generation but Jericho didn't care about that. He had realized over the last few days when he'd been alone how much he loved Maggie.

He heard the sound of boots on the stone patio and turned to see Maggie walking toward him. She wore a pair of faded jeans and a scoop-neck top, and her long black hair was braided, falling over her shoulder across her breasts. She had on a straw cowboy hat, which she tossed on one of the chairs as she walked toward him.

Her expression was guarded and she looked tired. He thought she looked hurt as well and he hated that he was responsible for that. He stood up, taking the papers he'd brought with him.

"What's that?" she asked.

"The agreement we signed," he said, tearing it in half and dropping it in the firepit that was near the seating area.

"So no more dates?"

"No more doing things for anyone other than ourselves," he said.

"What do you mean by that?"

"From the beginning I wanted you, Maggie. I mean before the app," he said.

"We didn't even know each other."

"I saw you at the TCC," he said.

"So, lust… Well, you were certainly right about the chemistry between us."

"But it was more than that. Yes, you're hot and every time I see you, I want to pull you into my arms find a private place and make love to you. But it's more than that," he said.

"Really?" she asked. "The other night it seemed it wasn't even lust."

"I'm sorry. I should have led with that and I should have said it when we were outside of the sheriff's office," he said.

"Are you sorry because they found the real culprit and she confessed so you don't have any doubts?" Maggie asked, but there wasn't anger in her voice—it was hurt.

He took a deep breath.

"I'm sorry I ever doubted you. I have no excuse."

"No you don't," she said. "So why are you here?"

"I want to start again. Not because we're put on the spot by the k!smet app or because we want to make our families happy. I want to do this because I love you, Maggie."

She put her hands on her hips and gave him a hard stare that was reminiscent of the one that Gayle had given him.

"You love me?"

"I love you. I thought… Well, I hate how vulnerable I feel when I say those words to you. Other than my family, I've never said them to a woman. I didn't believe that I could be in love with you until…" He trailed off.

"Until when?"

"Until you walked away."

He loved her? He loved her. She was just giving herself time to process everything he said. She looked over at the torn-up dating agreement, which she'd never really cared for to begin with, and then back at him.

Loving Jericho hadn't been easy in the last few days and more than anything she wanted to yell for joy, but she was cautious.

"You love me even though you thought I was a criminal," she said. She needed to understand where he was coming from.

He took a step closer to her and she saw him reach out toward her but drop his hand before he touched her. She wanted his touch. She wanted to be able to believe he really loved her because she'd missed him so damn much and she knew that if he was lying to her…

But Jericho wouldn't lie about this. He'd always been blunt and honest. Even when he thought she'd broken into Winters Industries he hadn't hedged. He'd told her.

So that meant…

"You really do love me."

"I do," he said. "I know it's going to take a long time for

you to forgive me. It's going to take me a long time to forgive myself as well."

"No," she said. Knowing it wasn't going to take that long to forgive him.

"No?"

"It's not going to take any time at all for me to forgive you, Jericho," she started. Then paused trying to find the right words.

"You can't?" he asked, sounding forlorn.

"I can. I love you, too," she said. "Now, it is going to take me a minute to get over being mad—"

Jericho pulled her into his arms and swung her off her feet as he brought his mouth down on hers. Everything that had been tense over the last two days seemed to finally relax as she felt his tongue moving over hers. The kiss was intense and passionate and then he gentled it, setting her on her feet. His hands moved up and down her back as he lifted his head.

"I love you," he said, looking right into her eyes. "I was so afraid to tell you that I was willing to believe anything that would prove I was wrong about these feelings."

She put her hand on his face, looking into those deep brown eyes of his that made her melt. "I love you, too. I was afraid to trust my gut and let myself fall for you, but it happened anyway."

"Will you marry me?"

"What?" Being engaged again. Having the town of Royal know she was going to be married. Could she do it? She knew that this was Jericho and he'd never leave her the way Randall had. But could she trust herself enough to wear his ring and walk around town planning another wedding without… Could she trust him?

That was what he was asking her. She could say she loved him and say she forgave him but the truth was she had to trust him.

And she knew in her heart and soul there was no other man she trusted the way she did Jericho Winters.

"Will you marry me?"

"What about our families?" she asked. She knew the feud was still going strong due to the break-in.

"I don't care about our families, sweet Mags. I love you. I want to spend the rest of my life with you, have kids with you. I want it all and I'm asking you—"

"Yes. I'll marry you," she said. Then realized what she'd agreed to. She waited for the panic to set in, but it didn't. There was something about the way Jericho had stated his desires for the future that had made her believe in it and want it, too.

"Thank you for agreeing to be my wife," he said. "I don't have a ring on me."

"That's fine. We both know what we want from each other," she said.

"We do," he agreed. "Come home with me so I can make love to you and we can plan our future?"

"Yes."

They left her brother's ranch together in Jericho's sports car. As he drove with his usual speed and skill, she couldn't help remembering the first time they'd made love at his house. He let them into the gated community he lived in and drove to his house. They barely made it inside before they were in each other's arms, ripping clothing off. It felt like it had been ages since he'd been inside her, and they came together, long and hard. Then he carried her into the living room and they cuddled naked on the couch.

She looked up and saw the painting she had made for him hanging over the fireplace.

He saw her looking at it and hugged her closer to him. "From the moment I saw this, I knew I had to get you back. No one has ever seen my work as art but you did from the beginning. You might be the one person in the world who actually gets me."

"I definitely am," she said. "You got me, too. You saw that even though I wasn't cowering around town, I was still shy and damaged from my past and you never did anything but try to help me heal from it."

"I did but I had ulterior motives," he said.

"Did you? Why?"

"I must have been falling in love with you even then. I knew there was no way you could fall for me unless you could trust me. So I did everything I could to show you that I was trustworthy until…"

"Until that night that really tested us. And you stumbled. I did, too. I'm sure it won't be the last time, but I think we both know that what we have is worth fighting for."

"It definitely is. Always know that I love you, Maggie Del Rio."

"And I love you, Jericho Winters."

* * * * *

THE RANCHER MEETS HIS MATCH

J. MARGOT CRITCH

This book is dedicated to anyone who might be looking
for connections in unconventional places.

One

"Love is in the air as Jericho Winters and Maggie Del Rio have been seen together all over Royal, Texas." Trey Winters shook his head as he read aloud from the screen of his phone. Trey rolled his eyes and looked at the sign on the building in front of him. k!smet. Because of the dating app, his brother Jericho was now in a relationship with Maggie Del Rio, despite the bad blood between their families that went back almost one hundred years, when a woman named Eliza Boudreaux left her fiancé, Fernando Del Rio, and instead married his rival, Teddy Winters.

He got out of his SUV and strode up to the door. He had a bone to pick with the one running the show—Misha Law, the woman who created the whole app. He strode into her office, expecting to see an assistant sitting outside of the private office, but instead, he saw Misha, the woman herself, sitting alone at the center of a large boardroom table. It seemed that she'd unpretentiously taken over a boardroom instead of setting up a traditional office space.

Her fingers were flying over the keyboard of the laptop that was in front of her, with two large monitors connected, a tablet at her elbow and several plastic cups that he imagined had held iced coffee at a point earlier. Her eyes were locked on one of the monitors, and he would have assumed that she hadn't even known he'd entered, except, still typing with one hand, she held up the first finger on the other hand, instructing him to wait.

Trey glowered. Not many people ever told him to wait.

Finally, Misha looked up at him. Trey had been filled with a fiery anger, but when her hazel eyes met his, it transformed to a heated flush of lust, just like it always did when he faced her. Even though he was a key investor in k!smet, Trey had not spent much time in Misha's company, one-on-one. Sure, they'd crossed paths before, most recently at ByteCon, around town and at tech events. And every time he found himself in front of her, he was always completely taken aback by her beauty.

"Trey Winters, my biggest investor," she greeted him with a playful smile. "What an unexpected surprise. What can I do for you today?" she asked with a bright smile.

Her smile was welcoming as she looked up at him from the table, her eyes amused. Distracted, transfixed, by the way the sunlight reflected off her auburn hair, he found himself wanting to reach out and wrap one of the short, wavy strands around his finger. He straightened, however, forcing himself to remember why he was there, and he looked past her stunning beauty and cleared his throat. "There's a problem with your app," he said simply.

Her smile fell into a frown, and she narrowed her eyes at him. Her bubbly energy was gone, and she turned serious.

"Come in," she told him, her voice low and serious. "And close the door behind you, please."

He did as she asked. As he walked farther into the room, he caught a whiff of the floral scent that lingered in the air. It was pleasing and he inhaled again.

"There's a problem with k!smet?" she asked him when he took a seat on the opposite side of the table she was using as a desk. "What makes you say that?"

He didn't have any proof, of course, and in that moment, he felt like a complete blockhead for even barging in there, but he had to let her know his dissatisfaction. "Well, I don't believe that there's any reason why it would have paired my brother Jericho with Maggie Del Rio."

She sat back in her chair, her eyes moving, as if she was trying to work through what he'd just told her. "I'm sorry, what was that?"

"You heard me. Maybe not the whole app. Maybe just the Surprise Me! function. There must be something wrong with your code, or a funky algorithm, for it to have had that result. They share no common interests— they want different things. There's no reason why they should have been paired up. Unless there's a problem with the app, or it was sabotaged."

She let out a humorless laugh. "Are you serious?" she asked. "You come in here and accuse my app of being faulty when it made a perfectly good match between your brother and Maggie?"

"A *perfectly good match*?" he asked, incredulous. "She's a Del Rio."

"She's also my best friend and an amazing person, so if I were you, I'd watch what I said."

He crossed his arms, knowing that he'd obviously gone too far. "Okay, I'm sorry for insulting your friend."

"And my work?"

"I know you do good work," he told her. "I wouldn't have invested in the platform if I didn't. But I feel that with the match between Jericho and Maggie, there is something weird going on."

"Just because there's some family feud between the Winterses and the Del Rios, has nothing to do with k!smet. It did what it's supposed to do," she told him. "It took their information that they provided and matched them based on compatibility."

"What could they have in common?" he asked. He knew he was grasping at straws. He'd been frustrated by his brother's new relationship with a Del Rio, and he'd made Misha the target of those feelings.

"Maybe you should ask them."

"Okay, let's clear the air." He was feeling stupider and more inarticulate by the second. Misha had the ability to put him off-kilter, to make him lose his train of thought. He couldn't remember the last time a woman had made him feel like that. "I feel like I got off on the wrong foot here."

She raised an eyebrow. "Did you even try to get on the right foot?" she asked.

He'd really stepped in it. He had to turn it around.

"What I'm doing here is offering my services. Royal is on track to become a technology hub. I don't want a faulty app to tarnish that." He had a lot of money on the line.

"Faulty."

"Maybe that was the wrong word to use," he admitted. Her smirk told him that she was enjoying him coming into her office and looking stupid. "As one of your key investors, I want to take a look at the platform. Maggie and Jericho agreed to go on some dates so the app doesn't look bad before IPO launch. In the meantime, I want to know if there's something wrong with it and fix it before the problem gets too huge."

Misha Law blinked several times. *Trey Winters.* How dare this guy, investor or not, come into her office and claim there's a problem with k!smet, the app that she poured her life and soul and energy into creating and launching. "There's nothing wrong with my code, or the algorithm. What you're saying is completely unfounded."

"There has to be something."

"The only *something* is that your family has been feuding with the Del Rios for so many years that you feel like it's outside the realm of possibility that they could be compatible."

Misha was frustrated. Trey was one of those unobtainable guys. They'd met several times and had had pleasant enough conversations in the past. Interest in him had always given her a flutter in her stomach. He was perhaps one of the sexiest men she'd even had the pleasure of seeing, but he was also quiet, mysterious.

Like there was also something at work behind his dark brown eyes.

But having him come into her office was another matter. His unexpected visit had surprised her and pissed her off. But it was also stressful to her because there was a small part of her that wondered if he might have been right. Misha would never tell Trey, but for a moment, she had also wondered about the veracity of the app when she saw the pairing of Maggie and Jericho— on the surface, they were quite different. But seeing her best friend happy with a good man from the moment they connected made her forget about any questions she had about the app. *It clearly worked, right?*

"There isn't a problem with k!smet," she told him firmly. His determined stance told her that he didn't believe her, and the stubborn clench of his jaw told her that he wasn't appeased by that response. He sure was cute, though.

"Okay," she relented. "I don't think there's anything wrong with the app. But you're one of my biggest investors, and if we can work together, to look into anything you think might be wrong, then we can."

Trey was a rancher, but he was also known for his tech proficiency. If there was anyone whose skills she trusted to dig around in the backend of the app, it was him. He nodded. "Okay, fine."

"But there's another thing."

"What?"

"In exchange for access to the app and my code, I need you to promise that you'll leave Maggie and Jericho alone. No questioning their match, or their relationship. They're happy to give this a chance. Leave them alone to see where it goes. I certainly can't have you out in public raving about how the app doesn't work, okay?"

"I wouldn't do that," he told her. "I have as much riding on k!smet's success as you do."

She gave a short laugh. "No, you certainly don't." He had no idea how much of her time, energy, money, *life* she'd put into developing k!smet. "Sure, you've written a check, and a large one, at that. I appreciate it. But there's so much of myself in this app, this business. No one has more to lose here than I do."

He was quiet for a moment, and then he nodded. "You're right. When do you want to get to work on this?"

"Why don't we start tonight? When the rest of the staff goes home, you come over. I don't want any of them thinking that there's something strange going on with the app."

He nodded. "That's fair."

"Does around eight work for you?"

He was quiet for a moment, and the way he stared into the distance told her that he was considering. "My son is staying with his grandparents tonight. That'll work for me."

"Great," she said, smiling. "I'll see you then."

Without another word, Trey turned and walked out of her office. She couldn't help but notice the way the denim of his jeans clung to his lower body as he closed the door behind him.

She let out a heavy breath. "What was that?" she said to her empty office. How *dare* Trey Winters just barge into her office and tell her that her app didn't work. She woke her computer, which was already open to her email, displaying a High Priority email that had been forwarded from k!smet's PR firm. "How should we deal with this?" they'd asked.

Dear Ms. Law,
I downloaded k!smet hoping to find the love of my life. Unfortunately, that isn't what happened. When I matched with Steve, our differences were noticeable immediately. Not only did we disagree on most topics, even many of the deal breakers that we'd included in our profiles, but when I excused myself to go to the ladies' room, he made a quick exit. When I came back my purse was also gone. Did he take it? I can't say for sure. Maybe it was someone else. I've heard a lot of great things about k!smet and your matching process, and I thought that it would be a great way to find a future part-ner, but instead, I ended up alone, needing to can-cel my credit cards.

I just wanted to let you know that even though the k!smet app has been touted as the next big thing in dating apps and making foolproof matches, in this case, your app matched me with my complete opposite. Maybe it didn't get it right this time.

Misha reread the email from an unsatisfied customer. It was only the latest in a list of complaints from users who had been paired with incompatible matches. She would never admit to Trey that maybe he was right; maybe there was a problem with the app. But what would admitting that mean for her best friend, and the happiness she'd found with Jericho? k!smet was set to be the cornerstone of creating a tech hub in Royal, Texas. Trey himself, had already invested so much money into her business, and Jericho had built the Winters Expo Center, in preparation of putting the town on par with Silicon Valley and other tech hubs. If there was something wrong with the app, it could ruin everything, cost everyone involved a lot of money and disappoint the people of Royal.

Misha trusted her work, and honestly, she had no reason to believe that there was something wrong with the code. They'd tested the algorithm and functions, and it worked for a long time. The code seemed sound, but it was the users, the way the algorithms were constructed and manipulated, that's what lead to unpredictability. But there was something strange going on when it came to the wonky matches being made, especially when it came to pairing users who gave incompatible answers on the personality profile upon signing up for the app.

These were things she didn't want Trey to know, and she had no plans of discussing them with him. But bringing him in could be helpful. Two hands were better than one, and if he discovered a problem that she'd missed, she would accept it. She'd rather have any glitches found before they launched the IPO. She looked to her closed office door, picturing, once again, him in her office, in all of his mouthwatering glory, and knew that it was better to keep him as an ally than a foe.

She hated the idea of having him checking her work, but she didn't want to tell her small staff that there may be problems. She didn't want to scare anyone or start any rumors to stir bad press. Even though she didn't want Trey looking over her shoulder, or checking her work, he would definitely be a help.

But not only that—as she thought about him, he might be an arrogant ass, but it could be fun to bring him into it, spend a little time getting to know him. And if she kept him busy with the app, then maybe he wouldn't yell from the rafters that there was something wrong with it. But even though Trey was an investor, she didn't want anyone else's input. k!smet was her baby, and she didn't want anyone fooling with it.

She had so many confused thoughts—about the app and Trey—that she knew there was only one person she could talk to about this—her brother, Nico. She picked up her phone and dialed his contact. Like he always did when she called, he picked up after one ring. "What's up?"

She smiled upon hearing his voice. She'd spent too many years not being able to contact him whenever she wanted or needed to, and now they called each other several times a day. It helped with the physical distance that was between them. "Nico, you will not believe what just happened here."

He exhaled, no doubt picturing any number of scenarios. "Tell me. Whose ass do I have to kick?"

"You'd have to come home to Royal to do that," she told him pointedly. She managed to bring up the topic of him returning to town during every conversation.

"Not much chance of that happening," he said, just like every time. "Tell me, what just happened?"

"Trey Winters just stormed in here."

"What did he want?" Nico asked.

"He's claiming there's a problem with k!smet."

"What kind of problem?"

Misha told her brother about the other man's visit. "He says there's no way his brother Jericho would be paired with Maggie, given the feud between their families."

"Screw that," he scoffed. Nico and Misha had worked closely together to create the code for the app, and she knew that her brother took these allegations as strongly as she did. "Well, the algorithm doesn't detect family feud BS. There's nothing wrong with the code," he maintained.

"Yeah," she said, trailing off, her voice low.

"What was that tone?" he asked.

"What if he's right?"

"You created that code and I double-checked it. Then we triple-checked it before the release," Nico needlessly reminded her. "Your work is brilliant. If neither of us caught an error, it doesn't exist."

"You're a lot more confident than I am," she said. "We're not omnipotent. We could have missed a problem."

"Not likely."

"But even so. He offered to help me figure out where the problems are."

"Oh, come on. You don't need him. The only reason he even thought there was a problem was because he's too pigheaded to see beyond a petty family feud. That isn't your problem."

"But I can't have Trey telling everyone in Royal that there's something wrong in the app. I figured that if he's helping me with the app, it'll help keep his mouth shut." She paused, unsure whether or not she should share her next thought. "But that's not all. I *also* had some questions about the app."

"What are you talking about? What kind of questions."

"There have been emails," she started. "User complaints telling of inappropriate matches since the Surprise me! function went live at ByteCon. Sometimes the algorithm doesn't get it right."

"That doesn't mean there's a problem with the app."

"It's in the way that the user application is designed. There are specific questions that people would answer and cause them to be paired in a way that their politics, lifestyles and beliefs align. That hasn't been happening. Imagine setting up a date with someone with whom you have nothing in common. What if the stranger they're meeting isn't safe? Or if someone used the networking option and their work or privacy is compromised? All because they trusted our vetting process when admitting new members."

"That's a good point."

She told him about the woman's stolen purse. The lady couldn't prove it was her date. Maybe it wasn't. Who knew? "But what if something even more horrible happened on one of our dates or meetings? I could never live with that."

"I couldn't, either." He paused. "Does this have anything to do with Maggie and her match with Jericho Winters? What do you think about what happened there?"

"I love Maggie. She's my best friend, and I know she's been happy with Jericho on their first few dates, but there was something with their match that didn't feel right with me at the time. Especially with how public the reveal was. You should have been in the room. Everyone was stunned. So, my question is—despite the family feud, why *were* they matched? They're so different. It felt weird, and even though I trusted the algorithm, it feels wonky. Like it was set up to happen that way."

"You have all these concerns and the user complaints. Why didn't you tell me sooner?"

"Because I don't want it to be true," she confessed. "I know there's something going on, but I'd buried it deep, trying to ignore my gut instinct. I just can't fail, Nico. I put everything I have into k!smet." It wasn't just her own personal pride at stake—she saw untold pressure being a woman in tech. She had already had to work so much harder to get a place at the table with the *big guys*. If k!smet failed, there would be no coming back. And that was why she would take all the help she could get, even if it came from an unlikely source. "Having Trey come in here and tell me he also thinks there's something weird going on, maybe I should have trusted those instincts."

Nico paused before speaking. "That makes sense. It's good that you've got him to help, but when it comes to Trey Winters, just be careful."

Misha felt the heat rise in her cheeks. There was no way her brother could have known the way Trey's appearance had affected her. "Be careful of what?"

"I know he's one of your investors, but that isn't set in stone. He could be grifting you. Using the promise of an investment to get close. If he starts examining and playing with the code, he could cause any kind of damage to the app. Maybe he has his own agenda to make the app exactly what he wants."

"He wouldn't do that," she said. But what did she know? She only knew Trey in passing. The conversation they'd just had hadn't exactly been a positive one. He'd shown himself to be domineering and interested in his own personal gain.

"No?" Nico asked. "He's already claimed there to be a problem with the app. Even if he's an investor, if he doesn't like that his brother matched with a Del Rio, then he's got an ulterior motive for compromising its integrity. If he can make it look faulty, he won't have to invest, and he can show that the match is illegitimate."

"Do you hear yourself? That's ridiculously convoluted."

"Probably, yeah."

"Why would he do that? His brother built the Expo Center to prepare for Royal becoming the next tech hub. He's put a lot of money into the app itself. Trey needs k!smet to succeed as much as I do."

"If you say so," Nico relented. "Just be careful giving control of all of your hard work to an outsider."

"I will."

"He is a Winters, after all."

"Oh, God, not you, too. Didn't you call the feud BS?"

He chuckled. "And if you're really that concerned about the app—even though you have no reason to be— I'll help you out with it, too."

"You're so busy with your own company," she told him. "But I appreciate it. Thanks." She paused and drew her bottom lip between her teeth. "If you're concerned about me being careful around this guy... You could always come home," she said carefully. Nico had been away from Royal since he went to prison. He'd taken the fall for a close friend, after a bar fight had accidentally injured the nephew of a. After getting out, Nico had kept a low profile and hadn't yet come back to their hometown.

"I wouldn't hold my breath, if I were you."

"That's what I thought." Misha looked at the time on her laptop. She only had a few hours before Trey returned, and so many things on her to-do list. "I'd better go and get back to work," she told her brother.

"Yeah, I guess you should. Love you, sis."

"Love you, bro." Misha hung up the call and turned her attention back to the email complaint. No matter what may happen to her code and programming, she had to get to the bottom of what was happening to her users. And if Trey was the man to help her, then so be it.

Two

"Are you looking forward to spending the night at Grandpa and Grandma's house?" Trey asked, helping Dez get down from the back seat of his truck.

"Yeah!" Dez said enthusiastically. "I can't wait!"

Trey knew that his son looked as forward to the weekly sleepover as much as his father and stepmother did. They never seemed to mind chasing after an eight-year-old. In fact, they loved it. Trey gripped the strap of his son's backpack and slung it over his shoulder. "This is heavy What did you pack in here?"

Dez ran on up ahead, before stopping about twenty feet ahead of him. "My laptop," he called back. "Ring light, microphone, my tablet. The usual."

"Did you pack any clothes?"

The precocious eight-year-old snorted. "I'm only going for one night, Dad," he said, before turning and running the rest of the distance to the door.

"Yeah, exactly," Trey said to himself, knowing full well that his son did not, in fact, pack one piece of clothing. At least Trey knew that there were several changes of clothing and pajamas at his parents' for Dez to wear.

Dez was the perfect son, and Trey knew that his computer and movie obsession came from his upbringing—Trey had more of his own tech toys than he could name—but he sometimes wished he'd raised Dez with a little more balance. While his son was more concerned with watching TikTok videos or filming his own projects for YouTube—under strict supervision, of course—Trey didn't have any interest in social media, or trending videos and memes. Maybe he ought to take the boy out on the ranch more often, get him out from behind the camera on his phone. But he had a happy, healthy, kind, well-mannered son, and to Trey, even if he didn't relate to his hobbies, that was more than enough for him. Despite the fact that Camille was his stepmother, he thought of her as his mother.

By the time Trey arrived at the front porch, Dez was already letting himself into his grandparents' house. Trey watched as Dez ran into the house and crashed against the legs of Camille, his father Joseph's wife and Dez's doting grandmother.

"Watch it, bud," Trey warned, but Camille laughed as she hugged the boy.

"It's okay. Why don't you head into the kitchen?" she suggested to Dez. "There's a fresh batch of peanut butter chocolate chip cookies cooling on the counter."

Those were Dez's favorite, and Trey knew that he was all but forgotten until time to pick him up the next day. "Thanks for watching him tonight. He loves coming over here."

"So do we," Camille assured him. "Sometimes I wish there were a few more pairs of little feet running around here."

Trey thought about his siblings and wondered who might be the next parents among them. He laughed to himself. That might be quite a bit into the future. "You might have to talk to Jericho about that," he told her. "But I wouldn't hold my breath on a sibling for Dez," he told his stepmother.

Being motherly, Camille looked up at Trey, cupping his jaw with her soft hand. "Trey, I hope you haven't given up on finding the right woman."

He stepped back from her, putting distance between them. "That ship has sailed, Mom. Thanks for your concern, but I'm fine. And so is Dez."

She shook her head. "So that's it, then? You get burned once, and you're done with love?"

"I wasn't only burned—" he pointed in the direction of the kitchen "—so was he."

Dez was a happy child, and when he asked about his mother, Trey gave him a sanitized version of what happened. He'd told him that his mother had to go away for work. That had been enough of an answer for the boy, but one day he would have to tell him the truth. How he'd fallen head over heels in love with a professional dancer during a trip to Dallas. When she told him she was pregnant, he'd asked her to marry him, and she'd accepted.

He'd loved her, and as far as he'd known, Cassandra had loved him, too. He'd been ready to settle down and spend the rest of his life with her, raising their son together. After giving birth to Dez, however, she skipped town—not ready to be a mom and wanting to focus on her career—leaving him with a *Dear John* letter and a newborn son. He'd been terrified, and some days, he still was. Raising a child was the most important job he'd ever had, and he worked hard every day to make sure he didn't screw it up.

His father came down the staircase. "Trey, why are you still standing at the door? Why don't you come on in for a drink while Dez gets settled," he said.

Normally, he would take his dad up on the invite. He always liked to catch up with the family. "I can't tonight. I have plans."

"Oh, really?" His father raised his eyebrows. "A date?"

"What is it with you people?" he asked, looking between his father and stepmother. He pictured Misha in his mind, her bright, red-lipped smile, smooth skin, generous curves in the right places. He should be so lucky as to have a date with a woman like her. He shook his head with a laugh. "It's nothing that exciting, I'm afraid. It's a work thing. Just me and a couple of computers," he explained, leaving out all references to Misha.

"Grandpa," Dez called from kitchen. "Come check this out."

"Sounds like I'm being summoned," Joseph said. He turned to Trey. "I'll see you tomorrow."

Camille leaned in. "You know, maybe a date wouldn't be the worst thing in the world," she told him.

"Wouldn't it?" Since the debacle that had happened with Dez's mother, Trey didn't make a habit of letting himself get close to women. Sure, he had casual relationships, but between being a father, Winters Industries, ranching and his tech and investing activities, he just didn't have the time or the interest to devote to a relationship. "That's just not me," he told her. "Not anymore."

"Just because it ended badly las time, doesn't mean it'll happen again."

Trey shook his head. "If it was just me, I wouldn't be so worried." He pointed into the kitchen, where he saw Dez and his grandfather sitting at the kitchen island, dipping cookies into glasses of milk. "I can't introduce him to a woman who might just up and leave like his mother did."

"Have you heard from her?"

Trey shook his head. Last he heard, his ex had ended up in Europe, traveling, not acknowledging the fiancé and son she'd left behind in Royal. "No, and believe me, we're both better off."

Camille smiled. "You sure are. You two are great together."

Trey took one more look at Dez. "I'd better go, before I'm late. Hey, Dez," he called.

His son was showing his grandpa something on his phone, probably the new video he'd made that afternoon. "Yeah?" he asked, without looking up.

"I'm leaving."

Dez still didn't look up, but he and Joseph burst into laughter at whatever was happening on the phone screen. "Okay, bye."

Trey shot a hapless look in Camille's direction. "I'll see you tomorrow. Thanks again for watching him."

"Yes, and you have *fun* tonight," she said, deliberately slanting her words.

"It's work related. There'll be no fun had," he told her, no matter the thoughts of Misha and the *fun* things he could do with her swimming through his head.

After a short drive across town, for the second time that day, Trey arrived at k!smet HQ. This time, he grabbed his laptop bag from where he'd laid it on the front passenger seat of his truck. He made his way inside. While on his first visit, there had been some of her staff milling about, this time, the building was close to empty. He walked down the hallway to her office. Her voice filtered through the air, getting louder as he got closer. He could only hear her, so he assumed she was on the phone, telling a story. But when he looked into her office, she was sitting on the long, simple table that she used as a desk, her back to him, her phone held above her, and she spoke animatedly to the screen. She wasn't having a conversation with another person on the phone, she was filming herself.

"So always remember," she told the reflection of herself in her phone screen, "when you go grocery shopping, never take the cart with the wobbly wheel!" She finished, and before she put her phone down, she tapped the screen with her thumbs at lightning speed, likely posting the video.

"What happened with the cart with the wobbly wheel?" he asked.

Startled, her shoulders jerked, and she turned to face him. "You scared me."

He came farther into the room and dropped his shoulder bag on a nearby chair. "Sorry, I guess you didn't hear me come in."

"I did not. I was just doing a few videos while I waited for you. Typically, I film in batches and schedule them for different times when I can expect the most engagement and reach more people."

"I didn't realize you were an influencer," he said, rolling his eyes a little. Trey didn't care for the reams of internet stars who found celebrity doing online videos of silly dances and showing off clothing hauls.

"Oh, I don't think I'm an influencer." She shrugged. "It's a hazard of the trade. It's all about reaching people where they are—their phones, tablets and computers. Most of my single day gains is from a viral post."

"You sound like my son. He's obsessed with TikTok and YouTube and all that."

She narrowed her eyes. "Isn't he pretty young for that?"

Having Misha question his parenting immediately set him on edge. "Probably," he answered shortly, his tone gruffer than he'd intended. "But he's a smart kid, and he's strictly monitored by me. I made a lot of rules around the use of devices. I limit his screen time, make sure he makes time for family, friends and other activities."

"How do you know he's being safe online?"

He grinned, quite proud of himself for how he'd handled that problem. "I created a clone of each of his devices, and I created an app so I can see at any given moment what he's doing."

"Wise," she said. "It gives him the independence to

branch out on his own online, but you can see exactly what's happening. That's impressive."

"I like to dabble," he said with humility. "But I had to get a little help on that one." He opened his bag and took out his laptop, placing it on the long boardroom table, just a few seats down and the opposite side of where she'd set herself up.

She looked down at his computer and nodded appreciatively. "That's a nice model."

He smiled. Her tone had almost been one of jealousy, and he couldn't blame her. His laptop hadn't even hit the market yet, but the buzz was that it was the next big thing. "Thanks. I got it a month or so ago," he added casually.

"That's the PF-962, right?" she asked.

"Yeah." He looked her over, impressed how well she knew her stuff. She was one of best in her field, and that, in its own way, was hotter than any of her very fine attributes.

"I didn't realize that it was available for purchase yet."

He shrugged. "It's not. I know a guy," he said with a smirk. In working to make Royal the next technology hub, Trey had been in close communication with many of the top names in the industry. He and his family had hosted some on their trips to Royal, and he now even considered some of them to be friends.

"I'm sure you do. I also know people, but no one's giving me exclusive access to tech that hasn't even been released yet."

"Maybe I can introduce you."

She visibly bristled. "Should we get to work?" she asked. "I don't have all night."

He caught the subtle annoyance in her expression. "Yeah, sure."

He took his seat at the table, and they both turned their attention to their laptops. "I just granted you access to the platform," she told him without looking up, her eyes glued to her screen.

"Thanks."

As he accessed the network, his gaze slid over the monitor of his laptop and landed on Misha. Her face was illuminated in the bluish glow from her monitor, and her features were delicate, in contrast to the intensity in her hazel eyes. He didn't know Misha well, but he did know that Misha was highly intelligent, independent and persistent. He was thankful and, frankly, surprised that she'd let him investigate and pick through the code with her. He'd expected to be thrown out on his ass.

Misha was staring down at her own laptop. Her hazel eyes were sharp, and she'd pulled her plump lower lip between her teeth. With his focus on her mouth, his body stiffened in response. Her presence affected him more than he thought she could have. She was gorgeous, and he knew he would have trouble resisting her, especially if they were going to be spending time together. The sooner they got down to work and discovered any potential problems, and it took him away from Misha, the better.

After several hours of scrolling and typing on her keyboard, Misha started to feel her eyelids get heavy. Last year, when she'd eventually finished version one of k!smet and started to see initial success, Misha had erroneously thought that her nights of working late were over. She'd been on her way to just running the business side and leaving the more technical aspects to her staff. It had been a tough decision to make; k!smet was her baby, and she wasn't sure she wanted to relinquish so much of it to anyone else. But as the company and the brand grew, she had to step away from some parts of it. However, Trey coming into her office and making her question her work put an end to that. She wasn't stepping away from the technical aspects of the app until she knew that it was working one hundred percent the way it should.

She lifted her fingers from the keyboard and rubbed her eyes. She'd been in front of her computer screen all day, and she could feel a band of tension forming around her forehead. She pushed back from the table. "You know what? I'm done. I can't look at this screen anymore." She took a deep, relaxing breath, taking in a lungful of Trey's cologne from his place across the table from her. It was woodsy, with a hint of leather, but still managed to be light and not overpowering. It was warm, comforting, and she sniffed the air again.

"Yeah, sounds good to me." He sat back from his computer and stood, stretching his arms over his head. Misha couldn't help but notice the way in which his muscles bunched favorably underneath his shirt, or how the hem pulled up, revealing an inch of smooth, tanned skin at his waist.

When her gaze returned to his face, Misha saw that he was watching her with a smile, telling her she'd been caught staring. She turned her attention back to her monitor. "What are your initial opinions?" she asked. "Find anything? Are you satisfied that the app is fine?"

"I'm no expert," he started.

"Oh, really?" she asked, smirking, interrupting him. "Because I could have sworn you walked in here earlier today like you knew better than anyone else."

He shot her a withering look that made her snort. "I'm no expert," he said again. "But tonight, the code looks good."

She nodded. "Yeah, I know. My brother and I did it together."

He turned his attention to her. "Your brother," he repeated, and she didn't miss the accusatory edge to his voice.

"Don't you dare." She pointed her finger at him. "Nico served his time, and since leaving prison, he's done quite well for himself. Dammit, he knows more about programming than both of us combined."

"That doesn't convince me that maybe he did something—"

"He would never," Misha insisted, keeping her voice steady, even though anger was tempting to waver it. "I trust my brother with my life, with k!smet."

Trey looked at her silently for several beats. She was unwavering under the intensity of his gaze, but he raised both his hands. "I'm sorry. If you trust your brother, then so do I. I shouldn't have said that."

"You shouldn't have, but I thank you for apologizing." Misha never liked to dwell too long on unpleasantness—her life had doled that out to her in abundance. She always tried to be happy, bubbly and look on the good side, to focus on the positive, no matter how she felt on the inside, as difficult as that was sometimes.

"Thank you for letting me come in here and work on this with you."

"I'm glad to have you."

He cracked a smile that made her stomach flutter. "You're lying."

"Believe it, or not. I'm just glad I'll have the chance to prove to you that the app works, and that your brother and Maggie are a legitimate love match." That was part of her motivation to have Trey working with her—she wasn't about to reveal to him that she had her own questions and doubts about the app.

"I'll see about that," he said, but his tone was good-natured, teasing.

She smiled at him from across the table. She'd thought that having Trey in her space, looking over her work, would be annoying, but she again inhaled the woodsy notes of his cologne. It wasn't so bad, after all. It surprised her that he deferred to her when he'd had questions. He recognized that he was still on her turf. It was her business, her office, her app, and he didn't try to take over in their task. Misha appreciated that. She stood from the table and went to the mini fridge in the corner of the room. She withdrew a couple of bottles of beer. "Now that the work is done," she said, "we can have a drink. That's the rule around here."

"That's an interesting rule."

"Actually, that was a bit of a lie," she confessed. "I don't typically make it a habit to mix alcohol and work. This was leftover from a small celebration we had here in the office before ByteCon. When we first decided to launch an IPO. That was a good night for us." She wrapped her fingers around the cap of the bottle and struggled to remove it from. She looked at the bottle and realized that the cap was not a twist off.

"Well, that's a good thing," he said, standing and coming toward her. "I was starting to think that my suspicions about the platform might be confirmed." He took the bottle from her hands, and, in one movement, he slapped the bottle down and used the edge of the mini fridge to remove the cap.

"Slick move," Misha noted, with a nod.

"I've got a lot of those." He did the same with the second bottle and extended it to her.

She accepted the chilled bottle from his hand, and when their fingertips touched, a frisson of electricity jolted her fingers and made her gasp. He looked down at her with a one-sided grin and a knowing twinkle in his eyes, and she knew he'd felt it, too.

"I'm sure you do have a lot of slick moves."

Just a few inches separated them, and they looked at one another. Unable to pull away from his gaze, Misha took a deep breath.

"Cheers," he said, raising his bottle to hers.

She tipped her own bottle against it. "What are we toasting?"

Instead of taking his seat at the table, Trey settled in the love seat in the corner of the room. Misha sat in the empty spot next to him. She curled her legs under her and sipped her beer.

"A new partnership?" he ventured.

"Partnership?"

He shrugged. "We're working together, aren't we?"

"How about we call this working with an investor to make sure the app is at its best before the upcoming

IPO call? You might be an investor, but k!smet is still my baby."

He tilted his head to the side and then nodded. "Okay, I'll accept that." They both drank from their bottles. "But I want you to know, I'm not trying to take over your *baby*." He drank. "I know I blustered into here this afternoon, making accusations. Thank you for agreeing to investigate my concerns, and for not tossing me out on my ass."

Misha was determined not to let him know that she'd had her own concerns, so she shrugged casually. "I want to thank you for not taking out an ad in the local paper about anything you feel may be wrong with the app."

"I wouldn't go public," he assured her, turning serious. "I know how gossip and bad news travels in Royal. I would never invite that kind of negative attention," he finished with a cringe.

"Not even with your brother in a relationship with a Del Rio?"

He cringed, but then grinned. "Well, I'm not crazy about it, but we'll see how it goes." He drank again and looked around her office. There were pictures of her, and promotional materials from her various other projects, apps and programs that had never had the promise of k!smet. "Let's switch gears. If we're going to be partners—"

"Working together," she corrected with a smirk.

"Working together," he amended. "But tell me, how did you get into this kind of work?"

Misha took a swallow from her bottle. She didn't want to get into the tragic story of her childhood with him. It was a story that everyone in Royal knew. After they'd lost her parents in a tragic accident, the people of the town had come together to support her and Nico, but she was no longer the helpless orphan. As a woman, she was now going to use k!smet's success to bring great acclaim to the town and build its reputation in the technology sphere.

"You know my backstory," she said, hoping he wouldn't want to dig deeper on the topic. "Our parents passed away when we were young. Computers were my escape. I spent all of my time in the computer lab at school. Until I got my own laptop. I played, I tinkered. I taught myself to code when I was in junior high. After college, I worked for several programming companies until I branched out on my own. I started a few different networking and dating apps, all precursors to what k!smet became, but none of them took off. But k!smet is the one that made the difference in my life. It's been hard, but worth it." She fiddled with her bottle, suddenly insecure at just how much her future depended on this one chance. "You're a Winters, I'll bet your life has been quite different than mine."

He gave her a wry smile. "Just so you know, my life hasn't been all rainbows and sunshine."

Trey and the entire Winters family had wealth that she could never have imagined. Misha had heard he'd run into some trouble with the mother of his son, but she didn't know the details, and she'd never ask. It just wasn't any of her business. Money was helpful, but it certainly didn't always lead to an effortless life. "Everyone's got a story, right?"

"They certainly do," was his simple reply.

Misha drank more of her beer, feeling a little looser

already in his company. The electricity, which had crackled between them only minutes earlier, still hummed in the background. The mood in the room had sobered significantly as they both likely considered their own vastly different stories. There was a comfort between them, however, that came from being vulnerable together. Desperate to turn it around, Misha pushed past her memories and smiled at Trey. "Enough dwelling on the past," she said. "Things happen. You can't change them. So that's why I always try to find the positive in life."

He looked at her. "That's a good outlook."

"There's no point in focusing on the negative when there's so much to look forward to, right?"

"No, I guess there isn't."

They watched each other for several moments in silence, until his phone, which he'd laid on the side table, vibrated to life, the screen lighting up. When she glanced at it, the caller ID photo was a picture of Trey and a young boy with glasses and dark hair. His son.

He quickly picked up the phone. "Sorry, I've got to take this."

"Go right ahead."

He stood and walked to the far side of the room and answered the video call. The grin on his face told her all she needed to know about what kind of father he was. "Hey, bud, what's going on?" He walked into the hallway, but she could still hear both sides of the conversation.

"I just wanted to tell you that Grandpa and I made some videos, and you should watch them."

"That sounds great. Do you want to send them to me now, and I'll watch them when I get home, or would you rather we watch them together tomorrow?"

"We can watch them tomorrow. Then we can discuss any notes we might have."

Misha stifled a giggle, and Trey, from the open doorway, looked in, amused at her reaction. She looked away quickly, not wanting it to look like she'd been eavesdropping. The fun and tender way Trey spoke to his son was a sharp contrast to the gruff public image he put out there. Being orphaned so young, she'd missed out on that kind of relationship with her parents. It made her smile, though, to see some lucky children had everything she'd wanted.

"I can't wait," he told his son.

"What are you doing?" the boy asked.

Trey looked over at her and grinned. "I'm doing some work tonight."

"What kind of work?"

"Programming, coding." He shook his head. "Nothing exciting like you're doing. Are you going to watch any movies tonight?"

"I found some Alfred Hitchcock movies in Grandma and Grandpa's DVD collection. And Grandpa said I could have his old VCR and all of his old movies."

Misha watched Trey's brow furrow. "I don't even know if I have anything to connect a VCR to your TV."

"He's already ordered some for me online. They should be here in a few days."

"Of course, he did," Trey said with a chuckle. "And I might have to talk to Grandpa and Grandma about that. Those movies aren't exactly age appropriate," he warned.

Dez sighed on the other end, and Misha laughed once again at the boy's impatience with his father. "Dad.

They're just movies, and you've said it yourself, I'm more mature than a typical eight-year-old."

"That is true, son. But if you get scared, you aren't sharing my bed."

Misha could basically hear Dez's eye roll on the other end of the call. "I'm almost nine, Dad. I won't get scared."

"Okay, fine." Trey seemed to relent. "You can tell Grandpa and Grandma that I don't approve, but I hope you have fun."

"Okay, I will. I'm going to go now. Love you, Dad," Dez said quickly, in an obvious attempt to get off the phone to continue the fun of the evening.

"Love you, too, Dez." He hung up the phone and came back into the room. She noted the way he passed the love seat where she was still seated and took his seat at the table. "Sorry about that. When he's at my dad's, I always ask him to call."

She waved him off. "Don't worry about it. Your son sounds like quite a child."

Trey laughed. "Yeah, he is. He's amazing. Before he was born, I never could have imagined what fatherhood would be like." Misha saw the way Trey lit up when talking about his son. The love and pride he had for the boy was apparent.

"He's into making movies?"

"Making movies, watching movies, writing movies," he said. "Of every genre. He loves all that stuff. TikTok is his newest obsession, though. He writes, films and edits these short videos, *movies*, himself, and he's really built quite a following. Like I said, I've made it as safe as possible for him, but I'm not sure I understand the appeal. Social media has never been my thing. But I want to foster that passion and not kill it."

"That's admirable. You're a good dad."

Trey dragged his fingers through his dark hair, tousling it, so it stood on end. "Thank you. God knows I'm trying. We're in it together, no matter what. I just need to give him the best life I can and raise him to make good choices and be a good man. Then maybe he won't find himself making the same mistakes that I did."

Misha frowned at Trey. There was clearly more to the man than she'd realized. "What sorts of mistakes did you make?"

As if the mood shifted, he put his bottle on the table. "You know, I should probably go."

She tilted her head to the side, wondering what had happened to turn him around. She wondered if her asking about his past caused it. If she could take it back, she would have, just to keep him in her office, where they'd been having a surprisingly pleasant conversation. "Um, yeah, I guess." She stood and walked to the door with him. "I guess we're done here."

"Want to get together another time?" he asked, putting his laptop in its carrying case.

"Yeah, sure," she said. "We can meet here again whenever is good for you."

He zipped the case and nodded at her. "Or we could do it at my place. I've got a pretty good setup, and we'll be able to spread out. We can be comfortable."

Misha looked around her clinically sparse "office." "What? This isn't comfortable enough for you?" she joked.

He looked around, as well. "It's not bad," he amended.

"But that way, I'll be able to put Dez to bed before we get to work."

"Right," she said. "That sounds good. Why don't you text me tomorrow and we can set up another time?"

"I'll do that," he said, as he walked past her toward the door. "Good night, Misha."

"Night, Trey."

For the second time that day, she watched Trey leave her office, leaving nothing but a light trail of his cologne and her fluttering heart in his wake.

Three

The next afternoon, Misha was running late as she made her way into the Royal Diner, the informal restaurant where the people of Royal gathered to eat the best hamburgers in Texas, gobble thick slices of pecan pie, and take part in the town's favorite pastime—gossip.

Misha was supposed to meet Maggie for lunch, but she'd run into yet another issue with a user of the app, who'd been a victim of an imperfect match. The complaints were beginning to pile up, and Misha felt every one of them on her shoulders. If she received many more complaints, the news would definitely affect the upcoming IPO call. She made a mental note to message Trey and arrange another work session. The sooner they found out what was going on with the app, the better.

Looking around the bustling diner, Misha saw Maggie at a corner booth at the far end. She waved and made her way across the black-and-white-checkered floor, nodding at people in greeting as she did. When she got to the table, she was surprised to see that Maggie wasn't alone.

"Hi, there," she said, taking a seat in the red, faux-leather booth.

"Misha, do you know Emilia Scott?" Maggie asked her. "She's renting the office space next to my design studio. You both work in the tech world."

Misha held out her hand. "I believe we've crossed paths before."

"At ByteCon," Emilia supplied.

"I know your work. I'm so sorry I didn't get a chance to stop and chat," Misha apologized.

Emilia waved her off. "It's no problem," she said. "That was a pretty wild event."

"Was it ever," Maggie added. "Lots of unexpected things."

Misha smiled. Maggie was glowing. She could see how well her friend's relationship with Jericho was going—despite the family feud that Trey had considered so important. She'd never considered romantic relationships to be a priority, but seeing how happy Maggie looked these days, she might be starting to come around on the idea.

"But I didn't mind," Emilia continued. "I know you were busy. I was just there to learn, not network. I like to keep to myself at events like that."

"Sometimes I wish I had that luxury," Misha told her.

"I hope you don't mind that I crashed your lunch date. Maggie mentioned that you were coming here, and I couldn't stop thinking about getting a cheeseburger, so I invited myself along."

Even though she had been looking forward to catching up with Maggie and picking her brain about Trey,

Misha still wouldn't be rude. "Oh, goodness, of course not," she told her.

"It's nice to finally meet you. Formally."

"You, too."

"We're more than happy to have you," Maggie added.

Amanda Battle, the diner's illustrious owner, approached their table. "Hey, ladies, how are you all today?"

"Just great, Amanda," Maggie answered. "And yourself?"

"Oh, you know," she said, with a look around the diner. "Any busy day is a good day."

"I hear they're all good days around here," Misha noted. She liked Amanda and was glad her diner continued to be so successful.

"We've got no complaints," Amanda responded with a wink. She turned her attention back to Maggie. "I hear you've been having some good days, yourself, Maggie," she said with a suggestively raised eyebrow.

Maggie laughed. Being the owner of the most popular diner in town, Amanda didn't miss much of what happened in town.

"How about I get you ladies some drinks?"

"I'll have a sparkling water," Misha told her.

"That sounds good," Maggie agreed. "I'll have one too."

"Same, please," Emilia added.

"I'll have those out in a jiffy and get your food order," Amanda told them.

"Thank you," Misha said. She turned back to the other women at the table. "Sorry I was late," she told them. "I got stuck at the office with something."

Maggie frowned. "I hope everything is okay."

Looking between Maggie and Emilia, for a moment

Misha wasn't sure how much she wanted to say. She didn't know Emilia well, but if Maggie considered the woman a friend, she must be a good person. But Misha had heard things about Emilia. Not bad things, but she was well-known for her computer skills, and consulted with many social media platforms. There were also the rumors. The world of tech was small, and there were murmurings that Emilia had a habit of finding her way into the backend of different platforms. If there was a problem with k!smet, she didn't want it to get out, and she certainly didn't want Emilia to find out either way. "Yeah, it's fine," she told them with a casual shrug. "You know how it is. We're just trying to make sure everything is perfect."

"Is there any reason to think there isn't?" Emilia asked, her eyes sharp. "I could help you out with any problem you might have."

Misha regarded Emilia from across the table. A person like Emilia Scott and all of the skills she would bring to the table could be a huge asset to her business, but she wasn't about to let someone she didn't know that well onto her team. "Thank you so much for your offer, but I think we have it under control."

Emilia smiled. "Well, let me know if you run into any trouble that I can help with."

Misha narrowed her eyes at the woman, trying to determine if there was any shade in Emilia's comment. Something about her demeanor rubbed Misha the wrong way. But she was Maggie's new friend, and that meant she would be seeing Emilia at social engagements. Misha smiled sweetly—and made a note to keep her eye on Emilia.

Four

The next morning, Misha woke, hearing the vibration of her phone before her eyes even opened. It vibrated again. Then again. Then again. Assuming that it was someone calling her, she sat up, rubbed her eyes and reached for her phone. It wasn't ringing, it was her social media notifications, dozens of them, from every app—Twitter, Facebook, Instagram, TikTok. Waking up to being the new main character in a social media scandal was never fun, and with a pounding heart, Misha opened Twitter.

Is this the end of @TheMishaLaw's front-running dating app, k!smet?

Matches not quite made in heaven? @TheMishaLaw @k!smettheapp

Not-so k!smet? What do you have to say @TheM-ishaLaw? @k!smettheapp

Bad Matches put @TheMishaLaw's k!smet in jeopardy.

Each of the dozens of tweets was accompanied by an article from a well-known tech blog.

Using her thumb, she stabbed at the screen to see what exactly was being said, and to come up with a suitable damage control plan. She read through the article, which detailed some of the things she hadn't wanted to get out—the mismatches and the associated problems. The article speculated that the bad press might spell trouble for the platform, and the upcoming IPO launch.

Misha looked at the time. It was just past seven in the morning, and already her day had gone completely off the rails. She briefly thought of the conversation she'd had with Emilia the day before. Someone like Emilia might be able to get to the bottom of whatever was happening on the backend of k!smet. But instead, she quickly dialed Trey's number, not considering that it might be too early.

Surprising her, Trey answered after the first ring. "Hello?" he said, sounding alert, awake, like she hadn't just woken him up.

"Hey. Sorry I'm calling so early. I hope I didn't wake you."

He chuckled, and the low rumble traveled through the phone lines, into her ear canal, to do a swan dive in the pit of her stomach. "No," he told her. "I've been up for hours."

"Early riser," she noted needlessly.

"Sure am. What's up?"

"Do you have any plans this morning?"

"No, why?"

How had he been up for hours but hadn't seen any of the articles about k!smet's potential problems? She imagined that being a dad to an eight-year-old kept him busy and unable to read all of the tech blogs or check his social media accounts. But she couldn't imagine that not being at the forefront of her mind. He really was built differently than her. "We have a problem."

Less than twenty minutes later, Misha was at her desk, when Trey knocked on the frame of her open door. She looked up from the email she was writing. "Hey, you made it."

"Sorry I'm late. he said, coming into the room. I had to drop Dez off at a friend's house. And I stopped for these," he told her, holding up the cardboard carry-out tray that

"You brought coffee!"

Smiling, he laid the tray on the table. "I wasn't sure what you liked, but the guy at the café told me that a vanilla latte with an extra double shot of espresso was your usual."

Misha's mouth watered. She hadn't had time to stop for her own latte on her way to the office. "That's perfect. I'll have to give him an extra big tip when I go tomorrow." She took a sip and let the delicious, caffeinated nectar fill her mouth, soothing her. She hummed in satisfaction and closed her eyes, luxuriating in the flavor. She leaned back in her chair and took another sip, feeling her problems slip away, at least momentarily. When she opened her eyes, she saw that he was watching her, amusement crinkling the corners of his eyes. "What?" she asked.

"Glad you like it."

"I know it seems dramatic, but caffeine is a necessity. This is amazing. Thank you so much for bringing it."

"It was no trouble," he said, settling in, unzipping his bag and withdrawing his computer.

"What did you get for yourself?" she asked.

"Just plain, regular, black coffee."

"Typical," she said, rolling her eyes, but still smiling. It made sense that he would take his coffee black. It was strong, no-nonsense, got the job done. Just like him.

He sipped from his cup, and nodded approval at his drink.

"Want to try mine?" she asked. He narrowed his eyes at her cup. "Come on, try it," she prodded, holding out her cup.

"Sure." He reached across the table and accepted it. He brought it to his lips and sipped cautiously. He closed his eyes and gave his own short groan of appreciation. He handed it back. "Damn! That's good stuff."

"I told you," she said.

He chuckled. "I said it was good. It didn't give me an orgasm."

Misha felt her cheeks turn hot. "It didn't give me an orgasm."

He raised an eyebrow. "No? I'm the one that just saw the look on your face. I'm sure it's one you'd use in *other situations*."

Her mouth dropped. Her heart rate ratcheted up, and

her temperature rose. She was at a loss for words, and all he could do was look at her with those dark eyes, boring into her, stirring awareness in her core. Misha wondered about those *other situations* and knew that Trey could definitely be the man to bring her far more satisfaction than her first coffee of the morning.

Outside of her office, the noise of a couple of her team members walking by her open office door startled her. This was not a topic of conversation that she should be having in the office, with Trey Winters, of all people. She tore her attention away from the man, and, sitting straight in her chair, she cleared her throat and turned her attention back to her computer and the problems at hand. "We should get to work."

"Sure thing. Why don't you catch me up on what's going up?"

"I feel like I'm hours behind on my morning already. I'm already on damage control. Something like this can really spook investors."

"Aren't *I* one of your biggest investors?" he reminded her, sitting in the same place he'd sat the last time they'd gotten together.

"Bad press can affect the success of the IPO launch."

"Okay, I do care about that," he conceded. "But you know how it is these days. You're on the trending timeline for twenty-four hours, by then some celebrity or social media *influencer*," he bit out the word, "will have said or done something stupid, and people will have forgotten about this whole thing. You don't have to acknowledge it, just let it blow over and users will move on."

"That's the thing—I don't want people to forget about

k!smet. This news shouldn't have gotten out. We need to turn the bad press into good press. That's the only way out of this. If we aren't at the forefront of people's minds, then we'll become obsolete before we even get off the ground."

She thought he might dismiss her concerns, call her hyperbolic or emotional, but instead, he booted up his laptop. "So, what do we do? k!smet means everything to me and I'll do anything to save it."

"We do what we've been doing—we search and pick through the code and backend for problems with the app. Nobody knows we're doing this, so I need you to keep it quiet."

"You haven't told your team we've been investigating?"

"No," she said. "I wanted to keep this as quiet as possible. I don't want any of the team thinking I don't trust them or their work."

"Were you doing this on your own before I joined you?"

"No," she said. "Some of the complaints had come in, and even though I know my work on the app is sound, I was concerned there might be some kind of problem, but not enough to check the coding because Nico and I had triple-checked it before launching it. Then you came in here, telling me there was something wrong…"

"So, I was right," he said, with a cocky grin on his lips.

"I never said that. You only have to look at Maggie and Jericho and see that when it came to those two, k!smet knew exactly what it was doing."

"Sure, sure," he said playfully, causing her to glare at him. "Okay, in all seriousness, let's get to work."

Trey had had plans to spend the day on his ranch. He'd been cooped up in his home office for the past few days and wanted to get out on the land. He hadn't intended to spend such a beautiful day at the k!smet office, behind his laptop.

His gaze drifted up from his screen to land on Misha. She had strands of her auburn, wavy hair tucked behind her ear, and again, her bottom lip was drawn between her teeth. He was sure that he'd stumbled upon one of her tics, and he smiled.

Despite his own need to concentrate, he couldn't stop replaying their earlier conversation in his mind. He knew that a video of Misha tasting her coffee would be at the forefront of his mind any time he attempted to conjure a sexy image. Misha was a beautiful woman, sexy in ways he hadn't realized. Remembering the pleasure she'd taken at drinking her coffee, Trey knew how to make her feel that again.

"How's it looking over there?" she asked.

Incredible, he'd wanted to say, but that wasn't the answer she was looking for. Misha's mind was clearly on the work at hand, and fixing whatever was wrong with her app. He shrugged his shoulders. "We've been going through the backend all day. I just don't see anything that might be affecting the algorithm and causing the mismatches."

She sighed. "Me neither."

"So, where do we go from here?"

"We keep looking," she told him. "I don't know what

else to do. I don't know what's going on. Since k!smet's earliest days, we prided ourselves on having the best matching capabilities of any of the apps, but now... I really think that something is manipulating the matching algorithm of the Surprise Me! function."

He thought about that for a moment. "Maybe there isn't a problem with the algorithm itself."

"What are you saying?"

"Maybe it's being manipulated by a third party."

"You're saying we've been hacked?"

"I don't know," he said. "There's a lot riding on k!smet's success. Can you think of anyone who would want to see it fail?"

"I can't imagine anyone being that malicious," she said. "And our security is top-notch. Not just anyone can break into our code. Unless it was a rival app. An organization might have the resources to recruit the best. I know HitMeUp! has been at our heels the whole time."

"Maybe HitMeUp! has a talented hacker on the payroll."

Misha shook her head. "I don't know. That's a pretty serious accusation. A hacker would have left us clues. Between the two of us, we'd be able to tell someone was messing around."

"Not if they're good," Trey responded. "If that's true, does it make you feel better?"

Her laugh was humorless. "You know what? Not really. A problem with the code, I can fix. I can't control anyone else's short-term manipulations, nor can you. I guess I'll put out some feelers in the community to find out what I can."

"I'll do the same."

She put her forehead down on the desk and lightly bumped it several times.

"You okay, over there?" he asked.

"Yeah." She leaned back in her chair. Her lips were turned down in a frown. "I'm just frustrated. Everything was in line for this to go well. We were on track. And now this. Why can't things just go easily for me? This one time?"

Trey frowned. The Misha he knew, the Misha that she'd always presented to the public, was positive, formidable, tenacious. But now, she looked defeated. "It's okay," he told her. "That's the industry. Nothing goes the way we think it will. As an investor, I've made bad deals, had them fall through. Came close to losing my shirt a few times. It's okay to fail sometimes."

"I appreciate those words, but they tell me you have a pretty huge safety cushion for all of those times you failed. I've never had that."

"You've got me there."

"And that's investing, but you're not creating something, putting your heart and soul into something and putting it out there. If I fail, I've lost everything. Not just money, but there are so many people counting on me. My employees, my investors, my brother, all those little girls in STEM. This means a lot to me."

Misha's eyes looked heavy, and he caught it when she swallowed a yawn. He knew that she'd been at the office since early that morning, dealing with the press leak. "I know that." He reached across and placed his hand on top of hers. He wasn't sure if the motion was too intimate, and he was afraid she would pull away. She didn't. Instead, her fingers lifted from the table against his. The warmth from her hand permeated his. "Tired?" he asked.

She grinned, looking embarrassed. "Yeah, a little. It's been a long day. How about you? You've been here as long as I have."

He stretched in his chair. "I could certainly use a session at the gym. Why don't we call it a day?" he asked, standing. He reached for his laptop case. "Or do you want me to get you another coffee?" he asked with a laugh.

She also stood. She came around the table to where he stood. "Why? So, you can see my bedroom face again?"

Trey leaned in. "I'm sure I could see it again without the coffee."

Her mouth dropped open. Maybe he should have been a little more delicate with his words, maybe not have used such innuendo when speaking with a lady. He almost took his words back, but he was glad he didn't when one corner of her mouth turned upward in a grin. She leaned in closer. Her breasts skimmed against his chest, and he felt his body tense involuntarily. "I'm sure you could."

It was all Trey needed. In one motion, he wrapped one arm around Misha's waist, pulling her close, while with the other arm he swept everything—her laptop, monitors, the empty coffee cups—from the table beside them, and he lifted her so she sat upon it. He lowered his lips to hers, kissing her without any delicacy or tenderness. It was a kiss borne of pure need, lust, desire. Whatever you call it, he needed her like he needed his next breath.

Misha's lips parted beneath his, and their tongues slid against each other. She tasted better than anything he'd had before, and he knew that if this was his only chance to kiss her, then he would spend his life trying to recapture the feeling of her.

Misha wrapped her arms around his neck, pulling him closer, and he lowered himself over her, so he was between her knees, lying on top of her. He smoothed his hands down her sides, and then pushed them underneath her shirt. Feeling her smooth skin under his palms almost made him lose control entirely. He was so taken up in desire for her, that he barely heard his phone ringing. He might have ignored it, but it was Dez's ringtone.

He regrettably pulled away from her. "I have to get that. It's Dez."

"Yeah, you should answer it," she told him, moving off the table to stand.

Trey looked around for his still-ringing phone, grateful for the chance to let his breathing return to normal. He finally found the phone underneath his chair—it was another victim of the broad sweep he'd made with his arm, clearing off the table. He picked it up and connected the call.

"Hey, bud."

"Hi, Dad. Are you still working?"

Trey cast a glance at Misha, who was dealing with the mess he'd made on the floor. "I'm just finishing up. What's up?"

"I was wondering if we could go to the diner for dinner. Amanda said she would make me a double chocolate and peanut butter shake next time I came in."

Was Amanda going to put his sugar-high son to bed after said milkshake? But he smiled, willing to indulge his son, yet again. "Yeah, of course we can go. I'll be by soon to pick you up, okay?"

"Okay. Bye," Dez said, hanging up before Trey could return the goodbye. He slid his phone into his pocket and turned back to Misha. She was still picking things up from the floor.

"Sorry about the mess," he said.

She looked up at him, her cheeks still flushed from their kiss. "It's quite alright," she told him, lifting a monitor that had landed on her laptop, snapping the computer in two pieces. "My laptop," she said with a playful laugh, the flush on her cheeks still present.

"Uh... Sorry about that." He took the pieces from her hands. "I'll buy you a new one."

"I don't need you to buy me a laptop."

"Well, I'm the one who broke it."

"You kind of did, didn't you? Maybe you can talk to *your friend*," she said, her eyebrow raised as she nodded at the black leather carrying case that held his specialized laptop. "You know it's a good make-out session when you consider the destruction of an expensive computer to be a small cost."

He laughed, pride straightening his shoulders. "Well, you're welcome," he said, brushing his knuckles on his chest. "I'll give him a call, see what I can do." He regarded the broken laptop in his hands. "I hope you saved your work."

"I did. I back up everything. I learned the hard way far too many times."

"Yeah, I've been there, too." They finished cleaning up and Trey was glad there wasn't any further damage. "Maybe it's best we call it a night. We should probably head home." He gave her a look, which he knew told her that he would like to be the person to go home with her. "Separately," she told him.

He nodded. "If you say so."

"Don't you have to pick up your son?" He nodded. She was right; he was due to get Dez, but if he hadn't have that parental obligation, Trey knew based on that kiss where the evening would have ended up—in his bed.

Five

Trey watched Dez ride on the back of his horse, Lightning. It was good for both of them to get out from behind a computer and out on the land. He waved as Dez rode farther out. Both he and the horse were getting more confident with every step.

"Hey," Trey heard someone call behind him. He turned and saw that it was Jericho.

"Well, look who it is," Trey said, holding out his hand.

Jericho also extended his own and they loosely shook. "I thought I'd come around and make sure you aren't getting into any trouble." He nodded at Dez. "He's looking better out there."

"Yeah, he is. He's a quick learner. In everything he does." Leaning against the fence, he looked at his brother. "You've been missing in action around here a lot lately," Trey said to Jericho. "I haven't seen much of you."

"Yeah, sorry 'bout that." Jericho's smile told Trey that his brother wasn't sorry about it at all. "I've been hanging out with Maggie any time I haven't been at work."

Trey nodded, leaving out the grimace that he would have normally had upon thinking about his brother's relationship with a Del Rio. "I noticed."

"Go ahead, say it," his brother told him.

"Say what?"

"Whatever it is you have to say about Maggie."

Only days ago, he'd thought that the only way his brother could have matched with the woman was through a faulty algorithm, or a problem with the code. And while the app's matching capabilities may still be vulnerable, he could see how happy his brother was—no matter how it happened. Maybe he'd softened to the idea. "I've got nothing to say."

"That's unlike you."

Trey was quiet for a moment. His brother was also one of his best friends, and even though the woman he was now with was from a rival family, he could see the positive effect she'd had on his brother. He wasn't jealous of Jericho and Maggie's relationship, but he wondered what it would be like to let someone get close to him again. And when that thought struck him, Misha was the woman he pictured. "She makes you happy, right?"

Jericho nodded. "She does. I'm very happy."

He shrugged. "If you're happy, then I'm happy for you. That's good enough for me."

"Thanks. I appreciate that. Maggie is the best thing that's ever happened to me."

"I'm glad to hear that."

"What about you? Is there any woman on your radar?"

Trey looked into the distance. His kiss with Misha from the day before was still fresh in his mind. He hadn't forgotten the way she tasted, the way she felt underneath him. The pang of lust that shot through him whenever he thought of her lingered in his nerve endings. She was the only woman on his radar at the moment, but after all of the grief he gave his brother about Maggie, he surely couldn't tell Jericho how he felt about her best friend. Instead, he shook his head. "Not a chance."

"Come on, you're not going to let being hurt one time affect the rest of your life, are you?"

Trey shook his head. "Christ, not you, too. Dad and Mom have both been on my case about it lately, too."

"Did you ever think that maybe they're on to something? Look at Dez. Wouldn't you rather raise him with someone else, a mother?"

Trey felt his jaw tighten. He didn't like to have his decisions questioned. "Are you questioning my judgment when it comes to how I raise my son?"

Jericho raised his hands. "Of course not. You're a good father. You have a great kid. You know, just forget I said anything."

"I will. Thanks."

"Let's just get past all that. Do you have any plans tonight? Why don't you come over and we'll watch the game?"

"No Maggie tonight?"

"Maggie's going to some k!smet dating thing at Silver Saddle tonight."

"She's looking for someone else, already?" Trey cracked.

"She's supporting Misha."

Misha hadn't shared with him that there was going to be a k!smet event. It was a singles event, to boot. He couldn't help but wonder if she was there to make a love connection for herself. The thought of that filled him with a gray feeling that he didn't want to investigate. Maggie was going to be there supporting Misha—maybe he should make an appearance, as well. After all, he *was* one of k!smet's key investors. He should be there to make sure everything went well.

He looked at his brother and shook his head. "I can't watch the game tonight," he told Jericho. "I'm going to Silver Saddle."

At Silver Saddle Bar & Tapas, Misha looked around at the crowd beginning to form in the lounge. Despite the bad press that had come out the day before, there was still sufficient buzz around Maggie and Jericho's match at ByteCon that had kept public interest piqued.

"Wow, this looks great!" Maggie said, coming up behind her.

Misha turned and hugged her friend. "Thanks for coming."

"I wouldn't miss it for the world. So, tell me, what's going on here?"

"Well, it's kind of like speed dating, but people are paired on the app." She hoped that none of the wonky matches would make an appearance and she would get through the night without incident. She checked her watch. "We've got to get started. I'll be right back."

She walked over to the corner where she'd had a microphone and speaker set up. "Ladies and gentleman," she greeted her guests. They quieted their various conversations. "Just take a look at all the sexy singles in the house tonight." The crowd cheered and raised their glasses. "I'm so glad you're all here for this event. You've probably heard a lot about k!smet in the last little while, and I know that many of you are members. If not, please see any of the k!smet staff on hand tonight, and they will help you download and create your own profile.

"For tonight only," she continued, "we've set up a special section on the app. Just sign in and we'll use your location data to enter you in the event, which is kind of like a speed dating scenario. Based on your preferences and your profile, the app will match you with an appropriate companion—" *one hopes* "—for two minutes of chatting. At the end of the night, you'll rate your mini dates on the app, and for the most compatible match made, k!smet will treat you to the date night of your choice." The crowd applauded. Misha held up her own phone, which was opened to the k!smet app. "Guys and gals, is it k!smet?"

In unison, everyone in the audience looked to their phones, signing into their apps or creating new profiles. Soon, the club was filled with the telltale ringing bells of matches being made. People coupled up and began their mini dates.

Misha smiled and left the corner, making her way back to Maggie. But before she reached her friend, she stopped when she saw Trey standing near the bar. What was he doing there? She hadn't thought to mention the event or even invite him, not thinking it to be his kind of thing.

He raised his glass in greeting. "Good evening."

"Hi, Trey. I didn't expect you here."

"No, especially since I wasn't invited."

"Sorry about that," she said with a cringe. "I know you like to be more of a behind-the-scenes guy. I didn't think this was your kind of thing."

"You know me too well," he said with a chuckle, reaching out to touch her arm. Like always, his touch lit a fuse of desire within her. "I'm not normally one for these. No hard feelings."

They were quiet for a bit, and she was aware of the fire that still sizzled between them. And from the way he looked down at her, he felt it, too.

She took a sip from her drink, breaking the hold between them. He looked around the room. "This is great, though. Quite a turnout. I told you that those articles wouldn't hurt us."

"Not yet," she said. "I guess we'll see how tonight goes."

"You're not optimistic?"

"I don't know. The fact that the app could be vulnerable is niggling at me. I've got the security team to work on bolstering the app against an attack."

"That's a good move. Despite your uncertainty, it's admirable that you still arranged this event. There's a lot of strength in that."

She shook her head. "I had to do something, you know. I have to do whatever I can to keep the positive buzz about k!smet alive, no matter what."

"I like the sound of that. We'll figure it out before the IPO launch," he assured her. "And everything will be just fine."

He looked around. She had really amassed a great group of Royal's most eligible singles.

"It looks like lots of people in town are looking for—"

"Love?" he asked, cutting her off.

"A connection, at the very least. In order to meet people, we used to go out to a bar, take a chance on talking to someone, going on a date. The beauty of an app is that you put everything out there—your picture, your likes, dislikes, your beliefs, your political affiliations. It saves time and takes the guesswork out of meeting people. You can take control over your interactions, your fate."

"Kismet?" he asked, with a grin.

"Bingo."

"So, you have a profile," he noted. "Are you looking to make *a connection* here tonight?" he asked.

Her eyes widened, and she sipped from her drink. "Why do you want to know that?"

"I'm just curious."

"Is that why you came here tonight?" she asked. "To make sure I don't match with anyone?"

"That's not it at all," he told her.

His words might be saying otherwise, but Misha was better at reading people than that. "I don't believe you," she teased. "You're here so I don't meet any other fine young men tonight. Tell me the truth."

His eyes slid over her and she stiffened in response, glad she'd worn the black bodycon dress that was always a hit. "If that's what you want to believe…"

"I think it is."

"I'm here for support, like I said. And to provide a united front against anyone who might be messing with k!smet. It's important to show Royal that you've got a Winters behind you." He raised his drink to his lips.

She leaned in, a smirk on her lips. "Well, that's good. It's always comforting to have you *behind me*."

Trey had to cover his mouth in order to not spit his drink at her. He choked, coughing, sputtering away from her, causing several patrons to look in his direction. When he stopped coughing, he cleared his throat one more time and looked down at her. "You're trouble. That wasn't funny."

She shrugged. "You're the one causing a scene in the middle of my event." She enjoyed flirting with Trey, and she could have done it all night, but in doing so, she almost forgot that she was supposed to be working.

So much was riding on getting k!smet to the IPO stage, that she couldn't help but think of the worst-case scenario at times. Misha couldn't believe that Trey showing up unexpectedly and flirting with her had stolen all of her focus. "You know, I'd better get back to mingling, but if you want to keep an eye on me, you can probably take a seat at the bar."

"Good idea."

She turned to walk away, but then stopped herself, pivoted back to him and leaned in close. She inhaled his cologne and almost closed her eyes to savor it. "I don't think we're done looking for weaknesses in the app," she said.

"I'm sure there's a lot more we could be doing," he agreed. "Why don't you come over to my place tomorrow night?" he suggested. "My home office is very private. We should be able to work without any interruptions."

She knew what he was suggesting. "Sounds good," she said, with a playful smirk. Say eight thirty?"

"That's fine by me," he agreed.

"Okay, I'll see you then," she said with a grin and turned away from him to rejoin the party, hopefully leaving him wanting more. Sure, they might do some work on the app, but she knew that, locked together in his private office, there was no way the night would end with their laptops.

Six

Dez looked up from his dinner with a frown. "Do I really have to go to bed before your friend gets here?"

Trey nodded. "Yes, you do."

"But I don't want to."

"That's too bad. We don't always get what we want."

"But I'd like to meet her if she's going to be coming into our house."

"What are you, personal security?" he asked his son, amused at his serious tone. "Are you going to be our bouncer?"

Dez rolled his eyes at Trey. The boy was only eight years old, and Trey would have to do something to curb the precocious attitude he was developing before it became a problem, but part of him also enjoyed the child's moxie. "Don't change the subject. Just because you have a date is no reason why I should suffer."

Trey stifled a laugh at his son's dramatics. He would

really have to do something about the attitude. And soon. "*Suffer*'s a pretty strong word for having to go to bed, don't you think? And it's not a date," Trey added. Dez raised a skeptical eyebrow, which made the boy look older than his years.

"What do you know about Misha?" Trey asked.

"I follow her on TikTok," he said, by way of avoiding Trey's question. Trey had noticed her account on Dez's following list. "But she hasn't followed me back."

Trey also knew that. There wasn't much his son did online that Trey didn't see. "It's because there's no reason a grown woman should follow a boy on social media."

"Well, you should tell her that my account is really entertaining," Dez told him. "I'm not like most kids on there."

"You've got that right."

Dez was quiet for a moment. "Misha's really pretty," he said after a beat.

That was understating it. Misha was more than just pretty. As she consumed more and more of his fantasies, she was beautiful, the sexiest woman he'd ever met. He swallowed hard, remembering that he was in the middle of a conversation with his son. "Yeah, she is."

"Is she married?"

"No."

"Does she have a boyfriend or a girlfriend?" he asked.

Trey shook his head, knowing what was coming next. "None that I know of."

"And you don't have a girlfriend, right?"

"I certainly don't."

"So, why isn't it a date?" he asked. "Did you ask her, and she said no?"

Trey didn't have an answer. "No, I didn't ask her." He liked Misha, and not an hour went by when he didn't think of the kiss they'd shared, the one that heated his blood, and how he'd swept his new laptop from the table in order to get closer to her. And even though he had a feeling the night just might end in his bed, taking care of that unfinished business between them, he wasn't at a point where he was okay with introducing his son to her. "Because we're friends," he explained. "And we're working together on her new app. We don't like each other like that." That was the first time he'd lied to his son.

"k!smet?" he asked. "Is that the app?"

"Yeah, she created it, and I've invested money in it. Now we're both working to fine-tune it before it gets even bigger than it is now."

Dez's whistle was low. "Wow, everyone is talking about that app online." He stopped. "And you invested in it? We're going to be rich, huh?"

Trey looked at Dez. If he had no idea that they were rich before, he didn't know what impact his return from the app would be. "We'll do okay."

"That's good, because I need a new laptop."

Trey furrowed his brow at his son. "What's wrong with your current laptop?"

"It's, like, a year old. It's outdated."

"There's no way I'm buying you a new one. Your laptop is just fine for your needs."

Dez sighed. "Yeah, I know it is. I just thought it couldn't hurt to ask."

"Good hustle, though, kid. But you're going to have to make do with what you have."

"Even though we're going to be rich?"

Trey regarded his son. He realized he was also going to have to instill a little humility in the boy, lest he become a spoiled brat. "We're already rich. But I can't just hand over everything you want."

"Why not?"

"Because if I do, you'll become spoiled, and you won't become a productive member of society. You need to learn to work for and earn what you get."

Dez seemed to ponder that. "What do I have to do?"

This was going better than he could have imagined. He was getting through to the boy. "There's always work to be done on the ranch. You're old enough now. You can do some chores, and I'll pay you a fair allowance."

Dez screwed up his nose, but then he nodded. "Okay, deal." He extended his hand, and, amused, Trey shook it. "So, I get to stay up late tonight?" he asked, after a beat.

"Not a chance," Trey told him. "Now, go clear your dishes."

Racked with nervous energy, Misha made her way up the walkway to Trey's door. She'd shown quite a bit of moxie suggesting that they get together once again, especially since both of them knew that work would not be at the forefront of either of their minds. She hadn't been able to get past the kiss that they'd shared a couple of days ago in her office. If she closed her eyes, she could still feel his lips on hers, the scruff of his five o'clock shadow against her cheek, the warmth and weight of him on top of her... She checked the time on her phone before ringing the doorbell. Eight thirty exactly, just like they'd arranged.

She raised her finger for the doorbell but pulled back. Maybe she should have waited a little longer, played it a little cooler. "What is wrong with you?" she asked herself, quietly. Misha had dated men, she'd had casual hookups, and hell, one of the first apps she'd developed was for exactly that purpose. She didn't normally get shy or bashful around men. She couldn't believe that somehow this one man had managed to turn her into a shy schoolgirl. "Get a grip," she whispered in reprimand, and decidedly pressed the doorbell.

She didn't have to wait long until Trey answered the door wearing a snug black T-shirt and jeans. He grinned, looking pleased to see her. "Hey," he greeted her. "I was wondering how long you'd stand out there, talking to yourself."

Misha looked above the door and saw that there was a small security camera mounted on the frame. "Of course, you have a camera out here. I should have suspected."

He moved away from the door and ushered her inside. "Come on in."

"Thank you," she said and looked around the foyer. It was spacious, and when she inhaled, she could smell leather from the boots on the nearby mat and a certain spice in the air that was reminiscent of his cologne. "Nice place."

"Thanks," he told her. "Come through here."

He led her down a hallway to a beautiful, luxurious kitchen. It was spotless, but for scattered toys and crayon drawings on the refrigerator—the telltale signs that a child lived in the house. She wondered about how Trey lived in this home. Did he cook meals for himself and Dez? Did he enjoy his morning coffee in the breakfast nook, in solitude, while the sun's heat poured over him? She looked into the family room, which was located just off the kitchen. Did he kick his feet up at the end of the day and read with Dez, or did he watch sports?

"Can I get you a drink?" he asked, intruding on her thoughts. "I've got water, beer, wine?"

"I'd love a glass of wine," she told him.

"Any preference?"

"Red if you've got it."

He plucked a bottle from the rack on the wall. "Good call." He poured them both a glass and handed her one.

Misha swirled the glass, the red liquid draining down the inside of it. "Should we toast to something?" she asked.

"What do you suggest?"

She raised her glass. "To k!smet?"

He nodded. "Sounds good to me." He raised his glass. "Do you mean the app, or fate?"

She shrugged. "Either? Both? Pick one."

He chuckled, and she forced herself to bite back the sigh that was born at the back of her throat. "Fine. To k!smet."

"Wait," she said, pulling back. "When doing a cheers, if we don't look each other in the eye, it'll bring seven years bad luck"

"Really?" he asked. He made intense eye contact that almost made her look away. "I've heard it similarly, but instead of luck, it's seven years of bad sex," he explained, his voice dropping an octave.

"Oh, really? I don't believe I've heard that one."

"Either way, I don't think we can risk it, now, can we?"

She grinned up at him. "We shouldn't. I don't believe in curses or anything, but we shouldn't push our luck," she agreed.

They clinked their wine glasses together, and as their eyes connected, they each brought their glasses to their mouths. The moment was charged, and he shifted closer, so close that there was just a hair's breadth of space separating them. Their kiss wasn't far from Misha mind. *Lips, scruff, weight and warmth. Lips, scruff, weight and warmth. Lips, scruff, weight and warmth.* She repeated the mantra in her mind. Misha felt her pulse jump in her neck, could see the desire in Trey's eyes. She moved closer, raising her lips to meet his, almost touching.

"Dad!" Dez called, his voice bouncing down the stairs.

Trey moved back from her. "I'd better go check on him."

"Yeah, you probably should."

"Sorry," he said, putting down his wine glass. "He went to bed just a little while ago.

"Don't apologize. It's fine."

He gave her a short nod, before turning and jogging up the stairs.

With Trey gone, Misha was able to think clearly. Maybe it was fate—kismet?—that had interrupted them. Whenever they were together, and let their hormones get the better of them, something came between them, and perhaps that was for the best. It was important for them to focus on the app. That was the priority, but whenever she was around Trey, she managed to forget that. She didn't want to fail. She didn't want k!smet to fail. She couldn't let down the people of Royal, or crush all of the expectations that hinged on the app's success.

She sipped from her wine glass and sought out the computer she'd brought as a pretense that she was only there to do work on the app. She picked it up as Trey came down the stairs. "Sorry about that."

"It's no problem. Daddy duty supersedes just about everything else."

"You've got that right." He picked up his glass. "But now that it's all settled, where were we?" he asked, his lips turned upward in a grin.

"Maybe we should head to your office."

That seemed to catch him off guard. He'd had other plans for the night, as well, but he recovered well. "Yeah, the app. Right."

"Yeah, the thing we've been working on."

"Alright. Let's get to it, then. Get it out of the way." He raised an eyebrow that shot need straight to her core.

"I've got the wine," she said with a wink, picking up the wine bottle.

"You think we're going to need that?"

She shrugged. "Would you rather let the open bottle spoil?"

"Wouldn't dream of it." He gestured to a staircase off the family room. "Let's head down."

She followed him as he led the way, and they headed down the stairs. They stopped at a closed door, and when he pressed his thumb against the sensor, there was a click as the door unlocked.

"It's kind of more than a man cave," he told her, pushing open the door, letting her walk in ahead of him.

Head on a swivel, Misha took in the vast room that must have been the entire lower floor of the house, with an incredible array of equipment and technology on display. There were computers, gaming systems, a virtual reality system, and a bank of servers obscured most of one wall. The other side of the room had three rows of theater seating pointed at the largest screen she'd ever seen, and an alcove held furniture placed in front of a fireplace, which was flanked by two floor-to-ceiling bookshelves, filled as much as they could be with books.

Misha had a lot of technology in her own home—a couple of laptops, a desktop computer, some tablets, the necessary things to run her business before she'd acquired office space—but compared to Trey's setup, it was an exceptionally modest collection. "Wow," she said, knowing that her eyes were wide, wishing she'd been able to play it a little cooler. "I wasn't sure what to expect, but this is wild."

He shrugged casually. "I like to play around," he told her. "And to have the latest gadgets."

"I can see that. I feel almost embarrassed by my lack of gear. And it's my full-time job."

"Don't. You can do so much with what you have. That's a skill."

"But still." She took a seat in a buttery-soft leather desk chair and smoothed her hands over the ergonomically divided keyboard in front of her. A large, curved monitor was in front of her. "This is quite a setup."

"After working all day for Winters Industries or on the ranch, this is my escape."

"I created k!smet at my kitchen table," she told him.

"I can't imagine the things I could accomplish with this type of setup."

"Well, feel free to come over anytime and put it to use."

"You shouldn't say that. I might come over and never leave." She'd said the words in jest, and even though it was still early in whatever was happening between them, part of her wondered what it would be like to be with Trey, in his home, with his family.

He smiled. "Is that a threat or a promise?"

"You tell me."

Trey looked at her for a moment, and she wondered where his mind was. He shook his head and turned to his computer. "We should probably get to work."

Two hours later, Trey sighed heavily and turned off his computer monitor. "Okay," he said. "We've gone through every bit of code, and from what I can tell, I'm officially calling it. The algorithm is sound." He was frustrated. Frustrated at looking for a needle that may not even exist in the haystack that was k!smet; frustrated because he was again sitting in such close proximity to Misha, in his home. They'd been so close, had shared such a charged moment before. He had been sure the night was headed in a different direction with Misha, but she'd been quick to suggest they get down to business... And not the *business* he was interested in. It wasn't too late. Maybe they could turn it around yet.

"So...?"

Trey sighed. "As far as I can tell, the app is fine."

Misha's lips turned upward in a cocky grin, and he was tempted to kiss it off her face. "I don't want to say *I told you so...*"

"I think you want to say those words, exactly."

"Fair enough. I told you so."

"You told me that you had your own doubts," he reminded her.

"I did. I still kind of do," she amended. "But with my security team covertly looking into hackers and weaknesses in the platform, and the two of us—" she waved between them "—being unable to find any problems, maybe I'm just being paranoid and there aren't any problems. Maybe the mismatches are just part of the business. Just statistical anomalies out of so many successful matches. It might just have to be something we deal with."

"Do you think you can just deal with it if it isn't perfect?"

She shrugged. "I guess sometimes no amount of technological advance can be swayed by the human condition."

He stood and reached for the bottle of wine. He refilled their long-neglected glasses. "Maybe you're right."

"So, now I can only assume you're going to drop this ridiculous campaign and admit that maybe the long-standing family feud doesn't matter when it comes to true love."

He laughed. "I won't go that far yet," he told her. "True love? Between Jericho and Maggie? It's only been a few weeks. I still don't really like that they're together. But I want my brother to be happy, and if Maggie Del Rio makes him happy, maybe I should just accept that."

"Finally. Smart. You've got to let people live their own lives and make their own decisions when it comes to their personal lives."

"When you're right, you're right." He handed over her filled glass, and she accepted it gratefully. "Why don't we take a seat over there?" he asked. "Get away from the computers for at least a while, so we can drink our wine."

"Sounds good to me."

Misha retrieved her purse and brought it with her, as they walked over to the overstuffed couch next to the fireplace. He pushed the button on the control panel that started up the fire. They sat in the quiet for several moments, drinking their wine in the orange glow of the flames, and she slipped off her shoes, then tucked her legs underneath her, pivoting her body toward his.

"I know I just kind of came crashing into your office that day, making demands, but still you let me work on the app with you. Again, I want to say thank you."

"I just wanted to make sure you didn't go around town talking about how the app is faulty."

"I wouldn't have done that. I have as much to lose as you do."

She shook her head. "I doubt that. Sure, you're an investor. You might have money on the line, but everything I have, everything that I promised Royal, is riding on k!smet."

"That's true. I misspoke." He drank from his wine glass. "But I'm mostly on the financing side of things, so I also appreciate the opportunity to flex my skills. It's been a while."

"Honestly, it's so interesting, There are so many sides of you—the tech guy, the investor, the businessman, the father and the rancher—and you seem to excel at everything."

He laughed. "Yeah, I've got many different sides. I

can choose wise investments, help run the family company, make sure Dez eats his veggies, program and code and saddle a horse."

She laughed. "Good to know." She sipped her wine. When she pulled the glass away, a small droplet of wine clung to the surface of her plump lip. He wished he could lean in and lick it away. Before he could, however, her tongue snaked between her lips and collected it. "I was actually grateful for your help," she continued. "I've since let the security team know, obviously, given the threat of a hack, but I didn't want it to get out amongst the staff, especially with the IPO launch coming up. It was nice to have an extra pair of hands."

"I'm glad I could help. Do you feel confident about it now?"

"Yeah, I guess so. Barring an actual outside attack, I have to say that k!smet is as close to perfect, foolproof and safe as it's going to be."

"You should be proud of yourself. You created a great product."

"Thanks. I just want to give back the best I can for Royal."

"You will," he assured her. The IPO launch will be a success. We'll make sure of it."

In the silence they drank more from the glasses. She turned in her seat, this time bringing her feet from under her, straightening her legs and bringing her toes to glance against his thigh. The touch burned through his jeans, and he felt his physical need for her grow. He shifted his body toward her.

"This is a comfortable couch. It's good to stretch out after spending so much time behind a computer desk."

"Yeah, after Dez goes to bed, if I don't have any work to do, which honestly isn't often, I like to come down here to flake out and read or watch a game."

"It's nice." She placed her wine glass on the end table and looked at him under long eyelashes. "You know, Trey, I feel like we could both stretch out here if we tried."

He knew exactly what she meant, and she didn't need to tell him twice. He gripped her ankles, which were delicate and small in his hands, and pulled her so that her body was in the center of the couch. She shrieked in amusement in response, but her giggles quickly quieted when he twisted his body and kneeled on the couch between her parted thighs. He leaned over her, looking down at her, and she looked up, her eyes hooded with desire.

Bracing his weight on his forearms on either side of her head, Trey lowered himself, and without a word, he took her lips with his own. Misha parted her lips under his and he brought his tongue to hers. He kissed her, hard. Her mouth was hot and tasted like red wine. But her own unique flavor came through with no trouble. This wasn't their first kiss, of course, but he knew it was the one that would leave him addicted to her. She wrapped her arms around his neck and pulled him closer, to lie more fully on top of her. He slid his hands underneath her but found the couch a frustrating barrier to touch her more thoroughly.

He wrapped his arms around her and moved so that he was back to a sitting position, with her thighs straddling his, her warm center brushing against his rigid need. His moan traveled from his throat to hers, and he thrust his hands roughly into her hair, tightening his hold, deepening the kiss. It just wasn't enough for Trey. He loosened his death grip in her hair and dropped his hands to her shoulders. He smoothed his palms roughly down her body to her hips. He needed to feel every part of Misha—her lean planes and luscious curves, her shoulders, her back, her ass, her thighs—and with every touch, he pulled her closer, making sure she could feel how much he wanted her. Her desperate moans, the frantic way she pulled at his clothing, told him that the feeling was mutual.

Misha raised his shirt, and he released her only long enough to allow her to pull it over his head, while he made quick work of her sleeveless button-down and her bra. Both of them topless, Trey took a moment to appreciate, *luxuriate*, in Misha's awe-inspiring beauty. She was all smooth skin and full curves as she writhed, her skin sliding against his. And he thought that if he didn't have her soon, he might just explode.

Misha heard the low growl that grew in Trey's throat as he lifted her and pivoted their bodies—all that finely-honed ranching muscle—so that she was again lying on her back on the couch and he was between her thighs. She could feel his hard length against her, and she ground her pelvis against him.

Her need for him was overwhelming, and she reached for him, unzipping his jeans and sliding her hand inside to grasp him. She gasped in shock, however, when he gripped her wrists and pinned them to the couch over her head. When she looked up, she saw the smile that had formed on his lips before he lowered again to kiss her.

"Too afraid to give up control?" she asked, breathless.

"I don't give up control," he rumbled, his lips finding the sensitive dip in her throat. "Ever. Especially in bed."

"We're not exactly in a bed, you know," she said, before shimmying out from under him and crawling over him so that she was on top. Misha had taken over for a brief moment, but Trey had had different ideas. He might think that he was in control, but if he thought she was just going to relinquish all the power when it came to sex, he was definitely mistaken. Next time—and there would be a next time, she was confident—she'd let him do his thing. She'd wanted this more than anything for the past week, and she was going to take it.

She stood for a moment and shucked her leggings, before pulling his jeans and boxers down his legs. Now that they were both naked, she straddled on top of him again. "Going to put up a fight?" she asked him.

"Wouldn't dream of it," he told her, sliding his hands up her hips to grip her waist with his strong fingers. "There's a condom in my jeans," he told her.

"I'm right ahead of you," she said, in a sultry whisper, as she reached for her purse which she'd placed nearby on the floor. She easily retrieved a condom from inside and proceeded to roll it over his substantial length.

He gave a moan as she touched him, and when she rose up and then lowered herself on him, it gave way to a groan. She rode him, and he smoothed one hand over the curve of her ass, as she set the pace while he stroked her with his other hand. Her leg muscles twitched, and her breath caught in her lungs.

Without breaking their connection, he sat up and kissed her again, plundering her mouth, and she matched his kiss in ferocity and strength. He took control of their rhythm and held her close. He roughly palmed her breast. He captured one of the buds between his fingers, and it was all she needed to tip her past the point of no return. She came with a thunderous crash that rocked her entire body. She shook in his arms and threw her head back and cried out. Trey, however, wasn't far behind as he held Misha close to him, as he kept the rhythm of his hips steady. Misha matched his pace, until she felt him stiffen below her, and he shuddered with a thick groan into her shoulder.

Several hours later, Misha drew leisurely circles through Trey's short, dark chest hair. She and Trey had long since retired to his bedroom, where they'd spent the rest of the night exploring each other, talking, then *not talking,* when the passion consumed them again. She was spent; her limbs felt like jelly, and she wasn't sure she could move if she tried.

"What time is it?" she asked him.

Without dislodging her from his chest, he reached for his Rolex that he'd left on the nightstand. He blew out a breath. "Whoa, it's almost four."

"Really?" she asked.

"Afraid so."

"Oh, it got so late."

"I'm pretty sure it's actually early," he corrected.

She smacked his chest and pushed herself up to a sitting position. "Either way, I should probably be leaving."

His arms were clenched around her, holding her tightly, and she thought he might ask her to stay. While part of her wanted him to hold her back, he didn't. Their eyes connected, and after several beats he let her go. He likely had his own plans the next morning. Which probably involved eating an early breakfast with his young son. Staying up all hours of the night would cause them both to have a rough morning.

She stood, letting the blanket fall away, and she felt his eyes on her naked body. Luckily, they'd brought their clothes from downstairs, and she pulled on her leggings and, skipping her bra, she buttoned her sleeveless blouse over her breasts.

Following her lead, he also stood and pulled on a pair of gray sweatpants. Her eyes were drawn to his midsection, as the light gray did nothing to obscure what was underneath. Misha pulled her eyes away from his form, lest she never be able to leave. "I'll walk you out."

"Sure, thanks."

"Do you have plans today?" he asked, walking down the hallway to the foyer.

"I've got a couple of conference calls in the morning." She consulted the time on her phone. "In a couple of hours, I guess. But then I'm hanging out with Maggie later. We're going for a hike."

"You didn't get enough exercise last night?"

"Ha-ha," she said. "That was a pretty good calorie burner, though."

"A full body workout."

"That it was." She picked up her laptop bag, and he opened the front door.

Together, Misha and Trey walked out onto the front porch. The sky was still dark, but she could see the sky beginning to lighten in the horizon. Despite the fact that it was still incredibly early in the morning, the air was warm and fragrant. "What a beautiful morning."

"It really is."

"I had a great time tonight," she told him.

He laughed. "I'm glad. I think it's pretty obvious that I did, as well."

"And we managed to finish poring over the app to see if it's clear or not."

"It was a productive night, all around."

She turned to leave, but Misha stopped herself and turned to face him again. "You know, I've been thinking. We worked together pretty well, on the app and otherwise," she added with a wink. "We both have a lot invested in k!smet. Why don't we keep working together? With the two of us, we can collaborate to maximize the app's impact before the IPO launch. We probably both have ideas how to make it a success."

"I agree. Although, I think we work better in person."

She didn't miss the truckload of innuendo in his voice. "Think you can keep your mind on the work?" she asked. She was looking forward to having him stay close—in a professional setting, of course—and she wondered how they would ever be able to get any actual work done. She anticipated finding out.

"Only if I can get whatever is between us out of my system." He leaned down and took her lips in a kiss. She savored the taste of him, as her tongue entwined with his.

She moaned and felt herself fall against him, but she had to pull away. She had to leave before she wouldn't be able to.

"It's out of your system now?"

"I think it's a start," he told her. "I might have to have a few more."

She almost said yes, but instead she took a step back. "I really have to go."

"Are you sure I can't make you breakfast?"

She smiled at him, rather enjoying that he was obvious in his desire to get her to stay. Even though having Trey cook her breakfast was enticing, she knew there was no way she could stay. "I'd love to, but what would Dez say if he woke and saw me at the table?"

He frowned. "You're right. Maybe we can work over dinner sometime. Then we can see where the evening takes us."

"That sounds nice," she said, placing a hand on his rough, stubbled cheek. She leaned in to kiss his lips again. "I can't wait."

She felt Trey's eyes on her as she made her way to her car. She waved when she opened the door, signaling that she was fine. But still, he didn't move from the door until she had started the engine and was out of the driveway.

Seven

Just a few hours after watching Misha drive away from his house, Trey was still awake, but now he was standing at the stove top. Chugging back coffee in order to stay awake. "Want to see my new video?" Dez asked, as he slurped chocolate milk and watched Trey make pancakes.

It didn't matter if Trey was tired, he still had to be a good, supportive father, and not take his exhaustion out on his son. "Yeah, Dez, I'd love to. Just give me a minute to finish this. We don't want the pancakes to burn."

Dez sighed impatiently. Trey knew how excited his son became when it came to his videos, so he plated the pancakes that were in the pan, poured some more batter and turned down the heat on the stove top in order to join Dez at the table.

He sat with his son and watched as Dez queued up his videos and pressed play on the most recent one. It was a short video. He'd set up his camera, stationary in one spot. It had been mounted on the front porch. "I set it up yesterday morning and filmed the entire day. I just edited it all together before I came down for breakfast."

Trey wasn't sure how he'd missed the camera that Dez had mounted on the porch.

"I let it go all night," Dez added.

Trey's eyes widened as he realized that if Dez's camera had been set up all night, then it surely would have captured his early morning goodbye with Misha. And as the video progressed, showing the flowers in the boxes twist in the sun as it glided across the sky, just as he'd suspected, eventually it showed he and Misha stepping onto the porch. They kissed. Trey blew out a heavy breath.

"Why didn't Misha stay for breakfast?" Dez asked.

"She had to leave," he said, stunned and unable to come up with another answer.

"I didn't realize she was sleeping over. But why'd she leave so early? She should have stayed for pancakes."

"Um," Trey started, unsure of what to tell his son. He'd been with women casually since Cassandra left him, but he'd never brought a woman home or to meet Dez. Misha was the first woman he'd allowed in his space, for fear of Dez seeing them and having questions. Despite how careful he'd been, it hadn't been enough. Now his son had questions. "We were working late," he finally answered, plating Dez's pancakes and handing them over the kitchen island. "On her app."

"Really late," Dez agreed, before digging hungrily into his food, the topic seemingly forgotten. Or so Trey had hoped. "You guys are friends?"

"Yeah, that's right."

"You kissed," he said simply, as Trey felt the blood drain from his face. "I don't kiss my friends like that."

"We were just saying goodbye," he told his son. "Nothing more than that."

Dez shrugged and went back to his pancakes, not saying anything else. He knew that, even though Dez was done talking about it at the moment, the topic was far from dropped. He would definitely bring it up again, and that was the reason why Trey hadn't been interested in introducing his son to any of his past romantic partners. He didn't want to risk Dez asking questions, or getting close to another woman, or placing feelings of familial love onto a woman who wouldn't be in their lives for long.

Trey watched Dez eat and drank his coffee. He had a full day ahead of him and would need the caffeine. He hadn't slept at all the night before, and while he should technically be comatose at the moment, he still felt energized, just thinking about Misha and the night they'd spent together. He didn't regret his night with her, but despite how careful he'd been, Dez had seen them together. And there was no way he was going to put his son in a position where he could be hurt. His family was everything to him.

Family. He dragged his palm down over the bottom half of his face as he thought of Jericho, and how happy he was with Maggie. Even though he was glad for his brother, it still bothered him that he was in love with a member of the Del Rio family. No matter how good a person Maggie was, and how much their families may be building a closer relationship, she was still a Del Rio, and when it came down to it, when the stakes were high,

Trey knew that Maggie's allegiance would likely be to her own family.

Maggie was also Misha's best friend, and he knew that she was close to the Del Rios, and had been for most of her life, as well. How far did Misha's own allegiances go? That was something he hadn't considered. By extension, Trey was also involving himself with a member of the family. He wasn't quite as trusting as Jericho. Would opening himself up to Misha similarly make his family vulnerable to the Del Rios?

Trey sighed into his coffee mug. He didn't like it, but maybe this was a lesson to keep his distance from Misha—to keep it strictly professional between them.

Misha pulled off her bucket hat and waved it in front of her face, hoping to avail of some of the cool air the movement caused. But it was no use. Her calls had run long that morning, and she'd had to stay at the office longer than expected. She had been late leaving for the hike and the high-noon sun had made the heat almost unbearable. And to make it even more interesting, Maggie had invited Emilia to join them. Misha still wasn't exactly sure how she felt about the other woman. She reached the peak of the summit and turned around to see Maggie and Emilia coming behind her.

Maggie sat heavily on a nearby rock. "This was such a bad idea," she said, before taking a healthy swallow from her water bottle. "We should have just gone for brunch in town. Bottomless mimosas sound pretty good right about now."

"Nature now, mimosas later," Emilia said. "We might be hot and sweaty, but look at that view."

Misha nodded, taking in the scenery. "Yeah, it is really great." She thought of the last time she'd been hot and sweaty, and that was with Trey. She'd had a pretty good view last night, too. She smiled to herself, remembering Trey, his perfectly honed body and the way he'd made her feel.

"You're pretty *day-dreamy* over there," Maggie said to her. "You're so quiet. What's going on?"

"Oh, you know, just thinking about work stuff. We've got a lot of things coming up."

"Yeah, I'm sure. But I don't think work put that silly little grin on your face."

Misha should have known that Maggie would see right through her. The woman knew her better than anyone else. "I'm passionate about my work," she explained, hoping she'd drop it. But the way that both Maggie and Emilia were watching her, they were clearly skeptical, so she decided to turn the conversation around to take the attention off herself. "How are things with you lately?" Misha asked. "With the exception of the other day, I feel like we haven't seen much of each other in the past couple of weeks. Since you started seeing Jericho."

Her friend grinned. "I know. I'm such a bad friend, and I'm sorry."

"It's okay, and you are a fabulous friend. Tell me, is everything good with Jericho? I'd like to know. I feel kind of responsible for the match."

"You were definitely instrumental. I know it's only been a couple of weeks, but things are going so well. I never could have seen myself happy with someone from the Winters family, but here I am."

"How is your family coping with the fact that you're with Jericho?"

"They've met him and liked him, so they're coping with the truce," she said. "Hopefully, we'll be able to bury the hatchet once and for all between the two families and just get on with our lives."

"That would be nice."

"It certainly would."

Trey had been one of the most vocal opponents to the relationship and the truce. But it hadn't stopped him from coming on to her. Even though she didn't share the same last name as her friend, she was closer to the Del Rio family than anyone. Maybe keeping him occupied—in the office, and the bedroom—would be enough to make him let it go. She knew that if she allowed him to get too caught up in the family drama, it would definitely pull him away from working on k!smet, which was what mattered to her.

"I'm glad you're so happy. I guess the technology knows better than people. Lord knows I trust the code more than most people." Misha cast a look at Emilia, who was watching her carefully. She wasn't about to tell either of them about the doubts she'd had recently, or any internal drama that might be happening behind the scenes. Maggie was her best friend, of course, but Emilia was essentially a stranger, and the fewer people who knew about the background problems, the better.

"Here, here," Emilia agreed. "You've got that right."

"I heard that you've been spending more time with Trey," Maggie said.

Misha's face heated, and it had nothing to do with the scorching rays of the sun. "He's my main investor. We're just putting some finishing touches on the app," Misha told them, not wanting to get into any feelings she may have been growing between her and Trey.

"Is there anything else you're putting the *finishing touches* on?"

"What is that even supposed to mean?" she asked with a laugh. "No."

"Lies."

"How did this turn around on me?" she asked and gestured to the stunning scenery around them. "Look at where we are," she said. "Can't we talk about that?" Maggie and Emilia both smirked and didn't, for a second, even consider looking at the rolling vista and the cloudless sky that seemed to go on forever. "Fine," Misha relented. "He's attractive."

Maggie smiled. "That he is. Anything else you want to share?"

"He's smart. He's been invaluable in making sure we have the money needed to ensure k!smet is a success."

"Nothing else?"

Misha shook her head.

"If you say so." Maggie paused. "I know he's Jericho's brother, but I just want you to be careful. The idea I get from Jericho is that Trey sees quite a few women, but he never introduces them to the family. He keeps them hidden. It's for Dez's sake, of course, and I won't judge how he chooses to behave around his son. It's probably for the best. But if there is something going on between you guys, I just don't want you to feel like his dirty, little secret."

That caught her off guard. She hadn't imagined that Trey had been living an abstinent life since his son was born, but he didn't strike her as the womanizing type. Misha's interpersonal relationships meant so much to her, that she was typically open with love and affection, and didn't believe it was something that should be hidden. She wondered if they continued to see each other, would he also keep her under wraps, keep their relationship private? She would have to figure that out if it came up.

There were so many things she wanted to say. Things she couldn't have said about his prowess in other areas of his life. Or how she had to force herself to get out of his bed that morning. She could definitely tell them about how she might be falling for him. "Nope. There's nothing else to say." Instead, she kept her mouth shut.

It was after 9:00 p.m. when Misha got home. It was yet another night of sitting at her computer at the k!smet office. As someone who had, until recently, spent most of her career in programming and platform development behind the scenes, being the CEO of a quickly growing social networking platform required much more face time than she ever could have imagined. The upcoming IPO launch just added to that. She was exhausted, and her condo was sweltering. She'd meant to call someone to fix the air conditioning, but she kept forgetting. There was so much swimming around in her mind—so many tasks, so many meetings, so many appointments. Maybe it was time to hire an assistant.

She put her laptop case and purse on the coffee table and flopped on the couch. She couldn't wait for the IPO launch, and then she could take a minute to think of anything but business and marketing and programming. It had been a few days since her night with Trey, but it was never far from her mind.

There was a knock on the door, and Misha rolled her eyes. Who could possibly be at her door? She considered ignoring it, but whoever it was knocked again. She sighed and pushed herself up from the couch. "Fine," she said, quietly. "I'm coming." She checked the peephole and saw that it was Trey. That was unexpected.

She opened the door. "Hi. What's up?"

"Hi, I was just driving by and saw that your light was on."

It had been a couple of days since she'd seen him. It had been just as well; work had kept her busy. But seeing him now, at her door, she thought he looked so downright sexy that she wondered how she'd been able to stay away from him. "And you decided to come in for a nightcap?"

"Well, I haven't heard from you." Her mouth dropped open. Was he sore that she hadn't called after they'd spent the night together? "And I thought we were going to collaborate on the app."

"Oh, right," she said. "I honestly haven't had time. It's been a busy couple of days."

"Yeah." He rubbed the back of his neck, awkwardly. "You know, maybe I shouldn't have come. I'm going to leave."

"Don't." Holding the door open, she moved out of the way. "Come on in."

"Thanks. I'm glad I took the chance that you were home and wouldn't show me back out."

She grinned. It was endearing to see him vulnerable

like that. His impromptu visit was romantic in a way she didn't expect coming from him.

He looked around. "Nice place."

"Thanks. It's not a palatial ranch house, but it's comfortable."

"It sure is."

After a beat of silence, she looked up at him and felt her pulse jump in her throat at the idea of having him in her space. "So, what can I do for you tonight? It feels a little late in the day to be worrying about work, isn't it? Are you here for some late-night booty call?"

He nodded, stepping closer, his eyes narrowing. "Yeah, I think I might be."

Misha took a step closer to him, as Trey's arm encircled her waist, pulling her in. She pressed her chest against him, so close to him that she could feel his desire against her abdomen. Teasingly, she tilted her pelvis against him, bringing her even closer, and she didn't miss the way he flinched at the contact. Looking up, she saw that his dark eyes were made darker with an intense desire that was likely a reflection of her own need. But what made her breath hitch were his lips, turned upward in the cockiest, sexiest grin she'd ever seen.

Using his index finger, Trey brushed a strand of her hair behind her ear, and she shivered when he wove his fingers through the strands and cupped the back of her head in his large hand, holding her in place. Misha closed her eyes and leaned into his touch. He rubbed her lips with the pad of his thumb, and she puckered them against it before her lips parted and she nipped it with her teeth. Her reward was his thick groan of approval.

She wanted Trey, needed him, and couldn't wait any longer. And seemingly neither could he.

She trembled against Trey, and he drew in a jagged breath, his jaw set. "I haven't been able to stop thinking about you, you know."

"Neither have I."

"In fact, I probably shouldn't be here right now."

"But you are." She wondered what he could have meant by that. But it wasn't the time to ask. The time for talking had past. Now it was just a time to feel.

When Misha stepped, naked, from her bed, she felt a light sting of pain on her backside, as Trey reached out and slapped it. "Hey!" she said, smacking his hand out of the way.

"Sorry," he said, his grin telling her that he wasn't sorry at all.

"Yeah, right, you're sorry."

He shrugged as she pulled an old concert T-shirt over her head and walked to the kitchen. At the fridge, she pulled out two bottles of beer and brought them to the bedroom. She handed one to Trey, and he accepted it. Misha felt a frisson of electricity that shot between their fingers when they touched, just like every time.

"Thanks," he said. He clinked his bottle against hers as she returned to her spot in the bed. He took a long swallow from the bottle, and she watched, transfixed, by the bob of his Adam's apple as he swallowed. When he pulled the bottle away from his mouth, he smiled at her. "That hit the spot."

She took her own drink from her bottle. The beer was light, cold and refreshing, and it quenched her thirst.

"Sorry it's so warm here," she told him. "My air conditioning is on the fritz, and I haven't had time to arrange to get it fixed."

"It's quite alright. Although next time we can meet at my place."

She raised an eyebrow. "Next time, eh?"

"Well, it'd be dumb to not do it again, right?"

"And we're both reasonably smart people."

"That we are."

She leaned against her pillow as they shared a quiet moment. But her mind hinged on something he'd said before they'd ended up in her bedroom. "Can I ask you a question?"

"Yeah, of course."

"Earlier, you said that you *shouldn't be here*. Why not?

Again, he raised his bottle to his lips. "Even though the other night was incredible, I told myself I was going to stay away from you. And limit our interaction to working on the app and IPO launch."

Misha hid her frown behind her glass bottle. "And why would you want to do that?"

"Because with you, I completely forgot myself. I'm normally so careful when it comes to women and letting my social life bleed into my family life. When I was with you, none of that mattered, at the time."

Trey might be naked in her bed, and had just talked about there being a *next time*, but she couldn't help the sting of rejection from his words. "And what brought this on?"

"Dez saw us," he said simply. "When we were saying goodbye. He had questions."

"Oh. Is everything okay? Is he okay?"

"Yeah, he's fine. But I haven't been letting him see that side of my life. Being a single dad, I don't want him to get any ideas about any woman I might have in my life."

"He's never met any of the women you've dated?"

He shook his head. "None. It's terrible to say, but they never seem to stick around long enough," he confessed. "And I'm wondering if you wouldn't mind keeping whatever is happening here between us?"

She sat back, taken aback by his words. She thought back to her conversation with Maggie, and her warning about Trey. The words *dirty little secret* repeated in her head, as she thought about his request. She didn't want him to know that it had affected her so greatly, so she smiled, playing it off.

"Probably for the best," she started, trying to keep her voice light. "Because, as you know, I might not be a Del Rio, but I'm pretty closely aligned with them. Can you imagine what people would say if they found out we were together?" She covered her mouth dramatically in a sarcastic fashion. "It would be a scandal that rocks the town, right?"

"Now you're making fun of me."

She nodded. "I am." She then turned serious and thought about his proposition one more time, and with everything going on in her life at the moment, she certainly didn't have the time to deal with public scrutiny of a new relationship—especially in a small town like Royal. With the rumors of him being a ladies' man, keeping his relationships secret showed that he cared about his public image and would not want his credibility jeopardized. Trey didn't trust easily, and he certainly didn't trust the Del Rios. Did that then mean that he didn't trust her?

"But if you want to keep whatever this is quiet, then that's fine by me. Although," she said, startled. "People are starting to talk. About us."

"Who's talking?" he asked.

"Maggie."

He rolled his eyes. "Of course, she is. The Del Rios are nothing but gossips."

"That's not true," she told him. "Maggie cares about me."

"And what is she saying?"

Misha shrugged, not wanting to get into what she'd heard about Trey. *Dirty little secret.* She shook her head. "Not much. She just warned me to be careful."

Eight

Trey parked his truck on the gravel lot at the k!smet office. The building was run-down, small and now cramped with the ever-growing staff at the company. With every day that passed, he knew that Misha needed more and more help. He was just glad that she'd realized that she wouldn't be able to do it all herself. If she was willing to let him, he'd help her find a new space befitting the platform, which was still on a steady incline of popularity.

He made his way to her office, waving to employees as he walked, finding himself at home there. He walked to the end of the hallway to the boardroom she still used as an office and knocked on the open door. In her office, Misha was surrounded by boxes, one of which was open in front of her. She was pulling out wrapped items. "Knock, knock," he said.

Misha paused, bent over, her arms inside the half-full

box. "You know, when you knock, you don't also have to say *knock, knock,* right?" She stood.

"What do you have there?" he asked. He nodded at her k!smet-branded baseball hat she was wearing. "Nice hat."

She smiled and pulled another out of the box, and she put it on his head and then handed him a k!smet tote bag. "Glad you like it," she said.

"I'm not sure it's my style," he told her. "I prefer cowboy hats."

"That's too bad, I've got one for everyone." She looked around at the boxes that occupied almost every square foot of floor. "Well, maybe I bought more than enough for everyone."

"So, what's all this?"

"Merchandise," she said simply, before poking a knife into the top of another still-taped box, slicing it open.

"I can see that. Where did it come from?"

She dug through the packaging materials at the top of the box. "Now that I have a marketing team, we've been working on some ways to maximize the impact of the app, and we've come up with a line of k!smet merchandise. We've got hats, bags, cell phone cases. But there's also this. The marketing team and I came up with this idea. Last month, I worked closely with a board game designer to come up with this prototype." She handed over the box.

"'Date in a box,'" he read from the top. "'You made a match. Now make a connection.'"

"Fun, right? We've also come up with versions for friends, networking events and, you know, a more romantic experience." She tapped the top of the box in his hands. "What do you think? Wanna play?"

"I don't like board games," he told her. "*Boring games,* am I right?"

"Holy hell, you are a grump."

He smiled. "Not always."

"Come on, open the box. Let's play a round or two."

He read some of the questions on the side. *What's your favorite sexual position? What's the wildest time you've ever had in bed?* Trey could feel his blood begin to heat and travel southward, and he wished that he'd closed the door when he'd arrived. "Some interesting questions there," he told her.

"Yeah, there's a good mix," she told him, still distracting herself with boxes. "Some sexy and playful, and some are a little more serious and introspective." He turned the box and saw that the other side of the box indeed showcased a more serious flavor of question. *What's your biggest disappointment? What's your worst fear?* They were all exceptionally personal, and while he'd felt himself getting closer to her, they were certainly not the things he wanted to get into with Misha.

"You know, I just realized that I've got somewhere else to be," he lied. He felt a pull of pain in his chest, lying to her. He was starting to fall for Misha. It wasn't just the sex, but just being with her, having her in his space and being in hers was comfortable. And in the spirit of not letting himself get too close to her, that was unacceptable.

"Oh, really?" she asked. Her eyebrows drew together, and he knew that she was confused. "I thought you were meeting me here to discuss the IPO launch."

"Yeah, I know. I messed up. I have a meeting to get to."

"That's a lie," she told him. "Sit down."

"Well, can we at least get to work and stop playing these games?"

"Sure thing."

Misha narrowed her eyes at Trey as he sat across from her at the table. What had caused his change in mood, so that he'd almost walked out on her? There was likely some personal stuff that the game had dared to dredge up, and he didn't want to get into it. And that was fair. They were business partners, albeit there was a little more to their relationship than that, but maybe it was for the best that they didn't get too far into their personal lives—traumas and tragedies included.

"I have an idea," Misha said. "If you'll go for it." When Trey looked up, he wore a look that combined concern and curiosity on his face. They were in his home office, where, Misha had to admit, she was getting used to sitting in his smooth leather chair, connecting her laptop to and using a curved monitor that likely cost more than her mortgage.

"What is it?"

"I want to make a series of videos," she told him.

"Okay," he said, drawing out the second syllable. "And what does that have to do with me?"

"Well, I want you to star in them."

Trey raised his hands. "I don't think so. That's not my thing."

"What, exactly, is your thing? You don't like social media. You don't like games. What are you bringing to the k!smet table, exactly?"

"Maybe you need to check your books," he reminded her. "I think I'm bringing quite a bit to the table."

She rolled her eyes at him. "Okay, besides your investment money, what have you brought to the table?"

He slowly slid his gaze to her. "I could bring something to *this table*," he said suggestively, gesturing to the tabletop.

Laughing, Misha balled up a piece of paper and threw it at him. "Okay, fine. But pretty soon, I think it'd be a lot of fun to get some videos of you wearing the new merch we have. Or talking about the app. Maybe we could do one together, where we're playing the game. I don't know, I'm just brainstorming. I'm just trying to think of ways to maximize our impact." He sighed audibly. "So dramatic," she mumbled to herself.

He watched her for a bit, his jaw set, but when he loosened it, she could see that he'd softened. "I don't know much about making videos and social media trends and all that," he said. "But I know someone who does."

Trey folded his arms across his chest as he and Misha stood on the back deck, watching Dez play in the garden. Although, *play* for Dez was quite different than it was for other boys his age. He'd brought Misha to his home to meet the boy. He told himself that it was because Misha would be able to understand his passion. They would relate better to one another than any other woman Trey had been with. It felt like the right thing to do.

Misha watched him, too. "Is he filming?"

"Yeah, it's all he does these days. He and a couple of friends get together and do all kinds of things. They know how to edit things to look new and flashy, and they even go old school with stop-motion animation."

"That sounds pretty fun."

"It's not what I was into when I was in third grade, but he's happy, so I'm happy." Misha smiled up at Trey, and, uncomfortable as he was under her scrutiny, he returned her smile.

He couldn't believe what he was about to do. He'd never introduced Dez to any woman he'd had in his life, but Misha didn't feel like the other women. Trey found that Misha was not only his partner—in and out of bed—but she was quickly becoming his friend. He reasoned to himself that it would be fine to introduce Dez to a friend, right? It felt right, and while he knew that he and Misha might not always be romantically— *no, sexually*—linked, he hoped that he could always count her as a friend.

He raised his hand. "Hey, Dez," he called out. The boy looked up, looking almost perturbed. As if he hadn't realized that Trey and Misha had been watching. "Come on over here."

"You just ruined my shot," Dez called back.

"Just get over here, would you?" Trey called back. The kid was precocious, that was for sure.

Thankfully, he listened and stood and walked over to where they were waiting for him.

"I don't have a lot of time," Dez said, looking up at the sky, gauging the sun's position. "I'm burning daylight."

He heard Misha stifle a giggle. Everyone loved a kid with an attitude, until it was their own. "Dez," Trey said, his voice firm, sending his son a warning. While he liked Dez to express himself, and he didn't want to dissuade him from his favorite activities, Trey also tried to instill a deep respect for other people. "Is that polite?"

Dez frowned. "No, sir." As if it was the first time he'd seen her, Dez's attention turned to the woman beside him.

"Dez," Trey said to his son. "I'd like you to meet my friend, Misha."

Dez looked at her for a few moments, as intently as if he were studying her. Finally, he held out his hand to Misha, and she shook it. "It's nice to meet you, Misha," he said.

"It's awfully nice to meet you, as well, Dez," Misha returned.

"You know, I told my dad that I don't kiss any of my friends goodbye."

Misha's eyes widened. "I—"

"Dez," Trey warned him. "Be polite."

"I'm just saying," he said with a shrug. He turned his attention back to Misha. "I've heard about your app, but my dad says I'm too young for an account."

"You are," Trey warned.

Misha laughed. "Yeah, I'm afraid so. k!smet is strictly for adults. There's definitely no children allowed."

"I've got a TikTok account," he told her.

"So I've heard."

"I follow you. I've got over five hundred followers. But Dad says there's more to life than follower counts," he said skeptically.

"I'm afraid your dad's right. There definitely is. It's important to not get caught up in all of that stuff."

"It's nice to hear I'm right," Trey muttered. He found it fascinating watching Misha interact with his son. Some sort of emotion grasped his chest in a tight hold.

"I don't interact with anyone, though," he said. "Dad won't allow that."

"And I don't allow him to post any pictures or personal details about himself."

"Those are good rules. The trouble with the internet is that you don't know if people are telling the truth about who they are."

"Isn't your app all for people who want to meet strangers?" he asked.

Misha looked up at Trey. He had her there. "Uh, yeah, I guess it is."

"How do you know if people who are meeting are who they say they are?"

"Um, well, the algorithm makes sure that people are right for each other. Plus, membership is limited. We have a waitlist, and there's a strict vetting process." Misha changed the topic. "What kinds of things do you post online?"

"I'm a filmmaker," he told her with a sense of gravitas that Trey knew was serious, and he hoped that Misha didn't laugh at how seriously Dez took his passion. "I don't really care all that much about social media. It's just practice for when I can make my own films."

It surprised Trey that Misha leaned in, interested. He appreciated that, while she was obviously aware that Dez was a child, she didn't speak to him like he was one, which was one of Dez's biggest pet peeves. "That's a great goal. What sorts of films do you make?"

"I left my phone over there," he said. Trey unlocked his phone and opened the folder that held Dez's videos and photos and handed it over.

"Lately I do a lot of stop-motion and time-lapsed recording. Then I edit them."

"On your own?"

"Me and some of my friends. It's not too hard when you know what you're doing," he said, as if it was the most obvious thing in the world.

Misha looked up at Trey with an amused smile, before turning her attention back to Dez. "I'd love to learn sometime," she said. "Do you think you could you show me?"

"I can teach you a few tricks."

"I'd like that. You know, we really need to make some promo videos. I'd like your input on what works." Another look up at Trey, her eyes narrowed, a teasing smile on her lips. "That is, if your dad doesn't mind."

He looked down at them. Seeing Misha with Dez didn't worry him like he'd thought it might. He wanted Dez and Misha to get to know each other. He didn't feel the same fear he'd had before when it came to women and his son. Then it hit him. He was interested in seeing where things might go with Misha. He was interested in a future with her.

Trey put a hand on Dez's shoulder, and when Misha looked up at him, he returned her smile. "I'm sure we can work something out."

"Are you staying for dinner?" Dez asked Misha, surprising both her and Trey. "That's okay, right, Dad?"

Trey didn't know how he felt about that. Introducing her to Dez was already a huge step for him, but inviting her to dinner? Sharing a meal?

She looked up at him, as if she was asking. She was leaving it up to him.

In response, Trey shrugged and smiled at them. "We'd be glad to have you," he found himself saying, and he meant it. If she were any other woman, he would have walked her to the door, but Misha had already gotten under his skin. He'd already introduced her to his son—what harm could having a meal together do? "If you don't have plans, of course," he added.

"Is your dad a good cook?" she asked the boy.

"He's okay," Dez said with a shrug of his shoulders. "He's pretty good on the grill."

"That's a ringing endorsement," Trey said.

"He makes an even better pancake breakfast," Dez offered.

Misha laughed, her gaze sliding up to meet Trey's. When she turned back to face Dez, she was still smiling. "In that case, I'd love to stay."

The sun had long set and Dez had gone to bed, but Misha still found herself sitting on the swing on Trey's back deck. She looked out at the pool and was transfixed by how the water moved in the evening air. She pushed herself with her foot and rocked gently, as she watched the darkening sky.

"It's great this time of night, right?" Trey asked, coming from behind her. He handed her a glass of wine.

"It's beautiful out here. Your own piece of heaven."

"I like it."

They sat together on the swing in silence, sipping their wine, listening to the wind rustling the trees and the sounds of the nighttime creatures coming alive.

"Thanks for inviting me for dinner or allowing Dez to invite me."

He'd fired up the barbecue and she'd eaten one of the most delicious steaks she'd ever had.

"It was nice to have you. It's not every evening we're joined by a beautiful woman."

"I had a great time." She put a hand on his forearm. "And you're much a better cook than Dez gave you credit for." He laughed. "You know, I think a lot of people are wrong about you—you're not as gruff and scary as you like to think you are."

He raised his arm along the back of the swing, but not directly over her shoulders. "Shucks, I've spent so long trying to cultivate my image."

"I know you're just an old softie on the inside."

"How do you know that?"

"I see how you are with Dez," she said.

At the mention of his son, Misha could see the change that came over his face. He softened. "That little boy is a handful, but he's the best thing that ever happened to me. It's just been the two of us the whole time."

"Can I ask where his mother is?" She knew she took a risk in asking.

His laugh was humorless. "You can ask, but I don't think I can answer. When she told me she was pregnant, I asked her to marry me. She said yes, but instead, she took off just after Dez was born."

"That's unreal," Misha said, shaking her head. She'd lost most of her family at a young age—she couldn't imagine walking away from a child. "How could she do that?"

"That's what I wonder, too. She just wasn't happy, and I wasn't the person who could make her happy. But in reality, she can think whatever she wants about me.

If she'd just left me, it would be a different issue, but I don't see how anyone could walk away from that little boy. I never will."

"I know you won't. And that's really admirable to me," she told him. "Family is so important to me. I don't know where I'd be without Nico, or my grandparents."

"While we're asking each other the tough questions— if family is so important to you, why haven't you started one yet?"

She couldn't believe that he'd gone there. But one tough question deserved another. "Wow, if I hadn't already asked you an intensely personal question, I might be offended."

"You don't have to answer if you don't want to."

"I will. I'm not embarrassed. The short answer is that I've been busy. It's a cliché, but I was married to my work, and the opportunity just hasn't come up."

"No suitors coming your way? I find that hard to believe."

"Believe me, there have been suitors. But none of them understood how important my work is to me. I don't exactly have a nine-to-five type of gig. You know how inconsistent the hours in this industry are, and how this kind of work can just consume you. It doesn't exactly allow you to build a great foundation."

"I guess not. But you said that was the short answer," he said. "What's the long answer?"

Misha blew out a shaky breath, about to say the words to him that she'd never said to anyone before. "I think it goes back to losing my parents so young, and then Nico went away to prison. I guess the long answer is that I'm...afraid?" She'd come to that realization in a therapy session several years ago. It had been the first and only other time she'd said the words out loud. "I've always been reluctant to give myself to someone, to love someone else so fully that the thought that I might lose them is crippling. I just can't let myself be that vulnerable. I force myself to be strong."

"I worry about Dez every waking moment of my life," Trey admitted. He took her hand in his in a comforting gesture. "But the kind of love you're talking about, it's worth it."

She thought about that. He was right. She blew out a breath and took a gulp of her wine. "This is pretty intense."

"I just want to know about you," he said.

"I'd like to get to know you, as well." She smiled. She turned in her seat and draped her legs over his thighs. He smoothed his hand over her instep, and she shivered at the touch, swallowing back the moan that formed in the back of her throat.

"So, losing someone else you're close to, that's your biggest fear?" he asked.

"That's probably the biggest one, but the most practical, everyday fear is that I'm afraid of disappointing people."

"Like who?"

"My grandmother, Nico, the entire town of Royal. We're setting this place up as the next tech hub in the country, and k!smet's success is a cornerstone of that. What if it's a failure?" She sighed. "I never had a lot of stability growing up. My grandmother and the people of Royal were so fabulous and supportive to Nico and me, but you just don't understand what happens to a child when their security is just ripped away from them when their parents die." His gaze on her was soft. "I need this for Royal and for myself. I want to carve out a life here, and while Royal is a successful town, this could bring all new attention to us."

"It's not. You know now that it won't be."

"I didn't always feel that way, especially when you came and insisted there was something wrong with k!smet—"

"I apologized for that."

"I know, and I appreciate that. But it struck a nerve and I had to work to keep cool. I'm desperate to not disappoint anyone."

"You could never disappoint anyone."

The way he looked at her, his dark, brooding eyes taking in every part of her, seeing things inside of her, was too much for Misha. Desperate to turn the attention away from herself, she cleared her throat. "Here's another one," she said, while she still had the ability to speak. "Have you ever been in love?"

"We are really getting into it, aren't we?"

"We can stop if you want."

"Wouldn't dream of it. No, it's fine. Have I ever been in love? *In love?*" He shrugged. "I don't know. If that's my answer, then I guess probably not. When Dez's mother told me she was pregnant, I was ready to spend my life with her, because of Dez. I liked her well enough. But it wasn't love."

"That was, what, eight years ago?" she asked. "There haven't been any women since then?"

"Well, there have been women," he assured her. "I haven't been living like a monk over here. But it's been more casual. With Dez in the picture, I didn't want to introduce him to anyone I wasn't sure about."

Misha's breath caught in her throat. He'd introduced her to Dez, and she knew that that action meant more than he was admitting. She nodded.

"But I'm like you," he continued. "I've been too busy, too distracted to form any long-term relationships."

"Do you think you've distracted yourself without realizing why? Are you keeping yourself at a distance because you're afraid of being hurt?"

"Are you a therapist now?"

"No, but I learned a lot from mine. Do you want to answer the question, or should we move on?"

He sighed. "I think I work so much to occupy myself. I work, and then when I'm not working, I spend my time with Dez. That's always been enough for me."

She nodded. "You know what, Trey, I think we might be more alike than we realize."

His hand slid farther up her leg. "I'm starting to think so, too."

"I have one more question," she told him.

"Fire away."

"Why did you try to leave my office earlier? When I showed you the game?"

"I guess it's a moot point at this moment," he said. "But I was afraid to let you get too close. I don't open up easily."

"But you ended up doing it anyway."

"Yup. I contend that you tricked me."

"I did no such thing."

Surprising her, he leaned over and grasped her by her waist, before depositing her into his lap so that she was straddling him. He leaned forward, allowing her to wrap her legs around his waist, locking him in. The swing groaned with the movement, but Trey didn't seem to notice or mind. When he kissed her, she parted her lips immediately for him, inviting him into her mouth. The kiss was similar to the ones they'd shared before. But there was more behind it—more passion, more feeling, more passion. Desperate with need for him, Misha ground herself into his lap, riding against the length of him as it pushed against her.

Trey pulled his mouth away from hers, and his lips blazed a hot trail over her jaw and down her throat. She sighed, and with her hands wrapped around his neck, she pulled him closer, as his lips skimmed her skin, and she cried out when his teeth sank lightly into the skin of her shoulder.

Trey pushed his fingers through her hair, then smoothed across her jaw down the column of throat. He reached the hem of her shirt, but before he down her ventured her hands came down on his, stopping him on his journey. "Wait."

He looked up at her. "What's wrong?"

Misha looked at him with uncertainty. "What about Dez?"

"Don't worry about him," he told her. "When he goes to sleep, he's out like a light. I checked on him before getting the wine. He's okay."

He pulled up her top and his eyes dropped to her chest, before he massaged her breasts with his hands. He squeezed and she arched her back against him, bringing her breasts close to his mouth. He closed his lips over one lace-covered bud, while he played with the other with his fingers. She sighed and pressed against him, relishing the feeling of him, even if it was through her bra.

She gasped, and he brought his hands back to her bare lower back, and then dipped down to her ass. He pulled her closer, bringing her against his hard length. Suddenly, he stood, and with her legs still locked around him, he laid her on her back on the wooden slats of the patio. He leaned over her, kissing her again. "Do you want this to happen again?"

Misha knew that this was her chance to end things there, go home and clear her head. She knew that, based on their conversation, nothing permanent would come about from whatever she was building with Trey, but she still wanted him so badly that she didn't want to think about whatever might happen in the future. She leaned closer to him and put her fingers in his hair, pushing through the thick strands. "I do."

"Do you have any other questions you want to ask me?" he asked, as he slid his fingers over her knee and up her thigh.

"Just one," she told him. "Do you want to go to your bedroom?"

Nine

"I'm having a chocolate milkshake," Dez said excitedly. "What about you, Dad?"

"That sounds good," he said with a nod. "I will have the same."

Dez looked from Trey to the woman standing beside him. "What about you, Misha?" he asked. "Are you having a milkshake, too?"

Trey was happy when he woke that morning and saw that Misha was still in his arms. She'd gotten out of his bed the night before and had started to gather her clothes, but Trey had pulled her back onto his mattress. When she shifted in his arms and looked up at him, he'd pushed aside any apprehension he may have had, and pulled her closer.

The three of them had had breakfast together. Dez and Misha mostly talked about YouTube and TikTok, while he brewed coffee and mixed batter for pancakes.

The decision to get milkshakes at the Royal Diner had come from Dez.

"I think I will have a milkshake," she agreed.

Trey turned to her. "I don't know if you know this, but Amanda makes the best shakes in all of Texas," Trey told her.

"I'd heard a rumor," she told him. "But I haven't had one myself. I don't think I've even *had* a milkshake in years."

He couldn't stop himself from taking an appraising look up and down her incredible body. "Well, you've been missing out," he told her. "They are even better than her pie."

Amanda, the diner's owner, came up to the counter. "What can I get for you three?" she asked.

"Three chocolate milkshakes please," Dez ordered, like he always did, holding up three fingers.

"Coming right up, handsome," Amanda said, before turning her attention to Trey and Misha. Trey knew she was about to ask questions, but luckily someone called her name from the kitchen, so she didn't get the chance. But he knew the way news traveled in Royal. By dinnertime, he would surely be fielding questions about his afternoon milkshake date with Misha.

"Well, if this isn't a nice surprise," Trey heard a voice say. They all turned and saw Maggie standing behind them, with Jericho at her back. "What are the three of you doing out and about together?" she asked.

"Amanda makes a mean milkshake," Trey responded without answering her question.

He watched as Jericho shot a look to Maggie, a secret smile passing between them. They were certainly settling into the new couple groove. They looked comfortable together; they made it look easy. When he thought about it, that was kind of how he felt when he was with Misha. But that wasn't the same as what his brother had with Maggie. There may be parallels between their relationships, but he and Misha weren't in love. Lust? Sure. Friendship? Definitely. Not love, though.

He couldn't help admire Jericho and Maggie, though. After k!smet had matched them, they had taken a huge risk in staying together and giving each other a chance, and they couldn't look happier together. He didn't know if he would ever be able to take such a risk. As an occasional tech investor, he loved taking a risk. But that was only money—there would always be more. He looked down at Dez, then at Misha. That was what he couldn't risk. He couldn't risk the hearts of the people he loved.

Love? That stopped him. He loved his son, there was no doubt about that. But when he looked back at Misha, he knew that whatever feelings he had for her were deep. *But not love,* he corrected himself mentally. He didn't love Misha. Did he?

"Do the three of you have a regular standing milkshake date?" Jericho asked. Trey noted the smirk on his brother's face.

"No, Trey and I were just doing some work together at his place," Misha supplied.

Trey jumped in. "We thought we could use a break, so we decided to take Dez out," he finished.

"You're still doing work on the app?" Jericho asked. "At your place?" Dez didn't miss the way Maggie narrowed her eyes, a playful smirk turning her lips upward.

Trey nodded casually and crossed his arms. "Yeah, at

my home office," he offered. Misha's office setup isn't conducive for both of us to work the long hours we have been to make sure that k!smet is as good as it can be. Making sure all of the code is ready, and checking for weaknesses before it gets too big."

"I heard it might be too late for that," Jericho said with a nod of approval. "I heard you've been that the waitlist is pretty long."

"It's very exciting. We were even called the Facebook of Matchmaking," she said proudly.

"And it's a good thing that Misha stayed over last night," Dez said before Trey could stop him. "If she had left in the middle of the night, like before, then we wouldn't have been able to come out for milkshakes."

Trey cast a look at Misha and saw her eyes widen with the same panic he was also feeling.

"What was that, Dez?" Jericho asked, his smile growing and crinkling the corners of his eyes.

"Sometimes when Misha comes over to work, she doesn't go home until the middle of the night. This morning, she stayed and we all had breakfast together."

Both Jericho and Maggie looked from Misha to Trey. Trey could feel a red-hot flush heat the tips of his ears. This sort of scrutiny was exactly what he was trying to avoid by keeping his private life exactly that—private.

"Is that so?" Maggie asked, amused.

"You know, I was checking out Trey's computer set-up, and we lost track of time," she insisted. "It got too late, so I ended up staying."

"In the guest room." Trey added a small lie, but it seemed that neither his brother nor Maggie believed him.

"I'll bet," Maggie said, her eyebrow raised. "You guys

must have been *really checking out all that gear* to pass the entire night without realizing it."

"You know how I am," Misha said. "It's easy enough to do to get so focused that you lose track of everything else."

"Especially down in that man cave of yours," Jericho teased. "There's a lot of comfortable furniture down there," he said, playing along with Maggie's game.

So, everyone in town was clearly enjoying toying with him, it seemed. Trey looked down at Dez, who was now playing a game on his phone, completely oblivious to the innuendo-laced conversation going on over his head.

He turned toward the counter. "Well, how about those milkshakes, Amanda?" he asked Amanda, who he'd noticed had been hovering nearby, likely hearing every word of the conversation.

"Coming right up, Trey," she responded with a knowing wink. "Don't be so impatient. Good things come to all who wait. Isn't that right?"

"Your investment is looking sound, right?" Jericho asked.

"I'll come out on top," Trey assured him, glad to be on the comfortable topic of business. He could talk about their investments until he was blue in the face. But he wouldn't reveal that he also cared about k!smet's success on a personal level. It was no longer just about the dollars they were sure to make. He cared about k!smet, because he cared about Misha. And k!smet was the most important thing in the world to her.

He lost himself in thought, however, reflecting on the number of times she'd said something to that effect. It bothered him. Of course her work, her creation, should be important to her. But *the most important*? He wondered how deeply that sentiment went.

"We'd better get to a table," Maggie said to Jericho, who nodded.

"We'll see you guys again soon, I imagine," he said to Trey, as he ruffled Dez's hair.

"Yeah, can't wait," he said to his brother, knowing full well that he would have many more questions to answer soon. The idea of having to answer them just for spending time with a woman was enough to sour his mood.

"Should we get a table?" Misha asked.

He looked around the crowded restaurant. Some of the patrons were looking in their direction. Were they already stirring the pot with their appearance at the diner? "We should just leave," he said. "Amanda, can we get those shakes to go?"

"Absolutely, honey," Amanda replied, switching the shakes to tall paper cups. She pushed all three across the counter.

Finally, Trey thought as he picked them up and distributed to Misha and Dez. He paid quickly. "Let's go."

Dez walked ahead of them toward the parking lot until he saw Timmy, one of his best friends, at the park next to the diner. "I'm going to talk to Timmy," he told them before running across the grass.

When they were alone, Trey watched intently as Misha wrapped her lips around her straw. Her cheeks hollowed as she drank, and Trey couldn't help but let his mind wander as it reminded him of…*other things.*

She raised her eyes to his and slowly withdrew the straw from between her lips. She made a seductive show of licking her lips and nodded her head. "You're right. That's a good milkshake."

He leaned in. "If we weren't in public right now, I might be doing something inappropriate."

"Then people might see us together," she warned. Her smirk fell. "I noticed it got a little tense in there. Are you okay?"

"Yeah, I'm just used to keeping that part of my life private."

"I get that."

"I hate lying, but it's not worth the headache of having everyone know my business. The last time random people had any idea about my life was when everyone knew that Dez's mom had left me. I got sick of the pitying glances, the sympathetic head tilts, the cocky smiles that my life had become much more difficult…"

"I know what it's like. I was a kid, but when my parents died, the community really came together to support my brother and me. Maybe they wanted to help, and you took it as pity and rejected it."

"Perhaps," he said, not quite believing it. "But either way, I don't think we need everyone to know…" he trailed off.

"Know what?"

"What we're doing?"

"And what are we doing, Trey? We're friends, we're working together, we're sleeping together."

He looked around to see if there was anyone around to overhear their conversation, but it was clearly the wrong move because Misha rolled her eyes and sighed.

"Trey, it's nobody's business what we do in our personal lives. Why are you so worried?"

"I have Dez—"

She gestured to the park where he was playing with his friend. "Dez is fine. He doesn't care. What happened this morning, then?" she asked. "What was that? Why did you ask me to spend the night?"

He didn't have an answer. He just knew what he'd felt at the time, and that was that he'd wanted her there with him. But being together at the diner, with the scrutiny turned on them, he was uncomfortable. But he couldn't find those words.

Before he said anything, Misha stepped back. "You know, I don't think I'm really cut out to be your dirty little secret anymore."

"You're not my dirty little secret," he insisted.

She raised her hand. "I should probably go," she told him. "I've got a lot to do before work tomorrow." She'd taken her car from the ranch to the diner, and she headed toward it.

"Okay," he said, resigning to the conversation. "Call me if you'd like to get together again soon."

"I will. Say goodbye to Dez for me, okay?"

"Sure thing."

She nodded, and despite the hurt he saw in her eyes, she smiled. He hated that he'd been the one to put the sadness there. That was why it was better to keep women at arm's distance.

Ten

"What's next?" she asked her team that had assembled at the table in her condo. She preferred to have the inner circle meetings off the k!smet premises in order to keep confidential information private. "Let's talk about new users," she said. "Where are we on that?"

David, her chief procurement officer, opened a document on his tablet and projected it onto the screen on her wall. "We were hoping for steady growth through the year," he started. "Our wait list is getting longer, but we're not rushing our vetting procedure. This was our projected growth." He pointed to the line graph.

"And?" Misha asked him. She'd seen the raw numbers, but without proper context, she couldn't tell how the membership was trending.

David smiled at her. "And this is a graph of how our membership has grown in just the past week." He handed her a printout from a trusted technology news site. "You are not going to believe this!"

"What is it?"

She read out loud from the article. "'The tales of strange matches have done nothing to affect the bottom line of k!smet. The dating/networking social media app's membership has increased by more than fifty percent, making it one of the fastest growing apps of the month.'"

Misha looked up from the printout to the graph and was amazed to see that the line that had been projected to rise steadily over time had shot upward at a steep angle. "Incredible."

He flipped to another chart. "I even took the liberty of looking into the market share of HitMeUp! And it would appear that their membership numbers are down, almost at the pace that we're gaining."

Misha narrowed her eyes at her employee. "How did you get those numbers?"

He averted his eyes. "I have my sources."

She snorted. "I'm sure you do. But this tells me we are definitely on the right course. It looks like people are leaving HitMeUp! in droves and signing up for k!smet." It made her think about what the leadership at the rival company might be thinking, and what they might do in retaliation. She looked down at her notes for the meeting. "And where are we on allowing international users?"

"Our lawyers are working with Canadian, Asian, European and Australian regulators and governments. Some are going better than others, but we'll be worldwide by our projected deadline."

"Amazing." Even though she held some doubts about the app and wondered if it had been the victim of a cyberattack or sabotage, it was hard to not feel optimistic about the future of her platform. "That's great, guys. We launched the merchandise store a few days ago. How were sales over the weekend?"

"It's going well," said Tamara, her senior associate of merchandising. "We'll have to restock the hats, bag and shirts by the end of the week. The game, k!smet/connect, is completely sold out and we're looking at developing a digital version and launching it in the metaverse. There's incredible room for growth."

Misha had amassed an amazing team. Every one of them were at the top of their game and they all had the same goal of making k!smet the best networking/matchmaking platform. "That's fabulous, folks. Thank you for all of your hard work. I couldn't have done any of this without you."

"There's more, though," David said, his voice now devoid of the excitement that had been there just minutes ago. Misha stiffened. "What is it?"

"You know those articles that were shared about inappropriate matches."

"Yeah," she said carefully.

"#KismetStories is trending on TikTok."

"Why?"

"People are sharing videos embedded with their own bad experiences."

Misha closed her eyes. She'd been hoping they were past this. "Not again."

"It's not the end of the world. Sure, it's getting more traction than the articles did, but it's only been a couple of days, and we're still seeing exponential growth in membership. But obviously, because of the way the algorithm works on TikTok, there's a lot of exposure for a short period of time and then it'll fall off the radar."

"Yeah, okay." She thought of the ways that she had gotten through the previous rough spot in the press. She'd managed to stay cool then, and she believed that she could do it again and hoped that the app's resiliency was enough to combat it.

Her phone vibrated to life on the table beside her. The picture on the screen was of Nico. "Alright, I guess that's everything for today. Let's meet again at the end of the week for another update. Thanks, again."

The team stood and said quiet goodbyes as she answered her brother's video call. "Hey, what's up?"

"I'm just checking in. We haven't talked in a while."

It had only been a few days, but for Misha and Nico, that was a long time. Even when he was in prison, they'd still managed to have daily conversations. His calls had a soothing effect on her, because even though things looked hard for her, Nico had gotten through a prison sentence with healthy stoicism and had come out mentally and physically strong. "Yeah, I've been so busy. You know how it is," she explained. "My PVR is getting full with unwatched reality shows."

"You're really behind on Real Housewives of Atlanta, aren't you?" he told her. "We need to talk about this season."

No matter what was going on, Nico, the closet reality tv viewer, always managed to make her smile. "I'm sorry, but you know how I feel. It's not the same since NeNe left," she said with a laugh.

"Yeah, I get that. And I knew that talking about tv would relax you," he said. "You look stressed. Everything okay? How's your investigation going?"

"I don't know. We thought it was going well, but apparently there are more stories out there of bad matches, and it's trending again on social media."

"That's rough."

"It hasn't affected new membership numbers yet, but I figure it's only a matter of time."

"And you and Winters couldn't find anything in the code?"

Misha shook her head. "No. I'm afraid it's a cyberattack, or someone infiltrated the backend."

"A hacker?"

"Maybe. I've passed my concerns on to the security team, and they're looking for any trace of a hack."

"Maybe it's…" Nico trailed off.

"What?"

"How much do you trust Trey Winters?"

Misha thought back to the last time she'd seen Trey, in the diner parking lot. She'd tried to make herself forget about how he'd made her feel—like he was embarrassed to be seen with her in public, that he was content to take her to bed, but hide her from sight. *Dirty little secret.*

"Why are you bringing Trey into this?"

"I don't know, but if someone has hacked their way into k!smet, then it might sound reasonable that it's the guy who bullied his way into working on the code."

"We've been through this, Nico. Why would he jeopardize his own investment?"

"The Winterses have money. Although it's a lot to us, and completely life changing, the amount he invested is a drop in the bucket to that family. You can't tell me that he still isn't pissed about his brother hooking up with Maggie."

She rolled her eyes. Trey might not be her favorite

person at the moment, but he wasn't sneaky. "It has nothing to do with Trey. He's been helpful."

Nico watched her for a beat. Even through the screen of her phone, she could feel his scrutiny. "Fine," he relented. "If it's not Trey, then who?"

"I don't know. Between Trey and me, we haven't been able to find any sign. I've got it passed on to my security team and hopefully they'll bring me some answers soon."

"Who do you think might be behind it?"

"We've won a large portion of HitMeUp!'s market share. Maybe someone over there is none too happy about it."

"It's as good a theory as any."

"To not even leave a trace that neither Trey nor I could find, they must have someone good on the payroll."

"Or an outside consultant."

"Fancy words for malicious hacker."

"I'll put some feelers out there," Nico said. "See if there's any word on the street about shady dealings over there."

"Okay, thanks," she told him. Misha knew how lucky she was to have her brother on her side. The support he provided her with every day was immeasurable. Despite his own busy life, he always took time to help her, no matter the issue. She just wished that other people could see that side of him. But in order for that to happen, he'd have to return to Royal, and she didn't see that happening anytime soon.

She disconnected the call and, with a groan, she brought her forehead to rest on the table. Things had been going well—according to the membership numbers, they were still going well, but for how long? Tech start-ups came and went. Misha couldn't afford to let k!smet be one of them. To save the platform, she needed help, and whether she liked it or not, she needed Trey at her side.

Eleven

Sitting behind his desk, Trey tried to focus on work, but instead all he could focus on was the image of Misha leaving him standing in the parking lot of the Royal Diner as she drove off. She'd had every right to do that, of course. He was certain he would have done the same if anyone had made him feel as little as he knew he'd made her feel. Several times, he'd picked up his phone to call her, but never followed through. He hadn't wanted to make her feel like his dirty secret, but he wasn't sure how to make it right.

He glanced at his security system in time to see her car come up the driveway. He watched as she got out and confidently made her way up the front steps to the door. She pushed the speaker button and turned to the camera. "Can I come in?" she asked.

From his phone, he unlocked the door. "Come on in," he told her. "I'm downstairs."

She looked again at the camera. "Thanks."

He listened as she came into the house and down the stairs. When she appeared in the doorway, she was wearing a small smile.

"Hey," she said, quietly.

"Hi." He stood from his desk.

"I want to apologize about yesterday—"

He held up his hands. "You don't need to apologize for anything," he told her. "I was a dick."

"It wasn't just you. I was being sensitive."

"No, it was me," he maintained, and felt the words leave his body quickly in order to get them out before she interrupted. "I was too worried about what people would say. I'm not embarrassed to be seen with you. I've just been so insistent on my privacy and protecting Dez that I lost sight of your feelings."

"Can we just stop with this?" Misha said. "We're both sorry. Let's put it behind us."

Trey nodded. "Okay, I'm glad."

"But that's not all."

He frowned. "What's going on?"

"I've got good news and bad news."

Despite the fact that they'd had a disagreement, she'd come to him with her news. He was glad that they'd put the nastiness behind them and could carry on... Depending, of course, on whatever the bad news was.

"Okay, bad news first," he instructed, and he braced himself, wondering what could be happening now.

"We're trending again, and not in a good way." She told him about the TikTok videos that were making the rounds. "The other investors must be freaking out. I'll have to be on the phone, first thing in the morning."

"Okay, we've seen that before. Nothing new."

"It's getting a lot of traction," she told him. I know you're not on the social media platforms, but when you're the main character and the top trend, it might not end so well."

He mulled it over. "Okay, fine. You're the expert on that, and I'll defer to you how we can combat it." Trey knew a lot about technology and stayed up on current trends, but when it came to social media trends, he may as well be a bull on a boat. "So, tell me the good news."

"Read this," she said, handing over a printout. He skimmed the words, and his eyes landed on the numbers. Despite the negative trends, user membership had increased. By a lot.

Trey's eyes widened. "Wow," he said, stunned. He knew there had been a lot of new accounts added, but he had no idea it had been so many. He pointed to the paper that was still in his hand. "And you thought that those news stories and the videos would cause problems for us, but I guess there's no such thing as bad publicity, right?"

She was smiling. The news hadn't fully erased the worry from her face. "I guess not. We still haven't gotten to the bottom of who hacked us. They need to be stopped."

"Your security team is on it, and they've reinforced any entry points. We're safe. There's nothing we can do about it tonight, is there?" She looked unconvinced. "Let's go out," he told her. "For dinner. Dez is with my parents. I think this calls for champagne." He was just as much celebrating the fact that k!smet was still succeeding as he was that Misha was in his home, actually speaking to him.

"Where?" she asked.

"I think we could get a table at Sheen."

She scoffed. "I think you're being a bit ambitious. Sheen is packed full every night, and you need reservations well in advance."

"Don't worry about that," he told her. "Why don't you let me make some calls."

Misha sipped from her water glass and looked around the restaurant. Sheen was the newest, and one of the nicest, most exclusive restaurants in Royal. Made entirely out of glass, the restaurant had a full house every night, and the bustling energy from the open, visible kitchen traveled throughout the air and resonated with the patrons. Sheen was sleek, sexy and frenetic and left Misha in mind of high-end restaurants in big cities, right here in Royal, Texas.

She looked across the table at Trey, and he smiled at her. They had certainly come a long way since the day he'd come into her office and told her there was a problem with the app. She'd been so unsure at that point and afraid that the app was going to fail, but now, she saw that *maybe* it wouldn't all fall apart on her.

"You look beautiful," he told her.

She smiled. Trey made her feel beautiful. "Thank you." Luckily, the little black dress she'd worn to work that morning made her appropriately dressed for the fanciest restaurant in Royal.

They enjoyed a quiet moment, then the waiter stopped at their table with the bottle of champagne Trey had ordered. With elegance, he opened the bottle and poured them both glasses, before setting the bottle in the table-side bucket and leaving them.

Trey handed over her glass.

"Cheers," she said, holding it aloft.

He tipped his glass to hers. "Cheers," he replied. "Are you feeling better?" he asked.

"I feel good," she told him. Her phone rang in her purse, and she reached for it. "Sorry," she told him. "I thought I muted it."

"It's okay. Answer it."

She looked at the screen and saw that it was the number of Victor, the head of her security team. "I have to answer this," she told him.

"Go ahead."

"Victor," she said, answering. "Do you have news for me?"

"I do," he told her.

And she felt herself still. This was it, the answers she needed. "Tell me."

"We've found evidence that the platform was compromised."

"Really?"

"Yeah, there were subtle signs, but nothing is untraceable. We feel that they manipulated the algorithm, and intentionally inappropriately matched users to their opposites."

"Any indication that users' information had been accessed or compromised?"

"We haven't been able to find any evidence of that. It looks like they bypassed the banks where the user and payment information was kept. It was intact and secure, and we did some searches on the dark web for names and email addresses and came up with nothing that had to do with us. I'd advise that you send out a warning to change passwords, but we think it'll be okay on that front."

Misha felt her blood run cold. It was reaffirming to know that the mistake wasn't something she'd done. But the platform had been vulnerable. The attack could have been so much worse. "Do you have any idea who's behind this?"

"We've been able to tie the location to Houston."

"Houston? Are you sure?"

"As far as we can tell. They covered their tracks. We only know because Sara is one of the best cyber hackers I've ever seen. So glad you hired her."

"Me, too. So, what now?"

"We're still looking into who is behind it, but on your end, there's nothing to worry about. The platform has been locked down and behind every security measure we have. It should be totally safe."

Misha nodded, taking in everything Victor had told her. "Okay, thanks, Vic. Let's talk more on Monday, okay?

"See you then."

When she disconnected the call, Trey was watching. "What is it?"

She told him everything that Victor had told her on the phone.

"Houston?"

"Guess which dating app is based in Houston?"

"How many guesses do I get?"

"None if you know it's HitMeUp!"

He nodded, taking in the information. "Interesting. They're behind the hacker."

"Stands to reason, right?"

"Sure does. The app is locked down for now. I'm going to meet with the team on Monday to see what our next steps are. Maybe Sara will have more information by then."

"So, you're saying there's nothing we can do about it right now?"

She shrugged. "I'll contact the other investors tomorrow and reassure them their investment is safe."

"And how do you feel about this news?"

She drank from her glass. "It's a huge violation, and really, users were so vulnerable in a space where they trust us to protect them. But it's over now. It's protected. But the fact that we were the victims of an attack makes me feel a bit better that I did create an app that works as it should. The mismatches came about because of the hacker, and I believe if we investigated, bots will be behind the social media reach of the negative press. Now it's just to figure out who, exactly, is behind it, and why."

"I agree. And just so you know, when the time comes to investigate and prosecute, you won't have to worry about paying any fees. I've got you."

"Thank you. I appreciate it."

"Let's move on, okay? At least for tonight."

They both raised their champagne flutes to their mouths, watching each other carefully. "How do you feel now?" she asked him. "We're here in a restaurant, surrounded by people. What must they all be thinking?"

"I'm sitting at a table with the most beautiful woman here," he answered simply. "I've realized that I don't give a damn what people say. You were right. It doesn't matter."

"And Dez?"

"Dez likes you, but I'm still a little apprehensive about involving him in anything."

"I understand that," she told him. "Don't rush anything you aren't ready for."

Neither of them were saying the words, but Misha knew that they were discussing pursuing a relationship together.

"Thanks."

"And to think we're sitting here tonight because the Surprise Me! function of the app matched Jericho and Maggie, and you were not impressed."

Trey laughed. "Please don't remind me."

"I've got a confession. Want to hear it?"

"Of course, I do."

"After all the scrutiny the app's been under, and all of the work that I've done on it, I've never used the Surprise Me! function."

"Oh, really?" he asked.

"Even more, my k!smet account is only on the networking section, and not even connected to the dating functions of the app."

"And why is that? You're not taken, are you?" he asked, slyly.

"The only men I've had in my company in a while are a tech enthusiast with the most amazing man cave I've ever seen, and an eight-year-old boy." She sipped her wine. "In the past couple of years, since I started working on k!smet, I never had much time for a relationship, or the energy. Back then, it was eighteen-hour days, surviving on iced coffee and hopes and dreams."

"It paid off."

"In some ways. But anyway, a relationship was

never a priority for me, especially since I had so much I wanted to accomplish."

"Well, now that we know k!smet is a resounding success, I have that chance."

She thought about her and Trey, and how they'd started working on the app together. K!smet had had a few stumbles along the way, but so had the two of them. Maybe it was worth them taking that risk together.

"There's time now, though," he reminded her. "Why not look for love on your own app? You know, if the algorithm is as flawless as you claim it is..." he trailed off, with a shrug.

That took her aback. She'd thought the underlying topic of conversation had been about them pursuing a relationship together. Was he actually sitting across from her in a romantic restaurant, suggesting that she look on her own app for a love match? She opened her mouth to retort, but he was grinning. "You're a jerk," she told him with a smile.

That made his smile grow. "Why not log in to the relationship function now?" he prodded. "While we're here. If it's as good at matching as you claim it to be, then maybe you'll find your happily after ever right here in this restaurant."

He was poking fun, of course, and without him even saying that they were beginning to build something together. She raised an eyebrow and pulled her phone from her purse. "Fine, I will." He was making a point to her that he still didn't quite believe the app to be solid, but she was prepared to call his bluff. She looked up to face him. "But first, you need to do something."

"What's that?"

"If I'm going to hit the Surprise Me! button, you have to do the same."

He waved her off. "I don't even have a k!smet account."

"You are such a liar," she said, pointing a finger at him. "I created the app. You think I don't know how to look up if a particular person has an account? You created an account before ByteCon."

"Are you saying that you looked up my account information? That has to be against the terms of service. Talk about an invasion of privacy."

"Did you read the terms of service?" she countered. When he shook his head, she continued. "That's right, no one ever does. I was well within my right to look you up."

"Sure, you were," he teased.

"So, what do you say, we both sign in and hit Surprise Me! and see what happens?"

"Sure." He pulled out his phone, and she watched as he opened the app.

"One," she started, her thumb hovering over the button. "Two. Three!"

They both pushed the buttons, and when she looked down and saw the profile that was displayed, she laughed. It was Trey's picture that met her on her screen.

He chuckled, and held up his phone, showing that her profile was also prominently displayed on his screen. "See? I told you the app was busted."

She playfully rolled her eyes. "The app works just as it should, and you know it."

Trey hummed behind pursed lips. "We're definitely compatible in lots of ways," he agreed. "I'll give the credit where it's due. You made a good app, and it's going to be responsible for bringing love to all sorts of people."

Misha held up her glass. "I'll drink to that." They touched glasses again. She liked being with Trey. She really liked him. Her gaze, however, drifted down to her phone screen. The same Surprise Me! function had already brought Jericho and Maggie together, and there was no doubt they were in love. Was k!smet trying to teach Misha and Trey the same lesson?

After dinner, Trey drove them back to her home, and when he parked in her driveway behind her own car, Misha noticed that he didn't cut the engine. She was confused, thinking they were both on the same page about where their night was headed. He looked down at her, his eyes questioning, and she realized he was waiting for an invitation. She put her hand on his thigh and leaned over the console, giving him a glimpse of the curve of her breast in the deep cut of her dress.

"Would you like to come in?" she asked, hoping, knowing, the answer was yes.

"I thought you'd never ask," he said with a smile and pushed the ignition button, finally turning off the car. They got out of the car, and he followed Misha closely up her driveway. Her porch light was on, and the golden light was shining down on them as he came up right behind her when she keyed in the combination for her electronic door lock. She got the numbers wrong and tried again. It took two more tries before she entered the correct numbers in their correct order, and the green light let her know they could enter. Before she could open the door, however, Trey dropped a kiss on the top of her shoulder that caused a shiver down her spine, and she leaned back into him, enjoying the way his body curled perfectly around hers.

In his arms, she knew that she was secure, protected. Anything could happen in her life—k!smet could fail, anything could happen—but it wouldn't matter if Trey was there. Her feelings for him had come about so quickly, so forcefully, and she hadn't even seen it coming. They had long since transcended physical desire, or even need, in a way she'd never experienced before in any of her other relationships.

"Are we going in?" he whispered in her ear, his lips skimming over the outside of her ear, shaking her from her trance. "Unless you want your neighbors and all passersby to see all the things I want to do to you."

Her abdomen quivered, and she exhaled a shaky breath. "Yeah," she laughed. Although, she was interested in finding out what sorts of things he wanted to do with her. On the porch, in her house, it didn't matter, she would let him do them. But at the moment, she couldn't seem to move.

"So, which is it?" he asked. "Out here, or inside?" He paused and smoothed his hands around her to flatten against her stomach. "Open the door, Misha."

She didn't need to be reminded again. She pushed the door open, and they walked inside. She turned around to face him, and he grasped her by the waist, tickling her sides and she giggled.

"Lead the way," he told her.

Taking him by the hand, she walked him to her bedroom. He was so close her, she could feel his breath against the nape of her neck, the pounding of his heart beat against her spine.

The normally short walk to her bedroom seemed to take forever, but when they finally made it, he grasped her hips, whipped her around to face him. He picked her up and tossed her in the center of her mattress, and he followed her down, lying on top of her, pressing his weight against her.

Misha wrapped her arms around his neck and pulled him to her, kissing him frantically. She couldn't get enough of his kiss, the way he tasted, the way his tongue felt against hers, the way his warm, strong body pressed against hers.

Her legs locked around his waist, pulling him nearer. It wasn't possible to get him as close as she wanted. They were still fully dressed, and she wished the barriers between their skin were gone. She put a hand between them, found his hard length, and grasped him through his pants. His lips were on hers and moaned into her mouth, sending a pleasant vibration through her.

Misha pushed on his shoulders, rolling them over so that she was on top of him, straddling his hips with her thighs. He chuckled at her, and she leaned over and kissed him briefly on his mouth. She rose up on her knees, and when he pushed himself upward to a sitting position, she took the opportunity to unbutton his shirt and pull it from his body. He reached behind her and lowered the zipper of her dress, and reaching for the bottom hem, she pulled the garment over her head, leaving her in just her bra and panties.

Trey smoothed his fingers over her ribs to the back clasp of her bra and reached back to unclasp her bra.

He discarded of the lacy material and discarded it on the floor. When he reached for her breasts, she playfully pushed his shoulders, so he lay flat down on the mattress.

Misha scooted back so that she was straddling his knees, and she pulled down his pants and boxers. Her eyes on Trey's, she lowered over him. Licking her lips, she took him in her mouth, tasting him, savoring.

His heavy groan filled the room, and she smiled up at him, to see that Trey was watching her, his eyes locked on hers. "Misha," her name rumbled past his lips, "that's so good. But if we want this to last more than the next few minites, you need to stop right now."

Without warning, he grasped her by her upper arms and pulled her up to face him. He kissed her and then rolled over so that he was on top of her, pinning her to her mattress. He reached lower, and pulled off her panties, leaving them both naked, and touched her in a way that made her entire body shudder, and a whimper escape as the air pushed from her lungs.

He groaned roughly in her ear. "You're so hot, Misha," he murmured. "So sexy. I just want to spend the night hearing you make that sound."

Keeping his body pressed against her, he reached for his pants, on the floor beside the bed. Misha was a ball of need, so tightly-wound, that she held herself still— afraid that if she moved, she might just explode. Just a touch from his fingers or his breath on her sensitive skin would be enough to bring her over the edge. Trey returned to her, after retrieving a condom from his wallet. Removing the latex from its foil wrapper, and then using one hand, he deftly rolled it over himself. He positioned himself between her knees and entered her in one quick thrust.

Misha cried out as he filled her, digging her finger-nails into his back. His hips pumped, forcing the breath from her lungs every time he filled her. She raised her hips, as well, in time with his, meeting him with every thrust. Their cries and the sound of her headboard crashing against the wall filled the room, and it didn't take long for Misha to feel the familiar swirl of pleasure in her stomach and spread throughout her entire body. Holding onto Trey's shoulders She gripped him tightly, allowing him to bring her to the full height of his orgasm. She arched against him, and he held her tightly, his hips still pumping. It was only a few more beats before he stilled, shouted his release and collapsed over her, his arms supporting his weight. He rolled onto his back and quickly disposed of the condom, before pulling her to rest on his chest. For several beats, they were silent, as they caught their breaths.

Misha swirled her fingers in his chest hair, and he chuckled.

"What's so funny?" she asked him.

"Earlier, when we matched on k!smet," he started.

"What about it?"

His fingers curled against her body, tickling her, making her giggle. "I said there must be something wrong with the app," he said. "Looking at us now, how compatible we are, I think we make a pretty good match."

Twelve

Trey wasn't sure why his father had summoned him to the Winters Industries building. Trey might be the second-in-command at the company, but he preferred to work from home, leaving his office on the premises empty most of the time.

Trey walked to the desk of his father's administrative assistant, Kelly.

"Hi, Trey, Joseph is waiting for you."

"Excellent, thank you."

He walked into his father's office, and saw he wasn't alone. Also seated were Jericho and Maggie. And Misha. "Hey, folks. What's going on?"

"Trey, have a seat." Joseph motioned to the empty chair next to Misha.

He passed Misha on his way to the chair. She looked up and smiled. He winked at her, remembering just the night before when he'd looked down at her.

Once he was settled, Joseph addressed Misha. "Misha, you've got the floor."

"Maggie and I were talking this morning," Misha started. "As we know, Defrost is tomorrow night," she started.

Trey nodded. Defrost was the annual black-tie charity event held by the Winters family at the Texas Cattleman's Clubhouse, which raised large amounts of money to give back to local farmers each year. It was one of the eminent social events of the year, with all of the town's movers and shakers in attendance with open checkbooks.

Misha continued. "Maggie and I thought it would be a great opportunity to hype up the app, in a brand sponsorship way, and push it across the platform, as a fundraiser."

"That's a great idea."

"But not only that," Maggie said. "Jericho and I, and also Joseph, agree that it would also be a great way to build the momentum of the truce between the Del Rio and the Winters families. I've been talking to some family members, and they would love to attend. It will make us all look like a united front to the public, but it will also bridge some gaps between the families."

"Is that right?" Trey asked. Misha's head whipped around, and she looked at him. "You're all in agreement?" he asked his father and brother.

"We are," Joseph said. "Now that Jericho and Maggie are together, it would be worthwhile to see the feud ended."

"Well, if you're all in agreement, I guess there isn't much I can add, now, is there?"

"You clearly have something to add," Jericho accused. "You may as well say it here."

"I'm fine with it," Trey said, a little short. He was unsure why he was upset. Perhaps it was that the family feud was deeply ingrained in him. Perhaps it was that he'd walked into the room as the only person unaware of the plan that had been building without his input. "Whatever makes more money for the charity."

"Great," Joseph said, clasping his hands together on top of his desk. He addressed Misha. "Is there enough time to do what you need to arrange with k!smet to make the brand partnership happen?"

"Yes," she assured him. "We'll make it a priority, and we can get everything in place this evening."

"Alright. I guess that's everything."

Along with Misha, Maggie and Jericho, Trey stood, and they quietly exited the office. In the hallway, Jericho reached out for Trey, stopping him from leaving. "Is everything okay on your end?" he asked.

"I'm fine." He faced the women. "Those were great ideas. I just don't like being blindsided. That was all very quick. I just don't like feeling like I'm out of the loop."

"You weren't left out of the loop," Misha told him. "Everything came together very fast this morning." *This morning*, meaning after he'd left her house. She had spent the night with him, planning to see his father about her ideas.

"I'm glad that got resolved," Jericho added. "This will be good for both of the families, and the charity." He clapped Trey on the back. "We'd better get going."

Trey and Misha held back, only walking when Jeri-

cho and Maggie were out of sight. "So, you'll be at Defrost?" he asked.

"I hadn't originally planned on going, but after strat-
egizing how k!smet could be a part of it, I guess I am."

"Well, I'm assuming you need a date, then."

She shrugged. "I was planning on going stag and
seeing where the night takes me. Can't limit my op-
tions, right?"

Trey laughed. "I guess not. But in the event that you
would like a date, would you consider letting me take
you?"

"I was hoping you'd ask."

"Great." He took her hand in his and brought it to his
lips. "I'll pick you up tomorrow at seven thirty."

Thirteen

Trey pulled Misha close as they walked into the Texas Cattleman's Clubhouse. The TCC, a large, single-story building, had been built in 1910 and was the social hub in Royal. Its high ceilings and stone and wood-paneled walls had been elegantly decorated with lights and crystals to resemble a winter wonderland. Even the hunting trophies and historical artifacts that lined the walls and its luxurious furnishings fit the theme. Pushing a finger beneath his collar, he pulled the material of his tuxedo shirt from his throat. Trey loved Defrost, but he hated the formal wear required for the event.

"You look beautiful tonight," Trey told her. She was wearing a black, floor-length gown, and her normal wavy bob was straight and sleek.

"Thank you," she said. "You clean up pretty well yourself."

When they walked farther into the room, they saw

that the party was already in full swing. Members of the Del Rio and Winters families mixed and mingled throughout the crowd. Trey knew that he and his family were coming around to the idea of making peace, but he was shocked to learn Maggie's family was coming around, too. He knew, though, that if they could get through the evening without any incident, they would be well on their way to peace.

Trey looked around and noticed that some appraising glances were being sent their way. People were, no doubt, interested in what was brewing between them, curious about Trey's very public dates with Misha. It surprised him, however, that he wasn't bothered by it. There were other things that picked at his gut about their relationship, but he no longer cared what random people thought.

"Maggie's over there," Misha said, waving to her friend. "I'm going to say hi."

"Should I grab you a drink?" he asked.

"A white wine would be great."

"You got it."

Trey walked over to the bar and ordered Misha's wine and an old-fashioned for himself. Jericho soon joined him and leaned against the bar, waiting for his own drink.

"This place looks great," Jericho said.

"It does. The decorators really outdid themselves this year."

Jericho accepted his drink from the bartender with a "Thank you." Trey followed his brother's gaze across the room to where Misha and Maggie were chatting. "Misha looks beautiful tonight," Jericho noted.

"As does Maggie."

"She does, doesn't she?" he asked with a grin. He drank from his glass. "It's interesting that you brought Misha here tonight."

"Is it?"

"You normally come to these types of events alone."

Trey shrugged. "Misha and I have been working closely on k!smet."

"Yeah, I heard about all of that overnight work, re-member?"

"Shut up," he said laughing. "I thought it would be good to show a united front for the app before the IPO launch. And to support your own very public match."

"Are you sure that's it?"

"What else could there be?" Trey asked, obtusely.

"You've been hanging out with Misha a lot, and watching you two tonight, I just thought there might be more going on." Trey said nothing, and Jericho laughed. "I knew it. You like her."

Trey sighed. There was no point in denying it any longer. People would talk—they'd wonder about the feud, with Misha being so close to the Del Rios. "Okay, fine," he admitted. "I do like her. A lot."

Trey couldn't remember a time in his life when he'd been more wrapped up in a woman. It had been quick, unexpected, but Misha had taken his life by storm, and he knew that there was no going back for him. Not even his relationship with Cassandra, which had been a whirlwind in itself, could have compared to the way he felt about Misha.

"It should have been obvious when I saw that you introduced her to Dez." When Trey frowned, Jericho continued. "And he seemed to really like her."

"He does, and she likes him, too."

"Is that problem, then?"

"It's all happened so quickly. Where could we go from here? I know that Misha isn't Cassandra, but she's talked about how hard it is to maintain a regular, consistent personal life with her job. Kids require a lot of time and attention. What if this goes further and he becomes attached to her? What if she decides that isn't the kind of life she wants? She could walk out. What would that do to Dez?"

"That's a lot of *what-ifs*."

"I'm realistic about the future."

"You're borrowing trouble, is what."

"I have Dez to worry about," he said. "It's not just me."

"And what would it do to you?" Jericho asked.

It would crush him. "Nothing."

"That's BS and you know it. I haven't seen you this way with another woman, not even Cassandra."

"She's not like Cassandra," he said, his voice firm. And that was true. After such a short time, Trey was beginning to feel closer to Misha than he'd ever felt with her. Was it love? He wasn't going to let himself go that far. Nothing good would come from it. It would just lead to Dez being hurt.

"Why not let yourself enjoy it?" Jericho asked.

"There's too much on the line. We're just so different," he said. He gestured at her across the room as she held court, speaking to a group of people, her charisma more than apparent. She shone brightly in a crowd, while

Trey like to stay to the side, keeping his distance from others. "She's so public and outgoing and has to display everything on social media. I'm not like that."

"It sounds like you're trying to find reasons to talk yourself out of it. So, what if you have differences?" Jericho asked. "That's the fun part. I've found myself in the middle of a long-standing family feud, and you don't see me complaining about differences."

Trey shrugged and drank from his glass. He'd never say it, but maybe his brother was right. "I guess."

Jericho pushed away from the wall. "I'm going to go ask my beautiful date if she'd like to dance." He stopped in front of Trey. "Listen, Trey, life is too short. Make sure you don't pass up what might be a chance at happiness, just because you might be a little different."

Trey didn't respond, as Jericho finished his drink. He would have to figure out his feelings for Misha. "Yeah, I guess," he said finally. "Maybe the most unlikely match is the best one."

Misha looked across the ballroom and saw Trey and his brother Jericho talking. She wondered how much he was telling his brother about their relationship. They'd agreed to keep everything between them secret, but neither Maggie nor Jericho was stupid and could likely see that something was building between them. Maybe keeping a secret was harder than they'd thought it would be.

"So, you're here with Trey tonight," Maggie said, a statement instead of a question.

"Yeah. After the meeting at Joseph's office yesterday, we thought we may as well come together. He's k!smet's main investor. It'll also help show off the united front of the Winters family and yours."

"I appreciate that. It feels like some of the heat from the feud is dying down for us lately," Maggie said. "The feud has been going for so long. It's hard for some to put the past to rest."

"And you know how small towns are," Misha said. "I love Royal, but there's no shortage of gossip to fuel the rumor mill."

"You've got that right."

Maggie leaned in closer. "And you have some gossip brewing yourself," she noted.

"Are you sure?"

"I see the way you look at each other. I don't believe there isn't anything there. Especially with you spending the night as his house. That can't be innocent."

"It's nothing. We're friends." *Friends who sleep together every chance they get,* she added silently.

"Yeah, sure," Maggie said with an eye roll. "It's great for me, though. It'll take all the heat off Jericho and me, if there's another couple involved in the truce between the families."

Misha ignored the remark. "Although, it's funny," she added. "Trey was so critical of the Surprise Me! function, so we both tried it the other night at dinner, and we were a match."

"Of course, you were," Maggie said. "I knew the app worked just fine. You and Trey may be fighting the truth, but I know there's something going on, whether or not you want to admit it."

Misha knew that no matter what the gossip mongers thought, she and Trey could keep denying that there was anything going on between them. She didn't want to draw too much attention to themselves before the IPO launch; she didn't want the business suffering because people were too busy trying to determine if she and Trey were together.

She gazed to where he stood across the room. At that moment, his eyes found hers, and the way he looked at her pulled the breath from her chest.

Maggie shook her head and gave a giggle. "I think you've both got it bad."

"We're just friends," she repeated softly, more to convince herself than anyone else. She was lying to her friend, however. She knew that there was more to their relationship than just friendship. In him, she could see the stability she'd always craved, the family, the love. She wanted all of that. With Trey and his son.

Before Maggie could retort, Jericho was at their side, asking Maggie to dance. She accepted and left Misha standing alone.

But Misha wasn't alone for long before Trey was at her side. "Having fun?" he asked.

"Oh, you know it. I love being grilled by my friends about our relationship." She'd said the word accidentally. "Or, whatever this is."

He seemed to have ignored her slipup, and he smiled down at her. "You know," he started. "I'm a little bored. Do you want to get out of here?"

There was nothing Misha wanted more than to go wherever Trey led her. Misha was in trouble, and she knew it.

Fourteen

Trey was a ball of need as he led Misha from the club-house to his car. He opened the passenger-side door and she sat. He pushed the ignition button, but instead of driving out of the lot, he reached for Misha and pulled her into his arms. He dropped his lips to hers and tasted her. He needed her like he needed air to survive. She moaned and leaned farther into the kiss. He sought out her tongue with his own. He smoothed his hands up and down her back, and her fingers were in his hair, grip-ping, needy. He reluctantly extricated himself from her, lest he take her then and there, in his car, in the middle of a busy parking lot.

"My place or yours?" he asked her.

"Yours is closer," she said, as breathless as he was.

"Good call."

"Is Dez home?" she asked.

"No, he's sleeping at a friend's house."

Exceeding the speed limit, Trey made it to his ranch in record time. Once parked, he came around and opened her door, and he rushed her inside. He shut the front door and pinned her against it, and, taking her chin in the crook between his thumb and forefinger, his lips again found hers. He wasn't sure what had happened earlier that night, but between his conversation with his brother at the bar and walking up to her, he'd become absolutely rigid with need for Misha.

Trey pressed a trail of kisses from her shoulder to the sensitive crook where it met her neck and clocked her sigh when he traced small circles over her sensitive skin with his tongue. The sigh, however, was followed by a quick gasp when he nipped her with his teeth. He inhaled against her neck. She smelled of lilacs and summer, and he didn't think that he would ever get enough of the scent mingled with the smell of desire on her skin.

He caught his reflection in the mirror on the adjacent wall and saw his own desire-flushed cheeks. Misha did something to him. This woman, this gorgeous, sultry, sexy woman was with him. She arched against the wall at her back and thrust her breasts toward him. He moaned and palmed her breasts through the soft material of her dress. She was absolutely perfect in every way. At that moment, he couldn't imagine not being with her for even a minute. He pushed down that feeling, unsure of what it meant, afraid that it meant something serious. He stopped, held still, closing his eyes and taking deep, careful breaths, needing a moment to compose himself. When he was with Misha, she controlled his senses, short-circuited his brain, so that his only impulse was to get her in his bed. His breath washed over her neck, warming her skin and hopefully sending every one of her nerve endings into high alert. His fingers traveled slowly, grazing up her neck to the base of her skull, into her hair. He lightly massaged her skull, and then he tightened his grip into fists, grasping her hair once again. He brought her face up to meet his, and he looked at her. He knew she could see the heat and the passion in his eyes, along with a hunger that he'd hoped she'd never seen on another man's face. He wanted her, only her, and there was absolutely no doubt.

He couldn't wait any longer, so he lifted her. The high slit in her dress allowed her the room to wrap her legs around his waist. Barely feeling her weight on him, he walked to his main-floor bedroom. He lowered her to the floor and shucked off his blasted tuxedo jacket, and she kicked off her heels. Without the shoes, she was about four inches shorter than him, and she reached up and wrapped her arms around his neck, pulling him to her.

He pulled her close, flattening his hands against her back, and he lowered the zipper on her dress. He crushed his mouth against hers and slid her dress down her body, and she was left in a nude-colored lacey bra and panties set, with matching thigh-high stockings. "My God," he muttered, looking down at her, his hunger for her growing by the second. "I want you more than I've ever wanted another person." His brain was too fogged with desire to determine what that feeling was—lust... Love? That thought gave him a pause that he could analyze all he wanted later. For now, he wasn't even able to string couldn't string two thoughts together that didn't involve how much he needed Misha.

She took several steps back, until she reached the

foot of his bed. She sat and smoothed her hands over his duvet. "Well, come and get me."

When Misha saw the way Trey's eyes darkened, Misha briefly wondered if she should regret her challenge to him. He came towards her, ripping his shirt from his body. He kicked off his shoes and pushed down his pants. He gripped her by the waist, and she squealed when he easily tossed her farther up the bed.

He joined her on the mattress, and took her mouth again. There was a ferocious quality to the way he kissed her. When her lips parted under his, he thrust his tongue into her mouth, and entwined with her own. She sighed into his mouth, and it seemed to spur him on. She caressed his cheek, and he took each of her wrists in his large hands and pinned them to the mattress on either side of her head.

He dragged his lips across her jawline and down her neck, across the swells of her breasts until he found her lace-covered nipple beading underneath the material. He closed his lips over it and nipped lightly, making her give a light, high-pitched cry.

Trey removed his hands from her wrists and undid the front clasp of her bra. The material gave way and her breasts spilled into his waiting hands. He hooked his thumbs underneath the edges of her panties and slid them down her thighs. But for her stockings, she was completely naked, exposed to him. She could *feel* his eyes on her, roaming over her figure just like a caress of his hand.

He took one nipple, between his lips and nipped, as he palmed her other breast, massaging her, teasing her until she arched her back, pushing her body against his.

He slid his hand down her abdomen. With every inch, as he got closer to her center, she became more and more tightly wound.

He finally reached his target, and he slid against her most sensitive bundle of nerves. *Finally!* She shuddered, crying out at his touch as he stroked her. Trey's touch was too much for her. Her pleasure drew closer, and she cried out her release, shuddering in his arms.

He kissed her deeply, and settled between her still-quaking thighs. She didn't know anything but her need for him, and she was desperate to get it, at any cost. Without thinking, she shifted her pelvis to line up with his, urging him to take her.

"Hang on, babe," he told her. "You have no idea how much I want you too, but just give me one second to get ready." He reached into a bedside table and withdrew a condom. Misha couldn't believe how she'd managed to forget one of her golden rules when it came to sex.

"Well, just do it, then," she told him, her voice impatient.

His eyes flashed fire at her orders, but then he grinned as he covered himself. "My pleasure."

He leaned over her and took her hips, lining up their bodies. Then he was inside of her. She wasn't sure how, but every time with Trey, he managed to shock her, steal her breath, sizzle her nerve endings. He pushed deeper, hitting that magical spot within her. She writhed underneath him, and she closed her eyes, overcome with the feeling. Trey touched her cheek, his fingertips so gentle and incongruous with the frenetic, wild way he was taking her.

Opening her eyes, she was back in the moment with him. Her eyes locked with his, as he thrusted, flexed, entering and withdrawing, bringing them both to the height of pleasure.

"Trey," she cried out, unable to stand the delicious feeling that came over her, and she watched enraptured as Trey threw back his head, his groan—loud and coarse. The cords of his throat straining, and he shuddered before collapsing, so that he supported his weight on his forearms on either side of her head.

"Misha…" he trailed off, whispering against her throat, tracing his thumbs along her swollen lips. When he looked into her eyes, it was like he was looking into her, and she knew he was leaving something left unsaid.

"I know," she whispered back, completely spent.

Misha was spent. And when Trey rolled over and gathered her close, she nestled against the strong wall of his chest. She and Trey had been together before, but this time was different. She felt her own heartbeat in time with Trey's, and for the first time, she felt an extra beat pulsate within her chest. And she didn't have to look too deep into her feelings to know that it was love.

Fifteen

Misha awoke with her cheek on Trey's chest, her legs entwined with his. She felt him shift and looked up to see that he was smiling at her.

"Mornin'," he greeted her with a sleepy drawl.

"Morning," she returned, snuggling closer. "Last night was...incredible."

"Yeah, it really was," he agreed.

"I hope no one minds that we left Defrost very early." She looked up.

He shook his head. "The event had a great turnout. My parents will be thrilled so many friends and supporters showed up. No one would've missed us. But I'll probably have to talk to Dez soon."

"What are you going to tell him?"

"The truth. That we like each other. But it's new, and we're talking things slow?"

She gestured to their naked bodies under the sheet.

"I don't know, Trey. I don't think we're exactly moving at a snail's pace here."

"Maybe parts of this are moving more quickly than others."

She glanced at the bedside clock and reluctantly pushed herself out of bed. "I should get going. I've got a meeting at nine that I should prepare for." She stopped. "I totally forgot, I left my car at TCC."

"I can give you a ride to pick it up."

"Thanks," she said. "I have a meeting, so I don't have any time for funny business, okay?"

He held up his hands. "Fair warning. I'll keep my funny business to myself."

After picking up her car, Misha walked into her condo, wearing her evening gown from the night before. She and trey had parted ways outside the TCC with a soft kiss in the front seat of his truck, and managed to separate before it went too far.

In her bedroom, she peeled her dress from her body and discarded it in her dry-cleaning pile, inhaling as she caught the scent of Trey's cologne as it lingered. Her heart rate sped up as her scent memory brought her back to the night before with Trey. There had been something different between them, as he looked into her eyes and held her. Their relationship was so new, so fresh, that it seemed implausible that she could be falling in love with him. How it had happened, she dind't know. But all she knew now was that she didn't think she could be apart from him.

They hadn't discussed what was happening between them in explicit terms, but last night had meant something, and the feelings just intensified every time they were in the same room. He'd even introduced her to his son, and even though she wasn't sure what it meant, she knew there was special.

Once showered, Misha pulled on her bathrobe and made her way to the kitchen to get some much-needed caffeine. The aroma filled her kitchen, and she knew she would take every ounce of caffeine she could get in order to function for the day and get through her meeting.

Her phone had been left, forgotten, in her purse, and when Misha retrieved it, the black screen told her that the battery had died overnight. Sipping her coffee, she plugged the phone into the wall socket and watched it come to life in her hand.

Misha sat at the table, the sun rays pouring into her kitchen, warming her. The large kitchen windows and morning sunlight were her favorite things about the condo and part of the reasons why she'd bought it. The morning was her quiet time, in which she could just sit and think about her upcoming day, without the noise and distraction of the rest of her life. For the first time in a long time, however, the only mental noise and distraction she felt like thinking about was Trey. As part of her morning routine, she thumbed the screen of her phone and opened the tech news website that was typically her first digital stop of the day. Casually, she brought her mug to her lips, waiting for the page to load, but almost spit her coffee out on the table when she saw the top headline in the Texas section.

"Is it k!smet for dating app founder and Texas tech investor?" the headline read. Misha cringed when she saw a picture of them leaving Defrost together the night before. It was only early in the morning, but already the story had racked up an impressive number of page views and shares.

Despite the recent social media storm detailing controversial and disastrous matches, it looks like founder Misha Law has made a love match of her own. Our reporters have been in Royal, Texas, since ByteCon and caught Ms. Law hurriedly leaving a fundraising ball on the arm of the tech investor and second-in-command at Winters Industries, Trey Winters. We don't need to mention what we saw the two doing in a car in the parking lot just after this photo was taken.

Misha couldn't even read the rest of the article. She had to talk to Trey, and it certainly wouldn't be an easy conversation.

"What kinds of things did you do at Timmy's last night?" Trey asked Dez as he poured himself a coffee. He'd just gotten back home after picking up Dez at his friend's house just a few minutes ago.

"You know, the usual," his son told him. "We watched some movies, played video games."

"Sounds fun."

"What did you do last night?"

"I went to the Defrost fundraiser."

"With Misha?"

Trey swallowed hard. He knew that he had to talk to Dez about whatever was developing between him and Misha, but he wasn't sure how. "She was there," he simply told him.

"Was it a date?"

"How would that make you feel if it was?"

Dez smiled. "Good. I like her."

"I do, too." Trey liked Misha. His son did, too. So why was it so hard for him to make a commitment to her? He was taking a huge leap, and if she left, if he drove her away, it would crush Dez, and he couldn't risk that.

"I've got something to tell you, Dez."

"What is it?"

"Misha and I have been seeing each other a lot lately. We do like each other, and if you're okay with it, she'll be coming around here more often."

"She's your girlfriend?"

"She might be," Trey answered him honestly. "Would that be okay?"

"Yeah, that'd be cool."

Trey smiled. He'd thought that would be the hard part. But he should have known that Dez would have taken any opportunity to spend time with a tech goddess like Misha. Trey drank his coffee, satisfied that his romantic life might start to turn around.

"Whoa!" Dez said from the table as he looked at his phone.

"What's up?" Trey asked, walking over to him, looking over his shoulder.

"My YouTube channel has, like, five thousand new subscribers."

"What?" Trey asked, holding out his hand for Dez to hand him his phone. He checked the subscriber list and saw that Dez was right—his subscriber count had gone way up, seemingly overnight. Unease trickled up Trey's spine as he opened Dez's TikTok account. The follower count had also risen dramatically.

"What's going on?" Dez asked.

"I don't know," he said. "But I'm going to get to the bottom of it before you get this back."

"But Dad…"

"No *buts*." His own phone beeped beside him. It was a text from Jericho, who'd sent him a link. He clicked on it and saw a photo of him and Misha leaving Defrost together the night before. "What the hell?"

"What's wrong?"

"Nothing," he said quickly. "Everything is fine."

There was a knock on the door, and as Trey walked to the foyer to answer it, he skimmed over the article. When he arrived at the door, he opened it without looking. And he wasn't surprised to see Misha standing there.

"Hi," she said, looking down at the phone in his hands. "You've seen it."

He nodded. He couldn't even speak.

"Misha, hi!" Trey turned and saw that Dez had come from behind him to greet her.

"Hi, Dez!" She waved back.

Trey turned to his son. "Dez, why don't you go out to the stable and see if there are any chores for you to do? You can start earning that allowance."

Dez pouted, but Trey was thankful he didn't argue. "Okay. Bye, Misha."

"Bye, Dez."

When they were alone, Trey ushered Misha into the kitchen. "Do you have any idea how this happened?"

She shook her head. "They have reporters in town. I never would have imagined that anyone would care what we do in our personal lives."

"'Trey Winters is known for his high-risk, high-reward investments in tech start-ups. When he's not second-in-command at Winters Industries, he is at home on his ranch with his son, Dez—'" Trey looked up at Misha "'—who has, at the age of eight, built his own large social media following.'"

"Trey—"

"They found and printed my son's social media handles," Trey said.

"It's bad," she agreed. "This reads like a gossip blog, I know. We've gotten publicity for the app before."

"Is this what you think it is?" he asked. "Publicity for a damned hook-up app?"

"How dare you talk about my work like that!"

"Is that where this came from? Are you so addicted to every story—good and bad—coming out and boosting your numbers that you don't see how royally screwed up this is?"

"No, Trey. I can't believe that you would think that about me."

"My son is eight years old, and I was afraid of him being dragged into this."

"Well, maybe your eight-year-old shouldn't be on social media," she said.

"Don't you dare question my parenting." She was right, of course. Maybe Dez was too young for the internet, social media and all of the gadgets he'd given him. He realized that he'd been giving in to Dez and fostering his hobbies because he didn't want his son to feel like he'd missed out on not having his mother around.

"I'm sorry. I shouldn't have said that."

"Maybe you're right." He sighed. "I didn't see it happening like this, though. I thought the worst thing in the world would be you walking away from us and breaking his heart. But instead, you've exposed me, and him, to public scrutiny. I can't forgive that."

"You think I did this. You think I leaked to a news site that we were sleeping together and that we'd make a show for anyone at the fundraiser?"

"No," he told her. "I don't think you leaked it. But it was released because of you."

"That's not my fault."

"I know it isn't. But perhaps it's a sign that I was right about keeping my life secret, and keeping Dez shielded. I think it's best we just go back to how things were."

"What do you mean?"

"Let's go back to only being professionally affiliated. It's best that way. We'll work together when it comes to k!smet, and my investment. But that's it. Before this gets too out of control and it's too hard to walk away."

She looked away from him, and Trey regretted every word when he saw the way tears filled her eyes, threatening to fall. "Okay," she said quietly. "Sounds good. Let's do that."

"Misha," he said, reaching for her, but she quickly moved away from his touch.

"I'm fine," she told him. "I'm going to go. I have my meeting soon. I'm really sorry about what happened with the article."

"Yeah, me, too."

"I'll be in touch about anything you need to know about k!smet, alright?"

He nodded. "Yeah, do that."

Without looking at him, Misha turned her back and walked out of his kitchen, and regrettably, he knew, out of his life.

Sixteen

At her desk, Misha tried to focus on the computer monitor in front of her. But instead of seeing the lines of code that she could typically read like a second language, she saw nothing but black squiggles and lines of gibberish. After leaving Trey's ranch, she'd come straight to the office, canceled her meeting and immediately called her lawyer to see what she could do about getting the story taken down, especially since it contained Dez's social media information. She picked up her coffee mug and brought it to her mouth but saw that the mug was empty. It was then she remembered that she'd drained it a while ago. She sighed and wished that she had the gall to ask someone to get her another.

There was a knock on the door frame of her office, and she looked up. She'd hoped it would be Trey and was equal parts disappointed and confused to see Emilia Scott standing there.

"Emilia, hi." She stood. "What can I do for you?"

"Can I come in?" she asked, her voice quiet. She looked away. It was surprising to see that she didn't look like the bold, confident woman she'd been on their previous meetings.

"Yeah, of course," she said, gesturing to the chairs lined up at the table.

"Misha," Emilia said. "I need to talk to you."

Emilia's tone put Misha on edge. "What is it?"

She took a seat across the table from Misha. "I'm about to contact media outlets, but I wanted to talk to you first about this."

"What's going on?"

Emilia took a deep breath, and she squared her shoulders. She clasped her hands together on the table in front of her. "I've spent the past few months doing some consulting work for HitMeUp!" she started.

"Really? What kind of work?"

"The usual stuff—user interface, security, you know how it goes. Several weeks ago, however, they contacted me for a confidential mission. It was all very vague, and it set my instincts on edge. I didn't sign anything, because by the end of the meeting I knew what they wanted. They were asking me to hack your platform, manipulate the code and the matching algorithm and create distrust of the platform."

Misha was shocked. She'd believed that HitMeUp! was behind the cyberattack, but she never would have believed that Emilia was involved. It took her several moments to compose herself. "What are you saying? Are you behind the wonky matches?"

"No," she said firmly. "I was solely consulting for

them. It was a job at the time, and a well-paying one at that. But then it became something else. They wanted me to use my skills to take k!smet down. They offered me a lot of money, and I have to be honest, I almost took it. And, as long as I'm being honest—" she looked down again "—I did get into your app. At ByteCon. I thought I'd have a little fun, sneaking around in places where I shouldn't be. But I swear to you, I didn't do anything malicious to you. I couldn't have. And I certainly wouldn't do anything to jeopardize your app."

"How am I supposed to believe you?" Misha asked. "You just admitted to accessing the back end of my platform. How do I know you're telling me the truth now?"

"You know I'm telling you the truth because I'm here. If I'd hacked your app, no matter the cyber security teams you had in place, there's no way you would know."

"You sound awfully sure of yourself."

"I'm awfully sure of my talent."

Misha knew in that moment that Emilia was telling the truth. "I believe you. Thank you for telling me. But what sort of reaction are you looking for? Obviously, none of this makes me happy."

"I know it doesn't. And I'm not looking for kudos here, but I want to let you know what you're up against. HitMeUp! wants k!smet out of business."

Misha nodded and looked away from Emilia. "Thank you for letting me know."

Even though Emilia hadn't admitted to hacking her app, she consulted for the company that contracted her do it. While Misha had been poring over her code to find out any problems, Emilia had been working with the company responsible. She'd liked Emilia, but she wasn't sure if she could trust her any longer.

"I'm so sorry that we're both wrapped up in this," Emilia said again. She stood. "I would understand if you never want to see or talk to me again."

"I need a little time to come to terms with it, I think," Misha said, in a more even tone than she imagined she could muster. "But thank you for telling me."

Trey was sitting behind the desk in his office at Winters Industries. He'd tried working from home, but every inch of his home office made him think of Misha, and the time they'd spent there together. It was the same thing as his bedroom, his shower, the back deck swing...

Their conversation replayed on a constant loop in his head, and while he regretted telling her they were over, he knew that it was for the best. Tell that to Dez, however. He'd heard them arguing, and as Trey had predicted, the boy had been upset that Misha wouldn't be coming around anymore. He'd accused Trey of driving away their friend, and then the boy had gone to his room, and then didn't re-emerge before he'd come to the office. Dez was upset, and that just proved to him that he'd been right about introducing his son to a woman.

Being right didn't fill the void in his chest where she'd taken up space. He opened another spreadsheet, this one showing his investments for the year, including the substantial amount he'd invested in k!smet. He couldn't escape her. She was everywhere. In his home, in his books, in his mind. In his heart.

His phone rang, coming to life beside him. He glanced over and felt his heart jump into his throat when he saw that it was Misha calling him. He reached for it, and, in anticipation, he almost fumbled the phone onto the floor.

He exhaled roughly and answered the call. "Hello?"

"Trey," she said. Her breathless voice put him in mind of the night when she'd whispered it into the darkness of his bedroom.

"Hey," he said in an affectation that was cooler than he felt. "What's up?"

"Something weird happened this morning, after I left your place. And I wanted to tell you before you heard it somewhere else."

"What's going on?"

"I was visited by Emilia Scott. She's a freelance cyber security specialist."

"And?" Trey listened as Misha told him about her visit. When she was done, he exhaled heavily. "And you believe her."

"I do. She didn't have to tell me anything, but she did. Why would she lie?"

"I don't know. So now we know that HitMeUp! was responsible for the hacking. I'll set up a meeting with our corporate lawyers and we can see where we go from there."

"I appreciate it."

"I meant what I said before," he told her. "I will help you and pay for any legal fees you incur."

"Thanks." She paused. "How have you been?"

"I'm well," he lied. "You?"

"Same," she said with a pause. "Actually, there's another reason I called you. It's better news."

"What is it?"

"We're moving ahead with k!smet's IPO launch. This week."

He smiled. This was it; this was where he saw his investment pay off. The IPO call was a huge deal, and taking k!smet public would launch the app into the stratosphere and place it amongst the big names in social networking apps. "That's incredible," he said. "It's everything you've worked so hard for."

"We worked hard," she corrected. "Me, you, everyone on the team. k!smet's success is everyone's success." Now that the conversation was on work, it flowed easily. They were right to limit their interactions to work-related topics. But the hollow space in his heart didn't feel any more fulfilled by it. But he could get over that. Right?

Trey didn't miss how they'd kept their conversation strictly to information about k!smet and the IPO launch. But what more was there to say? No matter how he felt about it, they were finished as a couple. He was still in love with Misha, but that wasn't enough.

"Oh!" Misha said on the other end, surprising him. "Head over to the local news site," she told him. "You'll want to see it."

He did as she'd instructed and loaded the news site. He was surprised to see a press conference underway. There was a podium set in front of a blue screen, with a scrum of reporters in front of it. He watched as a woman crossed the floor and stood in front of the podium.

He bumped up the volume to hear her speak. "Hello," the woman started. "My name is Emilia Scott. I'm a freelance cyber security consultant, and I'd like to make a statement."

Seventeen

With his drink in hand, Trey took a seat in one of the plush, leather chairs, across from his brother and father. He looked round the TCC clubhouse, and while the Defrost decorations had since disappeared in the days following the event, there was a buzz in the air as the events staff prepared for another event.

"What's going on here?" Trey asked.

"There setting up for the k!smet IPO announcement," Joseph said.

"That's happening here?"

"Yeah, it is. I figured that you had a hand in planning it, with how closely you and Misha have been working together on it."

At hearing Misha's name, Trey felt a clench in his chest. It had only been a couple of days since their fight in his kitchen, but after weeks of near-constant contact, he still missed her like she'd been gone a year. "With the exception of a phone call to let me know about the IPO, and the update on the security breach, we haven't exactly been in contact."

Jericho frowned. "Really? Why?"

"You all saw the pictures of us leaving Defrost the other night, and the article. They wrote about Dez, and I lost it."

"You took it out on Misha?"

"I said some things I shouldn't have," he said. "We decided that it's for the best if we only communicate and see each other when it comes to the app and our investment."

"Son, it didn't take a genius to see that something special was building between the two of you. You can't just drive her away when it's inconvenient."

"I didn't drive her away. I'm trying to protect my son. I should have stuck to my usual MO and not let him get to know her. Because now, after only a couple of weeks, she's gone and he's mad at me. It hurt him."

"And you?" Jericho asked, a sarcastic edge to his voice. "You're clearly doing fine and not upset at all."

"I'm doing just fine," he lied. "Things with Misha were a brief distraction, but now I'm refocused, and I know my instincts to not involve my son in my love life were spot-on."

"You look terrible," Joseph said bluntly. "When was the last time you shaved?"

Trey ran his hand over his jaw, the coarse stubble scratching his palm. "Just a couple of days," he said. "I'm trying a new look."

Neither his father nor brother looked convinced. "Why don't you talk to her, son?"

"She won't want to talk to me," he said. He'd said cruel things to her, and she had every right to avoid him.

"Try," Jericho said. "Humble yourself if you need to. If you've found someone you can see yourself falling in love with, then it would be worth it."

Even though he wasn't going to admit it out loud, he knew that the feelings he had for the woman, the love he had for her, were very real. "I have an idea," he said.

"Great," Jericho said. "How can I help?"

"You know, I might actually need Dez and Maggie for this."

Misha's palms were damp as she smoothed them down the jacket of her black suit. Normally, she hated such formal clothing, but as a woman in the tech field, she didn't have the luxury that her male counterparts might have, to stroll in wearing casual clothing, jeans, T-shirts... She needed to dress to be taken seriously, especially on a day as important as this one.

She looked around the TCC. In its normal, undecorated state, the great room was so elegant. She imagined the history these walls had seen throughout the years and thought of the men who'd made important decisions within them. The club had recently become more inclusive, and less of an Old Boys Club. When she thought of her own upcoming announcement, she knew that she and women like her were the future, and she hoped that they would find places where they belonged in these old-world settings, helping to edge them into the future.

Maggie came up to her and wrapped a supportive arm around her shoulders. "How are you feeling? Are you ready?"

Misha gave a nervous laugh. "I'm as ready as I'm going to be."

"This is such an amazing thing for you. I couldn't be prouder."

"Thanks. I actually can't believe it." She looked around the room and saw that Jericho and Joseph were both on hand, but there was a noted absence. "Have you seen Trey?" she asked Maggie.

She shook her head. "No, I haven't. Jericho has been trying to call him, but no answer. It's strange. I figured he'd be here. He is an investor."

"Yeah." She hadn't seen Trey since their fight a few days earlier, and while this was a triumphant day for her, it felt a little hollow because he wasn't there to share it with her. "This is important to him, as well. I didn't imagine that he'd skip it."

"And now here's the reason we're all here," the announcer at the podium told the crowd. "She's the creator and founder of k!smet, Misha Law."

Misha took her place behind the podium. The crowd was full of reporters and journalists that she recognized from the industry, but also those from the financial sector. From her vantage point, she skimmed the crowd, again looking to see if Trey had shown up. "Good morning, everyone," she started. "Thank you for coming. It's an exciting day for myself, everyone at k!smet and everyone who is looking for *the one* online. Today, we are announcing that we will be launching an IPO and making k!smet a publicly traded entity. Next week, we will be at the New York Stock Exchange to ring the opening bell. This remarkable success has come about through the tireless work of everyone at our organization and our investors to bring about a safe, authentic experience for every user. Information packets are currently being distributed for your use, but I will not be taking any questions at this time."

"What about Emilia Scott's allegations of sabotage against you, by HitMeUp!?" a reporter called from the crowd.

"That's still an ongoing investigation," she responded. "But I admire the strength and courage of Ms. Scott to come forward with the allegations, and she has my utmost appreciation. Thank you. I'll will now invite k!smet's controller, Jack LaSalle, to join you, and he will give you some of the key financial details." Misha took one final look at the crowd, and not seeing Trey among the faces, she stepped away from the podium.

"Great job!" Maggie told her and squeezed her in another hug. When they separated, Maggie was grinning. "You know, with the air conditioning up so high, it's chilly in here, don't you think?"

"Yeah, a little I guess."

"Want to step outside for a little bit?"

Misha looked to the podium, where Jack was handling all of the questions and details about the financial implications of the IPO. She wasn't needed on hand. "Yeah, sure."

They headed outside and took a seat on one of the benches in the garden of the clubhouse. The tall, thick trees kept them cool and shaded from the sun's powerful rays.

"I have to ask, have you seen Trey's TikTok video?"

The words, as Maggie said them, made no sense to Misha. "What are you talking about?" she asked her friend. "I know for a fact that Trey does not have a Tik-Tok account. He hates that kind of thing."

Maggie shrugged. "Are you sure about that? He must have changed his mind, I guess." She handed over her phone, and Misha took it. To her surprise, there was a video that Trey had apparently posted to his TikTok account, @TheTreyWinters. But before she pushed play, she saw the number of views it had gotten—close to two million. It had gone downright viral. It didn't make any sense.

She pressed her thumb against the screen, and she was treated to a video of Trey waist dancing to a catchy tune. She laughed at how awkward and uncomfortable he looked. Then the music stopped, and white text appeared on the screen. *POV: You were a complete fool for pushing away an amazing woman.*

"Okay, TikTokers, I need all of your help," he started. "I fell in love with a woman named Misha Law. You might have heard of her. She is the intelligent, beautiful, funny, caring woman that created the k!smet app—which you should all download, by the way—and I messed up. She doesn't follow me on here yet. I just made this account today, so I'm going to need you all to help get my message out to her. I'm sorry, Misha. I was stupid, stubborn, careless. Please forgive me. So, here's where you come in," he addressed the audience. "Like and share, duet or FYP it, and hopefully the message will get out and she'll see it."

Misha pressed the list of hashtags he'd used and saw that #MishaHesSorry was trending and led her to thousands of people who'd shared Trey's video alongside their own, asking Misha to forgive him.

"What is this?" she asked herself, amazed. She was stunned, almost speechless. Trey had a social media account, and he'd posted a video of himself dancing and profusely apologizing. It was the last thing she'd expected from him. Talk about your grand gestures... "This is ridiculous," she said, but when she turned her head, Maggie had disappeared. She'd been so engrossed in the phone that she hadn't even noticed.

She looked around the garden, and despite the flurry of activity that was going on in the clubhouse, the outside was quiet, and there was no one else around. There was movement to her left. She looked and saw that she wasn't completely alone. Trey was coming around the corner of the building, with Dez by his side, who was holding a bouquet of roses.

She watched as they made their way to her. When they were within a few feet of her, they stopped. "Misha, I'm sorry," Trey said.

"Misha, he's sorry," Dez echoed, holding out the flowers.

She laughed, accepting them.

"Did you like my video?" Trey asked. She would have expected him to be embarrassed, for exposing himself so fully, putting himself out there, online. But instead, he looked sure of himself in the knowledge that he'd done something brave for her.

"I did. It was unexpected, to say the least. I never thought the day would come that you would create any social media accounts," she told him. "But honestly, I have to say that the video was a bit cringe," she added with a playful wince.

"That's what *I* told him. It's so embarrassing," Dez muttered.

"And *The* Trey Winters as your profile name? Who do you think you are, exactly? Beyoncé?"

"I told him not to do that, as well," Dez added helpfully.

"Of course, you did," Misha said to the boy with a conspirator's wink.

"So, what else did you think?" Trey asked, clearly bracing himself for more criticism. He no longer looked like the sure and confident man he'd seemed to be before.

"I think that you've sufficiently embarrassed yourself in front of millions of people online, who must have taken pity on you in order to share it so many times."

"Not embarrassed," he corrected. "I prefer the word *humbled*."

She smiled and brought the flowers to her nose, looking up at Trey. "But it was also very sweet. You really put yourself out there, and I know how hard that must have been for you."

"It wasn't easy," he confessed. "But Dez helped a lot," he said, ruffling his son's hair.

"I'm sure he did."

Trey looked away and blew out a breath, before facing her again. "The most important question though is—are you able to accept my apology?"

She frowned at him. "You really hurt me."

"I know," he said, with a nod. "And I'm so sorry. I was being stupid and insensitive."

"And I also said some things I shouldn't have said. I'm sorry, too."

She took a step forward and looked up at him. "After all of that, putting it all on the line, how do you feel?"

"It was terrifying," he admitted. "And embarrassing. But only at first. Then I realized that it didn't matter because I needed you to know that you're the person I love."

"Love?" she asked, the air squeezing from her lungs. She had already been able to admit to herself that she loved him, but they had never traded those words.

He took a step toward her and slid both hands around her waist. "Yes, that's right. I love you, Misha. I know it's quick. And if it's too fast for you, then I understand. But there's no doubt in my mind that you're the person I want to be with every day and night for the rest of my life."

"What about everything that comes with me?" she asked. "The attention, the publicity, the social media stuff."

He shrugged. "I realized that I was wrong. And while it's not my favorite pastime, none of that matters to me. I just want you. I need you." He nodded down at Dez. "We both need you."

Misha felt tears rim her eyes as she looked at Trey and Dez in front of her—*her future* in front of her. This is what she'd wanted for her entire life—love, stability, security, a family.

"So, what do you say?" Trey asked. "Give me another chance?"

Misha nodded and took a step closer. She realized that giving him another chance meant taking a chance of her own, and letting herself be vulnerable with him. But as she looked at Trey and Dez, Misha knew that it would be more than worth it. Bringing her hands to his face, she drew him closer to her for a soft kiss on his lips. "Yes. Let's take another chance."

They kissed, and Misha had never felt something so right. She was at home in Trey's arms. He was her future.

"Do you have any plans this evening to celebrate your big IPO news?" Trey asked when they separated.

"No," she told him. "My job is done until it's time to ring the bell at the New York Stock Exchange. We were going to have some kind of celebration, but despite everything, I wasn't in a celebratory mood."

Trey frowned. "I can't believe I ruined that for you."

She reached up and cupped his cheek in her palm. "It all worked out in the end. Is there anything you'd like to do to celebrate?"

"It's nothing fancy, but Dez suggested we head out to the Royal Diner for chocolate milkshakes?" Trey asked, taking her hand, as Dez nodded.

"This time I want a large one, Dad."

Misha laughed. "Let's do it," she said.

"You know, I never believed in fate," he told her. "But I know that everything that we've been through has led us here. We're supposed to be together. You can't fight fate, I guess."

"Fate?" Misha repeated, as she reached down to take Dez's hand in hers, and together the three of them headed toward the diner and the rest of their lives. "I like to call it *kismet*."

* * * * *

COMING SOON!

We really hope you enjoyed reading this book. If you're looking for more romance be sure to head to the shops when new books are available on

Thursday 3rd August

To see which titles are coming soon, please visit

millsandboon.co.uk/nextmonth

MILLS & BOON

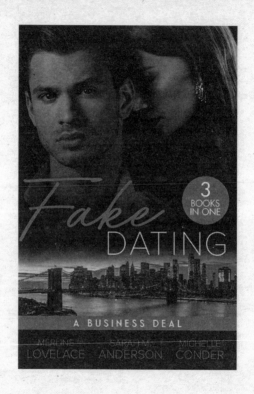

OUT NOW!

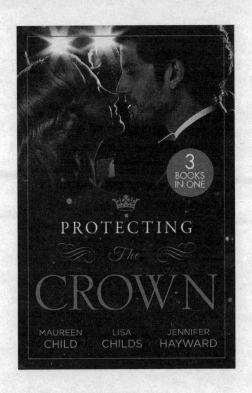

Available at
millsandboon.co.uk

MILLS & BOON

LET'S TALK
Romance

For exclusive extracts, competitions and special offers, find us online:

f MillsandBoon

🐦 @MillsandBoon

📷 @MillsandBoonUK

♪ @MillsandBoonUK

Get in touch on 01413 063 232

MILLS & BOON

THE HEART OF ROMANCE

A ROMANCE FOR EVERY READER

MODERN
Prepare to be swept off your feet by sophisticated, sexy and seductive heroes, in some of the world's most glamourous and romantic locations, where power and passion collide.

HISTORICAL
Escape with historical heroes from time gone by. Whether your passion is for wicked Regency Rakes, muscled Vikings or rugged Highlanders, awaken the romance of the past.

MEDICAL
Set your pulse racing with dedicated, delectable doctors in the high-pressure world of medicine, where emotions run high and passion, comfort and love are the best medicine.

True Love
Celebrate true love with tender stories of heartfelt romance, from the rush of falling in love to the joy a new baby can bring, and a focus on the emotional heart of a relationship.

Desire
Indulge in secrets and scandal, intense drama and sizzling hot action with heroes who have it all: wealth, status, good looks…everything but the right woman.

HEROES
The excitement of a gripping thriller, with intense romance at its heart. Resourceful, true-to-life women and strong, fearless men face danger and desire - a killer combination!

To see which titles are coming soon, please visit

millsandboon.co.uk/nextmonth